Connective Tissue

Eleanor Thom

TAPROOT PRESS

First published by Taproot Press 2023

ISBN: 978-1-7392077-0-0

Typeset in 11.5 point Garamond by Ryan Vance

Printed and bound by Severn Print, Gloucester, UK

Contents

This story is for my grandmother and her family members who were murdered in Auschwitz, Riga, Minsk and Zasavica. The historical part of the narrative has been constructed from the recorded events of their lives, and informed further by interviews, photographs, testimony, and archival holdings.

While researching this story, I found my grandmother's cousin living in Virginia, USA. Gittel was the baby of the family, born in Berlin in 1942. She survived against all odds, and was one of the youngest orphaned children brought to Britain after the liberation of Theresienstadt. Sadly, my grandmother never learned of her cousin's survival. She would be overjoyed that we are again connected.

Deborah Wilson 1916 – 1980
Ruth Rosa Tannenbaum 1937– 1943
Meta Lewin 1912 – 1943
Herbert Lewin 1910 – 1943
Dorothea Rowelski 1881 – 1942
Jette Rowelski 1908 – 1942
Hermann Rowelski 1910 – 1941
Max Moses Rowelski 1908 – 1943
Lucie Rowelski 1920 – 1943
Efraim Rowelski 1939 – 1943
Salomon Rowelski 1879 – 1942
Traute Taubine Rowelski 1932– 1942

ז"ל

Part I

20 May

Every room has a red push-button. They're halfway up the wall, yay wide, like a golf ball. Not a button you tap lightly, but one you slam as if you're in a game show. If you hit the red button, lights flash and bells ring. People come running. But the point is *not* to hit the button. That's why I think about it all the time.

A couple of years ago, Crosshouse replaced all the facilities in the smaller towns, and now everyone comes here, even the islanders. It's a modern construction, built on a curve so that long corridors won't seem as endless. Abattoirs have been designed the same way.

My son's heartbeat is recorded every morning and afternoon, its echo overheard through the murk of amniotic fluid. It's ghostly but comforting, like late night conversations in other parts of the building. Sometimes they want to know more, so they tie a band around me and attach me to a screen. I try to lie still, and a machine prints out a graph on a narrow roll of paper. These are taken away and filed along with scans of his body inside my body. They estimate the circumference of his head and the length of his folded limbs, try to determine his irregular origami.

My uterus is all wrong. I'm cocooning something other than the baby, amassing connective tissue of unknown origin. One mass is as big as a rugby ball.

Another has petrified inside me and will never leave. There are smaller ones too, clustering like grapes. No one can explain it. Is it purely genetics, or did I do something too much, or not enough? Eaten fruit without rinsing? Taken medication the wrong way? An internet search suggests suppressed anger. No one knows the reason, but because of it my baby is stuck at an angle and must not be born. If he starts too soon his umbilical cord could be crushed, or I could split open.

'Keep your mind on other things,' the nurses say. I try to do this. I knit. I look at baby catalogues and watch television. I'll even watch the World Cup and The Eurovision Song Contest. Anything.

'They're benign tumours,' my consultant says. 'Are you generally an anxious person?'

I shrug.

'They are very common.'

This is true, but usually they're no bigger than cherries.

Roberta is thirty-five weeks. She sits on the end of the bed, and I sit in the chair. Roberta's knitting a blanket for my son and I'm doing a pair of shorts for hers. It's unusually hot. It feels more like Texas or Tenerife, heat rising off the car park and the hospital helipad. The fields around Kilmarnock are yellowing. Ours will be June boys, born two weeks apart. I look at Roberta, cast on an extra stitch, and glance over at the red button on the wall. Days here drag. I wonder again at the feel of the smooth, red surface of the button, the click of plastic as I slap my palm down on it. I imagine the sounds of people hurrying towards me, sensible shoes scuffing wipe-clean corridors, a surgeon scrubbing under nails, blue plastic gloves snapping over hands, scalpels being arranged on a metal tray.

Roberta passes the end of her wool into her right hand and with a finger she draws the strand in a circle about the needle, which she holds tight under her elbow.

'We knit the same way,' I say.

'Oh?'

'Continental style.' I have to keep my needles still while I speak or I forget where I am. I'm a clumsy knitter.

'Continental? Jeezo.' She knits a few more stitches. 'I'm not *in*continent yet.'

She laughs.

'How come you knit like this?' she says. 'You're not continental.'

Roberta's parents are Italian, but she grew up here. Her grandmother owned a herd of buffalo, a story that sounded like a hallucination and ended up with stretchy mozzarella cheese that the family made out of buffalo milk. Roberta must have learnt to knit from her *Nonna*, continental style.

They do a sort of continental breakfast here: plastic tray, film wrapped croissant, state-controlled portion of marmalade with two grams of butter, yoghurt pot and fruit juice carton. It's the same every day.

'My grandmother was German,' I tell her.

I learned to knit from my mother, and she learned from hers. When I was a girl I would sit on the sofa watching television, and beside me my mother would knit colourful scarves for Romanian orphans. She knitted so fast it was like the sofa was shitting them out. Come December, she'd send hundreds of these scarves away in shoeboxes, and we'd imagine her colourful knitwear being worn all over Eastern Europe.

I didn't knit much till I was on maternity leave. I'm nowhere near as fast as my mother, or Roberta. Her needles tick away the minutes.

This will be my first child, but Roberta already has two sons and a daughter. Antonella, the middle child, likes me because my birthday is the day after hers, and because when she first saw me, I happened to be eating a cucumber like a banana, which is exactly how Antonella eats cucumbers. Almost every afternoon, Roberta's family visit the ward, bringing Big Macs and Tiramisù, the family recipe handed down through generations.

Funny how the past creeps into us, behind our backs, through a Tiramisù recipe, a saying, or the casting on of stitches. I can't remember my grandmother, but I knit the way she did. She was a Tannenbaum, a Jewish name that in German means 'Christmas tree'. I don't remember being told that, so I must have been very young. Everything about being Jewish was a mystery. It sounded nice, a religion of wishing, and of things that shone. Jewels. But nobody knew much about the Jewish side, and for years I accepted that. Dora Tannenbaum, my grandmother, passed on nothing. Only later did it become a feeling like peeling paint. I itched to pick at it. There had been clues all along, old photographs with Hebrew letters on the border, a Star of David necklace, a tune hummed absent-mindedly, and an extreme distrust of British sliced bread, apparently the cause of her losing all her teeth. But that was all they were. Clues.

I gleaned somehow that we were connected to unspeakable events of the past. Family conversations went back to 1939 and then petered out. There would be a shrug, a sigh, a staring out of the window at the grey expanse of Scottish sky. Sometimes my mother and aunts would stare instead at the patterned wallpaper, or into the bottom of a mug of tea, or at one of my aunt Annie's framed prints of a little girl playing. Annie has a whole collection of these little girls. Perhaps it was always a hint that someone was missing.

We're a family full of women, but I'm the only one with a dodgy uterus. Uterine Fibroid Tumors is the medical term. They can be intra, extra or sub mucosal. All sound equally disgusting. These benign masses can even hang down into the uterus from a thread of skin, like monstrous Christmas baubles. I think of them spinning themselves into fleshy, fibrous spools. Connective tissue. The thought makes me want to be sick.

I asked my consultant if it was genetic. 'No one else in my family has them.'

'Are you generally an anxious person?' she kept asking.

'Not at all,' I said. 'It's my job to be calm.'

This is the truth. I'm an ATCO, an air traffic control officer, and I'm trained to cope with pressure. On an average day it's busy, but for me it's straightforward work. The unexpected happens: mechanical failures, area violations, unexpected weather, bird strikes, passengers taken ill mid-air, all sorts. But I've been controlling for more than ten years, in area control and in the control tower. I can handle it all.

It was December when the fibroids were first revealed on a scan. My belly had been growing so fast that in the break room they were always offering more biscuits and insisting it must be twins.

I asked my mother if Dora had fibroids.

'Maybe,' she said. 'Her tummy stuck out a bit, like yours does, even though she wasn't fat. She always preferred her legs.'

My mother always hummed 'Oh Christmas Tree' in December. Sometimes she'd sing it in German.

O Tannenbaum, o Tannenbaum, Wie treu sind deine Blätter!

Whenever I think of my Jewish grandmother, Dora Tannenbaum, I always hear that song. Her married name was Dora Wilson. Not at all German and not at all Jewish.

My only memory of her also happens to be a photograph. It's hard to know if the memory is real or if it's just a figment I've peeled out of the gelatine layers of that old photo. Dora is fixing the camera. Her dark eyes are half-hidden by horned glasses, and you can see the curve of her belly through her wool skirt. Perhaps she's about to read me a story. I remember only the vague sensation of being pulled too close, pressed into the soft side of her, the prickly tweed skirt, and her shirt smooth against my cheek.

A few months after that photo was taken, Dora collapsed outside a locksmith shop on Elgin High Street. It was December. The window displays would have been full of trees: tinsel, baubles, fairy lights peeking on and off. Perhaps a tape of carols was playing.

A line of 'Silent Night' was inscribed on her gravestone: *Sleep in Heavenly Peace*. It was a song that always made her cry, but no one knew why. Another mystery. At the funeral there was no Rabbi and no-one left a stone on her grave, a Jewish tradition I had to find out about years later. Dora never taught the family these things. Instead, there is a small Christmas tree planted where she lies: a Tannenbaum. My aunt replaces the tree every year because the cemetery removes them when they get too big, before roots can develop.

I used to nag my aunties and mum, wanting to know more about Dora. She was too busy to tell stories, they said, working two jobs and raising four daughters alone. When she did get a moment's peace, they remembered her sitting silently in a haze of woodbine smoke. Inhaling, exhaling. The girls had to guess what she was thinking.

The idea of a lost sister began with a new doll.

'Call her Ruth Rosa,' Dora had blurted out, talking in code to tell a story she couldn't bear to speak of. Clues. It was just a hunch, but through a chain of similar moments that occurred over the decades that followed, my mother and her sisters became aware of an absence.

*

9

I'm frowning at my knitting and fishing between the strands for a dropped stitch.

'So you're German?' Roberta says, still clicking her needles. 'Just so long as you're not bloody Mexican, cause Italy are playing Mexico soon, and if they lose I'll have to kill you. Oh my God, I'll be screaming at the telly. I can't help myself.'

Roberta is mad for the World Cup.

'Tell the midwives to write it on the whiteboard,' I say. 'If the shift changes, they might think you're in labour.'

Roberta laughs with her whole body. She pushes her stitches back on her needles and, folding them in one hand, she checks her watch.

'Come on, honey,' she says. 'Feeding time at the zoo.'

I let her go ahead. I'll get to the canteen as soon as I've finished my row. I like to watch my stitches moving along, becoming even like a block of text. I see how fast I can add to the length, stopping sometimes to smooth a hand over my work, feel the tension, the little 'V's tighter. Continental, squarer than the English style. Dora's way is my inheritance.

It's roasting in this place. The windows only open enough to stick a hand out, and there's been hardly a breeze for days. The only time the trees move is when one of the helicopters comes in from Arran, or from another remote part of the South West. There's a yellow helicopter, and a larger red one. If they fly in during visiting hours you'll see hoards of kids pressed against windows, held up under the armpits by their dads. I suppose they prefer the bright, roaring helicopters to the milk-smelling blankets and quiet disturbance of new siblings.

I lay my knitting over my body and rest my wrists against my sides. I can feel one of the fibroids, the calcified one that's turned into a ball of chalk. It's hard and round like an apple but tender like a bruise when I press into it. The other masses should shrink after the pregnancy. Even the one that's as big as a rugby ball could shrivel to the size of a prune, they tell me. But not this calcified one. It's stuck there for good. I wonder if it'll roll around inside my coffin when I'm dead, like some curled up animal that could never be born.

I wind my wool and get up. I'm not uncomfortable. You'd think it, to see me, but my back is strong. That's my Scottish side. Dora was built like a wren. She put a little weight on when she got older, but as a young woman she had needles for bones. A 'wee wumman' they called her. There were other names that weren't so nice. No one protected her when my grandfather drank. My mother remembers this well. 'Who could blame him for his dark moods?' she'd hear the grown-ups mutter. 'She thinks she's better than us.' Then one night my grandfather took a drink too many and went to an early grave. For Dora, my mother said it was probably a relief.

*

A new patient was admitted this morning, due any day. She's the talk of the canteen.

'I saw it on the board,' says Roberta. 'It says T.L.C. beside her name.'

'T.L.C., like tender loving care?'

'I could do with some tender loving bloody care,' she says.

I pick up some extra pieces of food for Louise, one of the patients on bed rest. Louise's baby is trying to be born too soon. She says she can feel the amniotic sac starting to drop down, as if it's going to slip right out in the caul, the way a cat is born. She needs to get to twenty-three weeks, but the midwives are keeping quiet about her chances. If she goes into labour, we won't see her again. There's a room somewhere else for grieving, a place quiet and tucked away where you don't hear the newborns crying.

Stacey, who has the room opposite mine, comes in wearing her dressing gown. Sometimes Stacey wants to talk to us but other times she won't. She's thirty-five weeks and a social worker comes to see her almost every afternoon. They go in her room and the door is shut, and sometimes Stacey doesn't come out again till the next day. When she's having a better time she'll sit with Roberta, watching telly, or looking through her baby catalogues. Stacey takes a while stirring her coffee and goes back to her room without a word.

'Are you alright, honey?' Roberta calls after her.

After dinner we help ourselves to fresh linen from the cupboard and puddings from the fridge. There are always more newborns on the ward, so Roberta barges in on the mums and dads to take a look and get a cuddle. Inside the rooms, families are standing helplessly with new babies in their arms, their pink or blue balloons swaying with the sudden rush.

On the whiteboard by reception our names are written in a kind of table, with expected delivery dates to one side.

'Can you remove the fibroids at the same time?' I asked my consultant. I imagined a surgeon scooping out the rugby ball of flesh, grinning for a camera and cradling it under an arm. Then, once its size and weight was recorded, this inhuman twin that had grown beside my son would be incinerated.

'No,' they said. 'It would be too much of a risk.'

The board says it in black and white. There is a new patient who has been admitted for T.L.C..

'So *does* it mean tender loving care?' I ask.

The midwife on the desk is tight-lipped. They aren't allowed to say.

'Don't be stupid,' Roberta says.

We sit in the lounge till it's dark outside, but the air doesn't cool. The skin at the back of our knees sticks to the tacky fabric on the hospital armchairs. The lounge is right over the birthing pools, and when the women in labour scream, we listen. The noise swells and dips, and closing your eyes it's like being out in the desert, somewhere in Utah, near one of those roller coasters they build a mile high, the noise of the pleasure seekers all garbled together with the heat and the rushing of the ride. There's a woman down there tonight, swearing at the midwives and at her man, screaming that she can't take the pain. But what we're really listening out for is the baby. We want to hear the first cry, and till we do, the whole time we're holding our breath.

1937

Potatoes roll in boiling water, a pile of peelings lying cold on the table. Steam is misting the window. The baby will be born soon, hours not days. Dora throws salt into the water. The smell of starch is cloying. She rubs her brow with her wrist. Another pain, stronger now. She's packed her bag. The little suitcase is open on top of her bedspread, next to her coat and hat. She goes over to make a last-minute check, flipping the lid of the case, glancing over the contents, closing it. The catches shut with ease. There's not much she needs to take with her, just a change of clothes, her nightgown, a toothbrush, the blanket she has crocheted, a small bag of sweets, her papers, a change for the baby. If she needs anything else, her cousins will bring it. She lifts the case to feel its weight, then takes the time to go back to the stove and swivel with the hot pan of potatoes over to the sink, draining them into the colander. The boiling has made them rounder, smooth like eggs. They'll not be eaten warm, but they'll keep. Her head's fizzing as if she's forgotten something. It's time to go.

A door slams open at the bottom of the stairwell. Her cousins are home from work. She has already shut the apartment door and is half-way down the stairs. The smell of wood polish and potatoes is gone, replaced by a rush of cold air and Meta's laughter below. A voice you can't mistake, happy like bubbles, and her husband drinking in her every word. Dora has never seen a man look at any woman the way Herbert Lewin looks at her cousin. If she had found someone like that, things would be so different.

Realising that Dora's time has come, the Lewins fuss for a minute. Their neighbour from downstairs goes past without greeting them, opens his door on the landing, and slams it shut.

'Old Kokker,' Meta snaps.

Herbert's mouth turns up a little at his wife's sharp tongue and he touches her shoulder. He tries to hush her, but all the time looks at her with doting eyes.

'He's always coming up to kvetch,' Meta says. 'Too much dirt on the stairs or too much noise, whatever, he always blames us.'

'Don't think about that now,' Herbert suggests.

But Meta won't forget it. 'Imagine if we'd had a baby crying upstairs? He should count himself lucky.'

Herbert doesn't like Meta talking about babies, so he just agrees with her.

The air in the inner courtyard is damp and stale. They are surrounded by six storeys of grey stone and scores of small, grubby windows. At the top there is an opening of clean, pale blue sky. Herbert carries Dora's case and Meta takes her arm, and they walk with her across the cobbled yard and under the archway of the front building. They'll walk all the way to the hospital. Dora's insides twist like they're being wrung out, and she begs them to go quickly.

They walk along the side of the Red Castle. The police headquarters with its four corner towers takes up the rest of their block and casts a bloody shadow. At night, she thinks she can hear people locked in cells inside. She can't, of course. The noises of the apartments and the street drown out everything. Still, Dora always hurries past. She shies from doorways where black-uniformed men file in and out, and she listens instead to the traffic and the thousand conversations passing by.

Once they pass the corner, they reach the light, the view opening onto Alexanderplatz, the sky, the circling vehicles and the comfort of crowds, different accents, street dwellers and department store shoppers. Jews and Germans. A flag is flying high above a bus stop, looming over people heading home or going out for the evening. It's making a noise in the wind, but the people below don't hear it. They chat. They're dressed in best, charcoal suits and beige overcoats, herringbone and check, sleek gloves and purses with shiny clasps. The men wear ties with flashes of cream, cobalt and burgundy, and the women talk loudly and laugh. All of them so spick and span and proud of themselves, going dancing, hair-up, shoes shone, looking forward to a drink. The barbed cross flaps angrily above them, wanting to be noticed. Red. White. Black. There's one just like it on nearly every building. The red sea. The white circle. The arms of the black Hakenkreuz.

It's hard to remember a time when that flag wasn't everywhere you looked.

*

Meta and Herbert have been married since '35. After the wedding, they moved into the cross-courtyard building at Alexanderstraße, twenty six. It was neglected, small and dark and only two rooms, but theirs. They were downstairs from Herbert's older brother Benno and his family. Meta's mother Dorothea was only a few streets away. They renovated both rooms, clearing out cupboards where pigeons had been nesting. They got on with life. Dora leapt at the chance to take the small bed in the kitchen. This way she helps them with the rent, and the cousins keep each other company. They invite friends over, sit up late, and scatter crumbs on the windowsill for pigeons and sparrows.

If it weren't for the big event about to happen, Herbert would be having his cigarette about now. He'd let his mind wander over the events of the day, recount the important news in his paper. One cigarette per day is essential to his being, Herbert says. Later he would share a drink with Benno upstairs. Routine suits the Lewins. They take their shoes off at the door. Herbert sits in his socks and the girls go about in their stockings, and until Herbert has finished his cigarette he won't eat or drink, listen to the wireless or write letters.

But today is not a normal day.

By the time they've crossed Alexanderplatz, Meta says her fingers are sore from Dora squeezing them.

Dora winces as another pain comes.

'If I didn't work so hard you could squeeze them as tight as you want,' Meta laughs.

Meta's a seamstress at Anton Shulz. She sits for long hours at her machine and her fingers go numb. She's not a smoker like her husband. She talks too much to smoke, and anyway she prefers to eat. She has a soft spot for anything with cream in it, and anything with cherries. A sweet tooth runs in the family, and Dora is the same.

'Mrs Simonson is emigrating,' Meta says, trying to distract Dora with anything and everything. 'A dental practice in Chicago will employ her husband, but she's very upset. She doesn't want to go, poor Mrs Simonson. I told her I'd happily take her place.'

Talk of leaving puts a lump in Dora's throat. She feels it even now, through the pain of the baby coming.

'Are you alright?' Meta asks. 'You're holding your stomach.'

Dora shakes her head. 'No, it's nothing,' she says. 'Just the pain.'

'Oh, we wouldn't go without you!'

Herbert doesn't like Meta talking about leaving either. So far, he hasn't been able to find a way to emigrate, and however much Meta wants to go, she insists they take everyone, Dora, her mother, and her three older siblings. It's impossible. A distant uncle in the USA raised their hopes for a while, but the cost meant plans quickly fell through.

'Mrs Simonson is right. This is home,' Dora says.

'You're just like my mother,' Meta tuts. 'And Jette too. Am I the only brave woman in the family?'

'It's just too much money,' Herbert says. 'Let's not talk about that now.'

Dora turns away and there's silence between them for a minute, but Meta turns her mind to other things. She points out displays in shop windows, dinner services, cars, fashionable hats, records, and all kinds of other luxuries they cannot possibly own. She smiles even when she is angry.

'If we really *have* to stay, I will order one of those and one of those, and one of those,' she jokes, pointing at a twinkling display of cut-glass lamps. 'And our little nephews and nieces will all want lots of these,' she says, waving her hand at a display as they pass a toy shop.

When the men in black uniforms step into the street, it's Herbert who notices. A crowd is gathered on the pavement, and Meta calls out to everyone to clear a path. She thanks them loudly, oblivious to the stares they get or the officers just behind. Herbert takes the women by the arm and whispers to them. Meta falls silent, and a glance over her shoulder is enough for Dora to walk faster and forget the pains. She must reach the hospital. They don't speak another word. They head for the corner with the eyes of the uniforms on their backs, praying for all the world for them to cross the road and go the opposite way.

Dora can feel the ground through the soles of her shoes. She can feel every crack. The world is unstable. She knows they will be stopped, a sense she has picked up, as certain as the flutters in her stomach.

The man in charge shouts: 'Arms out! Legs apart!'

Two of the uniforms search Herbert, feeling his

trousers, patting around his coat. He stays calm and explains that they're making their way to the hospital, but the men tell him to keep quiet.

'Planning a trip?' they say, pulling Dora's case from Herbert's hand.

The officer opens Dora's case on the pavement revealing the female garments inside. A pulse is racing in her neck, and when he makes her stand facing a butcher's shop window and runs his baton inside her coat, she feels her throat redden. The people inside the shop are staring. The butcher is still serving customers, but no one will leave the shop until the search is done. She presses her teeth into the softness of her lips.

'Is there anything in your pockets?'

She can see the officer's face reflected in the window. He looks hot in his uniform, his face shiny with sweat. Dora can also see Meta. By the roadside, she's being searched too. She holds her head up, refusing to meet Herbert's glances.

'Check the belly,' someone orders.

The Uniform moves close enough that she could touch the handle of his pistol. She wonders what it would feel like to grasp the metal, to lift it and feel its weight, to pull a trigger, to be shot in the leg, or the chest. The officer puts his hands on her, scrubbed, pink, well-fed hands. Inside the shop, people's eyes flit to their shoes. They look back at the bloody meat, their place in the queue and the butcher's skilful cutting. The smell of that place and the sound of the Uniform's breathing make Dora's stomach clench and she has to hold her breath not to retch.

The baby must sense her unease. It twists suddenly and part of its body, a knee or a hip, pushes out against the man's hand. The Uniform's lip twitches and he quickly pulls back.

'Papers,' he demands, placing his feet wide apart. The other officers are already checking the documents Meta and Herbert have handed over. Meta's eyes won't meet Dora's. She won't want it discussed. That's Meta's way.

Their names are written up. Dora bends and chucks her nightdress and the baby's things back inside her case.

Another one of the uniforms comes over with her papers in his hand.

'You are Stateless.'

'I was born in Berlin,' Dora protests, her voice too quiet to be heard.

'Also husbandless,' he says, lip curling, his eyes again on her middle. She can hear the spit in his mouth, and inside her the baby is flapping like a fish on land. Her muscles harden, every inch of her belly tensing.

'The father's name?'

Marcus. Everything tightens around his name. When anyone speaks of him, something inside her runs cold and the skin prickles on her forearms. She's sure it shows, even when her back is turned. The man waits for more.

'He is Jewish,' she confirms.

'His address?'

'He has gone to Beuchen,' Dora says. She swallows the hurt, his silence still sticking in her throat. But there's still more to say. 'He's working there, as a locksmith.'

The Uniform bends again over her papers, chews his bottom lip and then straightens. He taps the edges of the document against his knuckles as he walks away.

Eventually, after the officers talk in a group, the papers are handed back. They are waved on. One of the uniforms stands watching as they go. Now it is Meta who squeezes Dora's hand too hard. Still, nothing needs to be said.

The hospital of Adass Yisroel is at number eighty-five, Elsässerstraße. It has a pink brick façade and arched windows. Looking up at it, Dora's mind drifts to the future. Things will never be the same after today, she knows, and even though everything will change, they must get on quickly with their goodbyes.

'I wish you could come with me,' she says.

Meta pulls one of Dora's curls and lets it spring back. Herbert puts an arm around his wife's waist.

'Mother says this is the best hospital,' Meta tells her.

All of a sudden Herbert says, 'I'll write to Marcus.' It must have been on his mind while they were walking.

Meta's mouth tightens. She doesn't like Marcus being mentioned. She doesn't want Dora to be upset.

'You'll let my mother visit soon, won't you?' Meta says.

Dora nods. She thinks of her own parents. Mutti, who gave birth to her in Mendelssohnstraße, just round the corner. Poor Mutti, gone so many years now. And her poor Vati too, only just departed. He loved babies. What would he say about all this? *Mirtsishem*, she thinks, and she laughs to herself because she can almost hear him praying with his cronies from shul. A child's life was always a good fortune, that's what he would say, no matter how muddled the circumstances.

Vati always said that Dora reminded him of Mutti, and that was why he spoiled her. He would save to buy her an extravagant birthday present each year, something special that she wouldn't expect. On her sixteenth, a brand-new copy of *Anna Karenina*, wrapped in green tissue. On her seventeenth, a silver locket. And on her twentieth, a pair of ice-skates. As soon as the winter weather arrived he came to watch her glitsh about on the ice, and he stood on the side with his hands stuffed in his pockets, laughing into his scarf.

'Daughter,' he chuckled. 'You skate like a tree in a gale. A true Tannenbaum!'

Soon it would be her first winter without him. Vati's illness was sudden, and whenever she thinks of that time she also thinks of Marcus. The two men are inseparable in her mind. Marcus was there the night Vati died, and back again the next evening after the burial, knocking on the door of Vati's apartment late after work. She remembers the look of him as he came in, the snowflakes in his hair, the leather jacket he took off, the smell of the cigarette he had just smoked and the way everyone in the room shifted around him. He didn't stay long. The apartment was full of mourners, but a week later when things were quieter and the temperature outside had dropped even further, he came back a third time, bringing gifts from the bakery, encouraging her to eat.

He lured her out to drown her sorrows in a local bar. She had grown up in that same apartment and walked past the bar a thousand times, but she had never drunk there before. It was warm, he said, and they'd sit by the fire.

The world had changed faster than the seasons. The winter cold would come back, but Marcus might not ever reappear. You needed money and friends if you wanted to emigrate: to London or New York, Chile or South Africa, or maybe Stockholm. His parents didn't want to see him trapped in Berlin. Dora had no friends or money, nothing that would help him escape, so they sent him away to forget her.

At a second-floor window in the hospital, a woman sits looking out. She has something in her mouth, tobacco or a sweet, and she's chewing as she stares over the rooftops of Prenzlauer Berg. Her arms are folded on the windowsill. Dora imagines doing the same, tomorrow or the next day, after the baby is born. She'll stare over the city that Marcus has gone from, and wonder about her life with the baby, wishing it were laid out in straight, easy lines like the streets below. Readable like a map.

Herbert forces a smile as he puts her case into her hand. She wraps her fingers around the leather handle, feeling the rough stitches and the swing in the hinges.

Herbert has been awkward with her lately, the way young men are about things they don't understand, side-stepping around her in the small apartment, apologising if he touches her belly accidentally. It won't be a big baby, not twins, thank goodness. Meta's brother and sister, Jette and Max, were born just two minutes apart. Dora can't imagine how it would feel to carry two babies. Already her buttons won't do up and her skin is pulled taught. If she had got much bigger, she would have needed Meta to alter all her clothes a second time.

'We'll wait till you're inside,' Meta says softly. 'Just think, it'll be over soon and you can go back to work in a couple of months. You won't like that!'

God willing, Dora thinks. She can't help hearing the voices in her head that sound like Vati, even if she puts no stock in the old-fashioned ways. What good had God ever willed for her? But she grew up with it, and so did Meta.

The cousins hold hands on the kerb till a wave of cars and buses and streetcars have passed. A bus to Hallesches Tor turns the corner, flashing adverts for Enver Bey cigarettes and Hildebrand chocolate. Behind the bus, a Stoewer Sedina Cabriolet purrs, gleaming new, the top down. Meta eyes it. The car swerves into the lane to the city centre, the big lights, the theatres and cinemas. Women in the back seat wear warm coats, hair tucked up, those fashionable little hats which almost look fit for swimming. Laughter overflowing. The car stops at a light. Coffee cream paintwork with a silver trim, the excitement of the city glinting in bright reflections all over it.

Dora crosses alone. She pulls her coat tight around her chest even though it isn't cold. She feels so slow in her body now. Her feet hurt. Shoes barely fit. Everyone she has ever known lives and works within a few streets of this hospital. She thinks of Marcus again, and how he would look at her. Him and his dark brown eyes. Whenever he laughed, he'd check to see if she was laughing too, and he kissed her without asking. People said he was aloof, but he hadn't seemed that way with her. Marcus with his thick, black hair. He wore it cropped short, and had a tiny birthmark on his cheek, a chocolate drop. Film star smile with perfect, white teeth and a lucky gap. He wasn't tall, but he was graceful, a good dancer. They had walked down this street on their first date, sharing pickles, and again on their second, and so many times after. Her feet had skipped along then, and she'd have followed him anywhere he went. A devoted puppy.

Another streetcar passes advertising soap and cocoa.

Dora looks back. Meta wishes it was her own event about to happen. Dora knows this. She and Herbert have been married long enough that people have started to talk about their childlessness, and Aunt Dotti is impatient to be a grandmother. Herbert's sister in Chorinerstraße has had almost a baby a year since she was married, five boys and three girls, and another on the way.

'Who would have a child, in these times?' Herbert said to Aunt Dotti.

'If you and Meta don't hurry up, my Max will beat you to it. He will marry soon and make his mother happy,' she grumbled.

Herbert was lying. He would do anything for Meta. A baby is the one thing she wants that doesn't come from a fancy shop, and that isn't illegal. Jews can still have babies with Jews.

From across the street, Meta raises her hand and smiles. Dora grips her coat. She feels a rush of affection so strong she thinks it might suck the air from her lungs. Sometimes she's jealous of Meta. She was always a few years younger, a few steps behind. But not now. She knows she'll always remember her cousin looking exactly the way she does in this moment, still amidst Berlin's evening traffic, everything about to change, and each of them wishing they could swap places.

21 May

The noise gets under my skin. A low, intermittent buzz that sounds out all the way down the corridor. It's been off and on all day.

We're standing at the window, looking out at the car park and the fields. The helicopter has just flown in. Sometimes I look out here and think about the control tower when I worked in approach, the monitors, the windows, all the activity on the ground, watching the planes as they lifted themselves into the sky, others slipping into view just below the cloud layer. I wonder what's happening right now in the terminal building, arrivals and departures, people from all over the world, the hugs goodbye, the welcomes, coffee in paper cups, suitcases on wheels. Controllers rarely see the passengers. Most of us don't even see the planes. If you work in area control, they're just pixels on a screen. But the idea of plane passengers is always there. Every bright dot on the radar represents incoming hopes and dreams, hundreds of people from every country in the world, a trip of a lifetime, a reunion, a stag do, a new career, a place of safety, a military manoeuvre, or someone hoping for a better life. A controller must never forget what those dots represent. That's why we have to renew our licenses every year. Being fit and healthy is crucial, and to only work the radar in short shifts. At work we focus on one thing only: guiding the bright lights through our airspace, bringing them home. Then we drink coffee.

The buzzers go off again.

'Wait till you have your wean,' says Roberta. 'That'll be you pressing the bloody buzzers all day and all night, and then I'll come and kill you.'

The buzzers are different to the red buttons on the wall. If you need help and it isn't urgent, you buzz. The people buzzing are mostly mothers with firstborns. You only slam the red button in a life-or-death scenario, and then you'll be rushed to a surgeon's table in twenty seconds flat. It's like the priority line at work. If that rings, everyone hears it loud and clear.

Matthew arrives. He always comes after work. He's not missed a day since I was admitted, even though it's a two-hour round trip. He works during the day, and some evenings when he arrives I can tell I'm the first person he's spoken to since waking up. He works for the estate, looking after trees. He's always been most at home there, up in the branches, listening to the forest, recording the birdsong and the rustle of the wind in the canopy, checking the boughs for stability and the leaves for disease and infestation. When a plane flies over, he says he looks through the canopy and thinks of me.

Before he comes to see me after work he drives home. He takes off his overalls and boots, showers, rinses the sawdust, cobwebs and aphids from his hair, rubs cream into his hands and picks out splinters. Even after showering, he smells of earth and roots and Atrixo hand cream.

'I've got your clean clothes,' he says, dropping a suitcase on the floor. He puts his hand in a carrier bag. 'I also picked you up some strawberries, a flatbread thing, and crisps. I'm having some. I'm starving.'

We pop open the cardboard tube of crisps and sit snapping stacks of them between our teeth.

Matthew reaches into his jeans pocket.

'I got an idea,' he says, handing me a packet of face paint crayons from the hospital shop.

I take off my shirt and lie on the bed, fiddling with the controls that move the mattress up or down. I do this till I get comfortable, and Matthew starts to dot a design on my belly with the face paint. I like watching him do this. He concentrates hard where the tip of the crayon presses into me, with more attention than you'd normally give a random inch of skin. He's not been to get his hair cut in ages, and the heat in the room has made his forehead slick with sweat. He flicks his fringe out of his eyes, careful not to smudge the paint onto his face. He uses all his fingers to blend the colours, covering every inch of my tummy. I have a line of stretch marks on both sides, ripples that start at my hip and point up to my bellybutton. Matthew paints them. He colours between the tiger stripes and his expression stays exactly the same. When he reaches the top he presses into the hard mass, the lump that's calcified and slightly protrudes.

'You're sure that's not his head?' Matthew asks.

'Definitely not. That's one of the fibroids. It's the one that's calcified.' I think of it turning into a ball of bone.

I put his palm over another part of my belly, letting him feel the different roundness beneath there.

'This is his head,' I say. 'That's where I feel him hiccup.'

Our son wakes up when the tips of the crayons smooth circles over him. We see parts of him moving, a hand or an elbow drawn right across me in a ripple. Once the paint covers the bowl of my belly, Matthew rubs shapes into it with his fingertips, swirls and clouds. He adds more, massaging layer upon layer of colour and shade until I look like Jupiter, the red spot floating right over the baby's head.

'I love it,' I say, peering down.

'I definitely should have gone to art school.'

Matthew's a tree surgeon because that's what his dad did. The family business has been handed down. He always knew that's what he'd do.

'The world probably has enough paintings of trees,' I tell him.

The face-paint massage is so relaxing that I fall asleep. When I wake up, visiting is over and Matthew has gone.

Before I came to the hospital, I taxed the van and paid the Council Tax. I cleaned the house. I left everything ready and just how I needed it for bringing the baby home. The tiny clothes were washed and folded and put away. Matthew's laundry was also done fresh. I even cleaned the windows and hacked some of the weeds back outside. Packing my hospital bags, I made sure I had ten days' worth of clothes for myself, exactly five days of dark clothing and five days of light clothing. I wear the dark colours for five days in a row, dark pants, dark bra, dark dress or t-shirt and jeans. Then I send all the dark clothing away with Matthew. All he needs to do is throw everything straight in the drum of the machine, wash it, peg it onto the clothesline that hangs across our garden from a birch tree to an oak tree, and bring the whole lot back. Really, his mum will probably come over and do it for him. While he's washing and drying the dark clothes, I wear my light clothes for five days. I go light and dark like the phases of the moon.

Matthew tries not to get angry about the sheep in the neighbour's field getting into the garden. I know he isn't sleeping well. Usually, it's me who'll kick him out of bed. I worry about him working in high branches when he's tired, balancing a chainsaw. I worry about him phoning to tell me that he can't cope with the house anymore and he wants to sell. The house isn't perfect, but I don't want the hassle of moving. It's an old house at the edge of the woods, and things go wrong. It's cold. But it was Matthew's before it was ours, and I know that really he's attached to the place, a rickety two-storey set all on its own and surrounded by trees and deer. Honestly, I'm not so fond of being remote, having nobody around to talk to and getting snowed in. Winters last forever. That's one thing the hospital has going for it. It's warm and there's always company.

The lounge is empty tonight, so I take a walk to the postnatal ward, but it's deserted too. Perhaps everyone's gone to bed. The newborns all went home today, and it seems like no more can be bothered to be born. The midwives have disappeared into their staff room to drink tea and eat cakes, pleased at having nothing to do. I feel like a cat peering in at the window, drawn to the laughter and the warm light. They're surrounded by bouquets of flowers that the new mothers have left behind. Swallowing a thickness, I head back down the dim corridor to my room.

I've nearly reached the window at the far end when Stacey's door opens. The midwife with the medicine trolley is coming out, her trays and pills in bottles rattling. She asks if I need anything. Someone to talk to, I want to say, but I don't. I shake my head. I don't need anything for sleep. I'm like a log at night. Matthew hates it.

Stacey is sitting on her bed with Roberta and I hover in the doorway hoping I'll be invited in. The gown Stacey always wears is hanging over the bottom of the bed and she's crunching down her medicine, a whole cup full of pills. She does it carelessly, barely wincing at the taste.

'You joining us, honey?' Roberta says.

I walk in and stand at the end of Stacey's bed.

'That's a nice top. Is that new?'

'Matthew brought it in,' I say. 'I sent him home with my other clothes.'

I feel bad saying this to Stacey. Her gown is thin and mucky, like something a child has sucked on too long. Her man never comes up to see her, and there's no laundry service.

'Men are useless,' Roberta says. 'Mine took just three days to break the washing machine. Tried to wash all the bed sheets and covers at once.' She breathes heavily. 'Can you believe how bloody stupid?'

I still have Matthew's astral face-paint pictures hidden under my shirt. I keep them to myself.

Stacey is here for a low-lying placenta, the same reason as Roberta, but there's more going on than the dark clouds the consultants look for on the scans. There are things on file that follow Stacey around. She won't tell us what they're holding on her, but she's often in tears.

We come up with names for Stacey's baby. Everyone here has a list of names, sometimes just in our heads and sometimes written down in a notebook or carried on pieces of paper in our pockets. I like unusual names and so does Stacey, but Roberta is more traditional. She laughed at Stacey's name list, and now Stacey doesn't want to share it with me in case I laugh too. Roberta and I fire off suggestions to her anyway.

There are drawings blue-tacked on Stacey's wall, kids' crayon lines and scribbles in yellow and red. Her other kids drew them, she says. She hands me a catalogue and asks me to turn to a page she's ticked down. It's a red sports holdall with white writing on it. She wants to buy it for the baby, to hold all the things she's bought for her. She's got the tiny vests, sleepsuits, a cotton hat, cardigans, and doll-sized socks. There's a mobile with birds and butterflies, nappies, wipes, creams and a soft-bristle hairbrush, all the usual things. They're all on display in her room. While we're looking at the catalogue she gets upset and Roberta reaches over and holds her hands. Through the window the streetlights flicker on across the hospital car park.

We're both knitting for Stacey's baby now, a winter bonnet, and a blanket.

'I know it's going to be the same,' Stacey says, her hand stroking her belly and her eyes on the crayon pictures. There's something stitching her up so tight she can't speak without the air rushing into her mouth. 'They're going to take her away too.'

She wipes a sleeve over her nose and swallows a sob, then tucks her face into her arm trying to hold her breath.

'It's not decided yet,' Roberta says.

But Stacey says she knows. That it's always the same. They won't tell you till the end. They wait till it's born, pretending you have a chance to mother your own baby, when really there's no chance. No real chance. I try to be positive, like Roberta, but I've seen the social worker who comes, and there's something unyielding about her, the tweed skirt, the file in her hand, the way her pointy heels clip clop on the lino floor. And she's left Stacey in that dirty gown.

'She's here for the baby, not me,' Stacey said when I asked why.

We get her calm again, or maybe she just tires herself out, or those pills kick in and make her drowsy. She tells me the top name on her list and I say it's good. An unusual name will be like a beacon, I think.

Whatever happens, Stacey will be able to find her daughter again.

I go back to my room and sit in the chair by the open window. I see planes in the sky and rub my hand over my belly. The sore, bony lump is getting harder every day, and I keep petting it by mistake. I don't want to touch it, but somehow I always end up running my fingers over the dead mass as if it needs comfort. I look over at the snacks Matthew has brought, but I'm not hungry.

Outside my window, someone's on the phone.

'The wee one's here… yes… it's a wee girl… aye…. Eleven-pound-twelve-ounces… Eleven!'

The man hangs up and makes another call, then another. The sun's low, and the birds are feeding on summer flies, going berserk over the fields between the hospital and the scheme. I could fall asleep. Each time the father tells his news about the big baby he sounds more excited. I can't see him from the window, but I imagine what he looks like standing there in the evening sun, glowing inside and out. That's a good sky to be born under.

If I sit too quietly, people ask what I'm worrying about. Everyone here has something going on, even if they're an ATCO, an expert at keeping their cool. With each person we meet, we hold our breath a little bit more. I'm not worried the way most mothers are. I haven't read any manuals on looking after babies, and I'm not squeamish about surgery. I do have strange dreams. I see him lifted out at the end of the pregnancy, the moment we've been waiting for. And instead of sticky baby skin, a fluff of hair and soft wrinkles, he's made of wood and bark and is already dressed. Handed to me like that, a stick baby wearing someone else's clothes, I don't believe he's mine. I don't know what to do with him.

If the masses of connective tissue and muscle and bone start to bleed, I'll be pumped with drugs straight away and knocked unconscious. I think about the huge rugby ball of flesh, the infant-sized thing that has been lifelessly sucking on me for so many months. What if they can't stop the bleeding?

It's in these quiet moments that I think about Dora, how her whole life was derailed, and the fact that I'm an offshoot of this insult, and so is the baby inside me. Our entire existence is a kind of mutation in the peaceful order of things, a violent jolt that led to an unlikely escape. Dora would never have met my grandfather if she hadn't first been expelled by Hitler. My mother, me, and this baby would have never been born. But around here, I keep thoughts like that to myself.

Matthew was working in Dunaskin one day last week, up near the dilapidated industrial site that's full of black dust, iron remnants and the tall brick chimneys. They used it in a film about a concentration camp. That night he came in with a smell of desolation on him, outdoors air and ash, and coal dust in his hair. There's a real darkness up in that part of Ayrshire, a deadness. It can stick to you, and if you're not careful you can walk it right home on your boots. Matthew brought it in here that day and I still can't get the blackness out of my head.

The Holocaust. A word I can barely say. I've started to feel like it needs to be written down, not spoken, so that the two pillars of its capital 'H' can be put in place first, bracing themselves to take the weight of the rest. Dora might have said *Shoah* instead, the Hebrew. I find that more bearable somehow, a whisper of a word. It doesn't have the wide eyes that stare out from the middle of the word 'Holocaust', nor the cold, empty space, the hollow. Actually, I don't think Dora called it anything, at least not out loud. She just saw it on the news at the picture house, before the films started. My mother remembers how she scanned every face on the reel, how they'd sit sometimes to watch the film and the news again, a second time.

When Matthew and I made a list of names for our son, I couldn't get Dora's own list out of my head. Dora's list had come in a letter from the Red Cross. When the war ended, she wrote to them. She sent the names, addresses and birth dates of her family members in Berlin, requesting a search for their whereabouts. She clung to the dream that they had remained safe, hidden away. Had a brave and good neighbour sheltered her daughter? Perhaps they had changed their identities? When the reply came, many years later, the girls saw Dora open the letter. They remembered the red cross logo in the corner.

She hid the list as if she was burying their bodies, folding the paper over and over and putting it into a purse, which was zipped into the dark pocket of a bag, and then pushed into the back of a wardrobe. The names stayed there, untouched, tucked in a dark pocket. They were still there when Dora died. Her things were tidied up and mostly thrown away. Her daughters were grieving and other relatives came to help with the task. No one remembered to save the Red Cross letter.

Making lists of names for my baby, I want to say Dora's list out loud, but those names are gone.

What traces of my grandmother have surfaced in me? Good legs, a potbelly, a fondness for silly hats and a sweet tooth; she always kept half a packet of Minstrels in her pocket. I also came across this medical fact: uterine fibroids are more common in Jewish women. Maybe something, maybe nothing. I asked my consultant if it was true, and she laughed in my face. I don't know if that meant a yes or a no, or if she didn't understand why I'd care. I gave up questioning her after that.

I call Matthew after midnight. I guess he won't be sleeping. I tell him about my theory of the fibroids being a Jewish thing, but he isn't interested. Matthew thinks of the fibroids as knots in a tree.

'Knots are natural,' he says. 'Part of a trunk growing.'

I tell him to bring me a packet of Minstrels tomorrow. I plan to eat them slowly, sucking the shell off the first one, nibbling it away from another, brutally cracking some of them in half. Later, I'll convince myself that my grandmother liked doing the same as me, stroking the smooth shells in her hand and imagining games with them on a chequered board.

We talk about DNA. I watched something on TV about a strand of DNA that only gets passed from mother to daughter, and as I'm telling Matthew about the programme I imagine it, this silk ribbon of Mitochondrial

DNA. It unwinds, travelling from hand to hand through thousands of years of grandmothers, mothers, daughters. Our son won't inherit it from me. I tell Matthew I feel a bit sad that our son can't grasp the end of this long ribbon, that this gift from the furthest most ancient of grandmothers can only get handed to a sister of his, and never to him.

'One baby at a time, please,' he says.

I tell him not to worry. I just have too much time on my hands. He agrees, and before we end the call he goes downstairs to open my post. He forgot to bring it in today. I hold the phone close to my ear and I can hear him ripping the envelopes. I picture him in the drafty hallway, throwing the torn paper on the permanently cluttered shelf. I have two pieces of junk mail, and an envelope from Germany.

'Open it,' I tell him.

It's an early postcard of a synagogue in Berlin. I've begun collecting possible snaps of Dora's city, buying them on eBay from my hospital bed. I want to know what it was like, standing in the streets where Dora stood.

'Bring it tomorrow,' I tell him.

A deafening alarm goes off. At first I think it's a fire drill, but as I'm swinging my legs, rushing to find my slippers, I see the red button. My blood runs cold. The same feeling I get at work if a pilot calls in a TCAS RA, a Traffic Collision Avoidance System Resolution Advisory. There's nothing worse than knowing that two planes are within touching distance. We've messed up, and in these last moments all we're allowed to do is watch the radar, praying that onboard technology will guide the pilots safely away from each other. For those thirty seconds, you can almost taste your heart in your mouth.

I throw open the door and lean out. The corridor is dimly lit at night, but there are blue lights on the walls, all spinning like sirens. I'd never noticed them before. The whole corridor swims in this sickly, wheeling blue. Two sets of double doors are swinging, and people are already hurrying to the other side of the ward, scrubs flapping and heels rapping the lino.

The new girl is standing opposite me. Tender Loving Care. It's the first time I've seen her. She wears a white nightdress down to her ankles. The blue light suddenly stops pulsing over the corridor and she stays there, just blinking at me. Stacey stands in her doorway too. Roberta's door opens and she sticks her head out, her eyes small and squinting without her glasses. I can taste it, my heart.

'Who was it?' I say. 'Did you see?'

'Wee Louise,' Stacey nods.

Louise was still on bedrest, still trying to reach twenty-three weeks so her baby could be born with a chance. Her door is closed. She usually leaves it slightly ajar, even at night. Roberta goes over and knocks, then pushes it open a crack. Inside, the bright overhead light is on.

'Honey?'

Roberta fully opens the door. We see the space in the middle of the room where the wheeled bed should be, where Louise should be. The bed has gone. Above there's a row of empty plug sockets on the wall. Louise's things are spread around: her suitcase, her sparkly grey cardigan hung over a chair, a half-finished bottle of water, a magazine open on the floor, a greetings card on the windowsill.

The alarm has stopped but I still feel the wailing. It goes cold, and I think about the new father I heard on the phone earlier, his sheer luck, whoever he was. He'll be home now. He'll have gone out for a drink, swelling as he tells his mates about the healthy weight of his girl, and how good it felt to rock her in his arms, keeping her safe.

Through Louise's window we see the huge building of the main hospital. Behind a thousand curtains and slatted blinds, lights flicker on and off.

Postcard

From the pavement people look towards the camera, eyes squinting in the afternoon sun: a family in a doorway, a man and boy in front of a shop window, a group posed by the entrance to the synagogue. Shades flutter over the windows of the building adjacent.

A man in a long jacket stands stock still in the middle of the tram car lines as a crowd of small girls cross nearby, all in white pinafores and black stockings. A woman in a pale dress walks quickly away, her waist tightly corseted, her posture guarded, camera-shy.

The Adass Yisroel synagogue is five stories tall, a building much like the others on the street, with arched windows and an arched doorway, a decorative balcony two floors up. The building is well proportioned, with panelled glass and stone carvings. Blinds are lowered inside. Through them nothing can be seen.

1937

The first thing she senses is dryness in her mouth. And the smell. All hospitals have the same smell. She remembers this from the wards in Wedding where Cousin Jette does the laundry. It's a smell of bedsheets boiled clean, and the starchy soup with strands of meat that comes round on a trolley.

Vati refused to eat in hospital. No matter how much she and the nurses begged him, poor Vati wouldn't touch the soup. She remembers his sickly palour and his bedshirt hanging loose. He didn't say much by then. He just lay awake. But perhaps he didn't recognise her. His thoughts had gone far back to his childhood, to a happier time, playing in the Cheremosh river, the farmhouse with the Carpathians on the horizon, his father Moses and his brother Leib, and his mother whose name Dora took.

There's a clock above the bed, but Dora can't see the hands. She squeezes her eyes tight. Opens them again. There is patterned wallpaper that makes her eyes blur, and prayers in frames on every wall.

The day Vati died, she waited in the prayer room. Soft light was filtering through the window shaped like a Star of David. At first she was alone, but there was Jette's hand in hers, her cousin's soap-smelling skin, fingers still cold and swollen from the wet sheets. Marcus came later with a car for them. Jews hadn't been stopped from driving yet and he was still wearing his chauffeur uniform. The car had impressed her. Her and how many other women? He'd put his jacket over her shoulders and drove her and Jette away from the hospital. She was comforted by the weight of the jacket, the smell of him, tobacco and leather and citrus cologne. She'd had thoughts she shouldn't have on the night her father died, but maybe having no one left in the world can do that to you.

There's a sting between her legs. Under her nightdress there's still a roundness to her stomach, but it's different now, soft as dough. She presses in her fingers and finds a lump. It's round, about the size of an apple. She can almost get her whole hand around it, hard as if she's swallowed a rock. Touching it makes her suddenly dizzy and she wants to ask someone what it is, but there's no one around. The white walls of the room are darkening and she's sinking back into sleep.

Dora wakes again. It's evening now, or maybe dawn. A pinkish light shines through the curtain around her bed. The place is still, but there are footsteps. Someone is coughing and women are whispering. There are people nearby, she supposes, so she calls out, but they don't come in. Beside her bed someone has left a newspaper, a glass, and a jug of water.

Dora pushes herself up a little, moves to pour herself a drink and spills some. She closes her eyes, lies back on the bed. Perhaps she falls asleep once more with the glass of water on her chest, but only for a few seconds. She startles. Water nearly tips out of the glass. Again, she puts her other hand down to her belly, expecting the baby but finding only the small, hard mass. Such an odd, left-behind thing.

The light is warm now, a deep pink bleeding in the sky over the city. She looks around for the baby, any sign of it, just a bottle or a small blanket. She listens for crying. She holds her breath. Echoes from somewhere in the building trick her for a second, a shriek outside on the street that could be a child, a creaky wheel on a trolley that could be a whimper. An urgent need pulls her upright, too sudden perhaps. Her head spins, but she steadies herself.

A window has been opened and she can see more of the sky. She gulps the fresh air raw. There are drops on the windowpanes, but she can't remember it raining. Outside everything sounds exactly as usual. Streetcars and buses pass by. Birds fuss on the roof or somewhere in a nearby tree.

It seems like only an hour ago that she was standing on the kerb with Meta and Herbert, and she crossed the road and came into the crowded reception. She remembers the feel of the floor tiles shifting under her feet, loose from too much cleaning. Meta and Herbert would have gone home to eat their half-cooked dinner. They start work early in the morning.

A man comes in, followed by a nurse. They greet her with a blessing. The nurse is pushing a small wicker cradle.

'It's too soon for her to be up,' mutters the man.

'The doctor wants you to lie back,' the nurse says. 'If you do we can let you hold your daughter. You've had a little girl, so precious.'

The basket wheels to a stop. The air feels thin in her chest and the tick of the clock is loud, raw seconds sliced off time like rings of onion on the chopping board, pinpricks of pain from the juice, joy like a sharp, red cut. She has a girl.

She leans back, deep in the pillows that the nurse is still plumping. She's not sure she even knows how to hold a baby.

'You smiled all the way through,' says the nurse. 'I've never seen anything like it.'

The doctor asks Dora what she can remember.

'Nothing,' she says.

'Perfect.'

The nurse shushes as she reaches into the cradle.

'She is a dot,' the doctor continues. 'But you are petite yourself, so we expected her to be small. She's only a little early.'

He takes a pen out of his breast pocket and starts writing some notes before he's called away.

There's a noise like a hiccup from the blankets the nurse is cradling. Dora sees now that the baby has a full head of black hair. They've put a little cap on her head, but the hair pokes out.

'Be careful,' the nurse says, at last lifting the baby into Dora's arms. 'Your medicine won't have worn off. I'll wait while you meet each other. Then I'll take her away.'

Her daughter is tiny and cross, with sore, animal-looking skin. She strokes the red rims of the baby's ears and it screws up its face. It opens its eyes to see her, just a little. Its eyes are dark, polished black stones.

'Your cousin came by,' says the nurse. 'She wants to know the baby's name and says she will go and register the birth.'

Dora looks for a second at her daughter's head, as small and fresh as a peach, the grazed skin, pink mouth, glossy eyelids, and perfect oval chin.

'Ruth Rosa,' Dora says. Rosa for her grandmother. Ruth for her.

'Sweet names!' The nurse pulls the sheets straight and tucks them around Dora's feet. 'Is everything alright?'

Dora isn't sure. She remembers arriving at the hospital, the loose clicking tiles, and a crowd of people, a woman in front of her, well-dressed, with beautiful shoes that Meta would envy, and a fur collar. There was a large hamper on the woman's arm. *Weltverbesserer*, Dora remembers thinking. Here to do some world-bettering by bringing picnics to the sick.

But why is that the last thing she can remember?

Dora lifts the baby's bonnet and runs her hand over the hair, two soft dark whorls, still sticky. She puts her face close to her daughter's tiny head. She wants to remember this, the smell of her own girl just born.

The aches come to mind again. Standing in line, the pain in her back had moved right up her spine and radiated down to her knees. Her thighs shook, and she'd felt her strength draining, an unsteadiness like being on ice. She had a vision of Vati at the edge of a frozen pond. She saw him clear as day, laughing at her terrible skating all over again, and then the same light-headedness that she felt when she took her blades off.

She'd been sick. The vomit had splattered all over the tiled floor and up the side of the desk. A bell rung fiercely. The *Weltverbesserer* very upset about her shoes.

'Good health on your bellybutton!' an old man shouted after her as she was pushed into a chair and wheeled away.

After that, nothing. She remembers nothing about the birth, not a single detail.

'Let's keep the baby warm,' she is told.

Dora lets Ruthie go. The baby moans and shifts a little as the nurse takes her and puts her back in the cradle.

'Why can't I remember?' Dora asks.

'Modern medicine,' the nurse smiles, wheeling the basket backwards and forwards to soothe the baby. 'It's like magic. No more pain.'

'Will I remember later?'

The nurse shrugs. 'Everyone feels confused at first,' she says. 'Try not to let it upset you. Drink some water. Rest. I'll bring baby back when she's hungry. You should be able to feed her yourself by then.'

The wicker cradle squeaks away gently.

Dora has forgotten to ask about the lump in her belly.

Light of day starts to fade. Dora realises she has been twisting the corner of her sheet, making her fingers hurt, wishing for things to go back to how they were, when evening was exciting because Marcus would take her dancing. She unwinds the cotton and wipes her nose and a stray tear from the corner of her eye. The quiet is unbearable. The idea of sleep and the restfulness of this place disgusts her, so she reaches up and turns the light on. She picks up the glass of water, takes a little sip. She runs her fingers through her hair and scratches at her neck and under her arms. She can't get comfortable. She unfolds the newspaper just to look at the front page, checks the date. It's Friday. A day and a night have passed since she arrived, and across Berlin families will be lighting candles and breaking bread. In Große Hamburgerstraße, in the home for the aged, residents will be gathering in the dining room. Some of them will notice her absence from work and the ladies will guess that her time came early.

HITLER WILL ADDRESS MUSSOLINI, says the newspaper headline. There's a photo. Dora curls her lip at Shitler's face. She never reads anything about him, but tonight more than ever. Just looking at the small, spidery print makes her skin itch even more. She turns a page.

'Any newspapers?' a voice asks. A young nurse is at the end of the bed. She's not offering. She's collecting them. It's the Sabbath.

The nurse takes the newspaper and asks if Dora would like her curtains pulled. Dora nods and the curtain swoops around the bed, the fabric swinging and settling. She closes her eyes. She puts her hand down and cups the mysterious hard lump in her belly.

*

Marcus will find out about the birth soon enough, whether Herbert writes or not. Dora wishes he could see Ruthie's face, her swollen eyelids and black downy hair, still sticky from her passage into the world, tufts and swirls all over her scalp, curls perhaps, when she grows.

Dora already misses the weight of the baby on her chest, holding the tiny hands, the fingers with their feathery nails. Just a few hours ago those nails were inside her, tracing the shapes under her skin. Ruthie's been with her all these months, and Marcus, because Ruthie is his child. They've been curled in the dark middle of her ever since she lost Vati, making her not one but three people.

Behind the white curtains, she's not sure what is left. In the hushed ward, where she is supposed to become a mother, she just feels less.

29 May

There's a big round moon over Kilmarnock and no empty beds. A full moon brings out the babies, the midwives say, like moths attracted to light. One of them joked that it should be written into the staffing plans.

The forecast is for more heat, not a single cloud on the map, and tonight is the televised final of Eurovision. While the singers struggle to hit their high notes in Oslo, the maternity unit will ring with atonal screams.

I don't want to listen to births anymore.

Not long after Louise went into labour and disappeared, Stacey got into trouble. Now both of them are gone for good.

Stacey skipped out of the unit to go shopping, and the next thing we knew, her name was erased from the board. The social worker probably had something to do with why they came down on her so hard.

'It's not prison,' Stacey had said. 'Why shouldn't I go shopping?'

Roberta had told her not to be so stupid. 'You can't go shopping,' she said. 'You don't have any clothes.'

I was the last person to see her that afternoon. She was sitting on the bus shelter seats, pinning her eyes on every bus that went past. I'd jump on a bus too, I thought, if I was her. They were going to take a baby from her. They'd been doping her up on pills, so most of the time she was wandering around like a ghost, but maybe she didn't take them that day. Sitting at the bus stop, she looked like she had her mind set on something.

It was after dinner when we knew for sure she was gone. I was with Roberta in the lounge, eating Maltesers and grapes. TLC came out of her room and decided to join us. She had her cousin with her and I don't think she wanted us there. She hadn't let on why she was in hospital, so we still called her TLC behind her back. Her and her cousin were slurping from mugs of herbal tea.

The door to Stacey's room was shut. Roberta had peeped in and the room was empty, but when the midwives came into the lounge we lied. We said Stacey was watching telly in her bed. TLC looked like she wanted to snitch, but she wouldn't dare in front of Roberta.

Stacey sneaked back in again, right past the midwives laden with green and white carrier bags. She was still wearing her Tweety Pie nightdress, with a disconnected cannula stuck in her vein and hanging off her left hand. She was looking better, not so spacey.

'It's not fair,' TLC said to Roberta once Stacey was back in her room. 'Louise loses her baby, but *she* gets to have hers.'

I felt Roberta shift, and the walls of the room seemed close.

'Louise should be given that baby,' said TLC's cousin. The two of them seemed oblivious to the change in the room, their eyes pinned on Stacey's door.

'Are you serious?' Roberta said.

I stared. I noticed the dew on TLC's upper lip as she blew on her hot tea.

Roberta stared too. 'Where's your hearts?'

They dropped their conversation for a while but then TLC started again.

'The midwives said she just goes and has another anyway.'

The cousin nodded.

'Wouldn't you?' Roberta asked them. 'Have another.'

TLC placed a palm over her belly. 'I can't believe anyone would defend her. She makes me sick.'

She took a deep slurp of her scalding hot drink and winced.

'It's probably drugs,' said her cousin.

They fidgeted in their seats, nudging closer.

'I don't know what kind of herbal tea that is, ladies,' Roberta said, getting to her feet. 'But you've had enough.'

I followed Roberta to Stacey's room to look at her stuff from the shops. On the chair by her window she'd laid out new baby things, adding to the pile of clothes she already had. More tiny pink outfits hooked over the arms, everything still on hangers. There was a shiny pink coat with a fluffy cuff around the hood, ready for next winter. A mobile was clipped to the windowsill. There were packs of socks, five tiny pairs in shades of pink and white and cream, and body suits with kittens printed on them. She had nappies and wipes and a changing mat with polka dots, and a pile of yellow and pink muslin cloths. There were hats, mittens, and a pure white cardigan, two pairs of tights and a dress with a collar and a bow. There were dummies and bottles, a steriliser in a huge box. Everything was spread out so we could see it. While we talked she picked things up and stroked them, unfolded them, pressed them to her face.

Someone told the midwives about the shopping trip. Not hard to guess who. A couple of nights later I had a weird dream. I was knitting, but the wool wasn't wool. I was teasing out these wet strands. Pink, shiny membranes. They were like gums, like the inside of cheeks, those stretchy bits under the tongue. And then I realised that I wasn't knitting. I was just winding this pink stretchy stuff. I was winding it round everything, all the way round my fingers, up my arm, loops round the chair leg and my ankle. I reached down into my knitting bag, wanting to stuff it all in there, but it wouldn't go away. It was all about my neck and in my hair. It was sticking to me like bubble gum, more and more strands pulling themselves up. When I raised my arms the strands went thin, like melted mozzarella, but there were always more. Roberta appeared.

'Where did you learn that?' she said. She found the whole thing hilarious, and I suppose it was.

'From my grandmother,' I told her.

I woke up with a burn in my throat, tasting sick. I knew I'd retched up stomach acid. It happened a lot now, and I'd started sleeping on a pile of pillows to try and prevent it. There was noise going on. At first I thought it was part of the dream still playing out in my head. Boots were stamping in the corridor. A van full of police were here, the sudden bass hum and bark of male voices. Through the slats of my blind I could see the shadows of them moving on the wall. Black uniforms, laced black combats. We'd been told to stay in our rooms that night, a curfew, but no one had known why. It was so they could do this: send these uniforms into Stacey's room uninvited in the middle of the night. They held her down while a doctor stuck a needle into her. I heard her call out in panic, sudden and high, instantly cut off. It sounded like a name. I think it must have been 'Roberta'.

Everyone else slept through it.

The next day I woke up unsure if it had really happened. But the auxiliaries moved in, just like they did after Louise, and they packed away and wiped down all traces of Stacey, the crayon drawings on the wall and the soft pink clothes, the trembling birds on the mobile. They swept and mopped and cleansed, and neutralized. We were supposed to just forget.

The midwives have been hiding away, scoffing tea and biscuits to calm their nerves. They huddle behind the flowers, the pink and blue 'thank you's and the 'it's a boy' and 'it's a girl' cards. They tell each other stories and laugh. We asked where Stacey had gone and we were told to let it go. They couldn't share information, they said, but Roberta stood at their door and bugged them for days, asking and asking till eventually one gave in and told us. Stacey had a little girl, small but healthy.

'End of story,' the midwife said.

She's still here, we think, somewhere in the hospital.

I'm letting the days pass slowly now, not bothering to take my meals in the canteen. I don't want to be friendly with the staff or make conversation with the new mothers. I miss going to work. I sit at my window and look for planes cutting through the sky to the airport or making a beeline up and away. I write an email to a colleague, the only other woman I work with regularly. It doesn't say anything I really want to say, but I tell her she should visit. I wish I had more visitors. She replies an hour later between her shifts on the radar, but doesn't get the hint. She says she can't wait to see me and the baby soon, and to let her know when we're home. I feel like one of the bright dots headed for the runway.

'Want to pick a country?' Roberta asks, busting into my room and making me jump. She's been trying to smooth things over between us and TLC. She says since we're all stuck here, we might as well try to get along, and the whole thing's getting her down. I don't like seeing Roberta so depressed.

'Go on and pick a country for the Eurovision,' she says.

'Italy's not in the Eurovision are they?'

'No, and if they were *I'd* be picking Italy, so I would,' Roberta says. 'I've got Spain. TLC's got Romania. The midwives have taken Ireland, Sweden, Portugal, and a few others. I'll put you down for Germany, alright? Same as the football. I was actually saving it for you seems as you've a German granny.'

Roberta writes me down on a piece of paper.

'What do I win?' I say.

She laughs.

'It's just something to do, honey. No prize.'

Later that afternoon I see TLC in the corridor. Through the window we can hear cars arriving and leaving, a busy shift about to change. She looks at me like she might say something, but then goes into her room. The door clicks shut like a full stop. Good.

Matthew visits. Today he comes straight from work and takes a shower here. It's probably against the rules, but I don't care. After that we lie on my bed and watch a programme together. He almost falls asleep. When he's gone I go into the bathroom and smell his shower gel, the one he's always used. I think about the day we met, just a few months after I moved here for work. I was out for a walk, and he had his mother's dog on a lead. Molly. She was old and slow. She kept wanting to stop. We got talking. Before either of us realised it, it ended up feeling like a first date.

Roberta knocks on my door. Eurovision's starting, and we go through to the lounge. TLC's already there. She makes her tea, weird smelling herbal stuff again, and then sits down blowing steam off the top of her mug. Romania, her bet, is up next. Roberta is reading the *TV Times*. We don't talk and I only have half an eye on the telly. I've brought my knitting with me.

The window's open, and there's plenty of screaming coming from the birthing pools. More than one birth in progress by the sound of it. I try and tune it out. There's traffic on the road and I can hear that too. I wish Matthew could have stayed later. At the weekend he brought the van, still loaded with logs, and I went down to the car park with him. We sat on the logs in the back and drank fizzy drinks. I looked at the insides of the tree trunks with all their concentric circles. He told me which was which. Oaks, Sycamores, Ashes.

'How old is that?' I asked, pointing to the largest.

'Count the rings,' he laughed, but there were too many to count.

I asked him why some rings are thick and some are thin.

'I've told you that before,' he said.

'It's about the sun, isn't it?'

'Aye,' he said. 'Solar flare and local conditions: damp, frost, toxins, air pollution.' He said some of those trees he'd cut down were a century old.

I wish he would pull into the car park right now, with his binoculars and the Celestron telescope. We could sneak out and go stargazing.

*

Romania's song starts. A man and a woman belt out the lyrics, and they accompany themselves on two transparent pianos that are conjoined in the middle. Around them backing singers, pyrotechnics and lights all fight for attention.

'Sorry honey,' Roberta laughs at TLC. 'I don't think you're going to win.'

TLC ignores her. She concentrates on the song, tapping her hand to the beat and reading the lyrics that jump along the bottom of the picture. When it finishes, she gets up and says that she's going back to her room for a while. She feels tired.

We stare at the screen.

'Have you met the auxiliary that only likes baby boys?' I ask Roberta. 'She came into my room today to clean the television.'

'She's a case,' Roberta says. 'You shouldn't have told her you're having a boy. She'll never leave you alone now.'

The auxiliaries wear turquoise tunics. One does sheets, one mops floors, and this one only cleans the screens that hang on creaky brackets above the beds. She moves from room to room, spraying and wiping.

'Boys are tremendous,' she said today. She stopped wiping for a moment and took a break, leaning against the windowsill. Her face was in shadow and the sun behind her made her red hair light up. There was a hard note to her voice.

'Boys love their mothers, so they do. If you do have a boy, he'll give you a lot of love.'

Right at that moment I could feel the baby inside me squirming. He's running out of space. Sometimes he seems to be pushing extra hard against my skin, not kicking or wriggling but pushing against the membranes. He's listening all the time, so I tell him what to do when he is born.

'Scream, so we know you've survived.'

Birth must be a shock. The sudden cold and the bright light.

'You think I'm talking nonsense but I'm not. Girls are fine, but boys are more loving. You'll see.' The auxiliary was folding the cloth over and over in her hands.

Not many boys have been born in my family. My mother only has sisters, and I'm an only-child. I wonder if Dora wanted a boy. Through all her pregnancies she kept working, manning a machine that rolled cloth in the Reid and Welsh woollen mill, shining a light and checking the cloth for broken threads. After work, she'd clean houses. Hard, sweaty work. I'm so weak by comparison. I spent the first three months of my pregnancy signed off work half the time, sleeping as much as possible on the sofa beside Matthew's shelves. For once we were on a par. I was full of the baby, nauseous, and Matthew had his insomnia, his creams for the rashes and insect bites he gets in the forest, and pills for his back aches and tooth pains. Both of us were shattered. It was January before I felt better. I already had an obvious bump but suddenly I felt stronger. There were three inches of hard-packed ice on the ground, and at the airport the planes were grounded. I went out with a shovel onto the road that leads to our house and broke up the ice and snow. I placed my feet wide apart and swung the shovel hard against the ground, feeling the vibrations of each blow and imagining the icy branches above me shuddering.

By then the doctors couldn't keep up with the fibroids. They described them as fruit. First they were apricots, then they were small apples, and then they were two grapefruits and an orange. They kept multiplying till they filled half the uterus. When we saw my insides on the screen, the tumours looked like a planetary system, with the tiny baby spacewalking between them. I was convinced it would be crowded out, but eventually things settled down. The baby was safer. I was told the tumours might shrink, a painful process called red degeneration, like dying stars, but this didn't happen. Mine held on. Multiplying, conjoining, calcifying. Growing and growing.

'Do you want anything from the canteen?' says Roberta, pushing herself up.

I shake my head.

The Russians finish singing on the telly, and after a couple of minutes of cheering and a short video about Norwegian mountains, the camera pans around the stage. Next is the Armenian entry. Roberta comes back with a plate of pastries and I end up taking one anyway.

'Germany's next,' I say, biting into a bun with icing on top.

The singer has long black hair and she stands alone on the stage, but just as she opens her mouth to sing we hear something weird: a long whooping call. We're used to hearing noises like this coming from the delivery ward, but this time it's much closer. Roberta goes to the door and sticks her head into the corridor.

The red button cuts in and almost immediately the midwives are in action, running this way. They go straight into TLC's room. For a second the pastry sticks in my throat, but the alarm stops as abruptly as it started, and right away we hear the gargling cry of a new baby. A midwife comes back out and hurries down the corridor.

'It's a girl!'

She grabs one of the transparent cots on wheels.

'All girls here at the moment,' she says. 'Blonde hair.'

Germany wins. Roberta comes into my room to see the singer crowned. We adjust the arm of the pull-down screen and sit back. In Oslo, the dark-haired girl is on stage again. She's smiling, with lots of German flags and balloons waving in the crowd around her. They cheer and throw shiny confetti. The song is about satellites. For the first time in days, I feel okay, like a plug's been pulled out.

'I really want to go to Berlin,' I say.

'You should,' Roberta says. 'We've not been to Italy in ten years. Antonella keeps nagging me about it.'

'Then you should, too,' I tell her. 'Show her where she's from.'

The credits are rolling. Another long list of names. As always, I think of Dora's list.

We knock on TLC's door and she says to come in. She's breastfeeding. The baby has a thick head of fair hair, just like hers. She tells us that she's fine, but that she's a little disappointed. She wanted a baby with dark hair.

'All my babies have had fair hair,' she says.

Roberta puts a hand on TLC's shoulder.

'Are you for real?' she laughs. She's smiling, but I know she's still thinking about Stacey.

Matthew phones late. He has taken some pictures of Saturn and he emails them over. The night sky has been keeping him busy all throughout the pregnancy. He's become obsessed with space and the relationship between trees and the universe. Not long before I became pregnant he bought the Celestron telescope, and he drags it nightly to the front of the house, leaving it to reach air temperature before pointing it at astral bodies. For most of the last nine months we've been using it to observe Jupiter, which has been unusually low and bright on the horizon. We watched the orange swirls on the planet's surface, and we tracked the clouds around its great, stormy eye. This week Saturn's trajectory has lined it up behind the moon, so that the two seem poised to kiss. In Matthew's photographs, taken through the lens of his telescope, Saturn looks just like the planet I've seen in cartoons. It's perfectly round and bright, encircled with rings and tinged blue-green.

I tell Matthew about TLC and the baby arriving at satellite speed. I wonder if the moon is responsible.

'Probably,' he says.

The next name on the midwives' delivery board is mine, and unless the universe interferes with our plan, I have just eleven days to go.

Infants and nurses in a Jewish Home, Nieder-schönhausen, Berlin. Photographs by Herbert Sonnenfeld, dated 1937.

A row of wicker cradles is lined up on the grass. Three nurses tend to the infants. The smallest babies lie on their backs gazing at clouds, but the older ones pull themselves up, peering over the sides of the cradles. They are dressed in whites that sparkle in the sun. The nurses wear striped dresses with sleeves rolled over their elbows. The dresses are covered with white aprons, straps that cross behind the shoulders and tie around their waists. Stiff, white hats with rectangle rims are pinned to the front of the nurses' hairstyles. The hats bob over the babies like folded paper boats on a sky-blue sea.

Behind the babies there is a flowerbed and a path that winds through young trees. Here the bigger children have thrown off their clothes and they play naked in the sunshine. They link hands around a fruit tree, arms thrown out, slim bodies stretching up like plants.

1937

Dora has visited once before. Niederschönhausen. It's a nest of green way out on the tram line that stretches north beyond Pankow to the fringes of the city. The district is easy to get lost in, with many side streets and dead ends, large gardens full of tall trees and mansion houses, high fences and gates, motor cars parked in driveways, rooftops hidden behind leaves, and birds fluttering and chirping in branches. It feels faraway but clean, a healthy place for a baby.

She leaves the hospital on Elsässer Straße holding Ruthie wrapped in a blanket, and they're put in the back of an ambulance. The upholstered seats and the silence are luxuries she remembers from other times, after hours in Marcus's car. Already forgetting the bland sensations of the ward, speeding through the streets she finds it easy to look ahead, imagining everything will be alright. She senses the itch, and with one hand she fumbles open the buttons of her blouse to feed Ruthie. The first minute of feeding always hurts. A cutting feeling, then the emptying sensation, tickle of her milk running into Ruthie's mouth, her heart widening. Dora looks at her as she suckles, content. Her tiny lips open and flutter.

Beyond Pankow the streets empty out, leaving the openness Dora remembers from her first visit: gardens and trees, and flat pavements with not a soul walking on them. A grey sky peeks through damp branches and October leaves. Rain begins to pour.

When they arrive, the driver carries Dora's case. He puts an umbrella up over her and the baby and they walk to the entrance. Ruthie has fallen asleep, and Dora tucks the blanket under her chin.

Even on a dull day, the home is full of light, with windows open and nursery rhymes on the breeze. The whole place has been modernised, they told her, with glass walls between the little dormitories, and views over the garden. The aunts are all young and smiling, and here they give every child its own personal things: a bowl, a cup, a towel, a brush. Each item is embroidered or painted with initials.

'You and baby will be right at the top,' Tia Anna tells Dora as they climb the staircase. 'And there are lots of us here to help you.'

Halfway up the stairs, a group of children comes down in single file, chubby fingers strumming the spindles. They pause to push their faces through the gaps and giggle. They coo and crowd around Dora till another of the aunts reminds them to keep walking.

'They are going down to lunch now,' says Tia Anna. 'We eat at one sharp.'

Tia Anna pets the children on their cheeks and hair. She tells one boy to stop swinging on the banister, but her voice is kind. When the children have gone, she continues up the stairs.

'You can have lunch in your room today,' she says.

There is a bed and a basket for them in the mother and baby room. Another white painted space, but here there are three beds, each one spread with a colourful quilt. Dora and Ruth are alone for now, Tia Anna says. It's been a quiet month.

She chooses the bed furthest from the door. It's tucked under the eaves, and the basket beside it is close to the window so Ruthie will see the clouds going by. The window is set into the roof, with a view into the treetops in the back garden. There's a little chest of drawers and a wardrobe, and inside it a shelf of clean, folded towels. On a small stand near the door there are folded white napkins and a pot of pins for changing Ruthie.

They like mothers to stay for three months, but Dora can only afford six weeks. When her time ends, she will need to go back to work, leaving Ruthie behind. Then, they will only see each other on Dora's day off. The date of their goodbye has already imprinted itself upon her. A weight in her chest, a constant hum, a burn behind her eyes. She knows she'll find this date waiting to catch her out and trip her up. It'll be everywhere she goes, in a lump in her bed, an ugly fleck in the mirror, a crust that makes her choke. Worse still, she knows she'll also find the sickness hidden in good things. Folding Ruthie's tiny clothes, the chirp of the birds in the morning, and the look on the face of the teddy bear that Cousin Jette sent to the hospital. Dora can already feel an ugly gap opening inside herself, like the space that will be left in her suitcase when Ruthie's things are removed.

'I'm going to show you how we do everything here,' Tia Anna says. 'How to bathe her, change her napkins, feed her, how to do her sheets. If you do things the way we do them, it will be easier for her later, when you go. She'll have a routine.'

The pulling ache. Later is already here, Dora thinks, a reminder not to love too much.

'If she is sleeping, you may as well have a bath,' Tia Anna says. 'When did baby last feed?'

'In the ambulance.'

A bath is a great luxury, but Dora doesn't feel like it. Even so, she isn't sure she is allowed to refuse. She puts Ruthie down gently in the little basket and sets her case on top of the bed. Meta has brought her more things, all the clothes she needs, some books, her knitting needles and some wool. There are dresses for Ruthie to grow into that Meta made from offcuts at work, and there's the teddy from Cousin Jette. It wears a bell around its neck.

Tia Anna covers Ruth with blankets, tucking them firmly around her body and nipping the edges under the mattress. Ruthie whimpers a complaint.

'She's fine,' says Tia Anna. 'Go now before she wakes.'

The hot tap is stiff. Dora twists till eventually there's a hiss and water starts to splutter into the deep bath. Dora watches it splashing around the enamel before she adjusts the temperature. She takes off her clothes. At the sink she looks at her face in the mirror. The rain has turned her hair into a wiry frizz and she has dark circles under her eyes. Her breasts are already hard and full with milk again, and the nipples are sore. Each time she feeds Ruthie she has the stabbing pain that lasts a minute before it becomes bearable. She grits her teeth, grinding her heel into the floor. Sometimes she'll feel a lurch inside her pelvis that makes her cross her legs, and then she thinks of the hard apple lump inside her.

Dora turns off the taps and lies back, her head resting on the rim of the tub, her feet starting to float. She sees the mirror begin to steam before she shuts her eyes, not quite relaxed, always listening for Ruthie. She wants this bath now. She strokes her hands over her breasts and down to her empty belly. The hard thing is still there. She has kept it secret. She pushes her fingers into it, and it shifts, but only slightly. Perhaps it will never leave. It will stay with her, like an oyster clutching some part of her daughter and Marcus, something precious under her skin.

Dora listens for any sounds. Tia Anna's footsteps, a drawer being opened or shut, or a tuneful humming to keep Ruthie asleep. The ache of later, the goodbye to come, is ringed with something more vicious. She wants to scream at the helpful nurses, especially the pretty Tia Anna, whose smile was like dripping honey to the little children on the stairs.

She opens her eyes and sees clouds of milk around her chest. It reminds her of the kitchens at work, pouring salt into boiling pans and seeing it swirl white. She rests her head again, feeling the hard edge of the bath at the nape of her neck. Ruthie has a birthmark here. It's right in the centre of her neck, a little triangle of darkened skin in the shape of a moth. A midwife told her it would fade, but so far it hasn't.

Dora wrings out her hair and stands up, pulls the plug, and reaches for her towel. Her hair drips down her back.

Tia Anna has gone away, and the mother and baby room is empty except for Ruthie, who's still sleeping in the little basket. Dora puts on fresh underwear with a thick pad, a clean loose dress, and she sits down next to her suitcase. Sometimes Ruthie makes funny noises in her sleep, but today she is silent. The rain has stopped, and the sun is streaming in through the open window. Some children have gone outside to play under the trees in the garden. Droplets of water cling to the window and drip from leaves. Dora goes to look out. There's a donkey and a little goat that the children are feeding with dandelions. The goat bleats and a small girl pats him and copies the noise, holding out a fist full of grass. When these children are six, if they haven't returned to their families, they'll be moved to one of the big Jewish homes in the city. Some of them will end up at Reichenheim, the place Vati chose for Dora after her mother died. She was there for ten years, always returning to Vati at weekends. Sometimes after school she would visit Auntie Dotti and her cousins, who were only a short walk away.

She is supposed to rest, but she can't. Ruthie seems too quiet. Dora lies on the bed fretting at the silence, and the hard lump in her stomach seems to sink into her. She gets to her feet and stares into the basket. Under all the covers that Tia Anna has tucked in, it's impossible to see if Ruth is breathing. Dora gently shakes the bundle, but Ruthie still makes no sound, so she peels the blankets off, pulling them out from under the mattress.

How can so tiny a thing make such gut wrenching noises? Dora tries to calm her, but Tia Anna comes rushing back in, offering to take Ruthie away.

'I thought she stopped breathing,' Dora apologises.

'Babies need to sleep,' Tia Anna says, flapping a hand. 'Just leave her and do something else while you have the chance.'

Ruthie is rooting at Dora's breast, so Tia Anna goes away to fetch Dora's dinner tray. By the time she gets back, Ruthie is sucking happily.

'No pain?'

'No,' Dora lies. She covers herself so Tia Anna won't see the sore skin.

'You gave me a shock,' Tia Anna says. 'You probably frightened her as well, poor thing.'

Dora leans over Ruthie, hiding her, curling away from the window where Tia Anna is silhouetted against the clearing sky.

Days go by more or less the same after this, feeding, changing, more feeding. Never enough sleep. The date draws nearer. A new mother who was supposed to come and share the room never arrives, and Dora wonders why. Perhaps the father came back or perhaps… No one mentions her again. The skin on Dora's knees rubs away from kneeling to change and dress Ruthie, and she has stabbed her fingers so many times with the ends of the pins they're now numb. At night Ruth cries unless she is held, her back patted firmly. The Tias tell Dora they'll do it, but she never fetches them to help. When there's no one around she sings to Ruthie under her breath, and Ruthie goes quiet and stares back into Dora's face. Dora puts her hand around Ruthie's head and strokes down to the moth-shaped birth mark.

'She likes this,' Dora says to Tia Anna one evening. She is swallowing her anger. She hopes that this will be remembered. Perhaps, when she has to go away, they'll use this trick to calm Ruthie and send her to sleep. They might do something her way.

Tia Anna smiles, watching Dora's thumb circling over the moth's wings.

'She is so pretty,' Tia Anna says.

Dora nods. 'I can't stop looking at her.'

When Ruthie is nearly a month old, Dora is told she can take her outside. It's a mild morning, and the gardeners in Niederschönhausen have created huge piles of fallen leaves on the pavement, perfect for children to jump through. Tia Anna leads Dora to the entrance of the infant home and wheels out a modern, expensive pram with shiny paint, wicker panels, gleaming mudguards and a long, slender handle. Such an expensive pram could dress a department store window. Meta would be speechless.

She tucks Ruthie under the satin cover, wraps her fingers around the metal handle, and feels how smoothly the wheels turn. She follows the long crocodile of children on the way to the park. The carriage glides over every bump, and Ruthie sleeps, her face a picture under her little wool cap.

'Isn't it a beauty?' Tia Anna says, moving her fingertips over the shiny paintwork. 'All the mothers love to take their babies out in it. A donor left it as a gift, a generous lady. She emigrated last year.'

After a silence, Dora asks her, 'Will you leave?'

Tia Anna shrugs. 'Someone has to stay with the children.'

They reach the park. The children will stop and play, but Dora is told she can keep walking round the path if she would like. She and Ruthie can go wherever they want now, as long as they're back for meals and Ruthie is in her basket by seven o'clock at night.

'The fresh air is good for her,' Tia Anna says. 'And you're doing very well, a natural.'

The words take Dora by surprise. She feels the burn behind her eyes and leans over and kisses Anna goodbye. The weight lessens a little that day.

Dora knows that she looks nice when she takes the pram to the shops. The lump left in her belly isn't visible. She can only find it with her fingers when she lies down, and in the early morning she feels it pressing, but most of the time she doesn't think about it. Her figure is flatter now and her clothes fit nicely again.

People turn to look as she walks along. Old ladies stop her and everyone admires the baby. Dora imagines Marcus driving by. He sees her pushing the beautiful pram and slows the car. Dora thinks about this day after day, every time she's out with the pram. She spends time imagining every word that Marcus will say to her when he gets out of the car, and how it will feel when he holds her again and tells her he has come back from Beuchen for her and for Ruthie. But he hasn't even written. At the very least, she thought he would write.

With each day that passes the bounce in the pram wheels feels less like dancing. The sickness gets worse. The nights also lengthen. Instead of sleeping she opens the curtains and stares at the sky, pinpricks of stars and clouds passing. When the final days come they bring with them a dismal spell of fog and mist and rain. The mist is so thick that in the evenings even the streetlights look defeated, their bright light rubbed out by the murk.

Dora has an appointment at a photographer's studio in Pankow on their last morning together, and for once the rain abates. She was told not to go out in the damp weather, but she wants to get a photograph made of Ruthie in the pram, and she won't let anyone stop her today.

It feels like the morning after Vati left her. She has no appetite. She skips breakfast, staying in her room, avoiding a young mother who has delivered a baby boy and taken up one of the beds. They don't talk much. This girl has weeks ahead of her before the days darken. She and Dora inhabit the same room but different seasons.

Dora dresses herself and puts Ruthie in the pram. They do exactly what they have done every morning, nothing different, though she feels heavy and clumsy today, unable to even dream of Marcus driving by. Trams pass. Dora thinks about getting on one of them, taking it to the end of the line, then walking again, pushing the pram further and further from Berlin, the sickness in her stomach lifting like the weather. She watches the tram numbers. She stops and looks at a timetable, working out where the furthest reaches of the line could leave her. Then she sits at the stop, watching clouds of her breath in the cold air. She lights one cigarette after another, and one by one she lets the trams rattle away.

She's too early to go to the appointment at the photographic studio, so she decides she'll look in the shop windows and buy a small gift for Tia Anna and the children.

Julius Moser Papier is just off the main street. Ruthie is sound asleep, so Dora kicks on the pram brake and pushes open the door of the shop. Inside there's a strong smell of blank paper, like starting school, the ink and the untouched exercise books, and the colourful cones that will be filled with toys and sweets on the first day. There are greetings cards, boxes, gift wrap, diaries, address books and notebooks with covers in colourful patterns. There are fancy pens in cases, and boxes of perfect crayons lined up in rainbows, unsharpened pencils, wooden rulers, tins of paint, and leather cases in different sizes.

At the counter an old man is reading the newspaper. He looks up from behind his glasses and asks if she needs any help. His accent reminds her of Vati.

Dora asks for a book of bedtime stories displayed in the window. The book has a blue cloth cover embossed with pink and green flowers and leaves.

The shopkeeper sets down his newspaper, unbolts and raises the counter, and slowly walks to the window. He leans on his walking stick.

'Here we are,' he says, reaching for the book and slowly walking back to the counter. 'The last one.'

Dora flicks the crisp, clean pages.

'A gift?'

Dora nods. The man offers to wrap the book for free, so she pays and then waits, watching as he expertly folds the book into a double sheet of green paper. Dora remembers, too late, that she had intended to write a message for Ruthie inside the book, something she could read when she was old enough, but the man is taking such pains with the gift wrapping that she doesn't want to stop him. He decorates the parcel with ribbon, and he glues a small label to the front. All of this he does with patience and enormous care.

The man is giving her change when a bell over the door rings and two boys walk in. The first could be sweet if it weren't for the uniform. Both Hitler Youth. The second is older, tall and handsome. They look around for a minute.

'Do you sell red ink?' says the younger one, coming up to the counter. He's about thirteen. His skin is still a child's, soft as silk.

The shopkeeper inhales slowly. He holds his hands together as if to stop them shaking. Dora hopes that Ruthie won't wake up.

'I sell every colour of ink,' the shopkeeper says quietly.

'Really?' says the boy. He picks up some pencils. 'I didn't see the one I want.'

Dora turns to look out of the shop window at the pram.

'Never mind,' says the older boy, his expression blank. He takes the nearest thing he can find, a blue glass weight, and clumsily juggles it from one hand to the other and back again. 'This is a Jewish shop anyway.'

The younger one stares at the man, waiting for a reaction.

'If you don't mind,' the shopkeeper says after a pause. 'I would just like to see this young lady out.'

Dora feels their eyes on her as she walks with the man. He opens the door and thanks her for her business. Behind him, something is knocked over and small items roll over the floor.

'Where are you going? I haven't paid you for this,' laughs the older boy.

The man shuffles back towards the counter, bending slowly to pick up the things the boys have scattered. Dora sees that Ruthie is still asleep, so she puts the present in the bottom of the pram and goes back into the shop to help the man pick up the pencils and inks that are rolling across the floor.

'He doesn't want our money,' the younger boy grins.

They push past. The small one sticks his tongue out, twisting it grotesquely in her face.

'We'll let you off this time.' The older boy spits.

Ruthie begins to cry and the two boys stop to peer into the pram.

'Aaah, look! Cu-coo,' the younger one says. 'That's a nice baby.'

'Don't,' says the other. 'It's a Jew.'

The boys wander off laughing and shouting.

The old man shakes his head. 'I have known them since they were that old themselves,' he whispers. 'They used to be a nice family. Don't ask me what happened. But they won't harm a baby.'

'They took something from you without paying,' Dora says.

She pulls a handkerchief from her pocket and blows her nose.

'I don't need trouble. Let it go.'

Dora takes the man to the counter and lifts it for him to go through. He sits on his stool again.

'Do you want a cigarette?'

'Yes,' the man says. He pats his hand over hers on the countertop. She gives him her last cigarette and lights it for him. He nods a thank you.

Ruth cries louder.

'Poor bissel thing,' the man says. 'Go and get her.'

'I have to feed her,' Dora says.

He gives Dora a stool in a little storage room, and she feeds Ruthie and lulls her back to sleep. The old man continues to tidy and rearrange. She hears the way his feet shuffle over the wooden shop floor. Dora fiddles with her blouse and Ruthie switches sides, knocking her forehead eagerly at Dora's chest. Dora will let her have her fill. The aunties have started giving Ruth bottles, in preparation for them taking over. Ruthie fights this ferociously, with howls of despair that Dora can hear even when she's pushed out of sight and the door shut behind her. Even as she walks away from the sound of Ruthie screaming, Dora's body answers. She feels the itch, right on cue, the tickle of cloth against her nipples, and before she's reached her attic room she's soaked and sticky with milk. She folds napkins and stuffs them into her blouse. She rinses away the clammy liquid with cold, clear water.

Take all you can, she thinks, and she feeds and rocks until Ruthie is dreaming in her arms, her mouth open but empty now, and lips still moving at the memory of sucking.

When Dora comes out the man is sweeping, one hand on his back.

'Do you need help?'

He frowns and waves her off.

'It's an old injury. I was a soldier once. Here,' he says. He takes something from the counter and hands it to her. It is a new photograph album with a bright green leather cover. 'A gift for you. You can put a photo of the baby inside.'

Dora's heart sinks a little. The appointment with the photographer.

'I would much rather give something nice to you,' says the man, 'than have those swines come in here and take it. I don't know how much longer I will be here.'

It rains heavily all the way back, so much that it's hard to see the street where the trams trail off to the North. She finds some shelter, already soaked, and sits on a wall, pulling the pram close. The drips from her wet hair run down her cheeks, hiding the tears she gives in to. She thinks of the man closing his paper shop, maybe for the last time, and remembers how Vati loved his workshop, the exact pattern of wrinkles on his forehead when he was concentrating, the polished cases, the clocks ticking on every wall, the sound of his voice. For once, it's not Marcus but Vati she wants to come, scoop her up, and take her far away.

Dora lifts the pram blanket and looks at the new photograph album and the carefully wrapped book of bedtime stories. She strokes the leather on the photo album like she used to stroke Vati's arm. The photograph of Ruthie that she imagined will just have to stay in her head. A memory of their walks with the pram.

Ruthie sleeps, lulled by the sound of the rain. So sweet now and untroubled.

Found Pictures 1

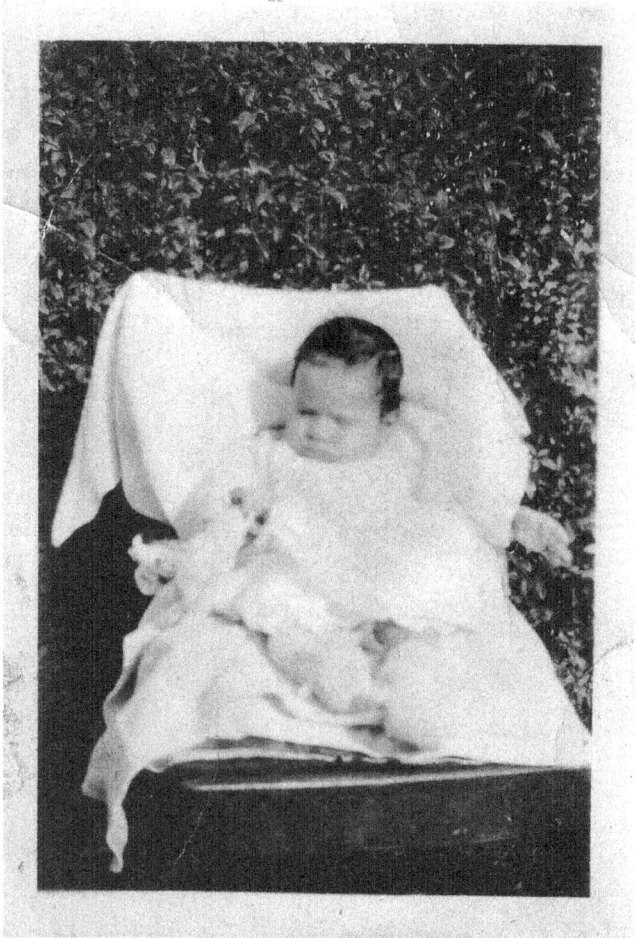

9 June

There are no windows downstairs and no way to know which way we're facing or what's happening beyond the smooth, whitewashed walls of the hospital. Like a departures lounge, we know we'll be here for only a short time. Matthew looks at me. We don't know what to say to each other. We are two passengers that have just met, boarding the same flight and discovering we're sitting next to each other.

The surgery isn't as clinical as I expected. The operating table is in the middle of the room, and it tips to raise a patient's feet slightly higher than her head, an angle that reduces blood loss. A large light is positioned over the table, and there are machines gathered at its foot, cabinets and trays to hold medical equipment and supplies for blood transfusions, a chair for Matthew and an area with an infant's weighing scales, already prepared with a cotton terry cloth and a clean paper cover. There is a sink and cupboards. Along the far wall I think I see chairs at a long white countertop.

After the operation starts, I see other things. Personal looking items cluttering the countertop along the wall, colourful cards, a music player, a domestic sort of mess that is comforting. Are those things real? At the top of the wall there's a narrow window. I can see part of the roof and a slice of sky. A plane cuts past.

So far nothing has been painful. I was asked to sit on the table and my gown was lifted over my back. I leant forward, curling my spine for the anaesthetist. Matthew held my hand as the man placed his hands over my vertebra and seemed to check a few bones, stroking my jutting spine with his fingertips like an archaeologist discovering a dinosaur. The injection, when it was done, was completely painless. We waited for it to take effect. I thought it hadn't worked, but they sprayed freezing compressed air onto my hand, and then on the skin of my legs. There, I couldn't feel a thing.

Our son's heartbeat is currently a regular one-hundred-and-forty beats per minute. Dubstep, Matthew says. This is a good deal slower than it was at the start of the pregnancy, when he made a sound recording of the home doppler hitting drum and bass levels of one-hundred-and-eighty beats per minute. Matthew watches the monitor. He hasn't shaved once in the weeks I've been in the antenatal ward. He looks as if he spent last night in the woods, stretched out like an animal, high up on an oak branch. But I can see his nervousness, the crazy smile he flashes me every few minutes, the way he doesn't stop stroking my hand.

My legs have been covered with surgical blankets and plastic and foam that reminds me of soft fruit packaging. Usually a curtain goes up, but I wanted to watch. I can't see anyway thanks to the masses of connective tissue, the rugby ball fibroid and the cherries, the stone apple, the oranges and grapefruit. My belly hides everything. Instead, I watch my surgeon's expression as she begins to work, the small movements of her lower arms, her white plastic gloves snapped high over the sleeves of the blue gown. Her hands are deft, long-fingered, precise. The others, a midwife, the anaesthetist, and a second surgeon, will step in if there are complications. It's the rugby ball they're worried about. They've also brought students. It's a small crowd, but for now everyone is still, watching as the surgeon slowly peels back layers, breaching skin and muscle to reach the amniotic sac. I wonder what this looks like. The first glimpse of a baby in his waters, separated only by a membrane, transparent like the skin inside an eggshell. I squint at the silver edge of the surgical lamp above me, trying to see something in the reflection.

It's then I realise someone else is here. She's sitting in the corner on a rocking armchair. My heart skips. I can tell from the machines I'm hooked up to, the sudden acceleration of beeps, and in the corner of my eye, the mountain range writing itself upon the heart monitor. My whole body is beating, the little v's tighter, like those loops on the knitting needles. Continental style.

'I've been looking for you,' I want to say, but I just watch her.

The armchair is an ugly brown velour thing from the seventies. She has slippers on her feet, her hair up in rollers, odd strands held under a net. She's not interested in the event going on, the birth of her great-grandson. She's smoking a Woodbine and reading a book, a slim thing, a romance. I swear it's her. Or it's the drugs. I am on drugs. But it seems so real. She's wearing her glasses, the same ones she has in the old photo, and the same scratchy tweed skirt.

I wave, trying to get Dora's attention, but she only glances up from the book for a second. I don't get another chance. The chair she sits on spins into a blur, and I see her body spiral away, silky pink ribbons that get thinner and thinner and then scurry all over the ceiling and disappear as fast as light into the cracks and the vents.

I'm blinking into the big circle of the surgical lamp, still waving. Matthew's laughing.

'What's so funny?' I ask.

'Nothing, don't worry,' Matthew tells me. He closes his fingers over my waving hand, holding it still.

'Just the medication,' the midwife smiles.

Matthew winks.

Minutes later, our son is born. He comes into the world right foot first. The surgeon's expression barely changes as she takes hold of his second foot, taking care that the knee isn't trapped in an awkward position before working the whole leg free and then clasping him by the hips. She gives instructions. Her voice is quiet and direct. The second surgeon helps to twist out his small body, and the first uses her palms to protect his soft belly, her thumbs meeting at the small of his back. Suddenly he's free to stretch and kick loose, but is tense with the shock of birth. I get only a fleeting glance, and his skin is a bluey colour.

I feel ice down my throat and some vague awareness of Matthew springing to his feet, his camera lens clicking, and messages being passed from one medic to another. But it's too quiet. I ask if he's breathing and no one replies.

Then they lift him and I see him properly. His arms are outstretched, fingers splayed wide as if he's trying to grab the whole world, the strong light of the surgery a halo over his body. His eyes are screwed tight, and then suddenly he does exactly what I asked him to, gasping air into himself, letting us hear the full sound of him. His cry is haltering and gargling, cat-like.

The surgeons place him on my thighs till the thick umbilical cord stops pulsing. Through the numbness of the anaesthetic, I can still feel his weight and the tension in his tiny body. The midwife checks his skin colour and counts his toes, and after a couple of minutes they clamp the cord. Matthew cuts it. Our son is slipped underneath my gown, still a shade of almost-blue. He hasn't stopped crying and gulping, and his hands are now clenched into strong fists, the nails already long. He's covered in a sweet smelling, white curd, like something from the sea. And to my surprise, he has jet black hair. It's wet and thick, and it clings to his head in sticky, galaxy-like swirls.

Matthew holds him for the first time while I am stitched shut, and the two of them sit looking at each other in astonishment. Matthew bleary-eyed but grinning, and our son: brand new, wrapped in white, the world stinging.

10 June

He is one day old. He cries when he's undressed and when he's held face down on the doctor's forearm. The doctor lifts him, shoogles him, pulls an arm first and then a leg, letting the limbs drop. He lies him down again, takes his tiny wrists and pulls. The baby screws his face as he's hoisted up, but his head doesn't lift. The doctor picks up his feet, looking at them from every angle. Maybe he does this to all the babies, judging them in silence, ready to pull a rosette from his pocket for the most pleasing infant. There are no congratulations.

A seed of uncertainty has been here all along, a dark thing with a sharp point that I've kept secret. Till now, it was small enough to tuck away.

Matthew's parents have already been in. This is their fifth grandchild. My parents are still here. It's a first for them. They've driven from the other side of the country, Mum behind the wheel all the way because Dad can't drive anymore. He gets confused. He takes the wrong roads and asks the same questions again and again.

'How is he feeding?' the doctor asks.

'Okay,' I say, but how could I know?

The doctor breathes deeply and turns my son's foot once more in his hand.

'I'm going to ask a colleague to examine him,' he

says. 'And we may do some extra tests.'

In the time it takes him to finish that sentence, the tiny, dark seed roots down. The doctor glares at me as if he can see inside my body. I hear my own breathing.

'Did you drink alcohol while you were pregnant?'

My tongue presses against the roof of my mouth and he stares, waiting for a reply. I try to straighten but my stitches pull, a reminder that I'm to stay still, bowed over.

'No.'

He doesn't believe me. He's got me, just like they got Stacey, in my shabby nightclothes, the thin cotton gown tied with a belt over my deflated and misshapen middle, my unwashed hair, the dark circles under my eyes.

'Nothing's wrong, is it?' Dad asks.

'I'm sure everything's fine,' the doctor says in a rehearsed tone. He won't look my father in the eyes. He mutters something about seeing us later and leaves.

I swallow, look over at my mother. No one knows what to say, except for my father who curses. He's forgotten how to do lots of things, but swearing is something that still comes naturally, and I'm grateful for it. Matthew comes back then, opening the door with an elbow and a grin saying he's brought four coffees.

'What?' he says, seeing our faces. But I'm sure he already knows, just like me. There's something different about our baby.

I tell Matthew they want to do some tests, and the whole time I can feel that little secret, the doubt I had all along, digging deeper. A midwife comes in to check my stitches. I'm glad when she pulls the curtain because

Mum looks like she might cry.

I want them all out of here. I want to sit alone with my son, curl over him, make my back into a hard shell. I know they want to spend time with the baby, but Matthew says he's had nothing to eat all day, and this is a good excuse to send them all to a pub for dinner. They leave after giving me a quick hug and kissing the baby on his forehead. Of course, they tell me not to worry.

'It's nothing,' my parents say. 'He looks fine, just a bit squashed.'

Matthew stares at me across the room while my parents get their bags. I've never seen him look this way before. His whole face has changed shape.

'Go,' I say. 'I'll be fine.'

I dress the baby and wrap him back in his blanket. I thought the doubt I felt was just a fibroid withering away, or my hormones. But what if it wasn't. I stare at the wall and at my legs under the sheet. I can already walk slowly round the room, but I don't bother. When it starts getting dark, I don't turn the light on over my bed. I stare into my son's face and try and get lost under the dark sky out of the window. I spot stars and the lights of planes passing. It's very quiet, and I realise then that the baby doesn't really cry. Instead, he makes that cat-like sound, or often just wrinkles his nose. Most of the time he sleeps.

Later that night we're moved into a private room, away from other mothers and babies being born. I stay awake. Midwives come in every few hours. They look at my son and whisper questions. They pussyfoot around me. When I talk to them, I'm short-tempered. I want to be left alone. I ask them why they need to know. I tell them I can do everything myself. Around dawn, finally one of them asks me if we've chosen a name. Ash. She writes it on a little blue card in a black pen and sticks it on the front of his cot.

Matthew and I debated the name for months. I wanted something Jewish. Matthew wanted the name of a tree, something strong. Ash is short for Asher. For months, his name was inside my head, a sound like the rustling of leaves. *Ash! Ash! Asher! Asher!*

11 June

I must fall asleep eventually. When I wake up, bright daylight streams through the window and a midwife is there, lifting Ash's limbs and letting them drop the same way the doctor did.

'We have to ask you to sign some forms. We do tests on all newborns. It's only a pinprick to the heel.'

I'm already wary. I can tell from her voice she's worried I won't agree. I wonder if she's lying.

'They all get this test?'

She nods and smiles, handing me the forms. Ash's details are already there, typed out on a sticker and stuck at the top. There's a section on ethnicity. I run my pen along the choices. I hadn't really thought about the fusion that is me and Matthew till now. There's a box for Ashkenazi Jewish. I want to tick it, but I don't. It's only one part of the mixture that is uniquely Ash. In the end, I leave it blank.

'That information helps us consider hereditary conditions,' the specialist says, before realising I'm not going to tick anything. 'Don't worry too much about it right now.'

I nod.

'I like his name,' she says. 'Where's that from?'

I hand back the form.

'It's kind of Jewish,' I say. 'That, and his dad's a tree surgeon.'

She smiles at that, but then she takes a breath and says, 'There are actually some extra tests we'd like to run for him.'

I go to the toilet and cry while his heel is pricked and blood is taken. Through the door I hear him making a new noise, a sound that is high-pitched and strange. The whole thing seems to be taking too long so I come out in time to see a needle much bigger than I imagined and blood being collected in a vial. A thick smear of red is taken away on a sheet of blotting paper, and three more tiny vials are filled to the brim. In his little cot, Ash's whole body is shaking with silent screams. I've done the wrong thing. I've already let him down, leaving him alone and agreeing that it was best to hide in the bathroom.

Matthew arrives early. My parents aren't with him and he tells me they've decided to head home. They thought it was for the best, and it probably is, but when I find out they've cut the visit short I sob into Matthew's shoulder till the arm of his t-shirt is soaked. Two midwives come in and check my incision, apologising, lifting the bandages and putting them back. They work quietly, not wanting to intrude.

Matthew leans over Ash's cot with his back to me. Ash is peaceful now, but I hear Matthew sniffing and a tear drops quietly off his face onto the blanket. I look over his shoulder into the corner, wishing that Dora would appear again, hoping for some sign that she will.

I've no appetite. Ash won't feed and I'm exhausted. Every time I try to feed him he messes around with a half-open mouth, trying but getting nowhere. I'm sure he's already lost the roundness to his cheeks.

There's a meeting at three o'clock in a small room with upholstered chairs and striped yellow and turquoise curtains. Notices are pinned on a board. Bottles of hand cleaner are hung on the walls. There are painted cottages in frames, a window with a bad view, and a small fridge humming in the corner. If I really listen, I can hear the beep and hiss of the monitors and ventilators in special care. The lights are left off, so the room is dimly lit by just a small window.

A box of tissues is placed on the table and I stare at it while the doctors start to speak about Ash. There's a paediatrician, the surgeon who did the caesarean, and a nurse. They keep their voices quiet, leaning towards each other. They only look at us when it's their turn to speak. Otherwise, they look down gratefully at their shoes, or at their folded hands in their laps. They say they want scans of his head and x-rays of his spine. They tell us the results of these tests could be bad news, and mostly very bad news, mainly because Ash's feet are curved at the bottom like a rocking chair, and he's floppy. They mention a few conditions, things they say they are ruling out. These conditions have medical names like spina bifida and muscular dystrophy, things that till now I've only been aware of because of television and charity fundraisers.

'We will find something,' the paediatrician says.

I stare again at the box of tissues on the table, but I don't take one. The room they've put us in is too dark and polite. It's like we're backstage, somewhere we have to hush. It doesn't feel real.

'Did you notice the abnormalities?' he asks.

Matthew squeezes my hand and I wonder again if he's been keeping the same secret, that dark, pinprick of doubt, just a speck, a seed, so easy to ignore.

'You didn't notice that when Ash cries his lips don't move at one side?'

The paediatrician straightens his suit jacket, frustrated by our silence. He sucks on his lips.

'We'll be moving him to Special Care for observation,' he says. 'We could place a feeding tube. It might help him.'

I refuse the feeding tube, and the doctors glance awkwardly at each other before admitting they have a few more questions.

'We'll talk again later about the feeding tube,' the paediatrician says.

'We won't.'

Silence, a clearing of the throat. He sits back and lets someone else take over. More questions. Was I ill? Did I take sleeping pills? I'm asked again if I drank alcohol or if I took drugs. The paediatrician leans in again, as if a thought has just occurred to him, and he asks if Matthew and I are cousins. I'm relieved when Matthew tells him to piss off.

They go, and we sit together for a few minutes in the dim little room. All I can think of is how I imagined

Matthew in the forest, climbing trees with our son, helping him up to the light of the high branches.

When we finally shuffle out of the room the paediatrician is on the phone in the bright corridor ordering tests from Glasgow.

'Genetics are coming to talk to you both,' he says, blocking our way. His voice is chirpy, as if he's ordering us all a pizza. We stand blinking at him.

'Many rare conditions are passed on in families, sometimes hidden for thousands of years. You just don't know till a baby like Ash is born.'

I watch him speaking for a second, the way he bobs his head and fiddles with a pen in his hand while he's on hold. It's there again, that edge of something that shouldn't be there. He's enjoying the suspense, drumming his pen on the side of the phone, talking too fast, biting down a smile.

We go into the room where Ash is sleeping and shut the door, pushing hard against the silencer to try and affect some kind of a bang, but this turns out to be impossible. They have a device on the doors to prevent slamming.

'I don't like that fucker,' Matthew says. He paces. I can tell he wants to shout but Ash is sleeping so he keeps his voice low. I can hear him breathing. 'I don't want him anywhere near the baby.'

Matthew stops pacing and we stand looking at each other, trapped in another quiet room. Ash continues to sleep.

'What if I did something to him?' I ask. 'I think they think I did.'

I stare into the cot. Wrapped up like this, he looks

just like all the other babies. Matthew comes and stands beside me and puts an arm over my shoulder.

'No,' he says. 'You're not to think anything like that.'

'I don't mean deliberately.'

I've been thinking about it, all the questions about our families, about genes that travel through generations for thousands of years.

'What if I let in some kind of, I don't know, bad energy?'

'Bad energy?' Matthew says, and he pulls a face.

'I know it's stupid, but I thought about so many dark things.'

I pick up one of Ash's nappies, unfold it and fold it again, rubbing my fingers against the dry crinkly surface.

'You did nothing,' Matthew says, and he pulls me close, forgetting about the stitches.

'Ow.'

Roberta comes down later to visit me in Special Care. There are other babies here, but none like Ash. The others were born too soon and they are less than half his size. I thought Stacey's baby might be here, but I haven't seen her. Maybe she's better, bigger already. Maybe they've sent her away.

Roberta brings sweets and a blue helium balloon. I'm pleased to see her. We tie the balloon on the arm of the chair and she sits in it cradling Ash. She blushes as she looks into his face, holding him up close. He stares back at her. He is going to have blue eyes. They're dark at the moment, like all newborn babies, but look closely and you can already spot the deepest inky blue.

'His feet don't look that funny to me,' Roberta says. 'Honestly, he's probably just a bit squashed. You had all those things inside you.'

She holds his foot in her hand. They've taped a wire to his toe, which links him to a machine. Every few minutes it starts beeping loudly. The number on the monitor drops at the same time, and when the number goes up, the beeping stops.

'I thought he was just squashed too,' I tell her. 'But the doctors acted like it was a stupid idea.'

Roberta must have noticed that Ash's legs don't move very much, but she doesn't say anything.

That night, Ash sleeps for an hour at a time, and in between I lay my head back in my chair and dream. Perhaps the morphine is still in my system. The dreams are crazy. A midwife hands me a baby with no face and no arms and legs, just a red, sinewy lump. I dress it all the same and hold it as if it were perfectly normal. I cradle it and try to feed it even though it has no mouth. In between dreaming I lie in bed and press my hands into my stomach. I don't touch the wound, which covered with a thick dressing, but I sink my fingers into the soft doughy flesh of my belly. I can feel the shapes of the fibroids inside.

I don't have to wait too long to see Dora again. She appears for me in the first light of the morning. I know she's just a figment, but I don't care. I'm relieved to see her. She's sitting in the chair where Roberta was a few hours ago, and the helium balloon is bobbing above her head. She's still in her slippers, knees tucked neatly together, back straight. She is knitting. She looks up occasionally as if she's checking the time on a clock on the wall. She doesn't seem to notice me. I don't think she can hear me, only the tick-tock of that imaginary clock on the blank wall in front of her. I can hear it too, this ticking. Not a hospital clock. It's too loud and too grand with an old-fashioned wooden stutter, a clock in a case. Dora moves her knitting needles in time with the seconds.

I whisper to her.

'Will he be alright?'

Nothing.

She might be deaf, I think, but before I try again the vision of Dora goes milky, and soon it slips away.

At some point later that night, or maybe it's early the next day, a nurse arrives pulling a yellow breast pump on a wheely stand. There are parts piled up on top of it, funnels in different sizes. Someone will explain how to use it, the nurse tells me. They are moving Ash into an incubator, and I won't be able to feed or hold him anymore. I'll only be able to touch his hands through the holes in the side.

Banknote

The fifty Pfennigs note is printed in blue and black on linen-paper that is greasy with age. A crease shows where it was once folded to fit inside a pocket wallet. On one face there is a picture of a black bear, the symbol of Berlin. It stands on its hind legs, arms outstretched, walking in a robotic fashion, a kind of automated teddy. The bear's pointed ears touch the blue border of the note, and it stares with a large round eye, claws unsheathed. The background is a complex geometric pattern.

On the back of the banknote there is an old scene of Weißensee, looking the way it was before the city of Berlin expanded and swallowed it up. In the picture there are three people and a dog. They stand in a group aside a dirt road, watching as six horses and a carriage pass by. On the horizon, tree branches touch the cloudy sky, and here in the town, medieval houses sit inside their fenced plots. The grandest of them stands out. It has dark beams and a steeply pitched roof.

1921

Weißensee is Dora's favourite place to spend the day. The buildings are new and the streets are wide, with enough space for trees and grass, which everyone keeps neat. There are buses and bicycles, and tramcars that trundle backwards and forwards. In spring, there are so many Elder trees around the park that the smell of the blossoms erases the stink of the breweries and the smoke. You can almost forget you're in a city.

They're building a chocolate factory. Once it opens, chocolate will be sold fresh in little boxes with the starry Trumpf emblem on the front. Weißensee folk will soon wake up every day smelling warm chocolate, at least if the wind is blowing the right way, and if it blows a little further south, to just beyond the Swiss Garden, the Tannenbaums will also be able to catch its scent. At least Dora hopes so. Dora has dreams of the chocolate factory. She imagines a pipe filling the round lake in the park with melted chocolate, and everyone going swimming in it, licking their lips and all the way up their arms.

Dora is five years old. She loves the walk up to Weißensee where there's room for things to grow, more space, more light, more air. Wildflowers sprout from gaps in the walls, and if Dora finds them she picks them quickly, before some proud homeowner throws them into a pile of weeds and scrubs away their roots with a bucket of water and a hard brush.

Dora's part of the city is older and not so well-tended, but she likes to play in the courtyard, caring for a dolly, trying to talk to the bigger girls, or sitting with her fingers all tangled up in a game of *etl-betl*. There are balls and bicycles, and skipping games, girls singing 'scissors grinding, scissors grinding, grinding is the finest art'.

There are always people coming and going. An old man that can make them laugh, or a lady worth chasing to the corner of Neue Königstraße in the hope of a sweet from her handbag. If a neighbour comes out to clean, pumping water up through the iron stand in the street, the children make a game for themselves, floating small sticks and leaves in the channels of water that trickle between the cobblestones.

The day Dora's father comes home, he doesn't recognise her. Till now, Vati has only existed in the frame on the sill. He is a man with a short beard, a small black hat, and a dimple in the middle of his lower lip. He has been away at war longer than all the other fathers, and most of the time Dora has hardly thought of him. She has been too busy playing games, and it's only lately that she has started to wonder what it would be like if he were here, if it wasn't just her, Mutti, and a man in a photograph.

He doesn't guess who she is. He goes right past her and stops at the door to their ground floor apartment. Mutti always leaves the door ajar for Dora, but Vati stops, takes a moment to straighten his hat and brush down the front of his coat, and then he knocks. Dora finds a hiding place. Neighbours are popping their heads out and calling to each other to come and see. Everyone knows her parents. Before they were married, they were neighbours, Vati on 9 Meyerbeerstraße and Mutti just opposite at 9 Mendelsohnstraße.

Mutti doesn't fling her arms around him like a character in a fairy tale. Instead, she puts a hand over her mouth, and then she takes a tiny step back, opening the door for him to pass. Vati says something in a loud, warm voice, a voice as warm as hot chocolate, but Dora can't make out the words from behind the steps.

They disappear into the apartment. Dora leaves her hiding place and goes over the street, into the bushes on the edge of the graveyard behind Mutti's old building. It's not long before she's called.

'Dorle!' Mutti shouts up and down the street. She knows all Dora's favourite places to play.

Keep dead still. Dora pretends she's one of the statues on the Märchenbrunnen fountain. She doesn't even blink, but she can feel the blood rushing from her heart. Dora doesn't want to meet Vati, or for Mutti to see her. Her dress is dirtied. Her hair has fallen out on one side of her face, and now it's tickling her neck. She twists the hair in her fingers and tries to stick it back under the pin. Mutti calls again, this time more hopeless, and then shakes her head and turns around.

Dora waits for a minute before sneaking back over the road and through the courtyard that leads to the apartment. The door looks squarely back at her. Mutti has shut it! It's a chocolate brown door, and if it really *was* made of chocolate, she could just eat the whole thing and go inside.

Dora goes up to the window and stands on her tiptoes. The lace curtains are drawn, and through them Dora can only make out the shape of Vati as he moves from the main room into his tiny workshop. He's taller than he looks in his picture. Vati has been gone so long, perhaps he's forgotten what the house looks like. Other fathers who already came back from the War, came back without any memories. Some had lost arms and legs. None of them had taken as long as Vati to come home though. Did he get lost?

Mutti had gone to work as usual that morning, dropping Dora off with Frau Tuch. The new dress was handed over carefully with instructions to keep it on the hanger until Vati arrived.

'You must be excited,' Frau Tuch said over lunch. Frau Tuch had a smiling face like a big yellow cheese.

Dora was excited, but only about wearing the dress. She had never had a brand-new dress before. She kicked her toes against the table leg, gripping her fingers around her glass of milk.

'Don't pull a face, Ketzele!' Frau Tuch laughed. 'Your Vati will think you are an ugly goose!'

Frau Tuch was cuddly, but smelled strongly of cabbage. She always treated Dora with chocolates and little toys or took her for picnics in the Volkspark. Dora liked the coloured glass ornaments that she kept on her windowsill. She also liked that Frau Tuch let her speak Yiddish, even when Mutti insisted it was wrong.

'You are not a country bumpkin like me and your father,' Mutti would nag her. 'You are born a Berliner.'

But Dora liked being Frau Tuch's little cat, her ketzele.

'You just want to wear that pretty dress, don't you?' Frau Tuch laughed.

The dress was hanging empty above them like a ghost. Aunt Dotti's friend had made it for her out of green velvet, Tannenbaum green like a fir tree. There were several trips across the city for fittings. Each time Mutti had taken her on the tram, another rare treat, and afterwards they had gone to Aunt Dotti's apartment. Dora collected the tram tickets because she liked the smell and the size of the little cardboard rectangles. Sometimes she gave one to Cousin Meta. The other cousins were older and they only wanted to pat her on the head and pull the springy curls in her hair.

The day the new dress was finished, Mutti, Aunt Dotti, and all of Dora's big cousins gathered around admiring her. The dress had ties that went in a bow at the back, and a golden ribbon sewn around the hem. Cousins Max and Hermann both said she looked like a princess, and everyone agreed, except for Meta and Jette who sulked. They weren't getting new dresses. Their Vati was staying in Königsberg, and even Aunt Dotti thought this was for the best. The adults never really spoke about Uncle Sally, not even Mutti, who was his sister.

'Can I dress up just to show you?' Dora pleaded with Frau Tuch.

'Finish your milk, Ketzele. Drink your milk to grow into a big cat.'

'Then will you let me put on the dress?' Dora sing-songed.

Frau Tuch told her to stop begging, since she had already won, and then she settled herself and wiped the corners of her lips with a napkin.

Frau Tuch washed the plates while Dora dried them, making squeaky circles on each one with the cloth. And then, because she had been a good helper, the dress was lifted down from the hanger over the door and Frau Tuch buttoned it all the way up her back. Dora did a little spin, making the skirt fly out, and Frau Tuch collapsed onto the couch and put her feet up.

'Let's have an afternoon snooze, Ketzele,' Frau Tuch mumbled. 'Do you want a story?'

'No,' Dora said, pretending to yawn. 'I'm ready to *plotz*.'

Dora closed her eyes and listened to the clock ticking on the mantel, counting down the minutes till the evening. She concentrated on it and tried to time her breaths.

'Did Vati make that clock?' Dora imagined him bent over it, his face wrinkled with concentration and fingers tweaking the mechanism. There was no answer though. Frau Tuch was already asleep.

Dora got up immediately and let herself out to play. Today she would knock on all the doors and show her new dress to the other neighbours. Frau Tuch would sleep and sleep because she was as lazy as a lion, especially on warm days. There was no need to hurry.

Dora told everyone that the dark green velvet was chosen to match her name, Tannenbaum. This wasn't true. It was Aunt Dotti's fabric left over after making curtains, but no one would know that. When there was no one around to talk to, Dora played with a ball. Next, she pushed along a cart that someone had left out, and then she found a silver coin. The coin was on the ground under one of the ivy plants that grew in the graveyard, a place she was not supposed to play, but she was good at hiding. She thought about taking her coin to the Märchenbrunnen, because there were often balloon sellers at the fountain, but she wasn't allowed to cross the big road alone. By the time Mutti came home from the shop, Dora was down in the muck to see what else might be hiding under the ivy.

After peering in the window for a while, Dora goes back across the road. She leans against the graveyard wall, listening. She hears a bird jumping through the twigs and leaves, families having dinner, talking, clinking glasses. There's a smell of meat and vegetables cooking, and Dora knows that soon her father will be eating too, his first meal with them since the War. She hopes it's cabbage with meat inside. That's her favourite, but they hardly ever have it. Only for a treat. Tonight, it should be a treat, and the thought makes her tummy grumble. All the other families in the neighbourhood will be talking about them right now, saying Uscher Tannenbaum has come home at last.

Suddenly, Frau Tuch is standing there, under the archway that leads to the road. Her red hair is standing in wisps on her head, and her old face, which is already funny, is even more hilarious when she is cross and sleepy. She peers at the evening sky, and her wrinkles pull together as she squints. She calls Dora's name, and then she spots her by the wall.

She comes over, dismayed at the state of Dora's dress. She says some bad words, and then turns around. It looks like she's going to stomp back into her house. She doesn't make it. Her hands fly up suddenly and she turns and starts again, kvetching and wailing. She grabs Dora by the hand, and Dora just laughs.

They go into Frau Tuch's main room and take off the dress. Then Frau Tuch takes a brush from under the sink and rubs Dora's white cuffs and collar, crying at her the whole time. Mutti must hear the commotion through the walls because she soon arrives to fetch her daughter.

'Rosa, I am so sorry for you!' Frau Tuch wails when Mutti appears. 'Look what Dorle has done!'

The two women console each other over the dress while Dora stands behind them in her underwear. For a minute or two they seem to forget about her altogether. They whisper about Vati. Does he seem well? Has he an appetite?

'You must want something to eat,' Mutti tells Dora at last.

Dora frowns and rubs her bare arms with her hands. She's not sure if she is hungry. Tonight, a stranger is eating with them, and she doesn't particularly like strangers. Mutti sighs. She holds up the dress again and looks over it, then decides that Dora should put it back on.

'It'll be alright,' Mutti says. 'It's not torn at least. Lift your arms.'

Together Mutti and Frau Tuch pull the dress back over Dora's head. Dora complains that her arm is stuck, but Mutti and Frau Tuch pay no attention.

'At least she looks like herself,' Frau Tuch says.

'Dorle will be Dorle,' Mutti agrees, and for once she doesn't even mention Dora's difficult hair, which always tangles as soon as it is brushed.

Snooping in Vati's workshop has never been allowed, but sometimes Dora takes something and moves it, or hides it and puts it back later. His books have no pictures in them. They are religious books, mostly in Hebrew, which go backwards from the end to the beginning instead of from the beginning to the end. Mutti is particular about these being left alone, so Dora only touches them a little when no one is looking. Once she turned one upside down, but she didn't leave it like that.

There are more exciting things than books in Vati's workshop. A row of clocks stand on the top shelf of another bookcase, each one made from scratch by her father, and on these shelves there are drawers that look small enough for a mouse. The drawers are full of tiny cogs and springs, tins of things that smell funny, and pillboxes full of arrows as small as pins, one box for gold, one box for silver, and another for black. Dora likes most of all to prise the lids from these pillboxes full of clock hands and gaze at them. Then she puts the lids back on and shakes them up. The hands inside seem to point in every direction, this way, that way, all glittering. The arrows point to the time before time and to things that haven't happened yet.

Standing in the small workshop, with the pointing arrows going this way, that way, and the books that go backwards instead of forwards, Dora thinks it's possible that this exact spot, at the very point where 9 Meyerbeerstraße meets 9 Mendelsohnstraße, is the centre of the world, the place where all of time begins and ends. A place where you could slip between the two, if you knew how.

The boys in the yard know about the clock hands, and sometimes they ask her to steal one, but she never does. Mostly she just stands in the middle of the small workshop and breathes deeply, imagining she can smell her father. When he left for war, his coat was still hanging on the back of the door, and his favourite hat was sitting on the top shelf next to his clocks. They are still there.

Dora has asked her mother a thousand times what Vati is like, and usually all she will say is that Vati is older than her, he goes to Shul, and he works hard. Dora is very disappointed with this, but when pressed, Mutti will also say that Vati is kind, he likes nature, and it was him who wanted them to take walks up to Weißensee. He thought the fresher air and walks around the lake would be good for them. *This* sounded like a better Vati, even though the swans in the park at Weißensee were frightening.

'Will Vati take me to the park on Saturday?' Dora asks Mutti when they leave Frau Tuch's apartment. She pulls the hem of her dress straight. She is about to meet him. Their house will be different forever, she thinks, with a whole other person living in it.

'Your father goes to Shul, Dorle.'

'He will still want a walk and a picnic in the park though.'

'Yes, maybe.'

Mutti says no more. She pushes Dora forwards, through the main room to the door of Vati's workshop. Dora feels her heart thumping. Of course, he would be waiting here, in this room, the middle of the world, at the centre of the universe. His chair is turned to face her, and he is smiling. He looks down at a small present wrapped in colourful paper in his hand.

Now that he's here, Vati is a bit like the man she has seen in the photograph, but he is also different. Dora stares, still holding Mutti's hand and trying to edge back behind her. Vati has the same small, round ears as the man in the picture, and the dark, glassy eyes. But he is older. In the photo he has a funny chin, and bottom lip with a crack right down the middle like a baby's bottom. Now he has a forest of beard and a thick moustache like a smear of ink, and his smile opens somewhere in between. The War has made him quite fat, Dora thinks, and this surprises her. He leans close enough to put his arms around her and lift her onto his lap.

'Is this truly *my* Dorle?' he says. 'I have something for you.'

He holds out the present. She smiles and takes it, but is too shy to open it in front of him.

'It's a necklace,' he says, taking off the paper for her and opening a little pouch inside. 'This belonged to your grandmother in Russ-Banila. Her name was Dvora Roll.'

Dora looks at Mutti.

Mutti nods, and Vati lifts it over her head. He taps her chest.

'From Dvora to Dora.'

He admires the dress, especially the shiny border on the hem that is also her favourite part. She can hear his breathing, loud as if his shirt was too tight, and when he touches her cheek, his fingers are warm.

'She almost ruined her dress in the yard,' Mutti says, but she doesn't seem angry at all.

'What have you been doing today?' he asks her.

Dora takes a long breath.

'I was digging.'

She puts her hand in her pocket to find the silver coin. She thinks about calling him 'Vati' out loud, but at the last moment she isn't sure.

'I found this,' she says. 'I want to buy a balloon.'

Her father stares at her for a moment, and then he laughs as if she has just told him the funniest story in the world. It's a laugh so loud she almost falls off his knee, but he holds her up. He folds her fingers back over the coin, telling her to keep it safe, and then tells her to look after the necklace. She looks down at it hanging over the front of her new dress. It has a pendant in the shape of a star, and she puts a hand up to it and feels the points with the tips of her fingers.

Mutti offers Dora a bowl of soup with pancakes, and when Dora admits she's hungry, her father stands up, lifts her, and spins her round and round. Dora holds tight to Vati's huge arms and screams. She lets her feet fall loose behind her and starts to relax. The air seems to be lifting her then, as if she has the giant wings of a goose.

'Careful!' Mutti says. 'Her legs are long. She's bigger than she looks.'

But Mutti's warning isn't heard. Vati takes a step away from his chair and Dora's toes swing across the shelf. Something is knocked. Dora shrieks as one of the tins somersaults. Vati makes a clown-like move to try and break its fall, sticking out a leg and almost falling over. The tin bounces off his knee and hits the floor. The lid flies open. Thousands and thousands of silver splinters explode around the room, each of the clock hands catching the evening sun and spinning into place. Dora holds her breath, wondering what will happen, now that time itself has just been blown apart.

Vati just laughs.

After dinner, he is still picking up the tiny clock hands when Mutti comes with Dora to say goodnight.

Many of the silver arrows have slipped beneath the floorboards, and into the gap at the bottom of the wall.

'Daughter, I am a fool!' Vati says smiling. 'I should have listened to your Mutti.'

'I'm sorry,' she says.

'No, no, Dorle,' he says, and he holds out his arms for her to come to him. They kiss goodnight.

Later, Dora hears him talking. His chocolate voice is filling the quiet that she used to fall asleep to while Mutti did mending and reading.

'Years from now, Rosa,' Vati begins in his loud voice.

Mutti hushes him and he drops to a whisper, but Dora can still hear every word, even with her head deep in her pillow. Her father, Uscher Tannenbaum, is as big as a bear, and maybe it's not possible for him to be quiet.

'Years from now, Rosa, when we are dead and gone,' he whispers, and then there is a pause. Dora imagines him licking a fingertip and bending down to dab another silver arrow from the floor. 'These pesky watch hands will still be hiding in the cracks.'

4 March

Ash is on his play mat, laid on his side, pressing his lips and chin onto a cloth book. I watch him, smile when he looks up, and fiddle with my necklace. I wonder if one day soon his little puffs and squeaks will turn into babble.

I've made some tea and I check my emails before the physiotherapist arrives.

You have one new message!

Subject: Your Baby is Nine Months Old

There's a twinge in my chest as I click on it. I should unsubscribe from these updates. They're full of photographs of babies grinning, sitting up, messy eating, finger painting, and lists of things Ash should be doing: clapping hands, blowing raspberries, waving and saying 'da da ba ba'.

Ash doesn't do any of the things in the emails. Right now, he's clutching the silky ear of a donkey in his cloth book. I take a loud sip of tea. It's still too hot.

The doorbell rings.

We had so many uniforms in the house after Ash was born. At first, hardly a day passed without the health visitor, a community nurse, a physiotherapist, or someone sent by a charity popping in. They arrived grinning with a list of things to say. 'How are you? How is baby?' and, 'This is a lovely house, but I had trouble finding you.'

I realise now that I'm grateful for the forest. It turns out I do like the thick canopy of trees that keeps our house a secret behind the main road. I do like being tucked away.

Mostly the uniforms don't take tea and don't give answers. Even after all the questions and tests, scans, measurements and consultations, no one knows why Ash is different to other babies. I've stopped asking and would rather everyone just leave us alone. I don't want to tell the whole story every time I open the door. The sound of my own voice is beginning to make me sick.

Matthew never wanted to talk to the uniforms either. When they came, if he wasn't already at work, he'd go out and chop wood for the fire. Eventually there were long, awkward silences. They were spying on us, I thought. One time a nurse took notes when she spotted a small birthmark on Ash's shin, just a little freckled patch. She said she hadn't noticed it before. The next time she visited she made a point of seeing it again and made another note.

The visits mainly tailed off after Ash's feet were fixed. It took a few months, with plaster casts and an operation to place pins. Now Ash wears a heavy brace with a bar between his feet that reminds me of a snowboard and boots. His feet are a normal shape now. They just don't move.

Alan is the only uniform that still comes a lot, and he isn't like the others. When I get to the door, I can see the turquoise of his NHS polo shirt through the patterned glass. He always sneaks a cigarette on the step before he rings the bell, and he always drinks tea.

I let him in and we sit down. He talks about a trip he took last weekend while he sits on the floor, cradling Ash's head in his palms and gently manipulating his shoulders and his neck. Then we talk about the woods, how they change from week to week. We talk about mountains, hiking, birds and music.

For months, Ash only wanted to look to one side, as if he thought something was happening just behind his right ear. He was stuck staring at the wall. Every visit Alan worked on Ash's tight neck, softened it, trained it to turn, relaxing one muscle and strengthening its mirror muscle on the opposite side. A balancing act. Thanks to that, Ash looks straight ahead now. He can turn to the left too.

'Let's have another quick look at these wee feet before I go,' Alan says. Ash is moved onto a pillow on the sofa. He's fallen asleep as usual and doesn't wake up when we move him. I take off the first leather slipper and tiny sock and we roll up the leg of his dungarees. Alan does the other side, then rubs a thumb over the hairline scars on the top of Ash's feet. That's where the surgeon placed the pins. On the back of his ankles, where they severed the tendons, there's not even a scar. The tendons of babies regenerate like magic.

Ash's feet are still tiny. One fits easily in the palm of Alan's hand. He turns the foot to examine the arch. He gives it a wiggle. It's as flexible as any foot now, but it won't wiggle unless we move it.

'Give him time,' Alan says.

Sometimes I miss the weekly visits to the hospital plaster room. The doctors there were nice. They talked about Ash's bones like parts of a puzzle, jumbled up but easy enough to sort out. I liked the white dust that settled on everything and the smell of it, like an art class, and the sound of the water splashing when they soaked off the casts. The nurses would bring a baby bath and cut the casts off with scissors while Ash floated in the warm water. I was given a few minutes to enjoy getting him clean before he was dried in hospital towels and his legs recast. Arches were thumbed into his feet by the orthopaedic surgeon. They wound the plaster around his feet and up the legs, warm, wet, creamy strips. Ash seemed to think he was getting a massage. When they cracked the last pair of casts open his legs were revealed, all pink and cocooned like seeds inside cotton fluff. They were warm and pink but still unmoving, hatchlings not ready to fly.

'Four months is a long time to be in stookies, isn't it,' Alan says in a baby voice to Ash, rolling his sock back over his toes. 'There you go, wee survivor. I'll see you next time.'

Lots of people call Ash a survivor. I think about that word after Alan has gone. One doctor said he'd only live for six months, but the diagnostic test he ordered came back negative and we never saw him again. There were more doctors after that, and all of them had theories. Everything they suggested was rare and untreatable, and for a few months, while this went on, I felt like I was sealed in somewhere, feeling the air slowly thinning. My skin went dry and I was so tired I could sleep standing up. I hardly cried at all. I just wanted silence, like I was scared crying might use up all our oxygen at once.

Some days were worse than others. A geneticist set up an appointment for Ash just after we came home. We took him along to her clinic and she stared at his eyes and his feet, and at me, and at Matthew. She measured all our heads with tape. A neurologist colleague tapped us on our noses to see if we would startle. Gazing into Ash's face, the genetics woman wondered out loud if his cheeks seemed too prominent. Was his jaw set back slightly? Was there too much of a depression around his temples? I was too tired to react. I just wanted to get out of there because I couldn't breathe. She asked about the past, as far back as we could go, first about Matthew's ancestors, then about mine. My mother's cousin had bad legs, I told her. He was on the Scottish side and he died young. She wrote something down about him. I told her there was a Jewish side too, and she took another note. In the end, no diagnosis had leapt out at her.

They wanted us to join a genetics study and the woman sent some forms. I held on to them for a few weeks, till one day when Matthew was at work and I was clearing up clutter. I made up my mind and stuffed them deep inside the wheely bin. When it was emptied the next day, I came out to watch. It was hooked up and shaken out over the rubbish lorry. I saw the metal teeth piercing our plastic sacks. I danced in circles at the bottom of the driveway as the lorry left, my arms tight round Ash, letting him spin. My bare arms were all goosebumps.

Now Matthew spends all of his time in the woods, even more than before. When he comes home he brings back hacked down bits of tree trunk, all the gnarled, knotted pieces of wood that don't stack. He's arranged these all the way around the house. They are huge, too big for me to lift. God knows what he's doing with them. It must be another of his creative projects. We don't need that much firewood. The Celestron telescope is gathering dust in the corner. I suppose he's too tired for stargazing.

It's baby bird season, so Matthew doesn't go up into the branches much. He doesn't want to cut down nests. At this time of year, he checks trees for disease and storm damage, keeps paths clear, looks for pests, and repairs or builds anything for the estate: fences, log stores, lookouts. He cuts and stacks firewood to be sold in winter. At weekends he watches TV. We visit his parents. We take Ash to the shops. We go for walks. We puree food and try to get Ash to taste it. He never does. He barely keeps weight on, let alone gains any.

'Give him time,' my mother says.

Matthew's mother said the same. 'He was just a bit squashed, if you ask me. He'll straighten out.'

When I told work I couldn't go back yet, they told me to do the same thing. Take my time. Every night I lie in bed and listen to the airspace above us. We're remote but we are under the flight path. I'll usually get up again and make tea. I'll snack. Matthew gets up too. He'll go into the back room to chisel the hunks of tree trunk he brings home. The whole house smells of his wood shavings. Sawdust coats everything. I'm comforted by the sounds of him working, the logs splitting, the pulse of Matthew's small hammer on the top of the chisel. It's the knots he likes best, slicing through them, exposing their cores, discovering the whorls. He has made a thin disc of wood out of one gigantic knot, and last night he was sanding it smooth.

'What's it for?' I asked.

He had no idea.

I'm upstairs later with Ash when I hear the van. Matthew's home early, pulling into the driveway. I count five pieces of tree in the back of the pickup. One is in the shape of a 'y', where a big branch has forked in two. There's a knot in it bigger than a football, gaping lips with a huge bulbous lump pushing out of it, like it's been trying to give birth. Matthew unloads the lumps of tree and takes them round the back before coming inside. He takes Ash and flings him round the room.

I kiss Matthew's cheek and put my arm around his back. His shirt is damp. He smells of moss and sawdust. 'You're early.'

'I'll do dinner,' he says. 'You can have a bath after I've showered.'

'Thanks.'

I want to ask him where he thinks he's going to keep more lumps of wood, but I don't.

'Can we eat soon?' he says. 'I'm starving.'

*

I lie back in the hot water, watching my body soak under the surface. Some of the fibroids must have shrunk, which is normal. I don't look pregnant anymore. I still feel a hard place, under my belly button and just right of centre. That's the one that's turned to bone. Sometimes I can feel more of it, sometimes less.

I come downstairs with my wet hair twisted in a towel. Matthew has laid the table. Ash is strapped over his chest in a sling, and he watches me with wide eyes, his head turned to the side he has always favoured. Matthew has tucked him in tightly so his head won't nod. He can't hold it up for himself yet but Alan thinks he is making progress. Matthew always says he doesn't see much progress at all, so we've stopped talking about the physiotherapy. It puts me in a bad mood when Matthew can't see any difference. It makes the air feel thin again.

I lean under Matthew's armpit to kiss Ash's cheeks. He gives me a gummy half-smile. He loves it when his dad carries him.

Matthew lights a candle. I sit down behind it and watch the flame flickering.

'You smell nice,' he says.

'You smell of the woods,' I say.

'Do you want me to blend some of this for Ash?'

We don't always sit at the table. Usually we curl up on the sofa with our plates on our knees, and Ash lies on his mat. Tonight, Matthew's being romantic. The food's good. Red onions, courgettes, brown rice, soy sauce, cream and pepper. Ash won't eat anything and starts crying, but that's no surprise. I put him on my knee, lift my shirt, and he sucks peacefully. His fists clench when he feeds. I don't know if all babies do this or if it's some reflex Ash has remembered from his first months, when feeding was hard and the threat of another feeding tube was constantly dangled. When he's got a belly full of milk he'll relax, let his hands open.

Matthew clears the plates. I stay at the table holding Ash, scared to move him in case he vomits, and watching the candle that continues to burn. I'm still hungry.

Some mail arrived earlier that I've not bothered opening, and I hear Matthew ripping an envelope. He comes back to the table and puts the post down in front of me. I know what it is straight away. The hospital has sent another copy of the permission forms, with another leaflet explaining the genome study. There's a note from the woman on top, telling us the study will close soon. It's our last chance for Ash to participate.

'Do you want something sweet?' Matthew says.

'I'm not hungry anymore.'

We don't talk about the forms at first. Matthew just asks if I want coffee and goes off to make it. I open the leaflet and read a few sentences. I stop to kiss the top of Ash's head.

'Do you think we should sign it?' I shout through to the kitchen. I want Matthew to say no, and when he doesn't, I swallow hard, my throat closing up as I wait for his answer.

'Maybe,' he says. 'What do you think?'

Panic rustles me out of my chair and I go through. 'Isn't it better when they leave us alone?'

'Then say no,' Matthew says.

'It says the results could take years.' I scan bits from the leaflet because I need him to really agree with me, not just pretend, but the pages fumble in my hands. Ash pukes a spoonful of milk onto my shoulder.

Matthew reaches over with a cloth and wipes the sick. He barely looks at me, just turns and throws the cloth into the washing machine.

'What if he's doing really well,' I say. 'If he's three, or four, and suddenly we get a phone call saying something's really wrong, something horrible like before.'

'Yeah,' Matthew says. 'But maybe we'd just know more about him. Get some answers.'

I slap the forms and the envelope on the counter in front of Matthew. I try to tell him I don't want answers, but my jaw feels slack, and the words come out in a stupid sounding wobble.

Matthew knows that I have the same bad dream all the time. In the dream, Ash is in his car seat and I'm at the till in the petrol station. The doctor who first examined him drives up in a sports car, the top down. It's the doctor that ordered the first tests, the one my dad called a prick. He has an empty infant carrier on the passenger side of his convertible, and while I'm paying for petrol he breaks into my back seat and steals Ash. I come out of the petrol station just in time to see the doctor's car pulling away, and Ash gone. I always wake up at that exact moment.

'Other people don't know anything about their children's genetics,' I snap.

Matthew takes a step away from me.

'Okay, fine. You make the decision then. Just like everything else. I just thought you came in here to discuss it.'

I go out of the kitchen and sit on the bottom stair. I start patting Ash on the back, maybe a bit too hard because a minute later he's sick again, just a little bit. The sick lands near my shoe and Matthew comes again with a cloth.

'Sorry.'

He sits on the stair beside me and puts an arm round my shoulder.

Ash looks up. He knows I'm upset. He watches my face, his blue eyes asking questions. Fingers opening and closing into fists. I keep quiet after that. I just stroke his head and look into his eyes.

'I agree with you,' Matthew says. His body sinks into the wall. 'I just wish you didn't snap. We never talk about it. You just fly off the handle.'

He fetches the leaflet and sits, reading in silence for a while. We agree to bin the forms, but I can't stop wondering if really Matthew wanted to know. Maybe I'm being a coward.

Ash sleeps like a kitten. He's always been good at sleeping, another thing you could say was abnormal. Once Ash is upstairs in his cot, Matthew tries it on with me. I knew he was in the mood earlier, but I thought I'd wrecked it. My nipples are still wet from Ash's mouth and I push him off.

'Give me a few minutes, okay?' I say, crabby again. I pull my legs up onto the sofa and hold on tight to my feet.

Matthew goes into the kitchen. I assume he's sulking but he makes me another cup of coffee and comes back in. He goes away again, then comes back with a piece of toast spread with blackcurrant jam. I know I'm being irritable. I just want to watch TV. I want to forget everything. The tea and toast is still nice.

The first time we had sex after Ash was born, we were frightened the stitches would burst. Matthew had seen the operation, and perhaps the memory of the open incision was on his mind too. He'd watched as the knife was drawn over my belly, a bleeding seam opening like an ink spill. We were told to wait six weeks. I think we waited more.

Matthew sits down and I stretch my legs over his lap. He takes off my socks. He strokes my feet. I feel the rough patches on his hands, the new callus he's got from the chisel.

'Do you want anything else?' he says.

'No.'

We watch a programme. When it ends there's nothing else on. Matthew scoots up and we lie next to each other. He nuzzles into me and puts his hand under my shirt. He strokes his hand around my stomach and rests his palm over the hard mass. I know he can feel it too. He presses round the sides of it, rubs warmth over my skin. It feels swollen, as if part of the pregnancy has refused to go away.

'Don't,' I say. 'It makes me think about it.'

He doesn't move his hand. 'I don't mind it,' he says.

'I don't like it touched,' I say. It makes me imagine I've got cancer. I'm scared to say this out loud. 'Don't, Matthew,' I complain, and I move his hand. 'Please just pretend it's not there.'

He growls and digs his fingers into my hip bones, making me laugh. I let him pull off my jeans and he scoots down and kisses my thighs and slides his hands under my bum. He rests his mouth on my knickers. I feel his breath through the material, the warmth spreading. He rubs a thumb over my section scar. I've lost feeling there. No pain, no pleasure, but I don't mind the scar being touched, not like the mass in my belly. Matthew kisses it. He moves his lips along the line.

The lights of the baby monitor blink on the coffee table and I hear Ash shuffling in his cot. The machine that monitors his breathing says 'pip-pip-pip'. I really hate the breathing monitor, the way its gentle tick can dictate the rhythm of my own heartbeat. I close my eyes and wonder about switching it off, but we never do. Matthew must have heard Ash waking too but he ignores it.

'Maybe I should go up?'

Matthew doesn't reply. He puts a hand over my belly and holds me where I am. The pip-pip-pip settles again to a sleeping rhythm.

Sometimes the muscles in my stomach clench like a vice, and in those moments I look down, open my eyes, and see the mass more clearly than ever. The fibroid is as large as a fist, and my skin is drawn tight around it, revealing the shape underneath like shrink-wrap. I don't want to see it anymore so I pull Matthew up. I put my arms around his back. There's a long scratch on his neck where a tree branch got him, and I rub a finger along it.

I know that later he'll go into the back room with his knotted tree trunks and chisels. Maybe he'll surprise me. Maybe tonight he'll dust off the Celestron, drag it outside and wait for a clear spell. I know that's wishful thinking. Either way, we'll both stay up for hours. I'll take my laptop to bed. Ash will wake up for milk soon, but once he's fed, he'll sleep soundly for a few more hours.

While Matthew's working on his tree knots, I'll trawl through old records online. I'm looking for Dora's family. I need to find names. Matthew says I'm obsessed and sleep-deprived, that it's not healthy, but I know I'm on the cusp of discovering something. The names must be out there, somewhere.

I've contacted archives and waited for replies, thinking about the chilled rooms where they keep rows and rows of boxes and files on tall shelves. Maybe one day I'll find someone who's still alive, a person related to Dora. If Ash has an illness that travels in families, that person might have better answers than any of the doctors.

In bed, with Ash asleep beside me, my head echoes pip-pip-pip. I turn from one side to the other, but no matter which way I face, I still hear the ticking. I start thinking about Ash's DNA, wondering what happened to Dora's family. I think of her baby, the little girl who was probably called Ruth.

Ash's downy soft curls have faded from jet black to golden, but his baby head is still small. I can cup it in the palm of my hand. I wonder how long we will have to keep using the pip-pip-pip machine.

I've seen Dora again, but not like before. Now it's only when I'm asleep. When I dream of her, she's always the same. She's in a chair, reading or knitting, or embroidering. Always a cigarette in an ashtray beside her. More recently, when I've been awake, I could swear I've gone into a room and smelled the Woodbines, as if she's just left a few minutes earlier. I want to ask her about the names.

Matthew's mother says I should get out more and join a mother and toddler group in Ayr. My mother says I should take up a different hobby, one a bit more sociable and a bit less morose. Perhaps they have a point. Looking for names in the records is the first thing I do when I have a moment, like an addiction, an idle reflex.

Ash always wakes up a few times in the night rooting for milk. It's exhausting, of course, but mostly I'm just relieved he is here and that we've made it this far. I put my face next to his and cover him in kisses. The 'pips' stop when the breathing machine is switched off, and in the morning's very first light, that's what I do. I sit up holding Ash and we listen to the silence. It's a kind of prayer. He smiles at me, and I feel a warmth filling my chest, a glow like candlelight before even the birds are awake.

1922

Chanukah is coming, but Mutti is in hospital. Number 9 has been full of people, all grown-ups. Dora doesn't know all their names, but she knows their faces. Even with all the comings and goings, the apartment is quiet. The grown-ups whisper. Neighbours have knocked on the door and asked in hushed voices how Mutti is, if she's getting any better. Vati's friends have come back after Schul. People keep coming, helping hands, to cook or to clean, praying with Vati, patting shoulders and backs as they come and go with warm scarves around their necks and hats frozen to their heads.

Vati has stopped saying that business will pick up. Even so, he keeps his workshop tidy and has never stopped fiddling with clocks. That is what Mutti calls his work. Fiddling with time.

The wind keeps changing direction today and sometimes the air smells of praline, the rest of the time of beer. The Trumpf factory opened its doors without Mutti, and other women were employed to fill the chocolate boxes. Dora still eats them, and so does Mutti, but today the smell is cloying. Since Mutti got ill, the neighbours have fussed over Dora, taking her on errands to give Vati some peace. She has played in the Bandmann's apartment and sat at Frau Schuß's kitchen table being treated with breads and cakes. Little squares of the famous Trumpf chocolate have been handed to her more often than usual. She has cried a lot. It is too cold to play outside.

Frau Tuch cooks every evening, but Vati only nibbles. His voice sounds different, too quiet. The only time he tries not to be like this is when he speaks to Dora, but he wears his cheerful look like face paint.

Their new family photograph, taken with the three of them, has been moved from its usual place on the sill. The portrait now sits on the mantle: Vati in a borrowed suit, holding a book, and Mutti with her dark hair pinned stylishly, her gloved hands resting on Dora's shoulders. They posed for the picture not long after Vati returned. Dora had worn the new green dress, Vati and Mutti borrowed clothes. In the picture they all look elegant. Now the dress is too small.

Vati is polishing the menorah with cream and a cloth. He works at it with his fingertips, pushing the cloth into the decorated relief until it gleams.

'Dorle,' he says when he's nearly finished. 'Put your toys away. We will leave for the hospital.'

He sets the heirloom back in the box and places it on the table, then checks if the right number of candles have been put in the box to last through the festival, counting out loud. He sweeps the cloth over the windowsill. He looks around the room for another task, but everything is already in order. She hears him sigh. The dishes are clean and the beds are made. The floor has been mopped, the rug beaten. He has wound the clock only the night before, and polished the boots, even Mutti's pair that she hasn't worn for a week. He has rearranged the knives and forks and mended a pot. He has completed the few orders he received for clock repairs.

Dora takes her boots from under the bed and her coat and hat from the hook behind the door. Frau Tuch has taught her to tie her own laces and brush her own hair, and she buttons her coat without any hurry. By the time she's ready, Vati is distracted, holding the lace curtain aside and looking into the yard.

The big door at the other side of the yard opens onto Meyerbeerstraße. It's a quiet road, but the shops aren't far away. Dora likes the shops. Here the streetcars stop and start. Bus drivers beep their horns, children freed from classes run to the Volkspark, and families doing their daily shop browse fruit displays and trays of rolls and pastries. Workers and businessmen buy newspapers, march along to their offices and factories, swing umbrellas and briefcases, go into bars, and only stop to buy cigarettes, or to catch a tram home, or to have their shoes shone. But here at number 9 Meyerbeerstraße, Dora feels almost invisible, as if their own corner of Berlin is just a light pencil tracing, slipped slightly off the map. Dora was born in Mutti's old apartment, right over the road at 9 Mendelsohnstraße, and she can't imagine living anywhere else. Mutti has put lace on the window in the bedroom and the main room, and she has kept their things clean and tidy. They have some wooden furniture, which Mutti and Vati are both proud of. Each of them has a chair by the stove, where one will read and the other will sew, and here they would normally sit and talk for hours after she goes to bed.

Mutti and Vati talk about money. Vati says they may as well burn money this winter. Maybe he's joking. Dora hasn't seen him do this, but she watches just in case. She lies in her small bed in the corner each night and pretends to sleep. She imagines Vati lighting note after note.

The collar of her coat itches. What is Vati looking at? The yard is empty, except for the clouds that sweep over the kilometre of sky above Meyerbeerstraße. Maybe he's spotted a broken gutter, or Frau Tuch putting out her rubbish, or a cat toying with a bird. Dora fiddles with the large round buttons on her coat until at last Vati seems to gather himself up.

'Let's go to Mutti now,' he says, speaking over her head to the clock on the wall and the photo in its new position on the mantelpiece. 'I want to get her home in time to see her Dorle light the last candle on the menorah.'

Dora feels angry at him for lying like this, pretending Mutti is nearly well.

'Do you remember how it looks, when every candle is lit?' he asks her. 'And do you remember the story of the miracle of the oil?'

She nods. She remembers it from the year before. She loved Vati's deep, sweet voice as he sung prayers with them, and the room getting brighter each night of Chanukah till eventually all nine flickering flames were reflected in the window-pane, each one so close to the next that they almost touched.

Vati had always told her to pray, but lately he never stops. Like the miraculous oil, Vati's prayers have gone on and on, and even when he isn't praying he talks about prayers. He says that if they pray together everything will be put right.

He straightens her hat.

'Mirtsishem,' he whispers.

Dora frowns at him. She doesn't see any point in praying.

'I think it might snow,' he says as they make their way to the tram. 'If it does, you can go sledging with your cousins.'

He is like a silhouette in the bright morning light. Usually, his tall black hat makes him appear so high up, but not today.

The hospital is covered in ivy. It's the biggest building Dora has ever been inside. Salt cracks under their feet on the front step, and their shoes make wet tracks over the tiled floor. Dora holds tight to Vati's gloved hand. She lets her arm swing and tries to concentrate on each of her limbs, the feet stepping and the arms swaying. She tries to feel them as if they were separate things, puppet parts.

Mutti has lost her arm. Dora has heard the grown-ups talk about it. Mutti won't work in the shop again, and she definitely won't work in the chocolate factory.

Dora is afraid to see Mutti without her arm. The grown-ups still won't let her, but not seeing her at all is worse.

Vati leaves Dora alone in a quiet waiting room with dark wooden tables. There are newspapers and magazines, soft chairs, a full bookcase, and a large, patterned rug on the floor. Through a window, she can see trees and grass, but Dora waits where she is told. She watches people come up the stairs or make their way to the exit, nurses and doctors and patients covered in bandages. She wants to find Mutti. Her absence is a heavy stone in Dora's coat pocket. She puts in her hand, but it's empty except for an old lollipop stick and a handkerchief. Hands become fists. What good are Vati's silly prayers? She'll make Mutti feel better if she can just find the right room. She'll give her the picture she drew with her wax crayons, a gift from Frau Tuch when Dora started school. She keeps them very carefully in their little cardboard box. She lines them up in rainbow order.

As the morning turns into afternoon, Dora does pray for Mutti, even though it's silly. Maybe children's prayers work better than grown-ups' ones. If Mutti gets well, Dora promises not to moan about going to shul. She also prays for Vati to hurry up and come back.

She has a plan to find him. She will peek through the door of each room, but she isn't feeling brave enough to leave the reception yet. An old lady with pure white hair sits down beside her and asks who she is waiting for. Dora explains that her mother cut herself on a nail and is poisoned, and the old woman puts her hand to her mouth. Her lips make an 'O'. A few minutes later the old lady rustles in her handbag and pulls out an ice-chocolate in a pink cup. She drops it straight into the pocket of Dora's coat.

Dora eats the ice chocolate straight away, sucking it and feeling the cool, melting bit trickle under her tongue. She smoothes the pink, shiny cup into a flat circle in her fingers, and then she folds it in half and rolls it into a cone shape, turning it into a goblet for a fairy. She plays with her doll for a while. The old lady is called away. Dora can't taste the sweetness of the ice chocolate anymore. She drums the toes of her shoes on the floor. She looks again at all the books on the shelves. They're all boring. In one corner there's a bucket of sawdust, and the damp in the air makes it smell nice. Dora sticks her hand into it and sprinkles a little on the floor behind the chairs, pretending she's feeding hens. She likes to pretend she lives in the countryside, and that she owns chickens and a horse.

It's well past lunchtime and her tummy hurts. Dora looks up and down the corridor. A nurse is helping a patient who's too wobbly to walk on his own, and Dora waits till the two of them pass before stepping out of the waiting room. She runs her hand along the stair banister the way Vati does, and she pushes open the door just enough to slip through.

'Vati?' she whispers.

There is a different smell here. It stings the back of her nose. It is almost a taste. The corridor is long and dark with a wooden floor, and there are numbered doors on her left and right, and a window at the far end lighting the way forward. An empty chair guards each door.

Dora stands for a minute between the two places, the dark corridor, and the landing that leads to the waiting room, the blood-red rug and the shelves of heavy books, and then she decides.

A cupboard is the first thing she finds. Inside there are shelves of white linen, perfectly starched and folded. She goes past a white, tiled room where a large bathtub sails through the middle of the floor like an iceberg boat. The next door is shut, but it has a window in it, so she stands on tiptoes to look through. She sees a desk, a cabinet, and a skeleton with dangling limbs, holes for eyes and the jaw pulled shut. A man is writing at a desk and doesn't notice her.

Dora thinks about going back. She has left her doll in the waiting room, lying on the rug. But she's hungry and she wants Vati, and this is worse than the creamy skeleton, and the empty chairs, and the black painted doors with little white numbers above them.

Further down the corridor, there's a moaning noise. Dora hears a voice she thinks she knows, like Vati praying. The deep, warm voice he hasn't used since the day Mutti got sick. She walks on to the next room where the door is open wide, and there is a terrible stink. The voice she thought was Vati's belongs to someone else, one of the old men from Shul, and in the bed, there's an even older man. The patient is so old he looks almost like a long, skinny baby, lost and hairless. The sheet is pulled to his stomach, and his chest is bare. Dora can see his ribs under his skin, a rack of bones draped with what's left of his long beard. The man groans, and he rolls away from the Rabbi, dragging his thin arms. He stares at Dora like a gull.

The smell thickens and the Rabbi keeps praying with the man, his eyes closed.

Dora runs all the way down the corridor to the window. She breathes against the cold glass. She tries opening the window, but it's stuck. She's still standing there a few minutes later, watching her breath on the pane, listening to her own heart pounding, when she feels a hand on her shoulder.

Vati.

Isn't he angry that she wandered off? He looks out of the window towards another building, where a round window is panelled in the shape of a star. It's a Star of David. Dora touches her necklace and feels the points of the star against her fingertips. Outside, a family is sitting on a bench. A boy in a wheelchair is opening a present, tearing the paper off, while a bird hops along the path. Dora feels strange, as if she is not part of things, and instead just watching, like a tree or a wall.

Vati lets his breath out in a long, broken sigh, and Dora's chin starts to shake. Mutti always says to think happy thoughts: birds flying in the sky, crayons, new shoes before they get scuffed toes, but right now she can't think of a single one. Outside, the boy in the wheelchair is playing with his new toy. Even this makes her sad. Vati turns her around. His face is blotchy, and his eyes are puffed up. Vati tells her he is sorry, and she knows what has happened. She crumples her face into Vati's jacket. Later, he will tear it for Mutti, because she is gone. Dora feels her feet off the ground and Vati holding her up.

'Come,' he says eventually. 'This is the men's corridor. You shouldn't be here.'

Back in the waiting room, Dora pulls her hand away from Vati's and kicks his leg. He wants to leave her again. A nurse shuts the door on them. Vati forces her into a chair.

'No, Dorle,' he shakes her. 'I will be back very soon, I promise. Then we will wash your hands. You have been near sick people.'

He is a ghost. He doesn't say anything about Mutti. He holds Dora one last time before he goes away and the nurse comes back in to stay with her. She sits quietly beside her and puts her arm over Dora's back. Dora wipes her face with a sleeve and stares at the pattern of black and red on the old rug. She wonders how they will go back to 9 Meyerbeerstraße now, knowing that Mutti never will.

Dora will never remember anything else about that day.

The men go to the cemetery the next day. Dora stays with Frau Tuch. They sit together by the window. They sit like stones. Frau Tuch has put the blanket over them both and they watch the rain pouring. They see Vati leave with Rabbi Munk and his friends, a train of men under black umbrellas going to the burial. Mutti will be buried in Weißensee, near the park with the lake, the place she walked with Dora.

'Why do we always have to wait?' Dora says. Her fingers pick at the dry skin around her nails. She's picking them all raw. She likes how they sting.

'Because while we are waiting, we can clean, and make food to help everyone feel better. Eating does us good. Do you want to help me today?'

Dora shakes her head, and for once Frau Tuch doesn't try to persuade her.

It does snow, just like Vati said, but not until five days later. Dora is asked if she wants to go sledging with her bigger cousins, but Vati isn't allowed to be with them, and Dora wants to stay with him. He lets Dora do as she pleases, but he follows the laws himself and shuts himself in their apartment, opening the door only to relatives who arrive with helping hands. The visitors cook and clean and tidy. They help Dora to dress, and even though she doesn't need help anymore with these things, she lets them.

About a week later, Aunt Dotti takes Dora on a tram. She hands Dora both the tram tickets, and Dora feels a lump grow in her throat as she takes them and drops them in her pocket.

She loves the busy streets. She likes the smell of the pickle stalls on Elsässerstraße, and the noisy buses, and feeling lost in the middle of it all. They go to Aunt Dotti's apartment on Linienstraße and sit at her oval dining table. Dora remembers standing here in this room the day her green velvet dress was finished. Now her aunt tells her stories. Dora listens. She holds a doll on her lap. It has tatty clothes, so they crochet a new dress for it.

'This doll used to belong to my Meta,' her aunt tells her as they dress it in its new clothes. 'And before that it was Jette's. It came with us from Lithuania.'

Dora frowns.

'No. It was Mutti's doll.'

Aunt Dotti smooths the doll's dress under her hand.

'Actually, it was your mutti that bought it for Jette when she was small. She brought it from Mühlhausen in Ostpreußen, where your mutti and your Uncle Sally were born.'

Dora doesn't recognise this mouthful of a place. Mutti had only cared about New York. That's where she wanted to live. She never talked about the past.

'It's a town,' Aunt Dotti says. 'Not far from Königsberg. You must have heard of Königsberg.'

Dora nods. The King's Mountain. This is where her Uncle Sally has gone, the husband of Aunt Dotti.

In bed later, she keeps thinking about the King's Mountain, how it swallowed up her uncle. It must be a bad place. She holds her doll tight. Aunt Dotti is wrong. The doll *was* Mutti's. One of Vati's clocks chimes gently in the other room. Her aunt comes in to check on her and her big cousin, Meta, who is already snoring.

'Are you asleep, Dorle?'

Dora pretends, but Aunt Dotti sits down on the bed, so Dora rolls up close. She puts her cheek on her aunt's thigh and lies awake as her aunt strokes her hair behind her ear with a warm hand. She smells of bread and apples.

'It *was* Mutti's doll,' Dora says quietly.

'Of course it was,' her aunt says. 'How silly of me.'

Aunt Dotti tries to go, but Dora squeezes her fingers.

'Auntie?' Dora says. 'What happened to Uncle Sally?'

'Nothing, Dorle. He just lives in Königsberg now and he has a new wife.'

'So, can I live here?'

'Oh, Dorle,' her aunt whispers. 'I have to work. So does your Vati.'

'I want to stay with you,' Dora says, holding tighter to Aunt Dotti's fingers.

'You'll go to a place with lots of other children. It will be nice, Dorle, and it's very close by. You can come at weekends.'

Aunt Dotti won't look at her, and Dora feels a pain in her chest. At the other side of the room, Meta turns over and moans, but falls comfortably back to sleep.

Dora cries and Aunt Dotti hushes her and strokes her hair.

'I know, Schatz.'

There is a wonderful, sweet smell and Aunt Dotti tells her there is something baking, a special treat to cheer her up. Dora eventually closes her eyes. Aunt Dotti thinks she has fallen asleep, but she hasn't. Alone again, Dora stares at the ceiling. She squeezes the doll against her chest and listens to Cousin Meta's deep breathing. Across the room, her boy cousins are snoring. Jette and her aunt must be fast asleep by now in the kitchen.

She can no longer keep her eyes open. The last thing she is aware of is her blanket pressing heavily on her, and a change in the air as if someone is watching. She breathes in the smell too, warm and rich, like melted chocolate praline.

Reichenheimsches Waisenhaus,
Weinbergsweg 13, Berlin

Writing on reverse:
Memento for Dora Tannenbaum from Reichenheim
Children's Home, 1932

4 November

I'm spreading butter on toast fingers for Ash while three eggs boil in a pan. He's on the floor, bum shuffling. Ash can go backwards, dragging his legs, but going forwards he tangles himself up. The legs don't play along.

It's toddler group this morning. The other toddlers are walking and some are talking. No-one really talks to me. I only go because Matthew nags me to get out and it's supposed to be good for Ash, but I don't see how.

We eat. Ash dribbles and licks butter off some crusts while I look through my pages of notes and spread them out between the plates and my mug of tea. A big brown envelope arrived this morning from Berlin, and I've torn open the seal and pulled out a piece of paper, a photocopy of an old record. It's impossible to read. The old handwriting is cryptic.

Sometimes I'm methodical when I stay up late and I search through records on my laptop. I squint at the scrawling writing on each digitised page until my eyes go blurry. The problem is that records are rarely transcribed or indexed. There are always too many pages, and too much of the handwriting is illegible. Inevitably, I start to gamble and scroll forward and back. If I find something, which I rarely do, I tell myself I have a good nose for this kind of thing. The printed documents are easier. I found

Uscher Tannenbaum, my great grandfather, listed in an old Berlin directory, and once I'd found him I looked for him in the years before and after. He was always at the same address: 9 Meyerbeerstraße.

The document in the envelope is a burial record. Along with it the cemetery has sent a map of where Uscher's grave is located. An 'x' marks his plot of earth.

I look over at Ash. His hair is growing in tight curls. The curls twist naturally around his face, and right now he has butter smeared over his lips and chin. He suits his name, so close to his great-great-grandfather's.

I type the places mentioned on the burial record into Google. One is the home address I already knew. Google Street View shows me the location again. It's not somewhere I can easily imagine as my grandmother's home. A long, wide street with big leafy trees. When I mentioned it to Mum she frowned.

'I'm sure she lived in the middle of Berlin,' she said.

This piece of the puzzle doesn't fit.

Uscher's town of birth is also named on the burial record, a place called Russ Banila. I type in the name. At first it doesn't seem to exist. I wonder how it was pronounced, turn it over on my tongue. 'Banila' like 'vanilla', or 'Banila' like 'tequila'? I find it after some more searching. Once it was in Austria, then Romania, and now it's in Ukraine. There it is on the map, a village near the Carpathian Mountains whose name has changed so many times over as the world has shifted around it. Russ Banila. Banila on the Cheremosh river. Banyliv.

I close the lid of the computer and look out at the

trees in the wood while Ash makes a mess of his egg. A host of birds visit the branches of the tall willow beside our back fence. We often get visitors from the forest, tawny owls and great spotted woodpeckers. Lately we also get big, ragged ravens that make a racket. I'm still saying the name of Uscher's town in my head as I watch the birds, linking myself to somewhere I'd not heard of yesterday. Placing a pin.

I look at the map of Berlin's Weißensee cemetery. It's divided into a huge grid. It's also full of trees, the tallest in the city. Left untouched in East Berlin for so long, the cemetery has developed its own ecosystem. Matthew would be happy there, I think.

Ash starts to whine, wriggling to the edge of his highchair and pulling at the straps. I take him into the living room and put a cartoon on. In half an hour we'll go to toddler group. Ash must do something with other children. Matthew's right. He shouldn't be sitting here surrounded by this.

I take my laptop into the kitchen and listen to the Jewish burial prayer as I rinse the dishes. The name of this prayer, *El Mole Rachamim*, is typed onto Uscher's burial record, something the family requested. Daffy Duck splutters through his beak in the next room, but I tune it out. The burial prayer and the lulling of the cantor are soothing. I lean against the worktop, looking around at the white kitchen units, the scatter of crumbs on the breadboard, the blades of light coming in through the slatted blind. I want the faraway sound of the prayer to inhabit my head. The voice is sorrowful, and the recording crackles and hisses. It's an old recording, made during Usher's own lifetime. By now the cantor himself will be in his grave. Even the prayer seems to come from deep within the earth, a sound you could imagine the ground itself making, not deathly, but the fullness of life, roots piercing their way down, shoots bursting up into the light.

I tilt the kitchen blind and strong wintery sunlight streams into the kitchen. I let it flood my eyes.

When the dishes are done, I put on Ash's shoes, strap him into his buggy and push it outside under the porch. He can listen to the birds singing for a few minutes while I finish getting ready. In the bathroom I look in the mirror. I'm wearing a new pullover. It's the first time I've worn it, and it hides my belly, which I blame on the fibroids. Lipstick hides my exhaustion.

I get the car ready and get Ash into his seat. He doesn't like drives and he's already crying. He'd much rather sit in his buggy on the porch, looking up at the trees.

We're late to the toddler group. The kids are sitting in a circle on their mothers' knees who are all singing Humpty Dumpty. I take off my coat, ditch the buggy, and squeeze into the circle. Ash likes music. When we do songs at home, he smiles a little and tries to do the actions, but at group he just sits and stares.

After the song circle finishes, the kids play. Other mothers stand in pairs or groups of three and four. They talk about teething and Halloween costumes. Next week they're all getting teenage neighbours to babysit so they can have a night out together. I tell them I live too far, glad to have an excuse not to go.

When we line up for biscuits and cups of juice to give the kids, one of the regulars comes over. I can't remember her name. Angie, I think.

'How old is he now?' she asks, nodding to Ash.

Her son and mine are the same age, almost to the day.

'I didn't realise,' says Angie. 'We must have been in hospital at the same time. It was a sad place, don't you think?'

'Definitely,' I say, wondering what she means.

'He was in the NICU for a few days and I had to share a room,' she goes on. 'They were taking this woman's baby into care, a girl. I often wonder what happened to her, poor soul.'

She takes a bite of her biscuit, and my throat tightens as I watch her chew and swallow. I still think of Stacey. That night when she came back from the supermarket, her arms full of the green and white bags, and then the way they came for her. I remember her baby clothes displayed on her chair and on the window ledge, and I wonder who took them after they fetched her away.

Angie asks if we're going away for the holidays.

Ash has too many hospital appointments for us to go anywhere, but I tell her I'm planning a trip to Berlin soon.

'Why Berlin?' I feel my pulse quicken. I don't know how much to tell her, but before I can say anything her son begins to squabble with another kid and she goes off to sort it out. I hear her telling him to share.

I pick up Ash.

'Are you alright?' says Tina, the mum who runs the group. 'You're white as a ghost. Are you sleeping ok?'

I tell her I have to go, and start stepping over toys. There's a pain in my breastbone. My new top is too tight. Except it isn't. It's the right size. I've had this feeling before here, but not like this, an invisible seam pulled taut round the top of my ribs.

I sit in the car across the road, thankful to have made it back, to be out of sight in case it gets worse. Instead, the pain starts to ease. It's raining on the windscreen, and I concentrate on the pitter-patter. If I drive home Ash will fall asleep and I'll go back to my laptop, scanning the pages on my screen, not able to read them properly. It'll help me relax.

A group of old people walk past the car. They're huddled under rain macs and umbrellas. Through the raindrops I see the other mothers leaving the hall with their buggies, faffing with rain covers. They wave to each other and dash through the wet weather. I think about calling Roberta. She doesn't live far away, but we never bump into each other, and I've not spoken to her since the babies were born. She'll want to know how I am.

Back home, I kick off my boots, take Ash inside and put him down beside the sofa. I get out all my notes and spread them around. Here, I can breathe more easily. The rain is softening, still tapping on the window, but gentle, a comfortable rhythm. I plug my laptop in beside me, grateful for the familiarity of home, my sofa, the hum of the fridge, toes warming up. The screen comes to life, offers its welcome, and I type in the password. My fingers are still cold, a little shaky.

There are always more records to look through. Archives are adding them all the time. Sometimes I print out the images, official forms with the jaggy arms of swastikas inked on the paper. There's something hypnotic about the shape, an almost-optical illusion. Looking at it closely I imagine it starting to spin, as if it could bore into the floor of my home and lie there, waiting to stick to the sole of my shoe or cut my bare feet.

Other records are stamped with the black eagle, the *Reichsadler* looking over its right shoulder. It longs to swoop off the paper, through the window and over to the willow at the bottom of the garden. It would look at home with the unkindness of ravens. The birds look back at me from its branches. I'm getting used to their ragged forms and guttural calls. Their assaults on the bird table no longer break my concentration when I'm trying to do something, but they are frightening away all the smaller, chirpier birds.

I put my head down and my eyelids go heavy. Air passes in and out of me. I've not taken my coat off yet, and the fuzzy hood is wet on my cheek, but I sleep.

One of Ash's toys lies on the floor in front of me, and I dream about it. It's a wooden thing, oblongs held together with elastic, and it squashes and pops back into shape. It's the shape of a double helix, like DNA, with each rung painted a different primary colour. In the dream, the toy is enormous, spiralling down from the highest branch of a willow. I try to find a footing to inch myself upwards, but pieces of DNA keep coming loose, rungs snapping like matches. Bits of it fall from my hand and spin down to the ground. I manage to climb a little way, and further up in the canopy I find pieces already missing where people have climbed before, leaving less and less to hold onto. Deletions. Some of the rungs are rotten, full of tiny holes. There's graffiti on the tree branches here, words and symbols scratched in with a penknife. Some of the dates are very old and I stop climbing to look for initials. A 'D' with a heart gouged out around it. I try to search for more, but lose my footing and wake with a start.

It's still raining. Ash is still quiet. If I listen very carefully, I can just hear the traffic on the main road. The toy remains the floor. I close my eyes again and go back to sleep.

1936

Dora looks in the mirror behind the door. Her hair is cropped below the ears. She wears it swept to the side, but a tight curl has freed itself. She pushes it out of her eyes. Her hair isn't as wild as it was when she was little, but she still spends a long time getting it to sit properly. She doesn't mind the rest of her appearance. Her cheekbones are high, and her features are neat. People never believe she is twenty. Meta says she could be thirteen if it wasn't for her hands, which are reddened from washing pots. Her chin has a dimple like her mother had, though she can barely remember Mutti's face now. She only has the photographs. Her chin must be like her mother's though. Vati has a deep cleft which runs right up through his lower lip.

There's a knock. He's here.

'Get the door!' Meta calls from the sink.

Marcus stands there smiling, looking first at Dora and then over her shoulder into the room to see if they are alone. Today he's here for her.

'You look nice,' he says.

'Is that Marcus?' Herbert says, opening the bedroom door.

Marcus is dressed in a loose pair of summer trousers and a short-sleeved shirt. His clothes are well-tailored and cared for. In his breast pocket Dora can see the outline of a packet of cigarettes. The shirt is a light barley colour and pale against his skin. Marcus smiles and rubs a hand through his jet-black hair. He won't come in, he says, and gestures to Dora. She feels the heat in her face, and silence hangs there as Meta works out that Marcus is here for Dora. The three-and-a-half years between Dora and her cousin suddenly feel like a generation.

The door is left ajar behind them. Stepping down the stairs, her hand tucked in the crook of Marcus's arm, Dora tries to forget Meta. Her cousin won't ask questions, but if Dora doesn't tell her where they go and what they talk about, her curiosity will sit between them like something uneaten on a plate. Meta hates secrets.

Marcus has visited them in the apartment ever since Herbert and Meta married last November and moved in. They got the place done up and gave Dora the bed in the kitchen. She's lost count of the evenings Marcus has come over and stayed late, drinking with Herbert while Dora sits on her bunk in the corner, her hand curled round a glass of spirit. Meta would go to bed, saying she had work in the morning. Dora had work in the morning too, but felt a strange kind of electricity in the room whenever Marcus appeared, and she knew she wouldn't be able to sleep.

At Reichenheim, there had been twenty girls in the dormitory. They had single beds in long rows. She left at sixteen and spent three years living with Vati, walking each day from Meyerbeerstraße to her work on Große Hamburgerstraße. Their only visitors had been Vati's friends, and she'd had no reason to stay up late.

It was here in Meta and Herbert's home on Alexanderstraße that she discovered how much she likes the night. The street is always teeming with life, even in the small hours. Bars and clubs spill out, till for just a few hours before dawn, the whole building goes quiet. All of Berlin seems to be sleeping then. Everything lies still, the windows black and the outside disappearing, but at their table, Herbert and Marcus keep talking. Sometimes, Dora feels as if the boys and their voices and the warmth of the drink in her mouth are the only things that exist. Marcus always refills her glass with a smile, and when they've drunk too much they eat bread with cherries. She noticed, early on in these visits, how he fixed his eyes on her. He had a girlfriend, Margaret, but in February she had emigrated, promising herself to an American. Marcus shrugged it off.

'Life goes on,' he said.

Dora has said goodbye to people too. A few school friends and colleagues left for Palestine and France and Vienna, but mostly she just hears about people leaving, a friend of a friend, or a cousin of someone. If the city is emptying, it's mostly from the top. The managers, homeowners, the rich and the famous and the people who want better jobs. The people who go leave things behind too, things that are too difficult or costly to ship, or items that Jews aren't allowed to leave with. This is how in Herbert and Meta's kitchen, a dentist's chair has taken pride of place, left with Herbert for safekeeping, along with a bag of dentist's tools. Dora never sits in it. It feels haunted.

'Do you believe in ghosts?' Dora asks as they step into Alexanderstraße. Marcus holds the door open.

'I don't think so,' he says.

They don't hold hands. As they pass the Police Headquarters they keep their heads down and Marcus tucks his fingers into his pockets. He relaxes as they cross Alexanderplatz and walk up Alte Schönhauser Straße, past the apartment where Aunt Dotti now lives with Cousin Jette. She sold most of her belongings when she moved from Linienstraße, but she kept the old oval dining table and four matching chairs, the same table Aunt Dotti and Mutti drank coffee at, where Dorle swapped her used tram tickets with Cousin Meta. Something delicious is always waiting on that oval tabletop. Aunt Dotti makes Pflaumenkuchen, and she will sit watching while Dora and her cousins fill their bellies and lick their lips.

They go into a record shop where music is playing. They smoke and browse the records, and Dora sways and shuts her eyes.

'Do you dance?' Marcus asks. 'Do you like Swing? I know a great place to dance. I could take you on Thursday.'

She steps outside to tap the ash from her cigarette. She has no money to buy anything, and has never been taken dancing before. She agrees. He touches her hand.

At Elsässerstraße, Marcus gets pickles from one of the sellers. He stabs one with a toothpick, bites it, and holds the other half to her lips. She feels the brine dribble down her chin. They both eat messily beside the pickle stand and she wipes the juice away on her chin and his.

Then they wander further along the street, taking up too much space on the pavement, their hands close.

It's late when they get back to Alexanderstraße. Marcus takes her into the dark hallway of her building. He pushes her against the cold stone wall. They spend a long time there, standing close and whispering. The old kokker from the floor below catches them. He usually doffs his cap to Herbert, but he never says hello to the women, and he bangs his stick on the ceiling if Meta and Dora laugh too loudly.

Marcus grins at Dora once the old man's door slams shut. Heat washes over her face and prickles under her scalp, but Marcus shows no sign of embarrassment.

Eventually Dora and Marcus climb the two flights to the Lewin's door. He kisses her quickly as her key slides into the lock.

'Meta will see us!' Dora wriggles free, afraid to be caught again.

They say goodbye and Dora closes the door. Behind it she looks at herself in the mirror again. She wants to catch a glimpse of herself the way he has just seen her, her hair a mess and her lips bitten, her coat buttons undone.

21 November

The doctor is reading Ash's notes and clicking a pen.

Click click. Click click.

Ash is already in a bad mood, arching his back, trying to get off my knee and onto the floor. He doesn't like these places, waiting rooms, consultant's offices, elevators. Maybe it's the starkness, the enclosed space. He always starts fretting.

Click click. Click click.

I notice a box of toys under a side table, so I drag it over and put Ash down on the floor. I rummage through the toys and children's books. I put a lift-the-flap *Handsel and Gretel* down in front of him, but he's more drawn to something bright and noisy, a toy ambulance that'll drown everything out. Then I sit myself back down and wrestle my arms out of my coat.

The toy's siren blares.

Click click. Click click.

I need to distract myself from the sensations of the room, my guts uneasy, the floor dropping away. The office is oddly cluttered. A family portrait is propped against the medical books and there are pot plants and more photographs on the wall. A window right in front of me looks onto fields. Fierce sunshine today, despite the freeze. Not a rustle in the trees. It's often like this after a storm. Matthew's been kept busy by it. There are usually two big hurricanes every winter, and we've just had the first one. I had been thinking about work and texted a friend. They had diverted all incoming flights. I went out yesterday morning to see the wheelie bin blown about. It had opened its trap, spewing rubbish the length of the path. In the town, people's trampolines and fence panels have been blasted off. Near us there are trees down and roads cut off. A woman was taken to hospital when a two-hundred-year oak fell on her roof. She survived with cuts and bruises. It made the news.

Matthew's been out every morning before it gets light. He gets a lot of domestic calls after a storm, anxious messages left on the answering machine from people ducking under creaking boughs. He's up at Dunaskin again today. When Ash and I are done here I've some lunch to take him, and a flask of coffee. Something nice to look forward to after Ash's appointment. Matthew refused at first, saying he was too busy, but then changed his mind and sent me a text to come up.

At last, the doctor swivels on her chair to look at me. Her voice is slow and monotone. I wonder if this is part of a technique, something she was told to do at medical school. Like the pilots when they talk to the passengers. Sorry about that, folks, just a spot of turbulence.

'You decided against the genetic study, did you?'

I nod.

'In terms of diagnosis,' she says, even slower now and glancing down at Ash, 'sometimes we just don't know.'

She's going to tell me again to 'watch and wait'. We do

nothing else. She tells me to see how quickly he progresses, to hope that he doesn't start to lose skills.

'But he's sitting up now,' she says, trying to sound cheerful.

I smile. 'He can pull himself along too. Backwards, at least.'

She's chewing the end of the pen while she watches him.

'Do keep an eye on things, especially if he starts to find any of this hard again, if he's regressing.'

Sunlight continues to pour through the window and she gets up to close the blind.

'I just need to check his spine.'

I lift Ash onto the bed and hold up the Hansel and Gretel book, turning the pages to keep him calm. Most of the flaps have been torn out. The doctor takes off the top my mother sent him and leans him forward, feeling each vertebra with her fingertips, then lies him back and pulls him up again by the hands. It's the same routine the doctor did the day he was born.

'He still has a lag there, do you see?' she asks.

Ash's head dangles.

Of course I see. Ash still hangs like a lifeless cat when they do their tests. I look out of the window again while she checks his feet. The sun is about to disappear behind a bank of clouds. Maybe it'll rain. I want it to. I want to be cosy in the van with Matthew and our boy, listening to the radio, lunch together, a snooze with the seats pushed back. If it's bright we'll get the camera out and have a walk round the old mine. It's a creepy, dark place, and normally I avoid it, but I've barely seen Matthew this week and I miss him.

'Are you going back to work?' she asks.

'I want to. But you can't just walk back into air traffic control. It's been too long.'

She gives me a sympathetic nod.

Honestly, all that feels like years ago. I'd love to have nothing but planes on my mind, to focus on a single task: keep dots from colliding, greet pilots when they arrive in our airspace, pass them on when they leave. Safe journey. Ninety minutes on the radar, overseeing easy flight paths, smooth curves, neat pathways. With the headset on, the glare of the screen in my eyes, and the pilots in my ears, the ground never threatened to suddenly drop away. To be honest, I don't know if I'd still be deemed competent. I'd have to go through retraining and pass a medical assessment. Without that there would be no license, and to look at me now, I don't think I'd be validated. I don't tell that to the doctor. There's no point.

'Well, that's all fine,' she says.

I drop the book back in the toy box, put Ash's clothes back on, and pick up the plastic ambulance. The doctor makes more notes on a form and starts tapping into her computer. At the last minute she calls me back and prescribes a daily vitamin supplement. She says we must come back in three months' time. I agree to it without complaints, but feel flat, a flight grounded at the gate. I thought he was doing better. I hoped she'd cut us free for six months, or even a year. She has nothing to tell me anyway, only that my son is delayed. The doctors all use this word for him: delayed.

*

Matthew doesn't ask about anything when I get out of the car. He just puts his arms around me for a bit. He knows the appointments set me off. I bury my face into his collarbone and breathe in the smell of bark and earth.

'They want to test his hearing again,' I tell him. 'I just wish the doctors would say something positive.'

'I know,' he nods. 'I couldn't do what you're doing.'

I scrape the toe of my boot on the mucky path. Lots of debris has come down in the storm, russet red leaves and small branches, and the canopy above has thinned, letting a little more light through to the ground.

'Shall we eat in the van? It's freezing. Ash is asleep.'

While we eat our sandwiches I tell Matthew everything the doctor said, how we're to watch for signs of Ash going backwards, not just missing milestones that other babies reach, but dropping them. I look into the forest and think about Hansel and Gretel getting lost, the path disappearing behind them.

'Hm,' Matthew says. 'That's not going to happen.' He chews and thinks for a while. 'Doctors aren't emotional, you know? They only deal in facts.'

'I suppose so.'

'They can't tell you he's fine, so they have to say he might not be.'

We think our own thoughts for a while. I feel a little better for Matthew's logic. I tell him that the doctor asked about the genetic study, but he doesn't want to talk about it again. He just nods.

We share the coffee. The steam of it swirls up and mists the windscreen. A song comes on the radio, a big hit when Ash was born. The nurses listened to the radio day and night on the ward, and every day it was this song over and over. It's supposed to be uplifting, a rousing orchestral intro, the whole thing gathering pace as the voice cuts in, but I can't bear to hear it. I turn the radio off.

I'd rather stay warm in the van and sleep, but Matthew wants a walk. He insists the fresh air is what I need and that it's good for Ash. It'll help me sleep tonight, he says. It'll help me forget about the appointment.

Matthew's sleeping better than me these days. He's started selling the things he made with the knots of wood. We need the extra money while I'm not working, and people want the knots for seats or to hang on the wall, or just to decorate the garden. It started with just a few people, friends of his parents or old classmates, but word is getting around. We've started to get calls from people we don't know, all asking for the 'wood guy'.

Half the time I end up crashing on the sofa. Matthew wakes me up in the morning, not the other way round like it used to be, and I struggle upstairs to bed as he heads out to work. If I'm lucky I get an hour before Ash wakes up.

I'm tired, but I agree to the walk. Matthew wants to take pictures.

'Say cheese for Daddy!' he calls. 'That's my boy.' He grins and takes the shot.

Matthew soon has to get going. He puts Ash in the sling on my back and points me down a circular route that'll lead back to the car. Ash settles quickly and Matthew kisses me and puts the camera round my neck so I can take more snaps.

Everything in Dunaskin has an atmosphere, as if the sun hasn't broken through cloud in seventy years. There aren't many birds. A few scratchy cries. Drips fall from the leaves that have survived the storm, and my boots thud on the tightly packed mulch. Matthew's chainsaw roars in the distance. On then off again. This path goes past the old ironworks. First they made pig iron here, then bricks, and then coal, a last ditch attempt to save the place. There's an information panel near the car park. It's all been stopped for nearly a century now. The remnants are rusting away. Even the museum about the history of the place has been boarded up. There's a tall brick chimney and old walls that are blackened in places with soot. Everything is incomplete, half standing, piles of rubbish and disintegrated engines, all forgotten and frozen. I walk along a single railway track that comes to an unsettling stop. There's an uneasiness here, where grass grows between the sleepers that have sunk almost out of sight.

I lift Matthew's camera and position myself to take a photo. There's a chill against my face. I pan along towards the tall chimney of the old works. Nothing at the top but cloud.

Then movement through the camera lens, someone hunched over, a coat flapping close to the rear wall of the brick building. The opposite wall has fallen down so you can see right inside. But there's never usually people here. It's a dead place. I feel the taut belt around my chest, pull open the straps of the sling. I need to take some breaths.

'Are you awake?' I'm asking Ash, twisting my neck. My voice sounds weird and high pitched. I can't see his face when he's on my back. He must be sleeping.

I sit down on the trunk of a fallen tree. My breathing is too fast. The strap of the sling, which was fine until just a moment ago, is constricting everything. I try to picture Matthew, imagine what he'd say to calm me down. You can breathe, he'd say. You are breathing. You just need to relax. Go back to the car where you feel safe. Put on the radio. Loosen your clothes. Close your eyes for a bit.

I lean forward and let elbows sink into knees, try to distract myself with the camera. I press review and look through the shots, though my hands are starting to shake. Ash smiling in the mud and leaves. One of me rummaging in my bag just before we walked away from the van. Matthew took that when I wasn't looking. My hair's a mess. It needs a brush. I've gone to the doctor's office without once looking in a mirror.

Never mind that now. Breathe. Feel the earth underfoot.

I flick through a few more of Matthew's shots till I reach the one I just took. Zoom in, look around the old walls. There's no graffiti on the building. No one bothers coming out this far, and whatever I saw moving, if there was anything there at all, isn't in the picture.

I feel a bit better now. I stand up and tighten the

straps on the sling again, not too tight, just enough to walk back to the van.

But there is someone there. I can see them again. They've moved further along the wall. They straighten and duck down, as if they're searching for something on the ground. I get the camera and put it to my eye, zoom in, focus, concentrate on my breathing and watch for a while. It's an old man. His head is uncovered and he has a thin coat on. He moves forward, stumbling on rubble, but he doesn't fall. I squint through the lens and take another picture.

The tightness in my chest gets worse when I walk, but I keep pushing forwards, telling myself that I can breathe, that the suffocation isn't real. I can feel the warmth of Ash's hands on my neck. I have to look after him. I can't let my head get carried away. It's just adrenaline. I put a hand up on my shoulder for Ash to take, push his little nails into my fingertips. His hands are wet with saliva. He likes to chew his fingers.

The uneven ground is harder to cross with Ash on my back, but I have to make it back to the car, and this is the shortcut. There will be coffee still in the flask and I can put the heater on. I can catch my breath.

'There was definitely someone there,' I tell Matthew that evening. I can't find the old man in any of the pictures.

Matthew says he's never seen anyone there before.

We watch a space documentary in bed before trying to sleep. For the first time in months, Matthew says he might set up the Celestron, and asks if I want to take a look, but I tell him to go ahead without me. I can't concentrate on anything except the man in the woods. I get out of bed again and clean the kitchen, pack a lunch for Matthew to take tomorrow. He does go outside but he doesn't move the telescope.

'I've got a surprise for you,' he shouts through from the hall. I can feel the cold rushing in through the door and I tell him to shut it quick.

When I come through from the kitchen I find him at the bottom of the stairs arranging the branches of a small Christmas tree.

'I had it on the van. Do you like it?'

'It's a bit early,' I say, but he looks so pleased with himself it's hard not to join in.

We've not had a tree before. There are plenty of them right outside. But Matthew says he thought Ash would like looking at the lights and the baubles on an inside tree, and this year there will be presents for him to put under it. I tell him it's a good idea, and he says I should decorate it. I'll have to get some decorations from the shops.

'Go to town tomorrow,' Matthew says, and he kisses my forehead before going upstairs, back to bed. I don't follow him up. I sit on the stairs by the tree touching its branches, breathing in its scent. It has long, soft needles, and each branch ends in a mysterious bunch of knotted twig, a full-stop. Up close, these knobbles seem oddly assembled, a bit of a bodge, like the masses inside my belly. I pull off a few of the needles and roll them till the sticky resin coats my fingertips.

1938

Six weeks after Ruthie was born, Dora was back in the kitchens. The weather turned cold, and all through November and December she cried into the boiling pans. But people were good to her, even when she was distracted, even when she dropped a bowl of soup into a gentleman's lap. Cook wasn't angry. She sat her down in the kitchen and gave her some.

It was a long winter. Dora still carries the sadness, but since her milk dried up she has quietened down.

And already it's summer. July 1938.

Every Friday since Passover, Cook has given Dora an egg. It has become a ritual to begin each weekend. Dora takes off her hat and uncrosses the straps of her apron. Her uniform is bundled into the laundry with the other whites and she says goodbye to Cook, who'll be making final preparations.

'*Gut Shabbes*, Dora. Don't forget Ruthie's egg.'

She carries the egg in her hand. Tonight, Dora takes her usual route down Oranienburgerstraße, and she steps quickly, cupping the egg close to her chest. The crowd nudges along, glad for the weekend but struggling with the heat. There is no breeze. Heat like never before in Berlin. Flags droop from their poles. Dora follows the raised railway along Dirksenstraße. A train rumbles overhead and she imagines the egg yolk trembling inside the shell.

By the time she reaches Alexanderplatz, the egg feels warm in her hand. Here the buses, trams and trains follow the curves of the streets and the rails. They loop in and about each other, and then somehow disentangle themselves to follow their own routes out of the busy square.

She passes the two turrets on the west side of the Police Headquarters, the Red Castle. One more block and then she's home, through the yard to the cross building, and up the stairs.

She cooks the egg as soon as she gets in. Tip-tap. Tip-tap. She watches it boiling. It has a bright, pale shell. Dora simmers it with her fingertips on the handle, feeling the gentle tapping, watching the bubbles form in the water. At domestic school they taught her the surest way to protect the egg from cracking: a spoonful of salt in the pan. It works.

The egg dances in the heating water. Cousin Meta isn't home yet. Perhaps she's taking time to be alone with Herbert. When they come in they'll bring noise, the chirp of Meta's stories, Herbert's whistling, the smell of his cigarette. They never change. She's glad they never change.

Tip-tap. Tip-tap. Faster now. Sweat is slick on her face. Dora's surprised she has any sweat left. At work the kitchens are unbearably hot and Fridays are the busiest day. Pots are set to stew overnight while preparation is made for the evening's dinner. Three meals have to be ready for all the home's elderly residents. It's a feast for kings every week.

The egg spins like a moon in the black pan. Should she take it out? As usual Dora's forgotten to time the cooking. Three minutes is all it takes to get lost in her thoughts. She lets it simmer.

According to the dietary laws you have *fleischig* and *milchig*, and then you have eggs, somewhere in between. This has always puzzled Dora. They taste more like dairy, but they come from flesh, and could be flesh again. But eggs look nothing like flesh, and so they are Pareve. If they are laid by a kosher hen, they can be eaten with meat or with dairy. Not that it matters to Dora. She would eat anything at all.

Cook tries her best to nourish the residents with alternatives since the kosher meat ban. The kitchen stocks cheeses, nuts, eggs, and milk. But the elderly are stuck in their ways and this means they get thinner. Some of them have been getting sick. Dora misses the ones who were livelier once, who are irritable now, no longer laughing. But it is no good trying to persuade them. They are stubborn just like Vati was.

Cook still makes a kind of cholent for Saturday, following as closely as she can the old recipe, just without the meat. She throws the ingredients into pots as big as barrels: potatoes, beans, paprika, onions, barley. Just before the end of Friday a whole basketful of eggs is placed gently into the mixture, left in their shells to slowly bake, and by Saturday afternoon the onions have dyed the eggshells a deep russet red. The shining shells remind everyone of Pesach, the egg on their plate, a symbol of how hard life was. And because of the brightly dyed shells they also think of Easter, when the Germans paint their Paschal eggs. Easter and Passover. In Spring, eggs are on the Seder plate and hanging in the trees.

Dora takes a large spoon and lifts the egg from the pan. She leaves the salted water to cool. She puts the egg in a cup on the table, and from a drawer takes out a pocket paint palette with a thin brush. She fills a glass with cold water. On the palette she sees the dried swirls of colour she made the previous week. While Dora goes to wash, the egg waits on the table.

At first Ruthie was too young to eat the eggs Cook gave her. Instead Dora made pinholes in each end of the shell and carefully blew into the hole at the top, emptying the insides into a bowl. She painted the empty, unbroken shells. Dora used the insides to make a treat to satisfy Meta's sweet tooth, *Eierkuchen* with a spoon of sugar and flour, spreading it with a little jam if they had some.

The empty shells were painted for Ruthie. Dora had to make sure she didn't crush them as she rode the bumpy tram to Niederschönhausen. At the infant home the aunts tied a branch to a bar of Ruthie's cot, and the eggshells were threaded and hung on the branch so the babies saw the decorations spinning and bouncing. Each weekend, Ruthie's tree would get a new jewel.

But Ruthie is nine months old now and she has developed a good appetite.

'*Mutti* brought you an egg!'

This is what Dora will say to Ruthie as she lifts her out of the cot, the moment she longs for all week.

Friday nights drag, but painting the egg helps pass the time. At first she wasn't very good at it, but since Meta found a special tiny paintbrush, Dora has been more precise. The paintings get better each time.

'What a shame,' Meta always says. 'That is far too pretty to eat!' But Meta doesn't see Ruthie's face when the colourful egg appears from Dora's bag. She hasn't played the game of rolling the egg along the ground to crack the shell, or watched how Ruthie eats, smacking her lips, licking each fingertip, with crumbled yoke sticking to her chin.

Meta and Herbert still aren't home. Meta used to wait for Herbert every day at the gates of a little park just south of the Spree. On nice days they would sit on the grass, but this isn't allowed anymore. Dora misses swimming in the baths behind the same park. Jews aren't allowed there either. Tonight the Lewins might be strolling by the river, or walking under the conker trees behind Unter den Linden. No-one can stop Meta and Herbert from walking together. If only Marcus could have been more like Herbert, then Dora would have had someone to walk beside her as she pushed Ruthie's pram.

The Lewins arrive home just as Dora finishes rubbing a wet cloth over her face and neck and under her arms.

'Post for you, Dora,' Meta calls.

'Did you walk far?'

'No. It's too hot,' Meta complains.

Every day Meta checks the letterbox when she comes home from work, and brings the letters upstairs. She takes her shoes off, and she will leave the letters on the table. She will go and change out of her work clothes. While she does this Herbert will be making coffee and looking forward to smoking a cigarette. He will be hungry, looking around the kitchen, already wondering what Dora's going to make and when it will be ready. Dora wraps a towel around herself and tucks a corner of it under her arm.

Herbert looks tired. He greets her in a rush and, taking his coffee, follows Meta into their bedroom to give Dora some privacy. Dora's clothes are kept in the corner of the kitchen, just above her bed. The letter is on the table.

Her name and address are neatly typed in heavy, official ink. The paper is crisp in the heat. Dora's insides lurch as she turns the envelope over and pushes a finger under the seal. There's a black eagle stamp and a single sheet of paper inside.

Dora reads a few words. Her skin is cooler after the wet cloth, but she feels the heat dewy on her already. She wet her hair and combed it through, and now a drop lands with a tap on the words.

> *According to the police order of 22.08.1938 regarding Jewish aliens residing in the territory of the Reich, you are ordered to leave the Reich within one month and may not return without permission.*

You have a right to file a complaint within two weeks of this instruction, which would have to be submitted in writing.

I also point out to you that you will face imprisonment for one year and fines, should you return to the Reich without permission.

Dora stares at the rough opening her fingers have slit through the envelope. The heat is rising in the room, and in Dora's head, and in the rock in her belly. A moment later Meta comes back in and reads the letter.

'What is this?' she asks. Her voice is thin and strained, like someone being held round the neck. They know what it means.

Dora holds the torn envelope over her chest.

They were half expecting it. Others have received them. They hoped she would be missed, but no, here it is. Dora folds the letter and presses the creases hard between her fingertips.

'How can I just leave? I've never been anywhere else.'

Herbert takes the letter, and as he reads she sees in his face that he can do nothing. Even so, he tells her he will think of some plan, and not to worry. They will write a letter, quickly. He lights candles. They light the candles every Friday even though they don't pray, and Dora puts the food in front of them, but tonight no one eats much. They just sit.

'*Vati* was not German,' Dora breaks the silence. 'He was Stateless, so I am too, even though I was born here. You didn't get letters, did you? Because Herbert is German.'

'If you were married to a German,' Herbert shrugs. 'Maybe Marcus.'

At the sudden sound of Marcus's name Dora feels a burn behind her eyes. She hasn't said his name out loud in a year, not since Ruthie was born. Is that Herbert's plan?

Meta snorts. 'Marcus only does what his parents want. He isn't even in Berlin.'

Herbert clears his plate noisily and goes to the window.

'What is there to stay for anyway?' he says, looking out at the yard. 'Everyone else is trying to leave, Dora.'

The window is open and outside the neighbours are having a fight over the rubbish bins.

Dora has never seen Herbert angry before. He goes out, slamming the door, as if he's annoyed with her in particular. Herbert would like to emigrate with Meta. They tried, but it was too expensive, and they had no contacts. Meta eventually said she would never leave without her mother anyway, and that made it final. Old people never got visas.

Even more than emigrating, Meta and Herbert want a baby. They've been married three years and people have started talking. The doctor says Meta's anxious and that's why it hasn't happened, but Meta says plenty of babies are being born and *everyone* is anxious. Meta would be so good with children. Even when Dora was carrying Ruthie, Meta seemed more motherly than she did. She's more mamish than Dora in every way.

'I wish we could all go together,' Dora says.

Her cousin hangs over her like a coat. She wraps her hands over Dora's fists and they cry as if they are trying to melt into one. Like this they sit as the candles burn short.

Dora can't keep her hand still enough to paint the egg. She was going to paint a ship, clouds swirling at the top, lilac and grey, a curl of yellow at the edges. The calm waves would ripple with a thousand tiny arcs.

Meta paints it for her. She cleans the brush with a swirling motion in the glass of water. It rings like a tiny bell. Every so often Meta gets to her feet and goes to the kitchen. She brings back clean water. Meta does this without a word till eventually, the ship is sailing.

When Herbert comes back in he squeezes Dora's shoulder.

'I'm sorry, Dora,' he whispers. He doesn't have a plan. 'I asked around. We might be able to extend it a bit, that's all. Six months.'

Dora takes the ugly letter with the eagle and the Hakenkreuz off the table. She hides it in her bag. When she gets into bed she wishes she could reach right over the city. She imagines the cot, the white blankets, Ruthie's tiny hands tucked below her chin, her face relaxed. Most nights Dora can trick herself into sleep, but tonight it doesn't work.

She thinks about Vati, how good he was at praying, his gentle voice. Dora hasn't prayed in such a long time.

She doesn't even remember her Hebrew lessons. She isn't a very good Jew and she's not a real German. As Stateless a person as one can possibly be. She and the egg are the same. Not quite dairy, not quite flesh. A mother, but *not quite*.

There is nothing left to do but pray.

Dora's thoughts blend like the paint in the water. Where will she be sent? She feels seasick, and wonders how it's possible. She's never even seen the sea.

23 November

When Matthew got up for work I was still awake on the sofa. He told me off because he doesn't understand. As soon as I close my eyes I see everything all at once, the hospital, the gene study, pages of notes and old postcards of Berlin, and planes coming in to land and taking off. I should be back at work by now. An old colleague emailed asking when I'd be back, and I haven't replied. I don't know what to say.

We need to do something with the day. For Ash's sake. Even though my chest is already tight, exhaustion weighing me down like the ever-growing laundry pile. I open drawers and rummage for whatever's clean and fits. I put Ash into a fresh outfit, feed him something, and then we get in the car. I take him up the fast road to the supermarket. We'll get some Christmas decorations for the tree. Maybe, on the way home, we'll drive to Prestwick and park up somewhere near the runway to watch the planes wobble out of the low cloud and touchdown. The last hundred metres of their journeys over oceans always seem so hesitant. I'll sit and work out what to tell work.

The supermarket is a twenty-four-hour giant, and you can lose yourself for hours, not knowing if it's day or night. There's a café and a pharmacy, and a glasses place and a photography shop, a post office, and a place next to the kiddy ride-ons where old ladies tie up their doggies. More than once this year, when Ash has refused sleep, we've driven here at two o'clock in the morning and I've walked around the shop in pyjamas with a coat over the top. Ash is so small he still fits in the infant bed on the top of the trolley.

Today Ash is quite happy lying in the trolley bed, staring at the tinsel and the lights on the warehouse roof, seeing the colours go by on the shelves: tins of sweetcorn and tins of beans, tins of soup, tins of canned meat, toilet paper, aluminium foil, bin bags, frozen peas, frozen pizzas, fish fingers, brown bottles of beer and green bottles of wine, bottles of blackcurrant and orange squash. I wander back to the magazines but there's nothing I want. I browse the baby clothes. There are onesies for Christmas with elf ears sticking out the hood and glitter writing. I pick things up and put them all back. I can't remember what I'm here for. I've not brought my handbag. It'll be sitting on the passenger seat in the car.

Ash has no coat on and it's probably raining. We're going through a spell, and it rains every day. He'll get cold and upset if I go back for my bag. Old ladies will come up to me in the car park and ask why he doesn't have a hat. Someone always comes up to us in the supermarket. They lean in and wiggle their fingers in knitted gloves.

'Where's your smile?' they say. They wait for a reaction, but it doesn't come. They get in closer, cooing louder. When Ash still doesn't smile, they take a step back, and I see them wondering.

'What's wrong with him?' some of them say.

Sometimes they try again and again, and I have to say before Ash gets upset that his muscles aren't very strong. He saves his smiles for special occasions and special people, me and Matthew, and Alan the physiotherapist. I'm not sure people understand. They just nod and walk away.

I follow a mother with a little girl. She goes up the aisle of fresh meat, commenting on the sizes of the turkeys. The child is bored. While the mother reads the labels, the girl picks up a polystyrene tray and presses her finger down on the see-through wrap.

'Don't do that!' the mother snaps. She takes the tray from the little girl and throws it back in the fridge. They cross over to the seafood section and the little girl puts her hands in her pockets and rocks on her heels. She stares at the row of raw salmon and torn strips of flesh.

I pick up the tray the little girl touched. Fillets of steak. It's expensive and lean. I can still see the dent in the meat from the girl's finger and I watch the flesh moving back into place, gradually plumping itself against the plastic. I stroke my hand over the cold meat and watch the blood at the side of it start to pool. There's a petrol blue sheen on the side of the cut. I wonder if the masses inside me are surrounded by something like that. Fibroids are all connective tissue, aren't they?

A rush of nausea makes me put the meat down. It lies there among packs of sausages and trays of pork loin medallions. Fleshy and human looking. I can smell it, and I can see the threads of fat running through it, strands of white greasy tissue. Another wave of nausea, and without any warning this time, my pulse starts hammering. Drumming in my neck. I look down the white aisle, and I'm like a jet on the approach, wheels down, clumsy, reaching out desperate for land after a mechanical failure. My top feels clammy, itchy and stuck to me, as if it's coated with something hard and sticky like the half-peeled bark of a tree.

I tumble on the floor next to the trolley before I faint. Someone asks if I need help but I don't look at them. I just keep my head down on my arms until they walk away. The fibroids are growing, pushing everything else out. They'll push up into my lungs and burst them. I think of the mother of the little girl, going home and piercing the meat with a knife, slitting it open, rubbing in butter and herbs.

A voice behind me is talking into a walkie-talkie. It beeps loudly and they talk in code. I don't know these codes. A carton of milk has burst open. I don't think it was me, but I've wheeled and walked right through it. The code is repeated on the crackling tannoy and someone comes with a mop. She asks if I dropped the milk and I tell her I don't think so. She sweeps it around in circles on the floor. She doesn't believe me. They start clearing the aisle. They put up yellow cones. Men in black jackets come up to us and one of them tickles Ash in the trolley. I want to stay on the floor but the milk's running everywhere as the woman mops it, and she's telling me to get up or I'll get wet. I put one hand on the trolley so they can't wheel Ash away from me, and I pull myself up. They're whispering to each other.

'Are you going to buy that?' a man asks me.

I look at Ash. I've completely covered him in tinsel. He's grinning, dribbling all over it, almost laughing as he pushes his hands through it, rustling it, watching the tiny ribbons of plastic and saliva shimmer in the light, his little fingers splayed like stars.

Someone places their hand gently on my arm, another on my shoulder.

'Are you okay, honey?'

Roberta. She takes one look at my face and wraps her arms around me.

'I'm getting it,' Roberta tells the man. She grabs the handle of the trolley and tells me to walk, shouting over her shoulder that we're on our way to the tills.

She takes me back to my car. I get my purse out to pay her back for the tinsel, but she won't take it. I try to talk to her, but I can't. Like that time in the woods, but worse, much worse. She asks if I need to call someone. I manage to shake my head.

'I should go home and sleep,' I say, and I put my arms on the steering wheel and my head down on top. She tells me to call her when I'm home.

I watch her walk back towards the supermarket. I'm safer in the car, the windows wound up and all the sounds of the outside muffled. Roberta stops by the doors, talking to a woman in a supermarket vest, and they stand chatting for a second. I see her looking back at my car, speaking about me to the other woman. I turn away and shut my eyes. I don't want anyone coming over.

My whole body jumps when my phone starts blasting, but I can't find it in time. Ash is on the front passenger seat, still playing with the tinsel. He stares at me while I root around, and eventually I find the phone down the side of my seat. The missed call was Matthew. I don't call back. Instead, I look up the number of the surgery. I dial, listen to it ringing and hang up again. They'll put me on pills, will send me off for a scan to measure the fibroids. This could be reassuring, but maybe not. They might send people to spy on me and Ash again. They'll think I'm going crazy, not coping, and I won't be able to tell them what's really in my head. I'll never get back to work.

I call Matthew. He wants to know what there is for dinner. I haven't done any actual shopping.

'Chinese,' he says. 'Fine by me.'

I tell him I was in the shop for hours and didn't buy anything to eat. I start to cry. After a while, he asks what I've eaten today. Nothing. I tell him I'll sort it and we say goodbye, and I dial the surgery again but there are no non-emergency appointments till January. I'm relieved. I tell them I'll call another time. Maybe I will.

When he gets home, Matthew hands me a box wrapped in green paper. He says he was going to keep it till Christmas, but thinks I need a treat so I can open it now.

'Tickets to Berlin?' I say, only half-joking.

He shakes his head. I open the paper and find a patterned box, and inside the box there is a bottle. I roll it between my fingers. The design on the box is a double helix.

'It's one of those ancestry things,' Matthew says, but I already know.

'Do I pee in it?' I laugh. 'It's a bit small.'

I kiss him, smelling the earth.

'Thank you.'

I move the bottle between my fingers some more and watch the double helix spiralling fast. It's a DNA test. Tightening again, right around my ribs, like a drawstring.

'It's not like a doctor's test,' Matthew says. He can read my mind. 'Don't look so worried.'

I don't have to pee in it, just collect a little tube full of spit, which is harder than it sounds and leaves my mouth dry. Once it's full, Matthew screws the lid on and seals it in a return envelope.

Ash cries, so I go to him, and Matthew takes the envelope to the van saying he'll jump out now, drop by the Chinese for a carry out and drop the test in the post-box on the way home. I feed Ash next to our tree, now covered in tinsel, and I can still feel the slippy DNA pooling under my tongue. I try to imagine the web of people that are about to be linked to me, try to picture its shape. Tannenbaums. Rowelskis. Roots and branches and twigs. A frizzy hair gene, a fibroid gene, a long fingers and toes gene, a legs that don't work gene, a good at maths gene, genes for worry, for love, for anger, for patience, everything. Genes colliding with other genes in billions of combinations, jostling and rolling through millennia like a giant game of pinball and finally forming a set, falling into line, two by two, a complete deck of chromosomes that's unique.

I think of my saliva glistening inside that tiny bottle in the dark post-box at the end of the street. All of the answers are in there.

25 December

Matthew cleans and prepares Christmas lunch. He does all the trimmings, even though it'll be just the three of us till we get to my parents on New Year's Eve. Matthew's parents have gone down to his sister's family in Shrewsbury, like they always do.

The huge knot of wood that Matthew sliced and sanded and varnished now has table legs, and is sitting in the living room taking pride of place. We sit at it and unpack Ash's stocking for him. Matthew brings tea and toast. He puts it on a coaster on the piece of wood. The ravens rasp in the tree in the back, and I slurp the tea a bit too fast. It's still hot. Ash smiles at some of his toys.

'He's getting stronger,' I say to Matthew.

I speak to my mother on the phone. I know that Matthew has told her about me not sleeping, and about the panic attacks if that's what they are. He wanted me to get an emergency appointment to see the doctor, but I refused. Instead, he's breathing down my neck, telling me to go to bed every night and putting food in front of me whether I'm hungry or not. My mother says everything will be all right, and that when we come up to their place, she'll spoil me. I tell her not to worry.

'Do you like the new table?' Matthew asks when I get off the phone.

'It's great. Where are all my notes?'

My printed pages and scribbled notes covered our old table. Now they've vanished.

'I'll set you up a desk in the back tomorrow,' Matthew says. 'I don't want you going back to working late on the sofa.'

Matthew hands me a package in Christmas paper before I can react. I unwrap the paper and find a set of DVDs inside, a series set in Berlin.

'I've not got plane tickets yet, but we are going to go. When you're feeling up to it.'

The DNA I sent off in a little bottle has come back early, and Matthew has intercepted the post and wrapped up the envelope with the results inside. We sign into the website. It says I have nearly four hundred cousins and am thirty-three per cent Jewish. My closest match is someone called Kitty. I click *contact*, but I can't decide what to say and know I should be taking a break for once.

My phone beeps. It's a text from Roberta.

Happy Christmas Hunny! Hope you are feeling better x

I text back that it would be so nice to see her. I haven't even met Wee Marc.

You did meet him! He was with me in Asda.

I didn't even notice. I'm not sure what to reply.

Don't worry about it, Hunny, you weren't well. Call me in the New Year.

I look at my phone for a while and then send back a Happy Christmas with a smiley face.

Matthew told me not to worry about presents, but I found him some bright yellow socks made of thick mohair that he can pull up to his knees under his work trousers. He gets cold feet sometimes, so I thought he'd like them. He opens this and two other presents I knew he'd want, a bottle of Macallan, and a book about campervans. That's Matthew's latest dream, doing up a van, then taking the telescope away for weekends, stargazing from the forest.

'Sorry,' I say as he opens them. 'They're not that exciting.'

He puts the socks on straight away.

I read Ash one of his new books. Afterwards, I put the book open on his lap and take his photo. He's wearing blue boots, and with them on he almost looks like a toddler, even if he isn't anywhere close to walking. Alan measured his feet a few weeks before Christmas, and he brought the boots round on his last day of work. They have laces and hooks, and they're tough. Strong and supportive.

'I'm never supposed to say this kind of thing,' he had confided after he wished me Happy Christmas, 'but between you and me, I'm quite hopeful for those legs.'

I've kept Alan's words to myself, like a wish. Matthew won't believe me if I tell him, and I want to hold on to them, not dull the feeling. When I said goodbye to Alan, shut the door and turned around, the tree lights were twinkling so bright I had to shut my eyes. There was nothing but the scent of pine. I thought I could hear everything at that moment.

I send the photo of Ash wearing his boots and holding his book to my mother, and then I dangle him down between my knees with the soles touching the floor. Alan made it sound easy: just let him feel the floor under his feet.

His soles skim the carpet, and I hold the moment in my mouth, scared to breathe. I imagine him pushing his feet firm against the ground, walking across the room to me, climbing a tree, or running in circles with his arms like a plane. I imagine it.

Part II

1939

The smell of London clings to her. This city feels different on her skin, different like the words in her mouth. Lumpy dumpling words. At home, the sharp winters are like pins pricking, but here her cheeks are damp and her nose streams with snot. It's impossible to stay warm even under her hat. She gets cold leftovers for dinner and shivers in the attic bedroom. It would help if she had someone to talk to, but the employers are sour and even the cigarettes are bitter. She has to speak slowly, thinking first about every word. When she doesn't know a word, she has to find another one. If she closes her eyes, the smell of chimney smoke and newspaper, and the sound of trains is not unlike home, but here there is an earthy smell as well, mouldering leaves and rotting rubbish. The car horns and train whistles chime a different chord to the Berlin traffic.

Londoners are taking down their Christmas decorations. Tannenbaums, stripped of their riches, leaning against fences, all browning and bare. Among the branches there's nothing left but a sprinkling of glitter dust and a few soggy paper chains. Dora walks up the road to Kings Cross, watching her breath make swirls of vapour. She's been sent to buy a chicken, and despite the chill and the words that get stuck in her mouth, going to the shop is her favourite task. It's the best thing to do on a long list of duties.

The cook had stopped her while she was cleaning the floor. She was taking care to push the mop right into the corners, the way she did at work in Berlin, the way she was taught. The cook wasn't happy.

'You're taking too long. Go and get the chicken instead, understand? I need to get it cooking.'

Dora's face went hot. She shook her head, hating the silence of the English household, longing for the chatter, the joking and the stories about the elderly residents that had filled the kitchens at Große Hamburgerstraße, the smell of Birches baking, all the anticipation of the meal to come, especially on a Friday, and the weight of Ruthie's smooth egg, the weekly gift from Cook, sitting in her pocket.

'Chicken!' The cook said again, curling Dora's fingers closed around a written note. 'I need to put it on soon. You can get it on credit.' She spoke louder and louder, tapping at the flabby skin of her wrist where a watch would be. Her arms were more than three times the width of Dora's.

The Franks are a family of seven upstairs. They need fed and kept tidy, three children, their parents, a plump grandmother called Mrs Davis, and her husband, a stern old man with one leg. The family does nothing for themselves.

'Is that our Fräulein?' Mr Davis always grunts when Dora comes into a room, his narrowed eyes following her footsteps. He never uses her name, and it has taken

Dora a while to understand that he is nearly blind as well as crippled. His ears are sharp though, and he hides his blindness. War injuries, the cook says. Mr Davis spends most of his day sitting in an armchair, but whenever he moves you hear him dragging the shoe on the end of his false leg.

'Chicken?' the cook shouted again.

'*Schinken?*'

The word for ham. The Davis family didn't keep kosher. Dora made the noise of a pig.

'No!'

Eventually the cook flapped her arms and clucked.

'Oh, thank God, we're getting somewhere!' she said when Dora finally understood, and Dora noticed the first hint of a smile on the woman's round, shiny face.

The walk to the shop isn't far, but they expect her to be quick. Run there and back, she's been told, but she doesn't. She takes her time. The list of jobs folded in her pocket, all tiring and filthy work, is long. It will take her till many hours past dark to finish, and she'll get no break. So now she takes time and gets some air while she has the chance. Perhaps they'll realise that they are asking too much.

The Franks could fit another bed into her room if they wanted to. They could take on another girl, someone she could talk to. Big Cousin Jette could come, red-haired Jette, who has never gotten married because no one has ever been good enough. Single women are ideal candidates for the visa, as long as there are no children. British invitations didn't extend that far, a fact that she'd been warned of at the start, before she even signed the forms. They needed domestics, not tots for nursery schools. Dora had pleaded and shown them Ruth's photograph, but there were no exceptions. The British granted Dora's visa and denied Ruth's, and nowhere else was taking Jewish refugees. Germany allowed Dora's extension on account of her daughter, allowing them a further six months to find Ruthie a British guardian, but it was impossible, even with the Jewish committee offering to pay in full for both tickets.

'Call for your girl as soon as you've found someone else to look after her,' was all the British officials suggested. 'You'll be expected to work. You won't have time for a baby.'

Two women in the street stand looking into the sky. One of them holds the hand of a little girl who's not much older than Ruth. The child is squeezed tight into a light grey duffle coat with a knitted helmet pulled low over her forehead and ears. She stands on chubby legs, dangling a doll from her hand and skimming it over the stone step of the house. The women pay no attention to her. They're talking about snow. *Schnee*. Words about the weather aren't hard to understand. The Londoners all talk about the weather and grimace at the sky in the same way. *Kalt*. Cold. *Warm*. Warm. Some words are almost the same, but others are confusing. Chicken sounds like ham. She will make the same mistake again because it's hard to do anything right when she is so frozen. Her hands and feet are stiff. Her ears sting, stomach aches, and her skin is rough and dry. Most of all she misses Meta, and Ruthie, and Aunt Dotti.

Dora joins the queue in the shop. She looks around at the pies and sides of meat, and the birds hanging in the window. Her boots sink into the soft mounds of sawdust sprinkled over the floor, and she breathes in the air. Animal fat and blood. The smell of an English butcher. Sausages lined up next to chicken legs. Between her fingers she holds the cook's greasy note. She unfolds the paper and stares at the words.

English handwriting is not like hers. When the boat reached England, they couldn't read her writing on her forms. There were hundreds of other passengers, all tired and seasick, and everyone just wanted to sit down. The officials couldn't read anyone's handwriting. Eventually, the people at the port made her spell out her name, and a man at a desk wrote it on a fresh form for her. He announced her name loudly. She had never heard it sound so stupid.

The butcher takes the note from her. He nods and a bird is chosen, the feet tied, and the bundle is wrapped in greaseproof paper. He hands her the package. No money is exchanged. The Franks have a credit account. Dora goes back into the street cradling the wrapped bird in the crook of her arm, the weight of it warming her heart, reminding her of something.

School children out for lunch walk by in groups. Dora listens to the strange music of their voices, but she doesn't look at them. The advice she has been given is not to speak German, especially in the street. It was the first thing they told everyone who arrived on the boat. Being foreign could get you in trouble, being German, worse still. Dora keeps her eyes on the ground. Frost is already glittering on the stones. Perhaps the Londoners are right, it'll snow overnight. There are heavy clouds over the city. It's rained every day since she arrived. She passes the house where the women and the little girl were. They have gone inside.

Halfway down the street, Dora slips. She feels the blood draining from her head and the solid ground slide from under her shoes, and for a second, she hears Vati, just like he used to say.

Daydreaming again!

She thrusts her left arm back to break the fall, and is surprised to find that her right arm is still cradling the chicken. It's wrapped in its cream-coloured paper, unharmed. Dora will have a bruise.

She lifts her hand to look at the sting on her palm, rolling over the ache in her hipbone. A man in a long coat runs from across the street.

'Are you alright?'

'*Danke!*' she says, and pins her mouth shut again, remembering she mustn't speak German at all. The man doesn't seem to have noticed.

'Oh, the devil! From over there I thought you were holding a baby!' he smiles, taking her hand and looking down at the wrapped chicken. He laughs and reaches out and she holds up the chicken.

Schoolboys pass and whistle. Dora pushes a lock of hair over her face, tugs her dress back down over her knees, and pushes herself onto her feet. She nods to thank the man again, brushing down the back of her coat.

The man has brown eyes and light brown hair, and

a bright scarf wound several times around his throat. The stubble on his chin is a couple of days old and he has faint lines around his eyes.

'Can I walk with you?' he asks.

She shakes her head and looks over to the door of number forty-one, aware of the schoolboys still glancing over their shoulders.

'I am here,' she says.

'Oh,' he says. 'Well, here you go.'

The man hands the chicken back. Dora's hip is aching, but she can walk. The man watches from the railings as she goes down the steps to the kitchen entrance and rings the bell.

Inside the laundry is being done and the windows are steamed up. Dora can't see through them. When cook answers she's wiping sweat from her brow with a dish cloth, and the smell of soap flakes is intense. It's the same smell that Jette always had on her, even on her day off. Dora dreams of Jette opening the door one day. She wonders what they would say upstairs if she suggested it. Cousin Jette has worked in the hospital laundry for years, and she's good at other things too, cooking and mending. She's used to hard work.

'You took your time,' the cook says. Glancing up, she notices the man and hurries Dora back into the house. She seizes the chicken and closes the door with a slam. 'Don't get any ideas,' she says, pointing a finger. 'You're in England to work, not for that sort of thing.'

The warmth in the kitchen is a comfort, but the cook's words sit hard like the rock in her stomach as she takes off her coat, hanging it on a hook beside the door. Behind her, the cook thumps the chicken down on the table. Dora goes back to mopping. She squeezes her eyes and clears her throat, holding back tears that would anger the cook even more.

The family have dinner at seven. By this time, Dora has tended the fires in the main rooms, wrung the laundry and hung it to dry on the pulleys in the kitchen, ironed yesterday's wash, peeled potatoes and carrots, beaten the hall rugs, mopped all the floors downstairs, tidied the children's bedroom and sewn name tapes onto their new school coats. While the cook slices the roast chicken, Dora polishes shoes, getting everything ready for the next morning. Mr Frank is going away on business. She doesn't know what kind of business he runs, but he wears a black suit, and most of the time he doesn't return till late.

'Here,' the cook says, and she hands Dora a potato. It's piping hot, but not enough. There will be leftovers later for both of them, chicken and cabbage. The bones will go into soup. The potato is good, but it only makes her mouth water.

While the family eat, Dora stands by the dining-room door, ready to fetch anything that is asked for. She tries hard not to stare at the steaming food. They act as if she isn't there, folding the meat onto their forks and chewing it in their mouths, speaking loudly. They don't ask Dora to do anything until the end of the meal. It's only then, as Dora is clearing away, that Mrs Frank notices she is walking with a limp after her fall in the street.

'I hope you are still able to work,' she says laughing. 'That looks quite nasty.'

Dora takes Mrs Frank's plate.

'I hope so too. I'm not sure I can afford any more staff,' Mr Frank chuckles.

The hard stone left in her belly after Ruthie was born is still there. Most of the time she forgets, but when she's homesick it seems to hurt. It swells and presses like something wrong she has swallowed. She feels it now. She feels it in the kitchen when the cook shouts.

Mrs Frank wipes the corners of her lips with her napkin and looks around the table at her family.

'I can't do all this work myself,' she says.

Glug-glug go the English words, like a noise at the bottom of a pond. Dora's mind races to find the right words to suggest another girl, to have Jette here.

'If she can't work,' says the youngest son, 'can we send her back to Hitler?'

For a few seconds, no one speaks. Only the clock on the wall responds. Dora swallows. She puts a hand in her pocket to feel the rough edge of the folded paper, the unfinished list of duties she must complete.

'Well, can we?' the child asks again, and this time the grandfather chuckles and raises his half-empty glass.

'To hard work!' he announces, and he swallows the contents of the glass in one gulp, looking across the table at Dora. 'And service to Great Britain.'

'*Mehr wasser*,' he says to her over the family's laughter. '*Bitte*, <u>Fräulein</u>.'

*

Dora takes her plate to her room. She has a single bed with a lumpy pillow. There aren't enough blankets and no heating, and in this part of the house, the only light comes from a small oil lamp. In one corner there is a sink, and above it an old mirror is fixed on the wall. Her clothes hang on pegs. She doesn't own much. She could fit everything that is hers into her case. She could go to the mirror and smooth her hair under a hat, and then she could walk out the door, all in just a minute or two.

Dora lights the lamp and puts it on the floor by the bed. Her photographs are hidden under her pillow, inside the little, green photo album. She flicks through them while she eats: Mutti and Vati and herself as a little girl, and her green dress, which is grey in the photo, but she'll never forget the real colour. There's a picture of her mother on a bench with Dora as a baby on her knee. It must have been taken in the Volkspark Friedrichshain, or maybe it was taken on one of their trips up to Weißensee, where Mutti would sit by the lake. In another photograph, her friends from school grin back at her, girls in rows with long plaits. Dora smiles as she runs her finger over their faces, remembering the sound of each of their voices. The last photograph is of Ruthie. Dora has just one photo of her daughter, but there are more pages in the album, blank and waiting.

Ruthie's photograph was taken in September, when Dora took the tram to Niederschönhausen to celebrate her first birthday with the nurses and the other children.

She'd pulled favours at work to borrow the camera. It was warm for the season, and the children had eaten lunch in the garden behind the infant home. Pears hung in bunches on the trees, ripe for picking, the flesh inside sweet and brilliant white. Ruth was sitting on the grass, holding a new toy, a knitted lamb that Aunt Dotti had made for her. She looked into the camera with wide brown eyes, a look of mischief that Aunt Dotti later said was just like Dora at that age.

Ruth seems suddenly a little girl, Cousin Jette had written in her first letter. *She walks confidently now. She doesn't need to hold your hand.*

Dora senses already that the Franks won't help Jette or Ruthie. She's anxious to move on and she'll do it quickly. All the Austrian and German girls are moving, swapping positions, switching about the city. The problem is that everyone is looking for a kind family. Everyone has someone they want to help back home. Mostly, it's impossible, but Dora will go back to Bloomsbury House on her free afternoon, and she'll search the notice board for another job. Maybe she'll be lucky, for Ruthie.

Dora pushes her empty plate under the bed, removes her shoes, unbuttons her dress all the way, and pulls down the top of her underclothes to see the bruise on her hip. It's the size of a rose, deep red and speckled with black and blue like a berry stain. She has her hand over the sore part, feeling the heat in it, when there's a knock. She has time to pull her dress over herself before the cook comes in. She has a list of jobs in her hand.

'Here,' the cook says. 'This is your list for tomorrow.'
She drops it in Dora's lap.

'I know you won't stay,' the cook says as Dora reads down the list. 'Your lot hardly ever last a week. I'll tell you something though, you're not as soft as most we've had.'

The bed sags as the cook takes a seat and leans back against the footboard. She sees the photograph of Ruth.

'You?'

Dora shakes her head.

'My daughter.'

The English word feels uncomfortable in her mouth. They say nothing for a few moments while the cook stares at the picture.

'You don't look old enough,' she says eventually. 'Not by a mile.' She puts her hand in her apron pocket and pulls out two cigarettes and a match. She sticks one between Dora's lips, the other in her own mouth, and lights them both. The smoke coils up from their fingers like plants heading for the light, thin in the cold, English air. The tendrils disperse over their heads, and Dora imagines them rising through the gaps in the roof, out into the sky over the city of London.

4 April

Blue skies. The wing tilts and I lean close to Ash, tucking his head under my chin and feeling his soft curls on my lips. We're circling over Berlin. Matthew's napping in the seat beside me, missing a view of the entire city through the window: wide avenues, parks, trees, buildings, and at the centre the tall silver needle and ball that reflects the sunlight. In a few minutes, we'll land in Schönefeld. I imagine Berlin below us as a living thing, its fibres and follicles already sensing our arrival. The city feels like part of our encoding. It knows who we are and why we are here, and my toes drum through the seconds, tapping the carpeted floor in front of my seat.

'Coming back' is what my mother called it, even though none of us have ever been here before. She's right though. Berlin feels stitched into me, a sort of legendary backdrop to our half-heard history. It's funny to finally arrive in this place that has always been on the tip of my tongue.

Berlin can make my mother twitchy. We told them about the trip one Sunday over lunch. We'd gone up for a long weekend.

'I wonder what would Dora say?' she said, and then tried to persuade me my health wasn't up to it, or the house would be burgled, or the roof would fall in if a tree came down.

'I'll be fine and so will the house,' I said. 'And I need to go.'

'Let them,' Dad had interrupted, bringing the discussion to a close with a rare, lucid comment. 'Don't try and stop her doing what she has to do.'

'I'm not stopping anyone,' she'd said in surprise.

I know that this visit will pick at the stitches, alter things. I don't know exactly what will come undone, what may be mended, but when the plane took off from Glasgow, breaking through the blanket of Scottish cloud into sublime, radiant sunshine, the worry poured away. It was like being pulled out of sand. The airport and the car parks, the houses, the cars and roads, and hotels and hospitals and fields below were shrinking. It was a sudden lightness, as if this possibility had been there all along, a book I suddenly realised I could read from back to front.

'Look!' I help Ash up to see over the bottom ledge of the window. He was eager to get on the plane, but as soon as the engines started the noise and power of take-off startled him. Ash clings to me. He's a cautious boy, nearly two years old. One day I'll need to tell him what happened here, what happened to Dora, his great-grandmother, and to the children like him, born floppy and squashed.

Touchdown. The wheels bounce and speed forward, pressing us back into our seats. It's a thrill, like winning a race or seeing a loved one after years have passed. Matthew's eyes open and he leans over to look out at the wet, grey ground. He kisses Ash on the nose and puts his hand on my knee.

Dora isn't here, except in my thoughts. I haven't smelled the Woodbine cigarettes for a while. I think that maybe she has gone forever. Maybe she just wanted me to look for her, and now that I'm here, she won't ever visit again.

My first moments in Berlin are consumed by Dora's last. The train station, the embrace of her cousins. Perhaps there was a hurriedly bought parting gift, that quartet card game that she kept forever in her embroidery bag. That was the kind of thing you'd buy at a busy railway station. There are photos of German cathedrals on the front of each card. They must have meant something to her. She never played with them.

The plane comes to a stop, and I wipe away the wet in my eyes. This was why I loved working in the control tower most of all. That was what I did before, a short stint in Manchester. In area control, I never saw the planes. I missed watching their wheels skim the tarmac, bouncing and settling back on the earth. I'd take off the headset, stretch as I walked off to the break room, smile, take a sip of coffee. I'd always give myself a minute longer by the window before sitting back down, time to look up at the clouds from where the next plane would soon appear, basking in the feeling. Safety. Return. I like flying, but even more, I like the good sense the ground makes. Half a cup of coffee later I'd sit down with the others and join conversations about the usual earthly things. Most of my colleagues were men, but we could get along. No one calls to catch up anymore.

Ash feels like an extension of my body. I carry him everywhere. He's no closer to standing for himself, but I hold on to the words Alan said to me just before Christmas. Ash still wears his blue boots. His feet haven't grown. I get out of my seat and swing him onto my back, strapping him into the carrier. Like this, we exist together, a single person. The warmth of Ash against my ribs holds me up. It was essential that I bring him. People still call him a survivor, and he has kept going forward, making slow progress. I can see it. Matthew tries not to. He doesn't want to get his hopes up, I suppose.

The main thing I've got to do in Berlin is visit the archive. I got a message from an intern who works there. He'd seen my letter, and recognised Dora's name from a brief mention in a history book published just a few years ago. I thought it must be a mistake. Dora was too ordinary to be in a book. But the next day, the intern scanned the pages and forwarded them. They were from a chapter about newly discovered documents, and sure enough, there was Dora Tannenbaum. There too was the daughter she lost. Ruth Rosa Tannenbaum. The archive had a file about them both.

The sleepless nights came back after that. I'd go into Ash's room and lie beside him with my eyes open. Ash slept, breathing slowly, and I looked at his hair, the swirls over his scalp, those galaxies floating in his own universe. I cupped the palm of my hand over his silky crown. As I listened to his breathing, I thought of Ruth.

I tried to imagine her face. I had to see what was in the file. I needed a photograph.

Matthew agreed to the Berlin trip. He suggested buying an old camper and driving, some old tin can of a vehicle that a mate wanted to sell him, but I put my foot down. We argued about it. I said he didn't know how tired I was. He was away in the woods all day every day. So, he agreed to let the van go, and the next day he came home with plane tickets.

'Another time with the van,' I said, relieved.

Outside the airport, I take Ash off my back. I already regret not bringing the buggy. Matthew says we should look for one second hand. We stand beside our luggage, waiting for a taxi, and the sky darkens and starts to drizzle. Matthew thumbs through our Berlin guidebook. I know what my mother meant now when she said we were coming back. It does feel that way.

'Some enclosures at Berlin Zoo are unchanged since before the War,' Matthew says.

'Great,' I say. 'We'll go if we can find a buggy. My back's killing me.'

Soon we're in the back of a taxi looking at the signs over the Autobahn that point to lanes on the left and right, and head straight on to Berlin. The city is pulling us in. I look out of the window and Matthew opens his phone and starts texting. When I ask him who he's talking to he says it's no one. Ash chomps the sweets Matthew bought him at the newspaper stand in the airport.

'You're missing the view,' I say.

I don't recognise anything as we reach the city centre, not till I see a large sign over Alexanderplatz. I have a few old pictures of this place in my postcard collection, but it was all bombed, and it looks totally different now, windswept and concrete. There are billboards, lanes of cars, and tall office blocks with stark facades.

If I see Dora here, she'll be different. She will be young, not an old lady knitting in an armchair. She'll have very short black hair and a dark polka-dot dress. Maybe I won't even recognise her, the ghost of her first life. Here, she was petite and pretty, with black shoes and a knee-length coat. She felt at home in the streets she had known since childhood.

The taxi stops at a red light. Outside, metal stalls are being dismantled and loaded into giant lorries. There are deck chairs and booths selling beer and sausages, and a few people are sitting, sandwiched between the tramlines and five lanes of traffic. German pop blares over a loudspeaker system, and the bright yellow trams run on sweeping lines in all directions. I can't work out which streets correspond to the shape of the old maps. I don't even know which way I'm facing. The light changes to green and the taxi moves on.

Our building is covered with pebbledash and painted a dark olive green, but giant pink and silver graffiti below the ground floor windows draws the eye. The graffiti has been daubed with small stickers and hurriedly sprayed tags.

My instructions are to buzz the neighbour to let us in. I hoist Ash onto my hip and with one hand fold the instructions and put them back in my pocket. I read the names on the doorbells. There are two sets of buzzers.

'Hurry up. I need a pee,' Matthew says. He's standing on the step beside me, leaning against the door that won't open. Our suitcases are lined up behind him.

I find the neighbour's name right at the bottom: Bosch, like the washing machines. Deep breath. The last time I spoke German was years ago in my school exam. I wish I'd tried a bit harder in those lessons. I sat between a girl called Emma and another girl called Claire, who never brought the right books. Claire wore dark berry lipstick, which she reapplied at the beginning of class and shared round the rest of us. I was fifteen and a muddle. I wore a khaki coat with a German flag sewn on the shoulder, and a clandestine Star of David, bought at the market. I wore it on a silver string around my neck. Sometimes I doodled a swastika and then scribbled it out or turned it into a flower.

My old German teacher had thick blonde hair and coloured fishnet tights. Some days her skirt was shorter, or her tights were brighter, and a whisper would go round the room. None of us knew where you bought sluttish tights like that, so we gossiped about it and stared at her legs. I remember her sighing while she waited for our answers, resting her hand on her thigh and pulling at her fishnets. The little diamond shapes all flexed together and sprung back into place.

The neighbour, Frau Bosch, eventually comes to the door. She has the same dyed straw-blonde hair as my old German teacher, and seems short of breath. She's saying something in German that sounds like a grievance. All the same, she helps us get into the building, holding the door open and reaching out a plump hand. She takes one of our smaller bags and now welcomes us enthusiastically, projecting her voice as if on stage. She grins at Ash and bellows what we can only assume are terms of endearment.

The apartment is up eight steps. Frau Bosch has left her door open, and I can see inside. A narrow corridor with a polished floor and a red runner, a wooden sideboard, knick-knacks, painted scenes in frames, and a smell of meat on a slow cook. A place that has been lived in for many years.

'*Schottland*,' I say, pointing at myself and Matthew.

She looks pleased. She's been to Scotland, she says, years ago. A trip to the Highlands. She waves her arms around the hallway, making mountain peaks with her hands.

'*Die Bergen!*' she says, her eyes wide.

'Berlin?' I say to her, and point to her and the ground. I want to know how long she has lived here, but she doesn't catch my drift. Other neighbours come down the stairs and she greets them as they go by.

I point at Frau Bosch again.

'Are you from Berlin?'

She puts a hand on Ash's head, ruffling his curls with excitement.

'*Nein. Schwartzwalde,*' she says.

'The Black Forest,' I translate for Matthew. I mime eating a Black Forest Gateaux, but Frau Bosch thinks I'm saying I'm hungry, which causes some confusion.

Ash twists and moans till Frau Bosch ushers us inside our apartment. Before I can say goodbye, she's gone. I hear her door close across the hall and hope I haven't offended her.

I hoist Ash over the cases in the narrow entrance and we open all the doors. There are two bedrooms, a small kitchen with a view into the courtyard where the bins are kept, and the living room with a window looking out over the street and the stop for the number 13 tram. At the stop there's a yellow sign that reads BVG, and people waiting for a tram to arrive. Matthew finds the shower and toilet. After that, he changes Ash, who already wants his toys out. I open the cases in the living room and show him the ones I've brought. He has dinosaurs and matchbox cars, tiny planes, books, and his soft toy hare.

At the end of the hall there's a little cupboard piled to the top with cleaning products, a vacuum cleaner, linen and an old pair of slippers. Half the furniture is antique, some of it as old as the building. In the large bedroom there's an old sewing machine table. I look at it but don't touch. I let it stand there like a piece in a museum.

I keep returning to the window in the living room. I watch a yellow tram come and go, almost without a noise. People disappear inside it. There's a poster at the tram stop, an advert for a museum exhibition.

Jude? asks the biggest word on the poster.

I've seen the same word in old photographs, daubed in dripping paint on the windows of Berlin's Jewish shops.

I turn on my laptop to translate the rest. My fingertips tingle. The city was waiting for me.

What makes a person Jewish?

The Whole Truth… Everything You Ever Wanted to Know About Jews

Matthew puts Ash to bed and joins me at the window. There are beers left for us in the fridge. We open them and clink bottles. The poster is illuminated in the darkness, and the yellow light at the tram stop spills into the room. I tell Matthew about the Jewish exhibition on the poster, but he doesn't think there's anything odd about it. He only believes in coincidences.

'What *do* you want to know?' he asks.

Maybe I just want to know what to do with the thirty-three per cent of myself that Dora folded up, pushed into a bag, and hid in the back of a wardrobe. I tell Matthew that I don't know.

He keeps going back to his phone.

'Mine's working,' I say, 'if your network is playing up.'

'It's not,' he says. 'I'm just dealing with a work thing.'

When we go to bed, I lie looking up at the ceiling. It feels like the five floors above us are pressing down. There's a dusty smell, like bricks. I fall asleep and do not dream. I do not see Dora.

1939

Snow makes anywhere new. Today London feels fresh, part of another place entirely. Flakes are still falling. From the front door, Dora looks up and watches them drift down in the cozy light of the streetlamps. She's on her first job of the day, scraping the ice from the steps, pouring hot water upon them and sprinkling them with salt. There's no one out, no tracks in the road, not a single trail of footprints along the pavement. Her name is called inside the house.

The cook lets her in to warm herself up by the stove. Normally she'd linger as long as possible in this comfort, but today she can't settle to it. She only wants to start working through the list of jobs in her pocket. She must help get breakfast ready. The bathroom must be cleaned, and the ironing finished, and lunch must be served and cleared away afterwards. But Wednesday is Dora's half-day, so she will get her wages in an envelope, and she'll be allowed out.

Dora reaches Bedford Square at two, her hand in her pocket holding tight to her pay. Not much, but enough for the café and a Shirley Temple picture. Bloomsbury House is not much further. The snow creaks under her boots and Dora's feet are numb. Students walk past carrying books, their chests buttoned into coats with warm scarves around their necks. One boy attempts to cycle to class, his bicycle slowly wobbling along the pavement. Near the gardens, a gang are building a snowman, rolling its huge body over the ground. They look like a picture on a jigsaw. Dora pulls her coat tight around her chest, holding herself together. The students' laughter is muffled in their scarves, and hats are pulled low over their foreheads. Dora remembers snowy days in Berlin, and an outing years ago, when her class was taken to sledge and throw snowballs on the pillowy slopes in the park. She stops for a minute to catch her breath and watch the students lift the head onto the snowman. No one notices her.

Bloomsbury House has tall chimneys and five storeys of reddish London brick that stand out against the white of winter. On the pavement nearby, someone has neatly scratched a name into the snow. Frieda. The name of a friend, or a wife, or a daughter, someone left behind. Dora goes up the steps, hearing them crunch.

Inside there's gossip in German, accents from Berlin and Cologne and Bavaria and Austria. They curse in Yiddish, but to Dora they sound posh. Most of these girls had servants of their own at home. They console each other about the English food, the damp, the mean employers and the lumpy pillows. They make their friendships on the stairs.

'Johanna,' says the girl below, sticking out a hand for Dora to shake.

'Zelda,' says the girl another step down.

People push on the stairs, and the three girls are forced closer to let others pass. Zelda looks newly arrived. The clean air from her family's home in the German countryside still shows on her cheeks, the smell of proper bread fresh in her memory. Her placement is in Hampstead, working as a nanny.

'The children are horrible,' she tells Dora, showing her the scratches on her arms. 'And I miss real bread.'

'We all miss real bread,' Dora says.

They nod.

'English bread is like cake,' Johanna tells them, pulling a face. 'Don't eat too much or your teeth will rot.'

It's always a long wait. Occasionally a volunteer comes down the stairs with arms full of files. People are desperate for news. One man loses his place to follow a volunteer through the corridor. He pleads for help for his son left in Hamburg, but the woman keeps walking. No one is surprised by the man's story. Eventually, he trudges up the stairs again, apologising to everyone as he is given back his place. For a moment everyone is silent.

Lines travel all the way up the staircase before finally reaching the desks. Dora starts to feel hot, her wool collar itching her neck. With every person who goes in and comes back out, the despair gets harder to ignore. She's still never seen a celebration here.

'We'll wait for you,' Johanna tells her, tapping her on the shoulder when they reach the top of the stairs. 'Afterwards, we'll go for a bite to eat. Will you come?'

'Yes. Good luck,' Dora says.

Zelda goes in.

Dora's only photograph of Ruth is in her pocket. She slips her fingers in, touching its papery edges. Zelda and Johanna's kisses still sit on her cheeks.

The woman at the desk is pasty white. There are a dozen or so other desks in the room and each one is the same, a chair in front and a chair behind it, brown paper files, and telephones that seem to ring constantly, typewriters, overflowing ashtrays, scattered pens, and cups of tea that go cold quickly because there's no heating and no time to drink them.

'You don't look old enough to have a child,' the woman says, lifting her glasses slightly. 'I wouldn't have thought you were a day over fourteen.'

'Twenty-two,' Dora says. She answers the next question before it's asked. 'I am not married.'

The woman's eyes are puffy, her fingers red from typing letters and appeals. She wears fingerless gloves, but still she must feel the cold. She rubs her hands together, blowing into them, and waits for Dora to tell her more.

Trains are bringing children to London, whole carriages full of them. Dora imagines these carriages snaking their way out of Germany, following the same track that her own train took. The problem is where she will stay, she explains.

'Does the father have contacts, or any assets?' the woman asks.

Dora doesn't think so. She isn't sure if Marcus is even in Berlin.

'A little money, maybe, "I don't know.' Since she arrived in London she's found it harder to picture Marcus, but she remembers how his clothes were always spotless, his fashionable leather jacket and sharply cut hair. His parents had some money, certainly, but she only met them once. His mother wore a smart coat with dark glasses and a little hat with a net that came down over her forehead. Dora remembers the faint wrinkles of concern on her face. Families had been trying to get their children overseas, and Marcus's mother was no different. Dora had nothing but the clothes she stood in, and Marcus needed money to get out of Germany. Money or rich friends.

The volunteer behind the desk taps the file.

'Your child will be two… when exactly?'

'September twenty-fourth,' Dora says.

The volunteer shakes her head.

'After she turns two, we'll find her an older child to travel with. You will need to pay for the ticket, fifty pounds Sterling, and find a sponsor. She'll need a guardian of some sort.'

It seems pointless to take out the photograph of Ruth. Instead, Dora puts her hand in her pocket, tapping her fingertips around the worn edges of the print as lightly she would her daughter's toes to make her laugh. Her throat burns. Dora looks away from the desk and notices it's snowing again. Thick, lazy flakes falling like feathers.

'This arrived for you,' the volunteer says, and she holds out a letter. Dora immediately recognises Jette's handwriting. She takes it and presses it to her coat, and then to her face. She breathes in, wishing for the scent of Aunt Dotti's apartment. The letter would have been written at the oval table. Perhaps while Jette wrote, her aunt made an Apfelkuchen or Birches for Shabbat. Dora starts to open it, but the volunteer tells her she must do this later. Too many people are waiting to be seen.

'Sorry,' she says quietly. 'I wish I could do more.'

At the bottom of the stairs, Dora and Johanna put their arms around Zelda, and Zelda blows her nose into a handkerchief.

'They won't allow my mother to come. They say she's too old.'

'My daughter is too young,' Dora says.

'There's never good news,' Johanna says.

Dora nods in agreement. London has darkened and dampened everything. With each day that passes, she thinks of Marcus less. But there are other things she wants to remember forever, like the smell of Aunt Dotti's cake. Now she is too tired to imagine that as well most of the time. What will happen if one day she forgets? What of her will be left?

She doesn't mention the letter in her pocket. She wants to read it when she's alone. The three girls stand and stare at the Positions Offered board, till eventually Johanna plucks a card out.

'I'm going for this one,' she says. 'St John's Wood. *Johanneswald*. It sounds nicer in German, don't you think?'

Dora looks at the board. She doesn't know any London neighbourhoods, but she knows she wants to leave the Franks. The next place could be worse, so picking a card is a game of chance.

She chooses one written in green ink with an address in Fulham. Dora's never heard of it, but she dreams of somewhere with trees, somewhere like Weißensee.

'Here,' Johanna says, 'stuff the whole card in your pocket so no one else will see it. Then the job's yours.'

The girls go down the street together. The warmth of their arms through hers reminds Dora of her outings with Jette and Meta, their feet stepping in time, making tracks through Alexanderplatz.

The Lyons Tea Room is on the corner. The girls go up to the first floor and take a table by the window so they can look out at the big red buses turning into Oxford Circus. The waitress comes over.

'Hello, ladies, I'm your nippy. Would you like menus?' she says with a smile.

She's their age, an English beauty with curled red hair and a round, friendly face. There's a picture of a nippy on the menu wearing the same uniform, a black dress, a white apron with a deep pocket, and a small, frilled hat pinned on her head.

The menu is huge.

'It's not that different to German food when you look at it, so why does it all taste of paper?' Zelda whispers.

'I heard this place is meant to be okay,' says Johanna. 'Try it.'

They all order and squeeze both thumbs for luck. Dora picks something called 'Welsh Rarebit'.

Vati would definitely not eat rabbit, but Dora still wants to try it. She isn't brave enough to ask the nippy out loud, so she just points to the item on the menu. Zelda orders fish, and Johanna wants chicken in a sauce.

The café fills up. Outside, the snow turns to rain, and Londoners disappear under a canopy of wheeling black umbrellas that sprout over their heads. Dora turns away from the window. The snowy scene has turned into a moving picture of black on white, with streaks of red as the buses drive by. The colours make her nauseous. She looks instead at the customers getting seated at other tables: a group of old women with pastel knitwear, a man with a napkin spread over his large belly, and a couple with two children, a boy and a girl who sit politely behind tall glasses of milk with long straws. There are cafes just like this near Meta and Herbert's apartment, but they would never be allowed in. The thought shrinks her appetite.

When Dora's plate arrives, her stomach groans and her face falls. On the plate are two slices of toast, cut into triangles and coated with a thick layer of melted, oily cheese. There's nothing that could be rabbit. She sinks a little against her chair and stares over at Zelda's plate. The battered fish looks better than anything she's eaten since arriving in London.

A second later, Dora feels a hand upon her shoulder.

'Miss, would you like something else?'

Dora's face flushes.

'Don't worry. It happens all the time. I should have warned you it was cheese on toast,' the nippy says with a smile. 'I'll bring you fish and chips.'

In a flash, she whisks away the cheese triangles. Dora taps the floor with her feet, listening to the exclamations of pleasure that her new friends make as they begin to eat. Dora doesn't have to wait long till her portion arrives. The nippy winks and places the plate in front of Dora, an extra-large helping of thickly cut chips and a plump fillet of white fish in a golden, crisp batter. It is so good, oily tears escape down her cheeks, and she has to keep turning towards the window to hide her face and wipe them away.

Postcard
Am Märchenbrunnen, Berlin

It is a summer Sunday, and half of Berlin has come out to wander in the Volkspark Friedrichshain and play beside the Fountain of Fairytales. The crowd wears hats and bonnets and best dresses. An older woman walking quickly, getting her exercise, holds her hand firmly on the handle of a black parasol.

At the fountain's edge, children abandon their hoops and lie over the low wall between the stone tortoises, sleeves rolled up and dipping their hands in the water.

'Don't splash,' they are reminded, as ladies pass close behind them or gather round the statues: Puss in Boots, the sister in The Seven Ravens, Hansel and Gretel, Snow White, and high up on the wall, fluffy lambs and four handsome stags who nose the clouds and pierce the sky with their long, sharp antlers.

The air is filled with chatter and the constant music of the water, which cascades gently from every level to the next and spews from the mouths of the frog princes. No one is in a hurry to move on. A photographer comes with his camera, but few pay him any attention. Only the father in the black hat who is waiting, not so patiently, for his children to leave their favourite place to play, looks over his shoulder at the camera.

5 April

Bustling out of the apartment on our first day in the city we meet a neighbour. Daniel lives higher up, on the fourth floor. We get talking for a bit, and ask him where we can find a second-hand pushchair.

'You'll find one here easily. There's something in the water in Prenzlauer Berg,' he says with a grin. 'Couples come here and they have babies.'

'Hope not,' Matthew whispers to me.

We explore the streets nearby, and sure enough, find a pushchair in a kids' second-hand shop. Then we go food shopping. Shop owners offer Ash little sweets and pastries, and these disappear under the hood of the new pushchair into his waiting, sticky fingers. A man at a fruit stall holds out a banana. At a delicatessen, where I expect to be told off for letting Ash touch the glass cabinet with his greasy hands, he's given a freshly cut slice of meat. The lady serving laughs as he pokes a hole in the middle of the slice and eyes her through it.

We stop at a playground. There's sand to dig in, and buckets and spades, and little toys that anyone can use. There are push-along bikes as well, but Ash can't ride them. The other toddlers wobble along the paths, learning about balance, and Ash watches them go by.

He points at the bikes and cries to go on, but can only sit on the saddles with our help.

Ash buries little pocket toys in the sand beside the swings and digs them up again. He does this for a long time. Parents sitting on the edge of the playground look relaxed, removing jackets, shrugging off the winter cold, strolling along and looking forward to summer. No one pays us any attention. The reason we're here is a secret I am keeping.

Ash starts to cough. Maybe he just has some sand in his throat. I watch his shoulders jump, his torso still not quite steady when he sits without support. I go over to him and pick him up, and I place my hand across his forehead. He isn't hot.

'Probably just a bit of dust,' Matthew says. We tell each other not to worry.

Later, we sit in a café and order coffee and ice cream. Across the street there is an unusual building on a little hill, a stout, round tower, seven stories of brick with dark windows encircling each layer. The whole thing is stacked up like a cake, with a roof on the top like the teat of a bottle, a tall chimney rising from the middle. Trees surround the tower and there's an entrance gate and a large information board.

Matthew has microphones in his bag. He likes making recordings, the dawn chorus and the wind passing through different trees. He doesn't take many photographs, but he collects lots of sounds. He has a microphone that he can attach to a tree. You hear it growing, the boughs creaking, all its internal life and the stretch of wood that has spanned centuries. Here he'll record the city too, voices in the street, announcements in the stations, the echoes of trains in tunnels, bicycle bells, the electronic beep of pedestrian crossings, the rhythm of trams on the tracks. In the evening, he listens to the recordings, mixing them together on the computer till he's relaxed.

'You pay. I might record over there,' Matthew says, nodding towards the tower.

The waitress brings the bill with three sweets on a shiny plate. I ask her about the tower, but she's young and maybe isn't from here.

Ash coughs again, so hard his face turns a funny colour.

'Is he alright?' the waitress asks. 'Do you want a glass of water?'

I rush to put a napkin over his mouth in case he spits food over the table, pretending everything is fine and hoping she'll go. I avoid her frown and force a look of calm, patting Ash gently on the back and wiping his mouth.

'Maybe it's pollen,' the waitress says.

I tell her it could be, but I know it's more likely his chest.

'Let's get you in the buggy,' I say to him.

The bill is settled, and we go over the road to meet Matthew. The panel says the building is an old water tower that Hitler used as a detention centre and later a torture chamber. Ordinary people are living here now. I notice lace curtains on some of the ground floor windows. I wait with Ash while Matthew mics up an old lime tree. He sticks earbuds in and listens for a few minutes to the boughs.

'If trees could talk,' I say.

'They can,' he says, and holds out the earbuds. I put them in and stand with my eyes closed, listening. The last time we listened to anything so carefully together, it was Ash's heartbeat inside my body. The inside of the tree is a hidden world, both earth and sky at once, and full of life. Groaning, clicking, sucking, whistling. I rest my head against the tree's strong trunk. It's like nothing I would have imagined. Matthew watches me, a proud look on his face, the way I watched him when he put an ear to my pregnant belly.

We wander and I whisper the street names under my breath, trying to pronounce them, form the foreign sounds. Ash falls asleep in his pushchair, relaxed at last. I follow the map in my head. I've looked at it for hours on a screen, but the real city takes me by surprise, and we make more than a few wrong turns. We stop behind a huge blue building on Weinbergsweg, the place where the children's home used to be. I stare at the sky and the blue walls, and a rainbow painted on a window. I take a photograph.

Dora had a photograph taken inside the home, a room full of girls at heavy desks, some of them looking straight at the camera, some of them ignoring it. She's there, reading at a desk against the far wall, looking up over her book at the photographer. There's a pile of books in the foreground and a globe, floral curtains, utility-style electric lights that extend from the ceiling on long metal tubes, pot plants, pictures in frames and a clock. Hearts and leaves are stencilled on the walls.

Here, the main street is wider and busier, a clutter of trams, traffic lights, pedestrian crossings, people eating sandwiches, tourists walking along with their heads hidden in maps, and bicycles chained to lampposts. Colourful post-war infills are squeezed next to older buildings. Peachy pink, sky blue, a bold shade of yellow. There is an odd asymmetry to everything.

Matthew fiddles on his phone. I'm here to get a feel for the spot, but I'm not sure what else I should do. I find myself thinking more about Ash's cough, hoping it isn't bad when he wakes up. He's lying very flat. I decide to keep walking, just so he sleeps longer. We find a passage behind the blue building where a large reconstruction of an older one is underway. Cranes are lifting in and manoeuvring the metal bones of an entirely new build, hoisting them behind the skin of the much older relic. The wall of the old building stands like a stage set, with doorways and windows that open onto nothing but sky.

We cross the road and go into another park. There are swings and slides and sports courts. It used to be a theatre. From the first-floor windows of the children's home, Dora would once have watched the crowds gathering to buy tickets to the shows, and cars dropping people off in their smart, evening clothes.

The trees here are tall enough to almost entirely obscure the five-storey buildings behind them. They must be the only thing that survived the bombs. I ask Matthew to use his microphones to listen to the biggest trunks. Their murmurs and whistles remind me of riding on underground trains, that electrical whooping, and the snap of a flash in the dark.

Ash wakes suddenly and goes straight into a fearsome coughing fit.

'Jesus,' Matthew says. He picks Ash up, holds him snuggled right into his neck and pats him. The coughing goes on and on. People stare and I can do nothing but watch, or stroke his tiny back as it shudders. I imagine an onlooker calling an ambulance, ending up back in the hospital. Part of me wants to run.

Matthew just about manages to calm him down, but I can tell his patience is tissue-thin. There's a tightening in his face, his eyes narrowing.

When Ash finally settles, it's almost as if nothing has happened. He's still a bit red in the face but he wants to play so we put him in a swing seat. Matthew sits on a wall and I shout over that I think Ash's back is strengthening a little. It seems a stupid thing to say, after the coughing, but Ash seems to balance better in the swing than the last time we tried. I'm annoyed when Matthew barely looks over and doesn't agree.

'I think you're imagining it,' he says. He takes a long breath and lets it go slowly, as if he's deflating. 'Don't push him so high.'

'He's fine,' I snap.

We stay late at the park. Matthew buys a couple of beers, and after a while the mood lifts. I sit on the swing next to Ash sipping my beer, and look over at the blue building standing where the Jewish children's home once was. Now it has smooth walls and small square windows, rows of dwellings each with a small balcony. It's a sheltered housing place for the elderly. There's a small coffee shop on the ground floor with a red sign flashing on and off. A garden out front with benches, sculptures and little features that remind me of a crazy golf course.

Behind us, the sun is setting over the rooftops. A church bell tolls, an old sound that Dora would recognise.

'Could you record that?' I ask.

'We just missed it.'

'We could come back tomorrow.'

We cross the road and stop just in front of the blue building. There's a bus stop where the theatre once was, and it's been graffitied in large, red letters. I read the drippy words, and take out my camera to photograph them.

Life Isn't Over Just Yet

Again, I get the feeling someone's looking over a shoulder at me, as if the city knows I'm here. It keeps asking me what I'm doing.

I don't really know the answer.

1939

Dora checks the address in the A to Z. The street is nicely kept. On the corner there's a school behind a tall brick wall, and she can hear children's voices shouting and squabbling, girls singing rhymes as they skip. The red brick house is set apart from the others. It's the biggest on the street but not the neatest.

The gate creaks on its hinges. Introductions always make her nervous. She doesn't like stepping into a stranger's house or standing in the narrow English hallways. From the outside of a house, you can never tell what people are going to be like. Owners with pretty gardens aren't always kind. There is paint peeling from the windowsills at this house, and the flowerbeds are stony. All she knows is that these people are called Wood. She straightens her clothes.

Dora's English is improving. She knocks, rehearsing the words, but the door opens almost immediately.

'Hello,' she says. 'I am here about the position.'

The woman looks her up and down.

'Hello,' she says, taking a step back. 'You look a bit young, but I suppose you'll do.'

She opens the door as wide as it goes and Dora steps inside. A man is standing further down the hall, his face in the shadow of the stairs.

'She looks like that vixen in the films,' the woman says over her shoulder to the man, as if Dora isn't there. 'Who am I thinking of? I can't recall her name.'

Mr Wood nods.

When the door closes behind her, the hallway seems to shrink. Mr Wood gestures to Dora to go into the living room, where they sit down and wait for her to speak. They are older than the last employers, and the house seems large for just the two of them.

'Do you have other help?' Dora asks.

The woman shakes her head and Mr Wood grins awkwardly.

'We've not had help here for a long time,' says Mrs Wood, 'not since the children were small.' She hesitates. 'Sorry, do you understand English?'

Dora shrugs. She puts her fingertips close.

'A little.'

'Well, not unless you count the last girl,' Mrs Woods goes on, speaking faster. 'She was one of your lot. Didn't stay long.'

Mr Wood grunts.

'Beate. From Frankfurt,' Mrs Wood says.

Both of them look at her as if they're expecting her to know Beate. She can hear the clock ticking on the wall while Mrs Wood gets out of her chair and goes over to a huge roll-top desk, a piece of furniture so immovable, it looks as if it must have been grounded in the same spot for a century. She picks up an envelope.

'This is for your first week,' she says.

'Are your children at home?'

Mrs Wood is quick to reply.

'I only have a son now,' she says. 'He's grown up. He doesn't live with us.'

Dora nods. Mrs Wood asks her husband to show Dora the room. He clears his throat and pushes his hands onto his knees to get out of his chair.

'It's a very nice room,' Mrs Wood says. 'Beate seemed happy with it.'

'Let me,' Mr Wood says, and he reaches out a hand to take Dora's bag.

'You don't have to start today,' Mrs Wood says just as they're leaving the room. 'You can go out.'

It seems good enough, even if the house smells of medicine. If silence had a smell, a bit like moths, or mice, or old library books, this house smells of that too. Outside it is cold, but it's better to go out than clean the house all afternoon. If she's lucky there might even be a cinema nearby, but she knows better than to ask about amusements. It'll make a bad first impression.

Mr Wood runs his hand along the banister as he goes up. He breathes heavily with every step. When he reaches the room, he goes in and stands by the window. When Dora says thank you, he nods and casts an eye down on the gardens behind.

'You can see my vegetable beds from this room,' he says.

It is the prettiest room she has seen since she arrived in England. The walls have a flowery pattern you can feel with your fingertips, and they're the colour of the milky tea the English like so much. There are books on a shelf waiting to be read. At the window, there is a wooden blind, and there is a chest of drawers and a wardrobe, and a small fireplace with emerald tiles. The bed is bigger than any bed she has ever slept in before. It's a double, made up with two pillows, one on each side, and on top of it there is a thick, satiny, feather-filled cover. In the corner there's a sink with a single tap.

Dora leaves her suitcase closed and sets it on the floor at the foot of the bed.

'I'll unpack later,' she tells him.

He nods.

'I think my wife put a front door key in the envelope, and the list of jobs for tomorrow.'

Mr Wood relaxes against the window frame and Dora realises he's going to stay there for a while. She is to see herself out.

Dora shuts the gate and walks quickly around the corner. She wriggles a finger under the seal of the envelope and rips it open. She counts the notes. It's more than they are supposed to pay, and she wonders if there's been a mistake. The list of jobs is also light. She could complete most of the days' tasks in just half a day, perhaps less. Dora turns the note over but there's no writing on the other side.

A young woman gives her the directions to a tea house.

'You want North End Road,' she says. 'Just there past the school.'

Dora buys a Cream Slice: two layers of pastry with a slab of whipped cream in between, and a shining iced top with chocolate marbling. They bring it to her on a plate, and her heart races as she plunges her fork down into the pastry and marble. The thick, bubbly cream oozes out at the sides. She hasn't eaten anything like this for ages. Cousin Meta would have loved to share it with her, but Dora tries to chase the thought away. She savours the sticky icing, letting it melt on her tongue. She sits there for a long time, keeping warm, looking through the window of the café and listening to the chit-chat of Londoners.

It's dark by the time she gets back to Halford Road. She takes the key from the envelope and slides it into the lock. It's not late, but inside the lights are all off. Alone in the hallway, the smell of the house is even stronger, and the sound of nothing even thicker. Dora steps up the stairs to her room and gets undressed for bed. Her case has been moved. It's pushed under the bed, and when Dora pulls it out and opens the lid, it's empty. All her things have been taken out. Swallowing, she stands up and looks around the room. She opens the wardrobe and finds her clothes hanging. Her nightdress is under the pillow, and in the drawer, safely tied with a new blue ribbon, is her notebook and her green album with her photographs inside. She takes the pictures into bed with her, holds them close, and pulls the eiderdown up over her chest, not sure if she will sleep.

*

It is much later during the night when something startles her. It isn't light yet, and the bed feels warm and comfortable. She wants to drift off to sleep again, but there's a strange smell in the room. Not the smell of the house. This is a new smell, strong and stinging. It coats the sides of her throat, catching at her tonsils. Mr Wood is standing at the window. He is in the same spot where he stood this afternoon, and he's pulled the curtain slightly open to rest an ashtray on the windowsill. A curl of smoke is spiralling up in the light from the moon. His smoking cigar is burning itself down and he is staring out at his vegetable beds again.

Peering through her eyelashes she can see he is wearing a gown made of some patterned fabric. Mr Wood smokes for a little while. He wanders around the room and looks at her bed and then he puts one hand around the foot rail. She feels the bed shift.

She can hear her own heartbeat, and wants to call out, but she can't. She has completely lost her voice.

Nothing happens. He stays at the end of the bed. Dora screws her eyes shut and pushes her face down into her pillow. She knows he's still there, holding onto the bed frame with one hand. After a while she hears him swallow and walk out. He makes no effort to be silent.

Dora keeps her eyes open all night.

She packs again in the morning. Mr Wood follows her to the front door. She'd waited till the breakfast was eaten and she had cleared away, and then she told them she would not be staying. The envelope of money was taken back.

'You think you are something special,' Dora hears Mr Wood whisper behind her as she walks away. 'Louise Brooks, that's the actress you look like. A common slut.'

She doesn't understand all the other words he is saying, but she doesn't stop. She walks through the gate and clicks it shut.

When she reaches the corner, the sun peeks out.

7 April

There's a scrap of paper lying beside the sink.

'Where's this?' Matthew says, pointing to the word I've scribbled on it.

'It's not a place.'

A woman came into the laundrette to give me this piece of paper with a word written on it: Feldenkrais. She said she could tell from the way Ash's boots fell sideways that he had problems with his movement. Feldenkrais had helped her with her spine, she said, twisting so that I would understand her. It's a therapy.

I tell Matthew about the woman and he drops the paper back on the table. 'Beware,' he says.

He's probably right, but I put it in my jacket pocket. We're about to leave for the zoo. We probably shouldn't go because of Ash's cough, but Matthew and I have been bickering all morning. Maybe we're just not used to city life anymore. Maybe we both need some fresh air, and it's mild out.

'That's not what you're here for,' he reminds me, stroking my back.

'I know,' I say, putting my hands up. 'It's supposed to be a break.'

I'm going to the archive tomorrow. I'll see the file they have on my relatives, and I'll read Dora's letters. I need to know more about Ruth. I should be focused on that, not therapies for Ash.

He's already sitting in his pushchair in his coat and boots, and we're ready to run to the stop when we see the tram approaching from the window.

'Do you still think his cough is ok?' I say to Matthew as we board the tram and find a seat.

'He'll be fine.'

His phone beeps and he takes it out of his pocket.

'I'll check the route,' I say.

We spend the whole afternoon at the zoo wandering around the enclosures. The fresh air helps Ash keep a clear chest, and we laugh at the hippos who swim past us in huge glass tanks. I guess which animal houses might be the oldest, and read about the history of the zoo while we stop for a drink.

'Jewish people were banned from the zoo the year before Dora left.'

Matthew nods. I can tell he isn't really listening. I keep reading quietly, and Matthew helps Ash, spooning yoghurt into his mouth and spilling half of it down his shirt. I wish he'd use a bib.

I read about the elephants, which we saw earlier. A ring of people pointed and took photos, and they hoofed in the dust, oblivious, looking strong and sorrowful, and now I wonder if they knew what suffering humans had inflicted on their kind on that spot. Only one elephant, Siam, and a hippo called Knautschke, survived the war. Their ornate house took a direct hit.

The sun is breaking through. I can feel the hint of a temperature on Ash's forehead, but tell myself he's on the mend. Other children climb on fences and hold onto ledges to get a better view. They clamber in front of Ash and push themselves up, brightly coloured and babbling in cheerful, high-pitched German. They're dressed for Spring, with stretchy cotton hats on their heads and daytrip sized backpacks. Matthew eventually lifts Ash out of the pushchair and puts him high up on his shoulders so he has a chance to see.

'Watch his head,' I say.

Ash stares into the enclosures. I point out the larger, slower animals, the bears and the rhinos, and the giraffes that live in an old brick building under tall arches. When we get to the monkeys, who are swinging and leaping with ease from branch to branch, I'm not sure if Ash sees anything at all. His eyes stare through his reflection and beyond it.

'Do you think he can see?' I ask Matthew. 'Are they moving too fast for him?'

Ash's expression doesn't give anything away and Matthew tries to encourage him, but soon gives up. Instead, he takes photos, and shows Ash the monkeys on the information boards.

Ash's eyes and ears have been tested half a dozen times, but the results were vague. Watch and wait, they said again, as if our boy was a rare, shy species of unstudied creature. We have to hide out and hope to discover him.

The thing that most interests Ash in the whole zoo is a large horse chestnut leaf, sticky with tree sap, which

Matthew breaks from a branch and hands him as we're walking towards the exit. Ash waves the leaf and pulls faces at it for half an hour or more before we realise that, somewhere across the city, he dropped it.

We try to have an early night. A new toy crocodile goes to bed with Ash. He can't say anything that sounds like 'crocodile' no matter how many times Matthew coaxes him, but eventually he does copy his dad, putting his hands palm to palm and making something like the sign for a crocodile snap. I can see Matthew's disappointment, even when Ash also makes the sign for 'elephant', waving his arm with his shoulder lifted up to his nose. Then he does 'monkey', hands up to his armpits. I turn round to see Matthew's reaction, but he's already left the room. Maybe Ash did see the monkeys after all.

'That's right!' I say. 'Monkey. Oo oo oo!'

My boy grins and puts his hands up to his armpits again. His lips make an 'O'.

'Monkey!' I say again.

I read him a story and he dozes off. Afterward I find Matthew in bed with his headphones on. He's editing the sounds he collected today. He reviews and cuts and pastes the high-pitched children, a zookeeper talking about the Serengeti, an underground train approaching the platform at Eberswalder Straße, the bells of all the bicycles that were parked outside the station, which we pinged one by one when no one was looking, the sounds of the tram and the people going home from work or going out for dinner, or coming home from the shops with bags full of groceries, or new shoes, or tourists with suitcases on trundling wheels, people making the most of the good weather, looking ahead to long summer evenings.

I go through to the hall, take the scrap of paper from my jacket pocket, and open my computer at the kitchen table. The webpage for the zoo, which I looked up this morning, is still on the screen. I check the spelling on the paper, and type 'Feldenkrais Berlin' into the search box. The zoo disappears and a list comes up beside a map of the city cluttered with red dots. I zoom into Prenzlauer Berg and click on one of the clinics. We must have walked past it a few times already.

'What are you doing?' Matthew shouts through.

I remember what he said this morning. Beware. But if I don't take a chance, no one will.

'Just getting a snack.'

'I can hear you typing,' Matthew says.

'I'm just emailing Mum some photos,' I lie. 'And making a snack.'

I take a slice of German bread from its plastic bag and I stick it in the toaster. When the smell of it warming up hits me I get the butter and the cherry jam out of the fridge. Dora loved this bread. She talked about missing it her whole life, and how the greatest treat of her childhood was a slice of this topped with black cherries. It was something they ate at the children's home.

The slice pops up and I spread the butter, watch it melt, then cover it with lashings of cherry jam.

I go back to my computer while I eat.

'Do you want tea?' I shout through to Matthew. He doesn't hear me, but I pour water into a pan and put it on the hob. The flat didn't come with a kettle.

I scroll down the webpage of the Feldenkrais therapist. There's a monochrome picture of the method's inventor in a black shirt. He has a ring of unruly white hair around his face and a bald, shiny head.

'Where's the tea?' Matthew shouts.

'Coming.'

I get milk from the fridge and try to read a little more while I stir it into the mugs. Moshé Feldenkrais was a Jewish scientist and a judo instructor, says the webpage. He invented his therapy during the Second World War after he injured his knee falling over on the slippery deck of a submarine off the coast of Fairlie in North Ayrshire.

I wipe some spilled milk with my sleeve. Fairlie is just up the road from Matthew's parents. I take the computer through to the bedroom and get Matthew to take out his earphones so I can tell him about the submarine in North Ayrshire.

'Don't you think it's amazing?'

He takes a deep breath, picks up his mug of tea, and blows on it.

'Didn't we say we were here for a break? It's just coincidence.' He puts his earphones back in. I sit across from him and go back to the email I was writing to the Feldenkrais therapist. I read over it once and press 'send'.

Later, as I'm trying to fall asleep, I imagine Moshé Feldenkrais on the submarine in the Firth of Clyde. I think about the soft Scottish rain and how it makes our garden deck too slippery. The deck of a submarine.

Tomorrow, Ash will spend the day with Matthew. I'll pack him a lunch and lay out clothes, one set to wear, and one for spare in case he gets mucky. With Matthew in charge, he's bound to get dirty.

Later, when Matthew senses that I'm having trouble falling asleep, he rolls over and strokes my back for a while. I think, just for a second, that I can smell something familiar in the room. It used to be there whenever Dora appeared, alongside the woodbines and the ticking of a clock. I hoped I'd see her again in Berlin, but so far no luck.

'Do you smell that?' I ask Matthew.

'Yeah,' he says. 'It's that toast you keep making.'

Ash starts coughing, but Matthew goes to him.

'Sleep,' he says. 'You need it.'

Postcard

*African Elephants, Lindi and Tempo at Berlin zoo,
postally used 1941*

*Lindi 01/01/1920 Tanzinia – 22/11/1943 Berlin
Tempo 01/01/1934 Kenya – 01/09/1944 Munich*

1939

Alvanley Gardens has houses down one side and large, blooming trees on the other. It's already Spring, but a late fall of snow has been partially washed away, exposing the grey slabs and the filth on the road. A family of snowmen built by children on the corner look like victims of a terrible disaster. Eyeballs lie at their feet and twiggy arms reach out of wasted bodies that have barely withstood the day's downpours.

Dora's room is in the attic. The Rosenthal family is out for the morning and the stairs are quiet, so she puts down the groceries, takes off her wet boots, and goes to clean the hall and then the stairs. She takes care with her work, pushing her broom into all the corners, light on her stockinged feet. There are two rooms at the top of the house, which she'll work her way up to. Her bedroom and a store.

The Rosenthals and their two sons sell furs, soft leather gloves, silk undergarments and other luxuries, and this is what they keep in the store next to her quarters. On her first sleepless night, when Dora thought she could hear funny noises, she listened outside the store and gathered the courage to peek inside. There were boxes of hats and stockings, the contents all neatly folded and divided with tissue. Dora shut the door in case they thought she was stealing. She soon got used to the noise, which was just pigeons nesting in the roof.

Time passes quickly when she has so much cleaning and cooking to do. The Rosenthals keep her busy, just like the other employers, but they are kind. She only thinks about doing her work well and pleasing them.

When the stairs are done, Dora makes soup for lunch. They all like their food, but Maurice Rosenthal savours it. He is the youngest son, the same age as Dora to the day. She will watch him lifting his spoon to his mouth, his eyes never leaving the bowl, a tiny dribble escaping the corner of his lips. No sooner has one mouthful gone down than the spoon is back in the bowl, scooping up more. Maurice is nothing like Marcus. He is tall and clumsy and quiet. She's noticed his eyes following her, but is still too afraid to look back at him.

'Was work hard this morning, son?' Mr Rosenthal laughs. 'Maurice always has an appetite,' he says with more than a little pride. Mr Rosenthal has a soft, Russian accent, and his laugh reminds Dora of Vati.

'When he was a child he would ask for seconds, then thirds, and sometimes…' Mr Rosenthal waves his hand over his head. 'But he didn't get fat. He got tall. Look at him and look at me. He is an English cuckoo!'

Maurice wipes his mouth with his napkin.

Dora is pleased. If they enjoy her meals, they'll keep her at least until the Autumn. Ruthie is depending on it. The ticket has already been agreed and Dora is counting the weeks till Ruthie's birthday, when she'll be old enough to board a train.

Elsa, the wife of the older son, sits behind a typewriter most days, piling up bills and writing and posting invoices for the Rosenthal's three shops. The work bores her. Whenever she gets out of her chair to stretch her legs, she'll go about the house looking for amusement or a snack. The piles of work on her desk never seem to get any smaller. But she is always cheerful, and in that way Elsa always reminds Dora of Meta. Every day, Dora sees people in the street that she thinks she recognises. She sees her family in the faces of strangers, and sometimes the resemblance is so strong she aches after they pass her by.

In her free moments, Dora reads her letters. She's read them all dozens of times but still carries them with her all day in her apron. The letters have brought news of Ruthie. In Cousin Jette's last letter she asked permission to take Ruth out of the infant home for good, since the fees could no longer be paid, and Dora agreed. By now, she thinks, Ruthie is living with Aunt Dotti on Alte Schönhauser Straße, and soon she will have a little cousin. Cousin Max met a girl, Lucie, and she is due any day with Aunt Dotti's first granddaughter. Dora's heart breaks a little for Meta and Herbert. Aunt Dotti's prediction really did come true, but it is still a blessing.

When they get home, the Rosenthals ask her to bring some coffee. They stay at the table for a long time, talking to each other about the family's shops, or playing a card game. Dora is asked to join in, and she offers to teach them Quartett, a game they've never seen before. Dora has a new set of cards. Cousin Jette bought them for her at the station. Each card has a photograph of a different German town on the front.

'Make new friends,' Jette had said, pressing Dora's fingers around the box, before wrapping her hands around Dora's.

Meta held tight to them both. They whispered to her that they would look after Ruthie, and that it wouldn't be for long. They promised.

'Write to us,' she had said. Her chin wobbled and she wiped her nose which was cold and dripping. It was late December. Other people were celebrating Christmas.

'Ruthie will be with you soon,' Jette called out, her voice pained over the sound of the wheels as the train ground into motion, and Dora pressed the palms of her hands to the window, trying to stop her cousins sliding away.

Dora goes back to Bloomsbury House many times to arrange Ruthie's journey. She's getting used to the noises of London, the soft ding when she pulls the stop cord on the bus, the ghostly whine of the tube tunnels as trains disappear inside them, the lullabies of the church bells, the songs of newspaper sellers outside the stations, and the best sound of all, the gush of tea pouring from a teapot. She wrote to Jette to tell her about the warm, sweet, milky tea. At first, she concentrated on this one good thing about her new life so that she wouldn't seem so ungrateful, but with the news that Ruthie will soon arrive, everything excites her. Dora saves her money to take Ruthie to the picture houses, the cafes, the department stores, the museums, and the zoo.

Today, as usual, Johanna and Zelda are waiting for her at Bloomsbury House. They take their places in the queue at the foot of the stairs and tell each other the week's news.

Johanna is going on a date with an Austrian. He knew her brother at university.

'You should also find dates,' Johanna says to Zelda and Dora as they take their place on the stairs. 'Everyone has their wages today.'

'No one will want to take me,' Dora says, but really she just wants to save her money for Ruthie's arrival.

Johanna tells her not to be so modest, but Dora says it's true. She's the only one here who held a mop *before* arriving in London. Johanna would have been studying law or medicine, not cleaning houses.

She has more post from Berlin, a thin, cream envelope, and as soon as it's handed to her, Dora knows that it is from Herbert. She recognises his writing, and the envelopes from his little desk. Dora puts it immediately to her face to try and detect some faint memory that might cling to it, the smell of Herbert's cigarette, or the smell of Meta's coat pocket. She breathes deeply.

'Thank you,' she says.

The volunteer also gives her a document for Mr Rosenthal to sign for Ruth's sponsorship.

'My daughter's birthday is the twenty-fourth of September,' Dora tells the woman.

'A train is leaving on the first day of September,' the woman says. 'I've just added another child's name to the list. Your daughter will probably be on the next.'

'I'm counting down the days,' Dora says, pressing her thumbs and crossing her fingers. The German way and the English way, just to be sure.

Dora gets straight back on the bus to Alvanley Gardens. She sits on the top deck right at the back, and looks out of the long window at the street disappearing behind her. She takes the unopened envelope from her pocket and touches the careful handwriting and the stamp that Herbert has pressed to the paper. The postmark has been smeared across it, but the ugly Hakenkreuz has not been wiped away. It stands out clearly at its centre. Dora turns the envelope over and runs a finger under the seal.

> *Dearest Dora,*
>
> *I hope you are finding some happiness in London. It must be hard for you being alone there.*
>
> *I have to tell you some difficult news. I have learned from a friend that Marcus is engaged. He will be married in April and he expects to receive 10,000 RM as a dowry. After the wedding they will go straight to*

London. If you can make contact with him urgently, perhaps Marcus will find a way to help us before he leaves. It is badly needed.

Life here gets much worse. In Marcus's good fortune, he must be made to think of others, and most of all, Ruth. Beg him to send something, Dora. We have not seen him for several years, as you know.

As for myself and Meta, your aunt and cousins, we pray to be reunited. We love you and miss you. Lucie and Max are excited for the baby. Ruthie is such a comfort to Meta and I, and we spend a lot of time with her. We have given her a horse on wheels. She is starting to talk now. Do not lose hope that we will all be together again. We are sure it will happen soon, Dora!

Your loving cousin,
Herbert

The letter is gentle, just like Herbert. He could talk Meta out of her anger using words like this. Dora pictures him sitting at his desk in the apartment. She traces a fingertip over the names, the curls of Herbert's ink. She thinks of Ruthie on the little wooden horse, her plump feet finding their place against the earth, testing the wheels, nudging her forwards. She remembers the little moth mark on her neck, her brown eyes and toothy smile, which will be so different now.

The bus lurches forward and snorts fumes. Condensation trickles down the windows. Suddenly she feels sick. She must get off. She can feel herself sweating, the vomit rising from her stomach, a twitch in her lower lip, saliva filling her mouth. She folds the letter and stuffs it into her pocket. Dora plummets down the stairs barely holding on, and shouts at the bus conductor. He doesn't understand her funny words, and he grabs her by the coat and pulls her back as she almost throws herself on the road.

'Wait for the stop!' he shouts. 'Don't you know it's dangerous? Go back and pull the string.'

Her mouth fills with words she can't spit out. In her mother tongue her curses are sharp enough they could break teeth. Dora turns to the staring passengers. Above their heads is the loop of waxy gut that must be pulled taut to ring the bell, but they're not at the stop yet.

The bus slows. Brakes screech. A traffic light turns red and Dora takes her chance. She jumps down, runs to the pavement, and takes a deep lungful of air. Her heart is racing and she sits for a minute on a garden wall till someone inside the house opens a window and yells at her to get off.

Dora walks fast to the next bus stop and sits down. She puts her hands in her pockets and bites small pieces of flesh from the inside of her lips. She used to put her necklace in her mouth, her grandmother's six-pointed star that Vati gave her, and she would feel the sharp points on her cheeks and tongue. Her parents used to tell her off for chewing it like that, but she never lost the habit, not till the necklace couldn't leave Berlin with her. She gave it to Jette as a keepsake. Now she bites her cheeks instead.

There's no point in crying. She pushes her fingers even deeper into her pockets, right to the bottom where the seams are grainy with crumbs and fluff and bits of old tobacco. She pushes her hands against her belly and feels that stubborn fist, the lump Ruthie left behind. Like a creature with a hard shell, it has burrowed down, cradled in her pelvis like it never wants to leave.

8 April

There's a queue to visit the synagogue. I wait to have my bag sent through an x-ray machine and then walk through a metal detector like the ones at the airport. I'm not going to the synagogue with the other tourists. One of the security guards calls a lift and tells me to go up to the archives.

I'm met by a woman who introduces herself as Margaret. We go through some doors, up a few steps and along a corridor. It's quiet. The building goes back in time here, somewhere up above Oranienburgerstraße. The fixtures are old, and I can smell the files and the shelves full of books, bound volumes of city directories that date back a century or more.

I'm taken into a room where there are special machines set up like old tape recorders. Margaret says they're for viewing records on film, but I don't need to use them. Family members are shown the originals. I am the only person visiting. The window is open and I can hear the hum of traffic on the street below. At a large desk there's a cardboard folder waiting for me, lying open so I can see the first page of the documents inside. A long German word is printed from one side of the page to the other. In old, inky letters it says *Sammelvormundschaft*, and I have to read the word slowly several times before I can guess at the sound of it.

I place my bag on the floor and sit down at the desk. Margaret moves the file in front of me, explaining that these are records of Jewish children in care.

'It is incredibly lucky that Ruth's file has survived,' Margaret says. 'It's one of only one hundred or so.'

She asks that I turn the pages carefully and says she will be next door if I need anything. Then she disappears, and I'm left alone with the sounds of the room, the creak and click of a door opening and closing on another floor of the building, the mumble of sounds outside, something electronic humming in a nearby room. I realise that since living with Matthew, I listen to the world differently, as if I'm recording all the time. I'm still looking at the cover of the file, remembering the phone call that came from the Director of the archives when I made the appointment.

'I want to warn you that the story isn't easy to read,' he said. 'You need to be sure you want to know the contents.'

I thought about it, but I always knew what the answer would be. I've always been decisive about everything in my life. Until recently. It's required for an air traffic controller. Indecision costs lives.

But that day in Asda shook me. Matthew said when I spoke to him from the carpark it was like getting a mayday call. But I know what it's like hearing a pilot say that word three times. So for once, I let Matthew be in charge. I did what he told me, as if he was my own collision avoidance system. Even though I knew any kind of anxiety disorder would disqualify me from ever controlling again, I followed his instructions and went to the doctor. I wasn't surprised when I was prescribed pills, and I dropped the prescription off at the pharmacy. Only then did I let HR at work know what was going on. It's a legal requirement. They said not to worry, to do what I needed to do and not to think about controlling till this was behind me. The only thing was, every time I set off to collect the pills, I changed my mind. I thought about all the pilots I had talked through sticky situations, how they took guidance from me and balanced it with the conditions in the cockpit. Really, the pilots in always charge. We just give them clearance.

The pharmacy left four voicemails telling me the pills were ready, but I never picked them up. You get pilots like that, the ones who'll talk back at you and always want to do their own thing just for the sake of it. I suppose I'm like that too. I like being the controller.

About opening this file, I'm stubborn. I always knew I'd look at the contents.

On the front page there are names. Ruth's, Dora's, and the father's.

Marcus.

I whisper his name out loud, feeling the shape of Dora's secret on my lips and the tip of my tongue. There are another hundred pages below this one. I wish for a sign that I'm doing the right thing. Nothing comes. I can't smell Dora's Woodbines, or the German bread.

His name was Marcus.

I've discovered a dark piece of the puzzle, plucked it from the place Dora left it. Now I don't know what to do with it, hide it up my sleeve, or tuck it behind my ear.

On the next sheet there are addresses beneath each of the three names. These entries are handwritten and some of the words are so small I can't read them. I take a note of anything I can understand. The rest will have to wait.

I find my grandmother's letters on a sky-blue sheet of paper that's thinner than tissue. I'm worried it will melt in my fingers. I can't understand what the letter says but I can see Marcus's name and Ruth's. There's another letter on the same thin paper, this time pink. His name again, and hers.

Margaret comes back and sits with me for an hour translating the small details. Ruth's general development: normal. A description of the family's apartment: two rooms, simple but clean. A social worker's note listing Ruth's needs after a home visit in late 1941: a warm jumper and new underwear. Ruth is four-and-a-half years old.

A pencil scribble in the margin makes Margaret sink back into her chair, and I notice her rolling a hankie she has tightly pressed into her palm.

'It says that Meta and Herbert love Ruth like their own child.'

For a second, she stops reading. We both sit listening to the clock, and I stare at the faint pencilled words, the message that didn't fit any of the official questions. The social worker's name is signed at the bottom of the page, and I picture her standing in the Lewin's little apartment, a stubby pencil in her left hand. I can just make out her name, Ms Silbermann. *Silber* means 'silver'. It's the right name for a messenger whose words, like silver solder, finally hold everything together. I wish I could thank her for her foresight.

It's still early when I leave the archives and step back out onto Oranienburger Straße. I walk up the street for a while, unsure what to do, then take a tram to Alexanderplatz. As always, it takes me a few minutes to get my bearings here. I walk the few hundred yards to the corner of Alte Schönhauser Straße. I look down the street from across the road, thinking it can't have changed all that much. It's a quieter side street with old shops and old apartments.

I walk along the street, looking for the glinting brass cobblestones called stumbling stones, *Stolpersteine*. Each is engraved with a name. These mark the homes where persecuted people last lived freely, memorials mostly for murdered Jews. Any of the stones on this street will remember my family's neighbours, maybe their friends. Although their friends, like them, probably go unmarked. Stolpersteine are often requested by surviving family and descendants, and most survivors came from the more affluent front houses, not the crowded side wings and back buildings that were accessed through the courtyards, pushed back from the street. If these households were remembered, with one brass nameplate for each member of the family, whole pavements of the city would be gold.

I don't have to go far to find the number I'm looking for. It is a wide, red brick building, grand at the front. There is an arched entrance with an open gate and a small fold out sign for a waxing salon in the yard behind. Here, the four sides of the building leave just a little square of sky at the top. A few plants and bushes decorate the yard, but it's mostly cobbled, maybe the same cobbles that have always been here, lifted and turned a dozen times. Cobbles with no names.

Aunt Dotti's apartment must have been in one of the smaller side buildings. I don't knock. At the foot of the stairs there are families of bicycles leaning against each other, buggies, children's scooters and helmets. Everything looks peaceful, as it always should have been. I don't want to upset things.

I wander outside a little longer. I touch cobbles and take photographs of the patterns of mortar and stone, and look at the names on the brass plates full of doorbells. After a while there's nothing left to do but leave things as they are, so I take another tram back to Prenzlauer Berg, feeling the weight of the photocopied file on my lap. I'm alert to everything in the tram: the quiet conversations and the gentle whirring and clacking of the track and the carriage. I look out the window to watch the buildings reeling past.

That night, I read Ash a Jewish tale from a picture book with bright illustrations. It's a very old story about a grandmother knitting for her grandson. I know I'll read it to him many times.

In the story, the grandmother knits the boy a long coat with blue wool. When he outgrows it, she unravels the wool from the coat and knits a smart jacket. Later, when he grows again, she knits a handsome waistcoat, till in the end when he's a fully grown man, there's only enough blue wool for a hat. By this time the grandmother is very old, and finally, the hat falls apart. When her grandson tells her he is sad that this time it won't be possible for her to make something new, his grandmother tricks him, pretending not to remember the tradition. So the grandson holds her hand and tells her the story of all the things she made for him with the blue wool, starting with the beautiful long coat when he was a little boy, then the smart jacket, then a handsome waistcoat, and finally a hat. The grandmother laughs.

'We have already made something new,' she tells her grandson. 'The blue wool is now a story, and it will last as long as there is someone to tell it.'

Ash is too little to follow the story, but I read it twice, adding a sheep and a spinning wheel, shiny brass buttons, pockets to hide shells in, and more things that are made with the blue wool. Most of all, Ash likes the picture of the skein, and the strand of blue that calls out to his tiny fingertip, inviting him to trace the maze of yarn in a wiggly line over the page.

Found Pictures 2

1939

London has changed in the last month. It's early June and the thick skin of clouds formed over the cold city has finally melted away. The streets are coming to life. Bare trees that Dora hardly noticed till now have blossomed, just like the trees in Berlin, bursting into crowded displays of pink and white. They shed petals in the breeze. Dora takes detours through the streets. She likes the neat gardens with plants in beds and tended grass, bushes shaped nicely behind their own little gates and fences: pots of flowers and mint, and decorated window boxes. In this corner of London, the houses are mainly two stories, and the streets are wide enough that the sun shines over everything. A different light to Berlin

Fortune Green is a short walk from the Rosenthal's house. There's a small park there with two fields of grass, lines of trees and a path down the middle. At the back there's a cemetery behind a high wall. Quiet, tidy graves stand with pebble paths between them, miniature gardens. At the other end, the park thickens with the smell of the fish and chip shop and the police stables next door. It's sweet and straw-like, and reminds Dora of the zoo in Berlin, a smell that used to waft over the Spree and into the school yard.

At the park gates, under the trees, four benches sit around a drinking fountain. People rest and arrange to meet here. Some feed pigeons, read the paper, or eat chips from newspaper cones.

The meeting with Marcus takes place completely by chance, even though she had a feeling that sooner or later it would happen. When she sees him, he's sitting on one of the benches, doing nothing in particular. He sits with a foot up, resting it on his opposite knee. His toes tap time. He has the same manner as before, the past three years hardly showing at all. A woman sits beside him, and his arm is slung over the back of the bench, behind the woman's shoulders. A handkerchief is just visible at the top of his trouser pocket, and he wears his usual smart shoes and a fashionable jacket. His face is tilted towards the branches of the trees, as if he's watching some bird that's perched there.

Dora and Zelda are crossing the road. Zelda talks. She doesn't notice Dora drawing into herself, or her shoulders shrinking back. Dora feels the hardness of the road beneath her shoes, black leather laced tightly, the soles starting to wear, already repaired twice. Each step seems clumsy. The sight of him is like a pressure, that hardness under her feet. She feels the same hardness in her stomach, a rope round her ribs.

She wrote letters after she heard about his wedding, but nothing came back.

'I saw Johanna at the weekend,' Zelda is saying.

Dora hears her but doesn't reply.

Marcus is still staring into the leaves. The woman, it must be his wife, sits with her back straight, her hands folded neatly over a small purse in her lap. Marcus shifts his weight, and Dora wonders if he senses her already, the way young men are sometimes aware of women walking by.

The pigeons swoop up, double back, and land again just in front of the benches. They rearrange their wings and peck the ground to see if the couple has thrown any crumbs. Marcus looks over now, seeing her at last. The shape of his face transforms, and Dora recognises that familiar flash of nausea. But Marcus doesn't look away. Dora forces her feet to keep stepping and she nods at the story Zelda is telling. She pins her eyes on the tall cemetery wall at the back of the park. She tries to hear some snippet of conversation between Marcus and his wife, but they sit in silence. There's nothing to hear but the city and the sky.

Small white clouds are hovering over the cemetery wall.

'You're very quiet,' Zelda says.

They sit down on the bench, reach into bags, and slide cigarettes from newly bought packets. The cool stone of the wall at the back of Dora's neck is a relief. The bench where Marcus was sitting is empty now, and there's no sign of him or his wife anywhere in the park.

'I'm sad you're going away,' Dora says.

'It's only a holiday,' Zelda says. 'It won't even be fun. I'll still be looking after the children.'

Dora wonders what happened to the letters she sent. They were scribbled in blue ink on thin sheets of coloured paper. She remembers folding them, and the feel of the paper between her fingers as she tightened the creases. She imagined them arriving in Berlin, hidden deep inside a sack of letters and parcels, sorted at the office on Alexanderstraße, right opposite Meta and Herbert's apartment, sent out on the postman's trolley, pushed through letterboxes, torn open by hands she had once held.

She didn't think she recognised his wife, a young woman with curled chestnut hair and a worried face. They couldn't have been in London long and she would be missing her mother every second of the day, just like Zelda when she first arrived.

Zelda takes a loud bite out of an apple, but changes her mind and hands it to Dora.

'You eat it. You always look hungry.'

They walk back towards the shops together. It's mild weather, and in front of houses, babies sit in prams under canopies while bigger children play and mothers chit-chat. A young tortoiseshell cat follows at their heels for a while, meowing for attention, slipping in between railings and running ahead.

Dora glances through the windows of the fish and chip shop as they pass, thinking Marcus might be there, but no one is in line and the tables are empty.

'That's my bus,' Zelda says suddenly. She kisses Dora on the cheek and runs, coat flapping open, over the road and onto the back of the bus. Dora watches it leave. She slides a single cigarette from the packet, lights up, and wanders back to Alvanley Gardens.

11 April

I wake before the alarm clock. I don't want to disturb Matthew, so I stay in bed and stare at the old sewing machine table. It has a black, iron shoulder screwed into the top. There are wooden pedals on a long lever underneath, and they turn like a little bike, powering the needle up and down.

I know now that Dora's cousin Meta was a seamstress, and her husband Herbert was a tailor. It said this in the file at the archive. By the time Ruth came to live with them they were both in forced labour sewing army uniforms.

Perhaps this machine once sewed uniforms.

'What time is it?' Matthew says.

'Early,' I say. 'Go back to sleep.'

He does. I get up and dress and eat a quick breakfast. I watch the early commuters at the tram stop till they're picked up, whisked away to the city centre.

An hour later a tram takes us in the opposite direction, north into Weißensee, which feels far from the city's tourist attractions. There are locals' shops, one selling watches, two selling stationary, a couple of small grocers, a bargain fabric shop, a second-hand shop, and an antique dealer. Some of the old buildings are derelict. There's a large park with trees as tall as the apartments and trunks wide enough to hide a whole family behind.

'Those trees would have been here when Dora was a child, wouldn't they?' I ask Matthew.

'Those are old men,' he says.

Sentinels, I think.

'Sycamores,' Matthew says.

We follow the map up the side streets till we find ourselves alone outside the locked gates of a small cemetery.

A smooth stone I picked up nearby feels cool in my fingers, and there's a nip in the air. I turn Matthew round with a hand on his shoulder so I can see Ash in the carrier on his back, and pull his hat down lower over his ears. His eyelids are oily with sleep. I walk up to the gate and peer through a gap in the metal railings, seeing if I can read any of the graves nearby. Most of the stones are undamaged. They're old but the Hebrew inscriptions are legible. Of course, I can't read any Hebrew. Some of the graves have little rocks placed on top, like the one in my hand.

Rosa's grave won't have been visited for a whole lifetime. It's a miracle it's here at all, and if we're lucky it will be inscribed with a detailed description of her. My stomach jitters at the possibility. It's not difficult to imagine the past in this place, Uscher standing over the grave in his long black coat, droplets of soft rain on his hat and in his beard.

I emailed the synagogue about visiting the grave weeks ago, but had heard nothing till yesterday.

Concerning your request to visit a grave of
your family at the Cemetery Adass Yisroel we

could arrange your visit tomorrow at 9.00h.
Unfortunately, another date is not possible.
We deeply regret. Hal would await you at
the entrance of the Cemetery and guide you.
If you like to attend we would be looking
forward for your E-Mail confirmation
no later than 14h in order to arrange
the necessary dispositions. We apologise for
the short notice.

At exactly nine, a car pulls up and parks at some speed. A tall man wearing jeans and a baseball cap gets out. He is younger than I expected. I'm relieved. He strides over to us, shakes hands, glances at Ash, and goes over a few rules about photographing graves. He also says he won't be looking, so what he really means is we can take any pictures we want. We follow him across the grass, still wet from the morning.

Rosa's stone stands out from the others. It's tall and grey with a rough, unpolished shape. I walk around one side and Matthew and Ash go round the other. It could be a small Scottish standing stone. There's something cold and northern looking about it, the rough texture and the colour, a darkened, dampened grey. Perhaps it was chosen for that reason. According to her marriage certificate, Rosa came from the wetter, colder north, from East Prussia.

On one side of the stone is her German name, Rosa Tannenbaum. On the other side an oval area has been polished, framed by the rougher rock around it. Here there is a long inscription in elegant Hebrew letters. Green algae has bloomed between the words, and there's a white line of bird droppings that we clear with a baby wipe.

The ribbon of mitochondrial DNA. The stuff that only travels in the x-cell from mother to child. Rosa's hand and my hand are on the ribbon, Rosa's mother who was a Grummach, and between us, Dora and my mother.

And so on for thousands of years.

Ash grumbles. He had another bad night of coughing. In the end I sat up googling medical journals, reading about diseases which are common mutations in the mitochondrial genome. What if all has something to do with me, with the ribbon passed on only by mothers. Symptoms of mitochondrial disease include poor growth, floppy tone, muscle weakness, delayed development, and vision and hearing problems. But most of the rare diseases I google seem to have some array of symptoms that fit, and others that don't. A mystery that never gets any clearer.

Watch and wait.

Rosa has waited nearly one hundred years for the three pebbles we place on the top of her headstone. I place them in a way that I hope will last. When Hal's not looking we take photographs of the grave, me and Ash in the frame. We also take a picture of the Hebrew inscription that I can't read. Hal says he can't read it either, but tells me there will be someone at the synagogue who can, and calls ahead to set up a meeting.

On the way back to the tram stop, we visit

Meyerbeerstraße. It's very close, but still I struggle to picture Dora here. The street is quiet and leafy, and far from the city centre. And yet the address appears over and over in the family documents. 9 Meyerbeerstraße. I ask Matthew to take a photograph of me and Ash stood beneath the street sign. Building number 9 is gone, replaced with a modern infill, but the others on the street appear old enough to be from Dora's time. I stop under a tree and kick the toe of my boot into cobbles where they've been loosened by the roots. It takes some effort, but I manage to free one from the set without being seen. I pick it up and weigh it in my hands. The size and shape of a Rubik's Cube, but much heavier. One last check that nobody's looking, and I put it in my bag. Dora never came back, so this piece of her childhood is going to sit on her headstone in Scotland. A reverse Stolperstein. I'll take it to her grave on our next visit to my parents.

We take a tram into the city. Matthew's hungry after skipping breakfast, so he goes to a café. I walk with Ash to the small synagogue on Tucholskystraße. There are policemen outside the entrance, and they watch as the door is gently unlocked for us. I get the feeling the door isn't often unlocked for strangers.

Inside is an atmosphere of quiet formality. The place is dimly lit and cool. Windows are veiled, but there are colourful decorations hanging on the panes of glass higher up, bright Stars of David in blue, yellow, green and red. The room feels separate from the rest of the city, belonging to another time.

An older man introduces himself, but quickly disappears to his office to reread my emails. He leaves me and Ash standing in the front room of the synagogue, which has a small café and kosher food shop. While we wait, I buy jam from a quiet young couple who stand behind the counter. The name of the synagogue is on the label of the jam jar. Ash stares at the colourful decorations and makes cooey sounds into the high-ceilinged space.

'Your grandmother was Rosa Rowelski?' the man says, returning from his computer with a wide smile on his face.

'No,' I say. 'She was my grandmother's mother.'

'On your father's side?' he says quickly.

'No, on my mother's side.'

He nods, opening his arms wide, and I realise that here the mythical mitochondrial ribbon is what matters most. From mother to daughter.

'So you are Jewish!' he says, as if this is the punch line to a joke. 'And your son is also Jewish!'

He takes us over to one of the café tables and relaxes into the back of his chair, smiling widely.

'Did you photograph the grave? Let me see,' he says. 'I can read what it says to you.'

I show the man how to zoom into the picture to see the letters clearly, and after a minute or so he asks if I'm ready. He speaks slowly so I can copy the translation of the headstone into my notebook.

Here lies an important, pious, and modest woman,
Ascended on high at an early age
Her death is mourned by her husband and daughter
Mrs.Reyzl
Daughter of our teacher and rabbi the late Rabbi
Shmuel and wife of our teacher and Rabbi Asher may
his light shine Tenenboym
Died on the 14 of the month of Kislev 5683 at the age of
43 years.
May her soul be bound in the bond of life.

I like the sound of the unfamiliar words, and I ask him to help me spell them, words like the month of 'Kislev'. It occurs to me for the first time that Dora had a whole other way of counting the passing of the days, weeks, months and years, and I wonder how often in Scotland she acknowledged Jewish festivals with only quiet thoughts.

'Asher is also my son's name,' I tell the man.

He claps his hands once together and then reaches out and tickles Ash on the cheek. He tells me about the temple built in the back, where Dora and her parents once prayed. The original was burned down on Kristallnacht. Perhaps Dora was relieved that at least her parents weren't alive to see this. She was still in Berlin, still living out the six-month extension that the Nazis had granted her. It was six months in which more and more Jews tried desperately to leave. Jewish shops were ransacked, synagogues burned down, and Jewish men were arrested and imprisoned. Already, parents in Berlin were saying goodbye to their children and sending them to the UK on trains to live with strangers, perhaps forever.

The man tells me about the synagogue's own hospital, the one Ruth was born in, and the high school on the banks of the Spree, probably Dora's school. All long gone. He shows me some photographs. But soon after that he appear to become more interested in talking about the present, his daughters who'd like to go to university in London, and a gathering of the community some weeks before, when small boys cut their hair for the first time. I don't ask him any more about Dora.

After the meeting I find Matthew in a record shop not far from the synagogue. He's texting on his phone. My head is still full of the quiet cemetery and the empty café with the coloured paper stars on the windows, but I've made an appointment for Ash, so it's time to go. I booked an hour's consultation with the Feldenkrais therapist.

Matthew and I make plans to meet later back at the apartment, and I steer the buggy through the crowd to the tram stop. Already I'm sceptical, and Ash has been coughing again. I'd rather sit in the park and breathe in the outdoors, or browse recordss with Matthew. I get on the tram anyway.

Walking the last few blocks to the clinic, I picture again Mr Feldenkrais on the submarine off the coast of North Ayrshire. Perhaps this was fate. Kismet. Is that a Jewish word, or does it just sound like the word on Rosa's headstone? I'm trying to find connections that aren't really there.

*

The therapy session takes place in a small, sweltering room. There are no windows and only a lamp that glows orange in the corner. I answer the therapist's questions and then she works with Ash, talking in a hushed voice, moving him with slow, exaggerated care. A few times I feel my head droop and startle awake. At the end of the hour I have to hand over sixty Euros. I know I'll keep this whole thing to myself.

'Sometimes it's like you're a million miles away,' Matthew says to me that night.

Later he wants to have sex, but I'm not in the mood. Instead I take a long shower on my own. When I do get into bed, I think about how Matthew smells different here, away from the mulchy Ayrshire forests and his chain saws and chisels. He's on his phone again, scrolling through images of campervans. I nuzzle close, but a few minutes later Ash starts to cough, and when I get up Matthew forces out a long, loud breath.

'Go on then,' he says. 'I need you too, you know.'

I don't go back through to Matthew. I lie down on Ash's bed. This room faces the street, and I fix my eyes on the yellow streetlight that creeps in through the cracks of the blind, and listen to the noises of the tram coming and going.

1939

Talk of war is in the Lyons Corner House, in the children's games as they run to school, and whispered up the stairs at Bloomsbury House where files are still towering on every desk. On the front cover of each one there's the name of a person trying to leave before it's too late. On the front of one file among thousands of others, there is her daughter's name. Ruth Tannenbaum.

Dora must watch and wait.

She gets breakfast ready for the Rosenthals every day. She lays the table and prepares a pot of tea the way they've shown her, and before they come downstairs she lays the newspaper on the sideboard. She doesn't try to read the articles yet, but she looks at the photographs and the headlines. She wonders what the headlines are in the papers back home.

Today the front page of Mr Rosenthal's paper shows Londoners getting ready. There are children running to an underground shelter, a pretend raid. Gas masks are slung across their bodies and people are ushering them along, telling them to hurry. It's only a drill. You can see from their faces and the way they skip along, that really there is nothing to be afraid of. It's a morning off from lessons, maybe a picnic for lunch. Even the adults in the picture are enjoying themselves. Berlin will not be like this. Hitler has had children lined up in formation for years now, stamping and saluting.

She has avoided Fortune Green where she laid eyes on Marcus and his wife. Today is her afternoon off, but she has been skipping her usual walks and going to the pictures instead. She'll do the same again today. She likes musicals and romantic stories, and more than anything she likes sitting in the dark. It takes her mind off the days she is counting, just weeks now, till Ruth's train will leave Berlin. The ticket has been paid for. Dear Mr and Mrs Rosenthal didn't hesitate. Ruth will take the same route north that Dora did, sailing from the Hook of Holland to Harwich. Dora still feels sick when she remembers the rough sea and the stench of vomit. She curled up small on her bunk, gripping her stomach. She counted the minutes until she would die. But Ruth's journey won't be in the middle of winter. God willing, the sea won't be so rough for the children.

Shirley Temple and Fred Astaire are her favourites on the big screen. It's nice coming out of the dark and finding it still bright outside, the sky blue above London and the strawberry-red buses shining in the sunlight. Dora likes to watch them driving in a long, straight line up Finchley Road. Finchleystraße, that's what everyone from back home calls it. There's a restaurant here too, The Cosmo, with old favourites on the menu for the Berliners and the Viennese. So many have found placements round here. But Dora still prefers the solitude of the picture house. On the way home, she likes to sit on the top deck. Her bus passes the spot where she saw Marcus on the park bench, and she only glances out to check if he's there again.

Last night, like always, she dreamed of Berlin. As usual Marcus was the only person there with her. In the dreams she wants most of all to find Ruthie, but Marcus never knows where she is. Vati isn't there, and all of her friends are gone as well. Even her cousins and Aunt Dotti have disappeared from the city. Apart from Ruthie, she doesn't look for anyone. It's almost as if the others never existed. The places are vague and empty, but otherwise the same. She finds herself under the trees by the lake in Weißensee, near the wooden deck, where waiting rowing boats nudge and bump each other in the water. It's so real she can hear the dull thud of the wood patting the jetty, and the water sloshing. This was where her mother took her to feed the ducks when she was small. It is real. The branches of the trees creaking, the ducks quacking.

Other nights she's been in the middle of Alexanderplatz, crossing the road, stepping between tram lines. It's silent. There are no trams or buses or trains.

Sometimes she stands outside her first childhood home, where 9 Meyerbeerstraße met 9 Mendelsohnstraße. The place she once thought was the centre of the universe. This dream is one of the worst. She still finds herself thinking about it until the following night as she closes her eyes, and she lies with her heart beating in her ears, unable to sleep.

Last night she found herself standing at a first-floor window in the old people's home, looking down on Große Hamburger Straße. It was the building she used to work in, but there was no one in the garden, and the kitchens were clean and cold. The residents' beds and chairs were empty. Cook, the nurses, and all the people she worked with had also vanished, leaving everything neat and tidy. Like always, she didn't look for anyone, no-one apart from Ruthie, frantically flipping mattresses, opening every cupboard, even trying to lift floorboards. Tiny clothes moths fluttered as dark corners were turned out.

Even if he's not there at the beginning of the dreams, at some point Marcus arrives. Sometimes he comes for her in a car, pulling up and beeping his horn. Other times he just appears, standing behind her as if he's been there all along.

All the dreams end in Vati's apartment on Meyerbeerstraße. The cupboards are emptied but the furniture is exactly where it always was, the beds made up by someone unseen. It is always winter, and a January frost makes patterns on the windows. The rooms look the way they did in the few weeks after Vati died.

Dora and Marcus locked the door that winter and stayed together every night. They lay on the bed that was hers as a child, and she feels again his warm breath on her neck, his body tugging at hers. In this part of the dream Ruthie is forgotten. Or maybe not yet created. Frau Tuch heard them and banged on the wall with her stick. They ignored her. She was too old by then to come to the door or cause any trouble, and it made them laugh. Not in the dream though. Frau Tuch is gone too. All the neighbours have disappeared.

Waking up is a sort of sickening. The dreams hang over her as she looks out over the chimneypots and the muddled angles of London's grey, early-morning rooftops.

Today she sits right in the middle of the screen with empty seats all around her. She doesn't really watch. When the picture ends, she walks up Finchley Road. Buses go growling past. She feels a pull to find Marcus. The pull comes from inside her, where the baby grew, where part of it remains. She would like to talk to him about Meta and Herbert, and about Berlin, the people and places, sounds of the city that once rolled off their tongues without a thought, Potsdamer Platz, Schönhauser Allee, Tiergarten and the Spree.

The air is cooler this evening. Dora wraps her hands around herself and quickens her pace. Women and men go by the other way, some of them arm in arm. They're dressed up for the evening, heading for the West End's theatres and restaurants. On a corner near the station, a group of men fall out of a pub and stagger over the road, stopping the traffic. A woman in dirty clothes sits on a piece of board at the entrance to the underground, shaking a tin cup. A group of men and women walk past and someone puts a hand into a pocket. Dora hears the coin drop.

Clink.

'Dora!' she hears, suddenly. 'Dora!'

She knows the voice so well she can pick him out in a crowd. He's out of breath, as if he's been running to catch up with her. He steps closer, holding his hands out, soft, warm, clean-looking hands, pure white cuffs. Exactly as she remembers.

'Yes,' she says. Now more than ever, they have to be careful speaking German in public, but neither of them speak English well enough yet.

'I've been to the park every Wednesday since I saw you,' he says quietly, almost a whisper. 'I needed to talk to you. I couldn't when I was with Vera.'

His wife's name is smooth and comfortable in his mouth. He's dressed in a thin sweater and tailored trousers that sit without a crease. A newspaper is tucked high under his arm, the same paper the Rosenthals get delivered.

'Share a smoke with me?' Marcus says, and he reaches a hand to his dark hair, pinching a cigarette from behind his ear. There's no awkwardness in him. He does everything exactly the way he always did. He nods up the street and they start to walk.

'Do you want a coffee?' He lights a match, draws on his cigarette and throws the match between his feet. 'We're close to The Cosmo.'

'I don't have much time,' she says, and keeps her hands tucked into the pockets of her coat. She strokes the smooth shells of her fingernails and the rough skin on her fingers.

'You look just the same,' he says with a smile. He breathes out smoke and passes the cigarette. There's a bench down a small side street, opposite another park, and they walk towards it while Marcus talks.

'A lot of friends were disappearing by the time I left,' he says. 'It was worse than you could imagine.'

'Did you see Herbert and Meta?'

'No.'

She gestures for him to give her back the cigarette. He takes a draw and holds it for a second before giving her another turn. She says nothing, and she knows the longer her silence gets the more he will tell her. She notices, then, that there is something different about his hands. They've started to shake.

'It was always the plan for me to marry Vera,' he says as they reach the bench. He sits down and looks over to the peaceful rows of symmetrical houses. 'Our families have been friends for a generation.'

Dora sits. A man with a dog crosses the road into the park. He unclips the dog's lead, letting the animal run free.

'Say something, Dora. You've hardly said anything.'

Dora tastes the cigarette in her mouth. She watches the dog.

'You didn't tell her about Ruth,' she says.

He wants the cigarette again, but she won't give it to him yet. She keeps her eyes on the dog running across the grass, the power in him, the happiness of his whole being as he springs around before shooting off after a bird. Dora takes another draw. Her throat burns, but it's not the cigarette. Marcus always did buy the smooth, expensive ones.

Marcus leans forward, studying the pavement.

'I was scared Vera would break it off,' he says.

He looks away, biting on a fingernail. The shake in his hands is more visible with every passing second.

'Our parents were so happy about there being a wedding. And we had to leave them behind, Dora. Vera had to leave her family too.'

He is thinner in the face. She sees it now. She hands him the cigarette.

'She's a good person. You'd like her,' he says, and he takes a long suck.

Dora looks at the back of his neck, the skin below the black arrow of his hairline. She wants to tell him about Ruthie's mark on her neck, how it's shaped like a little moth. She remembers lying beside him, stroking his smooth, black hair.

'Did you get my letter?' Dora asks.

'Yes.'

She sees him breathe in the smoke and swallow. Her jaw tightens and her shoulders ache. He keeps talking, faster now and in German, forgetting to lower his voice. He takes small, quick draws as the cigarette whittles close to his fingers.

'I spoke to my father and he said that things will change, and Ruth is only a child. She won't remember. My parents will try to help.'

Marcus sits up straighter. He takes the rolled newspaper from under his arm, laying it on his lap, leans back. His body adjusts to its usual, easy posture again.

Dora looks at the date on the newspaper. There are only a few weeks left till Ruth's birthday. It falls just after Yom Kippur.

'My employers have bought her a train ticket,' Dora says.

Marcus puts his hands over his mouth.

'That's amazing,' he says, and his chest lifts, as if a great weight has been taken off him.

'Unless the war starts before then,' Dora shrugs. 'Then what will happen?'

He sinks back down a little, reaches over and puts his hand over hers. She lets him keep it there.

'As soon as I knew we were coming to London, I hoped I'd see you,' he says.

They both look ahead, as if they're still in his car driving around Berlin, Marcus wearing his chauffeur hat.

He gives her the very end of the cigarette and she takes a last draw on it before dropping it on the floor. Dora stubs it out with the sole of her shoe. He smiles. It's something they used to do. He would give her the end of the cigarette and she would stub it out. His shoes were always too fancy.

'Did you get those shoes in London?' Dora asks.

'Yes,' he says. 'Vera bought them.'

'Not bad.' They used to tease each other like this, and laugh in a way that made old people mumble and tut.

They walk together towards Fortune Green. Boys are playing football while people shout on their dogs.

They stop under the tall trees. Here the air smells different, cold stone, cut grass.

'I have a photograph of Ruthie,' Dora says before he goes.

He puts a hand on the trunk of a tree and his fingers pick at the bark. She takes the photograph out of her pocket and holds it towards him.

'When was this?' he says, his voice small.

'Nearly a year ago. Her first birthday.'

Marcus looks at the photo for a few moments.

'She'll be alright,' he says, handing back the picture, refusing to look any more.

'Will you take it?' Dora says.

'Why?'

Because looking at the picture is even harder than not looking at it, she thinks. And because she wants him to take it home and really see it. And because maybe she'll have to see him again, to get it back.

'I don't know. Please, just take it.'

He is so close that Dora can smell his skin, his soap and shaving cream. His breath smells faintly of beer, which he never used to drink. He looks around as if he's afraid they might be seen, and Dora wonders if he lives nearby, if Vera might be watching from a window.

'Ok,' he says, screwing his lips. He drops the picture in his pocket. 'Have my address.' He puts a card in her hand. 'Are you hungry? I'm getting fish and chips.'

She says she doesn't feel like it, but that's a lie. She loves the greasy warmth and comfort of the batter and the chips all over her fingers and lips. It's one of the things she'll share with Ruthie soon, a newspaper poke stuffed to the top and drenched in salt and vinegar.

They say goodbye, and she watches him cross the road, one hand in the pocket where the photograph sits. She waves to his back, and he disappears round the corner.

14 April

Thunder rumbles and there's a sound of something snapping over the city. Huge raindrops splash onto my face and run down my cheeks. I dash under a shop awning and listen to it being pummelled by the weather, streams gushing down pipes and drains.

Ash is sleeping in the carrier on my back. His breath warms my neck, and his arms and legs are swinging, relaxed. He recovered from another night of coughing, and after a day inside yesterday, we've been wandering around bleary-eyed but relieved. His cheeks and hands are grainy with sand from the playground and the crumbs of his lunch. His lips are stained with chocolate dessert.

The traffic has stalled at the crossroads outside the underground station, pedestrians rushing for cover and a tram easing into a stop. The people make the cars wait. Drivers and passengers look bored, staring blankly at the lights from behind windscreen wipers.

I see Matthew in the crowd at the tram stop. He gestures for me to run for it while he holds the doors.

I'm surprised at how much Matthew likes the city. At home, he worries about global warming, planets colliding and the inevitable end of things. He chisels away at thoughts like this in the forest, but they're still on his mind in the evening, loitering, festering. Here, his restless pattern doesn't seem so unnatural. Maybe that's why he likes Berlin. He's taking pictures and recording the sounds, the rain, the voices, the car horns and the doors of the tram flinging open, beeping, and then sucking themselves shut with a thump. Sometimes he goes out at night and records the sounds of the dark, the trams now empty, a bar still open on the corner, or Berliners snoring from ground floor bedrooms with open windows. The glare of city streetlights hides the whole glittering cosmos above. It's true that the universe over our house back home is terrifying and beautiful. Nothing makes you feel small like a clear, dark night.

Passengers jump into the tram and stamp their feet to shake droplets from their clothes. It's dry inside, a little capsule, and we smile at each other, sharing our good fortune to be out of the weather. As the tram moves through Pankow, more and more passengers pull their hoods back up and ready their umbrellas. The tram empties out, and through the melting windowpanes we start to see patches of green, trees and parks, and old mansion houses behind hedges. I wonder how closely the tramlines follow those of the older city.

There's only a steady drizzle by the time we reach our stop. We walk up and down the street, peering through the gates and fences to see the houses hidden behind. Most of them are old, brick buildings with fancy extensions, all cloistered in wooded gardens. I walk ahead and Matthew records the birds.

'Go on. I won't be long,' he says.

I know that Ruth was here for two years, cared for in a big infant home on a lush green side street. The street name has changed, but I find the building.

'Should we go inside?' Matthew asks as he catches me up.

'I'm not sure.'

I stop near the glass doors. No one is coming in or leaving, and the ground floor windows are too high to see through. I take more photos than I need to, wondering if someone might come out and ask us what we're there for, but no one appears. The building has become a children's hospice. I wonder if the past and present of a place could be forever intertwined. Perhaps this will always be a place for endings.

Inside the reception is a list of Jewish children's names written down the wall on a memorial. None of the children survived, nor any of the nurses who stayed with them. Ruth's name would have been engraved there if Dora's relatives hadn't taken her home with them. At the archive the other day, I'd held in my hand Dora's short telegram, a message sent from London giving her aunt permission to collect Ruth.

She was returned to family.

I ask permission to photograph the wall, and as we're looking at it, Ash begins to wake and whine.

'It's okay. We like noise here,' says a woman behind us, who shakes our hands and introduces herself as the director. She reaches out and takes Ash's tiny hand, bouncing it up and down. 'We try to make it a happy place.'

When she asks if we'd like to take a walk in the garden I say yes without hesitation. I'm grateful for a chance to see more of the building, but there's a silence here that's uncomfortable. I'm not sure I've been anywhere that felt this quiet this since Ash was in hospital. Somewhere down a corridor a chair leg scrapes the floor and I feel that old, familiar tightening in my chest.

The trees Ruth played under in the garden have stretched high over the roof, and there's a small petting zoo in one corner that the director tells us has been here since the thirties. In the doorway of this little brick outhouse, a grey donkey with a gentle face is keeping watch.

We walk between the trees and come across a crop of hand-painted stones, each one a different colour, with names and messages written on them. They have been placed carefully, laid in a pattern that is constantly evolving as the hospice welcomes new children, and families say their last goodbyes. There's a wind chime in a tree that shines in the sun and twinkles with raindrops, and small statues of teddy bears, and fairies. There are many painted stones.

We travel back into the city. The rain is pouring again. As the tram heads down Schönhauser Allee I turn Ash into my chest so he can look out over my shoulder. The Meccano-like structure that runs down the middle of the street has his attention. The U-Bahn runs two stories over the ground in this part of the city, and the trains are lifted on a metal frame. Under it there are nests for pigeons, crowds of people crossing, drug deals, Currywurst stalls, sushi bars, and staircases leading to platforms. The busy city is a relief.

I put my arm around Ash. I stroke the nape of his neck, his skin like velvet, and feel the lightest push in his feet. With his stiff leather boots planted firmly on my knees he begins to lift himself up, just a little, bobbing his head up beside my head.

There's a thin ring of chocolate around his lips. The little wrapped chocolates he ate were a gift from the director at the hospice. They kept him content while we talked. Now he smells sweet, and I feel it again, that little push in his feet. He's trying to stand up. I put my smile close to his face. There's a rush of warmth in my belly I haven't felt for as long as I can remember.

'That's it,' I whisper.

I look across at Matthew. He's staring out of the window, holding his sound recorder in his hand.

The rain continues for hours. From our apartment window the road seems empty, except for a single pedestrian who exits the tram with an umbrella and runs for shelter. Other neighbours watch from windows and balconies. There are flashes of lightning in the sky and a petrol blue glow on the wet road.

Our visit today is still on my mind, the painted stones and the list of names on the wall. I can't shake it. The director didn't like the silence of the place either.

When I told her Dora's story, she became visibly upset.

I go to bed with my computer and browse a few webpages till I feel like sleeping. I'm just about to shut down for the night when an email flashes up from someone called Lucy. At first I assume it's spam, but the subject line catches my eye. *Kitty.*

Matthew's asking me something from the other room, but I ignore him and open the message. It's from my top DNA match. One of my hundreds of cousins.

> *My Mom's maiden name was Rowelski. She lived in Berlin, but she has no blood relatives left. I'm sorry I don't know much more. Any relation? We live in Virginia. We have a turkey farm.*

I reread the email a few times over. Could there be a connection? Then I get up, suddenly ravenous, and make a snack. I eat so fast I don't taste the food. Matthew's getting into bed, and I tell him about the email. He can't understand why it's important, so I try to explain it in a way he'll understand. It's like a rhizome, the stem of a plant that sends out roots and stems. Often this lies hidden under the surface, so even though the link isn't obvious yet, Lucy's mum has to be connected to me, attached to the same stem as Rosa, Dora's mother. She was a Rowelski too. I perch on the edge of the bed and email Lucy back, asking what else she knows.

A reply appears almost instantly, even shorter than the first message.

Her name used to be Gittel. She's Kitty now though. I'll ask Mom if she knows anything, but she was just a baby.

Gittel. It's not a name I've heard before. I lie back on the bed and stare up at the ceiling. Lucy and Kitty and the turkeys in Virginia.

My hands drift to my stomach. I'm eating too much here. I don't like touching my belly. I can still feel the fibroids. Are they getting bigger? When we get back to Scotland, I'll have a scan. The appointment came through before we left.

'Get me a beer would you, if you're not busy?' Matthew says.

Back in the kitchen I look out of the window into the yard behind. It's dark and empty but well kept. The residents have made a little play area with sand and swings, and there are buckets and spades left out. I keep meaning to take Ash out there. Every day it gets too late and we still haven't been. I promise myself we'll go first thing tomorrow, straight after breakfast, so long as the rain stops. I stare at the lights in the other apartments till the kettle boils and steams up the window. The light evaporates.

1939

The clothes on the line have dried in just an hour, and Dora's taking them in, dropping the wooden pegs in her apron pocket. The air is warm and lively with the sounds of Hampstead, neighbours enjoying their gardens, the whack of a cricket bat hitting a ball, women laughing, glasses clinking. She's almost finished when Mr Rosenthal calls her.

'Leave your work,' he says.

The Rosenthals are sitting together in the lounge. Her first thought is that they're letting her go, but no one speaks. Everyone is focussed on the fuzzy humming of the wireless being tuned. Mrs Rosenthal is gripping Frank's hand. Frank is seated next to Elsa. Maurice gives Dora a weak smile from the corner, where he sits upright in an armchair. The wireless comes to life and the voice of Neville Chamberlain splutters out.

Frank fixes the wall with his eyes and Elsa tilts her head to listen, hanging on the Prime Minister's words.

It surprises Dora that she can understand the broadcast. In less than a year she's learned English, and for just a few moments she forgets what she is listening to. She lets the announcement wash over her like a wave. The news floods the room. It floods the whole of London, the whole country, rushing over everyone all at once. The click that signals the broadcast's end makes Mrs Rosenthal jump, and then there is silence. The wireless is switched off. Only the clock can be heard from the mantelpiece, counting the first few seconds of the war.

In that moment, Dora remembers the day Vati came home from the last war, when his tin of silver clock hands flew into the air, opened and exploded. Would they have heard the news at the same time in Berlin?

'It will be a short war,' Maurice says. 'I'm sure of it.'

'Of course, Maurice. Hitler's days are numbered,' nods Mr Rosenthal.

'You are right, it won't be for long,' Mrs Rosenthal consoles them all. 'And look,' her voice is shaking, 'it's still such a lovely day. What a shame.'

Eventually Frank and Elsa get up and go out for a walk and Maurice wanders into the garden. He looks at Dora as he passes her, but says nothing. She watches him set out a deck chair and sit blinking in the sunshine, scratching the stubble of his beard, never quite relaxing back.

'We should leave for Luton,' Mr Rosenthal says. 'We'll take you, Dora, if you'd like to come. Have you heard of Luton?'

Dora shakes her head.

'There,' he says with renewed cheer, turning to his wife. 'No one knows where Luton is. It will be safer than London.'

*

Dora goes upstairs. She forgets the basket of washing in the garden and the mens' shirts still on the line, bleaching in the afternoon sun. She packs her suitcase. It's too hot for a coat today, but she puts it on and lies on the bed wearing it, waiting for Mr Rosenthal to call her downstairs to leave for Luton, or for bombs to drop.

But nothing happens. There is no sound but the pigeons, and no one leaves for Luton. Dora curls up on the bed and faces Berlin. She puts her hand in her coat pocket, her fingers expecting to touch the familiar, soft edges of Ruthie's photograph. Instead, she feels the sharp corner of the card with Marcus's address on it.

He doesn't live far away. Maybe she should just go and ask for the photograph back. She just wanted him to look at Ruth, to tell Vera about her. Perhaps she also wanted Vera to find it. But now she wants it back.

Dora lies on her bed for what feels like hours. She has never felt so tired. She thinks about the picture house, and scenes she remembers from romantic films. She watches dust spiralling in the sun and imagines things: the sound of Marcus's voice, and the mark on Ruthie's neck lifting up and fluttering away like the moths in her dreams. She sleeps, and wakes, and sleeps again. She dreams of the train that's supposed to take Ruthie to London, and wakes running a fingertip in a snaky line across her bed cover. The trains will stop, she thinks.

The trains will stop.

The Rosenthals go out for dinner, so there is no supper to cook. She hears them leave the house at six without a word. They probably think she's gone out. At her window, Dora watches the sun disappear behind the rooftops, the chimney pots and church spires becoming pathetic silhouettes jutting up into the sky.

It'll be another clear night. A few early stars have appeared, and a crisp crescent moon is rising over London like a slice of ripe apple. Dora thinks about Ruth on her first birthday, and the photograph taken under the fruit trees in the garden of the infant home.

In Berlin, the moon must already be high and bright in the sky, smiling down on the city. On trees, the apples will be ripening again. They will be gathered and sliced for the children to dip in honey at Rosh Hashanah. Wishes for a sweet New Year.

15 April

On the train to Potsdam we hold Ash up to the window and he watches drops of rain hitting the glass. He presses his nose hard against it, sticking his tongue out as if he can reach the water.

When we arrive it's still raining, and I hail a taxi. I read out the address on the piece of paper. Zum Windmühlenberg, which means something like windmill mountain. I form the word with my mouth a few times, the sound of something in a fairy tale.

Matthew and Ash get into the taxi too and I give some last-minute instructions to Matthew. He has to remember to let Ash rest, and make sure he wears his hat, and tell him to hold his hands in a fist when his arms go through his jacket sleeves. If he doesn't do that his fingers catch and bend back and he cries.

Matthew and Ash will get out of the taxi first. They're visiting an eco-dome where there's a dinosaur exhibition. Inside the dome there will be roaring, moving models hiding in the undergrowth.

The taxi drives over a small, white bridge. People are walking around under umbrellas and Potsdam looks very clean. We approach the eco-dome.

'Say bye to Mummy,' Matthew says to Ash, and he moves Ash's hand like a wave.

'Call me when you're on the way back,' Matthew says. 'Don't take too long.'

My stop doesn't look much further on the map, but the taxi drives on and on till it seems like we're deep in the forest. When the taxi takes a sharp left turn onto a single-track path, I glance at the rear-view mirror and try to see the shape of the driver's face. I don't even know what he looks like. I begin to feel car sick. I roll down the window and hear little pebbles and the gritty earth rolling under the tyres.

The taxi continues upwards through the lush trees and I take deep gulps of air. The smell of roots and wet leaves is pleasant, but it doesn't slow my heart. I open my bag and reach for my phone. Check for a signal. Not great, only one bar. I think about texting Matthew, but my fingers are all thumbs just trying to unlock it.

The track ends abruptly. There are some gates and behind them a compound of temporary buildings. Men stand around in workwear. I feel the taxi stopping so I stuff my phone back in my bag. I pay the driver and step outside, grateful to be out. The heavy rain has stopped and the soft ground underfoot is reassuring.

After Berlin, the density of the green and the cacophony of birds in the trees take me by surprise. The woods seem deeper than the ones at home, taller and healthier and endless, woods that need no one. Matthew would be impressed. My nerves haven't quite settled, but I ask the construction team where I should go. They don't know, so I wander into the complex further up the hill. For all I know I've come to the wrong place, but no one stops me. The taxi driver starts his engine, and the car disappears into the trees. I look back up the incline. The buildings ahead are container-like. There are no windows. I walk between them till I find an unlocked door.

'Hello?'

Inside the air is surprisingly cool. I go down a corridor and find a lady at a reception desk. She wears a sensible cardigan and glasses, and looks as out of place as I do. She takes my name and then gets up from her chair and beckons me to follow her along another corridor and into a small room. There is a row of lockers. I'm asked to put my things in one of them.

'Sorry you had to come so far from Berlin,' she says in perfect English. 'We're rather hidden away at the moment. This is only temporary. The archive is moving to new premises. In the meantime, here we are.'

I take off my coat off and hang it up. I keep only my computer under my arm. I'm shown into the reading room where two dozen people are already working at their allocated tables. I wonder who they could be, journalists, or historians, or lawyers working on cases? I don't interrupt anyone to ask. No one utters a word. No one even looks up when I appear in the doorway. The lady points to the one remaining space in the room, an empty chair in the middle of a long desk. Next to it there are folders in a pile, and I can see that they're full of documents, a tower of pages.

I sit down. The collection of files is presented to me simply, neatly. It seems almost as if it's been here forever, waiting beside a chair with my name on it. The lady leaves me alone.

I don't open the files immediately. Just like the last time, I sit for a couple of minutes. I listen to the almost-silence, pencils jotting notes, pages turning, a polite cough, and someone's stomach rumbling. The lingering anxiety of the taxi journey begins to ebb away.

Matthew told me not to dawdle. He doesn't like looking after Ash alone, especially when he isn't well-slept, when he gets whiney and clingy and only wants me. I don't have long. I slide the pile closer and look through the folders. These are all originals, the paper still chilled from storage. There is a file for Ruth, which is inside a folder with Meta's file and a one for Herbert. There is a folder for Dora's aunt Dorothea and her cousin Jette. Another full of relatives I didn't even know existed. I work out that it belongs to another cousin, Max, and his family. A family history in a chilled paper tower.

It takes me a while to work out what I'm looking at. Collection forms filled in by everyone who was going to be deported. They were filled in a rush, with light pencil markings and sweeping strokes. The same pencil may have been passed around a room of people, all awaiting a train. Possessions are listed. Rent and debts are declared. Finally, names are signed, in most cases, for the last time. Between November 1942 and March 1943, the dates on these forms, almost all the trains were going to Auschwitz.

The family's belongings are everyday items, simple contents of kitchens and wardrobes. Aunt Dorothea declares an oval dining table and four chairs. Herbert owns books, a standing lamp and, strangely, a dentist's chair. Meta notes various saucepans and a sewing machine. There are no toys on the list, but Ruth is present. Meta lists a child's bed, and items of children's clothing.

I trace their final signatures with the tips of my fingers.

I open the cover of Max's file, a name I'd never heard until today. He shares a birth date with Dora's cousin, Jette. Twins. Max's handwriting is fainter than the others, his form filled in even more sparingly. He lists no belongings and instead strikes through the entire page, but his wife Lucie, who is just twenty-two years old, lists underwear on her form, linen, and a pram. They have a boy, Efraim, only three years old.

I turn the pages a second time. Max's pencil marks are so faint they're easy to miss, and I nearly overlook the only question he's answered properly: *Are any members of your family not travelling with you?* In reply, Max scribbles three lines in the same slanting script, the same faint pencil. The couple also has a baby daughter left behind in hospital.

Gittel Rowelski.

I stare at the name. My throat is as dry as the document. It hurts to swallow. Max's grey pencil lines run off the page and seem to run forever, like steel rails, like train tracks. Time feels like it could fold and soften, like a piece of paper being crumpled into a ball.

Max's last words trace through generations, connecting everything, him and Dora, me and Ash, an old lady in Virginia. The day we were all separated.

*

When I leave the archive I decide to wait for a bus back to Potsdam. I know I'll be sitting at the bus stop for nearly an hour on the forest road, and Matthew wanted me to hurry, but I don't care. There are only trees here and the road is completely quiet, silent except for the birds.

I could sit here all night. The smell of the documents still coats my fingers. The birds sing, and the world is oblivious. I keep thinking of all the ordinary belongings listed in the files: pots and pans, bed linen, and various articles of children's clothing, the bric-a-brac and clutter that might have ended up in a car boot sale thirty years later.

Auctioneers' records were also in the files. Meta's cooking utensils, Herbert's books, the dentist's chair, Ruth's bed, and Aunt Dorothea's oval dining table and four chairs were all listed again a second time. On these pages, prices were assigned to everything, each handkerchief, each bowl and cup, each spoon. It was all tallied on headed notepaper, amounting to a sum that was still next to nothing. It was sold and the small profit noted. Letters were sent to the authorities that were signed off with a 'Heil Hitler'. Gittel's pram had fetched twenty-five marks, the most valuable item that Max and Lucie owned.

The bus arrives. It will take me back into Potsdam where I'll get on a train, but I'm still reluctant to board. The bus is bright and drives along stupidly. I stare out of the window and hold tight to the bag on my lap. I can feel my notebook inside the zip pocket. I wrote down some of the sentences in the files in German, and some of them I translated into English.

An hour goes by on the train. It's full of quiet passengers who read or stare out of the window. It's raining again on and off, and it continues like this until we glide under the glass roof of Berlin Hauptbahnhof. Suddenly there is noise: a bustling platform, conversations, announcements on the tannoy, and the boys waiting for me on the forecourt. Ash and Matthew wave through the train window.

I shake myself, take a deep breath, smile for the two of them and thank God for the city with its mass of excitable faces and sounds of life, the beep of the crossings and the popular music playing in shops, the pigeons, the speed on the underground, the greasy smells of fast food, the airports and the planes flying from here to everywhere else, all the noise drowning out my thoughts. Thank God for cities.

'We can pick up food on the way,' Matthew says. 'I'll cook.'

We get the tram. While I talk to Matthew, telling him what I've found, Ash falls asleep in my arms. He has chocolate round his lips again and a plastic dinosaur clutched in his hand. I can't take my eyes away from him. I listen to the noises of the wheels on the rails. Max's pencil lines trailing off into the distance.

1939

In Luton, people smile at strangers. Vegetables have proper flavour, and the smell of them when Dora comes home from the grocer fills the whole kitchen. Freshly picked lettuce, mushrooms still musty with soil, the sharp sweetness of an onion.

Dora goes from the living room to the kitchen, to the shop and back, to the bus stop, up and down the stairs, and in and out of the laundry room. Everyone tells her to relax. She's being clumsy, dropping things and forgetting what she's doing. At night she lies awake listening to her own breathing.

The Rosenthals still have a business to run, and they have brought work with them. Boxes of clothing samples are sent to the Luton house from the London shops, and Elsa opens all the parcels and chooses what she wants the stores to stock. No one knows if people will still be in a mood to buy, but Elsa has a sharp eye. Anything she likes, Mr Rosenthal will put on order.

Elsa has just announced that she's expecting a baby. She thinks talking of the war will be unhealthy for the pregnancy, so she chatters about everything else, and Dora is good company here in Luton, where Elsa knows no one. So Dora is invited to look through the clothing that arrives, luxury goods she could never afford.

Dora would love to send gifts to Berlin. Warm hats for the boys, and for Ruth a soft woollen scarf, shoes for Meta, gloves for Aunt Dotti and Jette. But no one can send a parcel or a letter now. The last news from Jette was that cousin Max and his wife Lucie had a baby boy. Dora hadn't even been allowed to send a reply.

I wish you could meet happy Efraim, whose bright eyes are so big. He's bringing us such joy! There is so much happiness in his soul.

Dora thinks of them all together, baby Efraim in the pram with Ruthie holding him. The apartment on Alte Schönhauser Straße will be full now. The family will hardly fit around the oval dining table. She knows the prayers and songs that Aunt Dotti will be teaching the children, and the stories she will tell.

The post office wouldn't touch her letter.

'You can send nothing but prayers,' the clerk had told her, shrugging his shoulders. 'Nothing to do now but wait for it to end.'

Dora tried pushing the letter back under the window. It was only wishes for a new baby, she said, and a birthday card for her daughter. She tried explaining everything to the clerk, but he slammed the window and told her to be off.

'If it's to Germany, it is a no. I'm sorry,' he had said, his voice softening as he saw her eyes filling up. 'Save your money, love.'

She still has Ruth's birthday card in her handbag, sealed in an envelope, the address written in blue ink.

The day Mr Rosenthal told her Ruth's train was cancelled, and not only that, but all the post stopping, he took both her hands in his and said the sooner the war started, the sooner it would end. He'd tried to say it in a way that sounded reassuring, as if the whole world could be packed for storage, like wrapping unsold hats in tissue paper, hiding them in boxes, and putting them back on the shelves as good as new the following winter.

Ruth's birthday card has her whole heart folded inside it.

There has been a delivery this morning. Three boxes. Dora unties her apron and rolls it into a ball the way she used to do on a Friday before she left work. She can't remember the last time she opened a parcel.

'Let's open that one,' Elsa says, pointing.

The address is written on the top in large, untidy letters. The name of Mr Rosenthal's company is spelled out: *Rosenthal Furriers Accessories and Silks*. Dora opens it and passes it over. Elsa pulls everything out and lines the accessories up on her desk. She doesn't look at them for long. There are calfskin gloves in brown and grey, lined with rabbit skin. There are leather belts and silk scarves and handkerchiefs, and a fur stole. Elsa hands it straight to Dora and tells her to put it on. She says that the style suits Dora with her close-cropped hair, but Dora doesn't like wearing it. The animal's paws are still attached, reaching down towards her breasts. She's pleased when Elsa puts it back in the box.

'I envy your hair. It's so black and shiny,' Elsa says.

'Everyone says pregnancy does that to you, but it hasn't happened to me yet.'

'It will,' Dora tells her.

Dora picks up another box. Inside there are two hats made entirely of fur. Dora takes them out. They each put one on their heads and look at each other. Elsa leans towards the mirror on the wall.

'You should keep one of these, Dora. You'll need it when it snows.'

Dora takes the hat off and pushes her fingertips into the soft fur. She would have loved to wear this in Berlin. Vati might have given her a gift like this for her birthday, if he were still alive, if things had been different. This year her birthday passed without anyone knowing.

Elsa looks through more samples, peachy silk underslips and packets of handkerchiefs. She holds them to the light to see how thick the fabric is, and she whistles each time she pulls out something she likes. She hands more of these things to Dora, insisting she keep them because they won't fit her this year.

The clothes Dora brought from Berlin hang off her now. Her collarbones jut out. She can't stop rubbing the skin over them. It gives her a strange feeling in her stomach, as if that hard lump in her belly that Ruth left behind was rolling around, licking her insides.

'Is it lunch?' Mr Rosenthal says, his head appearing round the door.

'Yes,' Dora says. 'I'll set the table.'

*

The Rosenthals have bigger appetites in Luton. They always hurry to the table and eat without talking.

'Eat up!' Mr Rosenthal says to her, noticing Dora's untouched plate. 'You'll need some fat to survive a winter in the countryside.'

Dora straightens and swallows down a few more mouthfuls of food.

'You will be too tired to do anything this afternoon,' Mrs Rosenthal says with a sigh, and Dora forces herself to eat a little more.

When they're finished, she goes around the table collecting the empty plates from the family and piling the cutlery on top. The crockery and cutlery makes more of a clattering than she wants it to, especially when a fork slides from her hand and lands on the floor against Maurice's chair leg.

'There's going to be a dance to raise money for the troops,' Elsa is saying.

'Dora, do you like dancing?' Mrs Rosenthal says suddenly.

'Yes,' Dora says, reaching over for her bowl.

Marcus had been a good dancer. He'd given her no chance to worry about her feet. With him leading, the steps seemed to unfold by magic.

'Maurice could take you,' Elsa says. 'It's for the troops. You'll take Dora, won't you Maurice?'

'Of course he will,' Mr Rosenthal says, looking over at his son. 'You are young, Dora, you should have a bit of fun too.'

'I'm not a good dancer,' Maurice says.

'It's true, Dora. Maurice has two left feet,' Elsa laughs, and she leans back in her chair and strokes a hand over her belly, even though she isn't showing yet. Dora looks away. She remembers what it was like when Ruthie was inside her, warm and safe and close, just under her skin. She wishes every day that she had kept that photograph. Her fingertips still reach for it inside her pocket.

Just before the Rosenthals took her out of London, Dora had visited the address Marcus had given her. It was too late to ring the bell, already dark. She stood in the street for a while, watching for him in windows, and eventually he looked out. She waved. She wanted the photograph back, nothing else, but Marcus said he needed to walk with her. They walked all the way to the park and up the path to the cemetery wall.

He'd argued with his wife about the photograph. Vera had taken it, furious. He didn't know what she had done with it. When Dora cried, because she knew it was her own fault for giving it away, Marcus had tried to put his arms around her. She could feel the cold wall at the edge of the cemetery against her back. There was a smell of moss and soil and freshly cut grass, and bits of the wall were crumbling under her fingers. She remembered their first date, how he had kissed her in the hallway outside Meta and Herbert's apartment, holding her fast with the folds of her clothes in his fists.

'Did you go dancing in Berlin?' Elsa asks.

Dora nods.

'So, you'll go with Maurice? Maybe you can teach him.'

'I will have a go,' Dora says.

*

Later, in her room, Dora tries to remember dance steps. She kicks off her shoes and hears the music in her head, sees the band with their polished shoes and shining instruments. She sways gently. Her stocking feet step out, side to side, passing her weight between them. The movement stirs another memory. She's back in Niederschönhausen, holding Ruthie in the darkness of the mother and baby room, rocking side to side. Ruthie had been so hard to get to sleep at night, as if she was afraid to miss a single moment of life.

When the first snow falls a week later, Dora thinks of Vati. It was snowing when he died. A headstone had been too expensive, so only the cold plot and the prayer was paid for. Herbert had made all the arrangements and signed the papers at the cemetery offices, and Vati was buried as soon as possible. Dora had stayed with Meta, Jette and Aunt Dorothea. The men went to the grave.

She also remembers the snow that covered London in the weeks after she first arrived. The longest year has nearly passed. In Luton ice is creeping over the windowpane.

Dora pulls a borrowed dress over her head and smooths it down over the silk under-slip. Elsa gave her this. Goosebumps cover her arms. The dress fits quite well with the sash tied tight, and Dora puts her coat on over the top. The fabric of the dress feels stiff and brand new. Dora would have liked to put a necklace on with it, but she doesn't own any jewellery. She comes downstairs with her coat already buttoned.

'Sorry,' she says, stepping into the room where they are waiting. All of them are in their dancing clothes. Maurice looks to the floor as he holds his arm out for her to take, and Mr Rosenthal waves them off to the bus stop. They step along the frosty pavement, arm in arm, their feet cold but impatient for the rhythm of music and dance steps.

The bus arrives on time. In town everything is decorated for Christmas, with paper chains and trees in the windows, and bunches of holly and mistletoe tied up. A brass band is playing as they pass the train station. They play a song that Dora sung to Ruthie when she was a newborn. A man at the front of the bus sings along, but Dora only knows the German words. It's strange, she thinks, how songs can slip across the world like the weather. Right now, in Berlin, they'll all be singing the same melody.

Stille Nacht, heilige Nacht, Alles schläft; einsam wacht.

'Dora?'

Frank has swivelled in his seat.

'You *are* a daydreamer,' he says. 'Father's right.'

'Did you go dancing in Berlin?' Elsa asks her.

She nods, clearing her throat and trying to suffocate the memories of the song.

'Not much.'

Dora looks at the reflections from the streetlights sliding over the bus windows, and at the people out on the pavement in hats and coats. A sleety rain has started to fall, and across the town heads are being covered by black umbrellas.

They danced fast in Berlin. Everything spun together, the glasses shimmering on the tables, the jewellery, the dresses, the black leather shoes, the brass, the music, Marcus. He had once asked her to marry him in the middle of a dance. She didn't know if he meant it. He was laughing as if it was a joke, and she didn't have the breath to reply.

'Who took you dancing in Berlin?' Frank asks.

Elsa pushes his shoulder and tells him off.

'You don't have to answer that,' she tells her.

Outside the dance hall, men and women huddle together sweet-talking under the porch.

'Tickets?' The woman on the door is slumped by the entrance and speaks with a cigarette drooping out of her mouth. Over her head a red paper ornament dangles and blows in the breeze. Frank, Elsa and Maurice push inside. Frank is already dancing.

'Aren't you coming?' Maurice says. He gives a nod to the dance floor. 'Don't mind Fred Astaire.'

'What?' Dora says.

'My brother,' he says.

'It's fine. I'll just be a minute,' Dora smiles.

She leans against the table where the ticket woman sits and reaches into her pocket for a Woodbine. She lights one and takes a long draw, feeling it go right through her body. A group of girls arrives, and behind them three young men with crisp white collars stare at Dora as they go past.

'Tickets?' the woman repeats.

Dora lets the music fill her up, feels the beat in her stomach. If she closes her eyes, she's in Berlin. Only the damp air and the voice encouraging the crowd to get to their feet spoils the illusion. She drops her cigarette and watches the embers of it glowing for a second before pressing the toe of her shoe down and scuffing out the light. The band starts playing 'Santa Claus Is Coming to Town'. She's heard it so many times from the wireless on Elsa's desk.

Dora takes off her hat and smooths a hand over her hair. She knows it'll frizz with the moisture. She should have pinned it back. She takes one last look into the sky and spots a few stars peeking out. She wonders what Zelda's doing in London. They wrote to each other a few times, but then Zelda met someone, a boy from Frankfurt who studied engineering. No letters have arrived for a month.

'They're saying it'll snow again later,' the ticket lady says suddenly. She nods up at the darkness. Their conversation is already over.

Elsa and Frank dance. A man comes over and asks Maurice for a cigarette, but Dora holds out a packet first. He takes a seat beside her. He's the first person she has seen wearing a British soldier's uniform.

'Davy,' he says. 'Thanks.'

She can smell drink on the man's breath. He slouches in his chair and lets his eyes wander around the room, lingering on the crowd and the women who are dancing. He lifts a hand to someone, and for a while watches a girl who's twirling near them in a black skirt. Tucked into her slim waist is a white blouse with little flowers printed on it. The girl is small, like Dora, with dark hair that's cropped around her face. She's the best dancer in the room.

'Are you and him an item?' Davy then asks, waving a hand between Dora and Maurice.

Dora shakes her head.

'Brother and sister?' he asks Maurice, offering him a handshake.

Maurice tells him that Dora works for his family, and that she's German.

Davy can't believe it. He leans back for a second. His eyes drift down to his army uniform and back to her.

'Before you say anything,' she says, 'I'm not a Nazi.'

He looks her up and down before telling her to relax.

'Can you understand me?' he asks. 'I'm not from here either. Can you guess where I'm from?'

It's strange. There's something about him, something that reminds her of Marcus. He has the same look about him, a curl to his lip when he talks, cocksure. She wonders if he's a good dancer.

'I'm from Scotland,' he says. 'Do you know where that is?'

She shakes her head, but he still doesn't tell her. He just laughs and goes back to watching the girl in the black skirt. The whole place is watching the same girl.

When the band finishes playing, she thanks her partner and goes to a table where she sips something clear and fizzy from a glass. Another man takes her hand a second later and the music starts again. The fringe of her skirt sweeps his knees when they twirl.

'Are you dancing?' Davy asks Dora.

She shrugs. Maurice hasn't asked her.

'I'm not as good a dancer as her,' she says.

'Oh, come on.'

Frank and Elsa come back to the table and sit down.

'That's enough for us,' Elsa says, stroking her belly. She takes a long drink and Davy nods hello but they ignore him.

'Go on you two,' Elsa says, looking from Dora to Maurice. 'You're supposed to dance.'

The band's singer announces the next number, a slow one. Some people go out for a smoke or return to their tables, but Maurice puts an arm around Dora's back and guides her into the middle. They go past the pretty girl in the black skirt, who's sitting this one out.

'Step up, you sweethearts,' the singer insists. 'Let's see some more couples on the floor.'

Maurice drops his hands around Dora's waist. They sway from side to side, and the buttons on his checked shirt brush against her face. The instruments play for at least a minute before the singer begins crowing.

They're writing songs of love, but not for me,
A lucky star's above, but not for me.

Maurice isn't as bad as everyone said. The song finishes but the band continues playing, a long instrumental that gets faster and faster. They keep dancing. It must be a big hit because the floor fills up again soon. Girls dance with other girls if no one asks them. Elsa gets back up with Frank. The girl with the black skirt clears a bit of space on the floor for herself and her partner. Dora looks over and realises it's Davy. He is a good dancer.

'You suit that dress,' Elsa says, sitting down next to Dora. The band has gone off on a break and a record has come on in its place.

'Doesn't Dora look nice?' Elsa says to Maurice.

Davy leans back in his chair and winks at her. He's lost the girl in the black skirt. She's moved on to chat up another guy, and for some reason he's followed them back to their table.

'Where's your girl gone?' Dora says.

He pushes his chin out like he doesn't care.

Elsa is impatient to dance again, tapping her feet and moving her arms about in time with the music.

'I've not felt this good in weeks,' she says. 'My appetite's come back.'

Suddenly, Davy downs the rest of his drink and slams the empty bottle on the table. He wipes his mouth with the back of his hand.

'I'm going home right now, unless you want to dance with me,' he says, and offers Dora his arm. 'One dance.' He nods to Maurice, a smile in the corner of his lips. 'I saw you. You're better at dancing than him.'

Everyone laughs. Maurice tells her to go on and

Elsa nudges her.

'Come on,' Davy begs her. 'I'm leaving soon. I'm going to fight Hitler just for you.'

'You really can't say no,' Elsa says. Dora gives in and gets to her feet.

The band plays a fast one and then a slow one and they move together in perfect rhythm. The steps take her right out of herself, away from Luton, and Berlin, away from bad dreams. For those two numbers the whole world is reduced to the dance floor. Words are notes, and the only person is Davy, with his army uniform and grey-green eyes.

They don't stop to say goodbye. Maurice has a blonde girl leaning over the back of his chair, and Elsa has dragged Frank back up to dance. The shoes Dora has borrowed are hurting her feet.

Outside, Davy asks her how old she is.

'Twenty-three.'

'Is that right?' he says. 'We're the same age. I thought you were just wee.'

At the crossing she asks if he wants a cigarette. She's taken her Woodbines out of her bag already, and is flipping the lid open and shut.

'Share?' he says, slipping one out. He lights it with a silver lighter from his pocket and hands it to her. She takes a slow drag and passes it back to him, the trick she learned with Marcus. It always gave their conversations an equal feel, talking between breaths.

A few seconds go by. He gives her another suck on the cigarette.

'Look,' Davy says. 'It's snowing.'

It is. Thick, beautiful flakes slow-dancing towards the ground.

Davy takes her hand to cross the road.

'Your fingers are freezing,' he says.

She nods. He takes off his gloves and gives them to her, then shoves his hands into his pockets and they link arms and walk.

17 April

We climb the hill and walk along what's left of the Berlin Wall. We're high above the flea market. The path glitters with broken glass. Berlin's East-West divide survives up here in a long section that's a spray-painted riot. The graffiti artists are working on new designs, and behind them I sit on a swing, listening to the chains creak as my feet fly out over the whole city. Berlin is stretched out below, silent cranes jutting into the sky like pins, marking out thousands of developments. Another city rising out of the ground.

Smells of the market rise in the warm air, Turkish spices, kebabs, incense and weed. On the grass people gather in groups and strum guitars. Someone has brought out their sofa and set it down in the middle of the park. A band arrives with amps attached to a three-wheeled bicycle, and they pick a spot and set up, plucking and tuning and twiddling with the balance and volume.

The market was crowded so we put Ash on Matthew's shoulders and pushed our way through the stalls. There were piles of 1970s furniture, chairs with bright yellow cushions, electric blue, rusty red, veneer tables and painted sideboards with handles shaped like sherbet flying saucers. Lots of stalls sold t-shirts printed with DDR designs and racks of old Adidas tracksuits, boxes of vinyl records and crates of clutter all lined up, stuff piled over and under tables and hanging on rails from above.

I took a photograph of an old wooden knitting doll packed in a bright pink box. On the next table there was a pile of magazines, someone's retro porn stash, some East European camera lenses, a disarray of electrical cables, and a few old pieces of electronic equipment that I didn't even recognise. Under the table was a box of worn trainers.

I let Matthew and Ash go on ahead. I knew which stall I wanted. Boxes I would lose myself in, orphaned photograph albums and piles of old postcards, dusty memories rescued from the cupboards of elderly Berliners. I cleared my throat and picked up a bundle: letters, diaries, photographs, faces that had somehow lost their way, eyes and smiles that could belong to anyone. I paused each time I found a photograph of a little girl, and turned it over hoping to find a name. Almost all the little girls were too well-dressed to be Ruthie, or they were wearing clothes either too old-fashioned or too modern.

I always know straight away when I find a photo I want. A girl no older than five. I like pictures best if they're damaged, faded, stained, over-exposed, half-hidden in shadow, or if the child is turning away from the camera. The faces I fall for are always partly obscured. I've been looking all over the city for these half-images. I didn't even recognise the impulse till I'd already collected half a dozen of them, and when I laid them side-by-side I noticed they all had this in common.

I stood at the stall today for twenty minutes before I found a photo I wanted and handed over my money, committing genealogical kidnap. I hid the girl away in my rucksack.

Matthew and Ash were already at the top of the hill by then, and I climbed up to join them. Ash is bored now and has rolled away from Matthew. He's trying to get onto all fours on the grass, and Matthew is watching him.

'That's it!' I say to Ash. 'Look, Matthew. He's trying.'

'He's not strong enough yet,' Matthew says, and looks only for a second.

Ash keeps trying but Matthew refuses to see it. We have a fight. He says I'm only seeing what I want to see, and I say he's not helping enough. I say his low expectations are holding Ash back.

'That's what you think, is it?' Matthew growls, and he gets up and walks off. He leaves with just one carrier bag swinging from the fingers of his left hand. It has a vinyl-sized square inside it. I get up quick, grab all our things, throw the bag together and struggle to walk with Ash in my arms before Matthew disappears into the crowd.

I catch up with him a minute later. We start walking back to the apartment without sharing a word. Our flight home is tomorrow, and this afternoon we'll have to pack and clean the rooms. But when we reach the road, Matthew decides to go off down Weinbergsweg instead. He tells me he wants a last trip to the record shops. I watch him crossing and he takes his phone from his pocket. He texts while he walks, and doesn't look back. He knows I'll be cleaning the rest of the day.

I breathe in the city. The smell of Currywurst and the weird mix of metal and feathers under the train station at Eberswalderstraße, the flashes of colour, the green steps to the platform and the bright yellow carriages. I could stay here. We could get on a tram right now, just me and Ash, and in a few stops we'd disappear into Berlin, into history, into family. It would be so easy to belong here, jumbled up with all the ghosts and all the boxes of misplaced and lost things.

Found Pictures 3

1942

When the bombs fall, Dora sits in the dark and wonders if air raids over Berlin smell the same: like sweat, dried blood, and newly plastered walls. Do the skies whistle at the same pitch, and do the old apartment buildings shudder like Luton's little rows of terraced houses?

Other mothers care for children in the shelters and somehow manage to stay calm. Dora shakes all over. She curls small as the anti-aircraft guns start firing, and when the explosions get closer and glass starts shattering, she can't move.

The Rosenthals had been preparing their shelter when she left them. Their house had a cellar with sand-bagged walls. They put oil lamps down there and books, cushions, blankets, and provisions. She often imagines them in there, a much sturdier structure than some of the shelters she's had to sit in. The worst was the thin, metal one, like a pig shed. You'd freeze to death long before a bomb hit you.

Elsa gave birth to a baby boy, and Frank and Maurice had gone to the front. Mrs Rosenthal was distraught. She wanted Dora to stay, but the visa rules had changed, and Dora was taken away and interrogated. She was treated just like anyone who had come from Germany or Austria, like a spy for Shitler! She was lucky they didn't keep her for long, but when they released her they said she shouldn't clean houses anymore. She would be of more use in the factories.

Dora still has to report weekly to the Luton constabulary. Luckily, it's nothing like the police headquarters she used to have to walk past in Berlin. Inside the policemen are always drinking tea. They're on first-name terms.

When she sits in the gloomy shelter, she thinks of the weapons she has made. She can always smell the metal on her fingers. The English still need girls to clean their houses, but that is less important now than the production of bullets and bombs, and the manufacture of helmets and guns and tanks.

With the better money she earns, Dora rents her own room. The house has stood for seventy years, and it'll stand another seventy if it isn't hit by a bomb. Lately, she and the other tenants have been down in the dark a lot. The factories nearby make them a target.

Right now, Davy is somewhere in Italy. He likes having someone waiting for him at home, he told her. This isn't her home, but she didn't correct him. Could it be? She doesn't know. In the dark she puts her hand in her pocket and holds his letter. She still carries Ruthie's birthday card in her handbag. A bomb explodes somewhere close, a street away, maybe less. She can taste the dust. Everyone presses themselves close to the walls and they pray.

In England. In Italy. In Berlin. They all pray.

18 April

I want to send a letter to Kitty from Berlin, so there's no time to wait. We're leaving today on a late flight. I've written one overnight, and after breakfast I fold the paper into a white envelope and take it to the shop on the corner. The stamp has a photograph of a red flower on it. I drop it into the post box, and imagine it reaching Virginia, Kitty holding it in her hands, noticing the German stamp. She might guess, before opening the letter, what it will say. Her daughter who contacted me first will have told her to expect it.

We spend our last hours in Weißensee. We try not to argue again. We take books, towels, sun cream, toys for Ash and money for beers and Flammkuchen. We roll up our jeans and sit on the little beach until the early afternoon, dipping Ash's feet in the water, watching the swing dancers practice, listening to their music. I'm sure I see a shiver of movement in Ash's toes. I ask Matthew to look, but they don't twitch again.

'I believe you,' he says.

Matthew has taken some work on an estate up north, something a mate has arranged for him. When we get home he'll be leaving. It's only a part-time gig. The rest of the week he and his mate are going to build interiors for campervans. He only told me last night, but I knew he'd been thinking about it for a while, arranging something secret on his phone. It's going to make good money, he said, and God knows we need it now that I'm not working. He's right, I suppose. He says it won't be forever.

Today he's acting as if it's nothing, leaving us behind. It's a weight off his mind now that he's come clean.

We wander back towards the apartment around three o'clock and decide we'll keep going and grab a snack. I recline the seat of Ash's pushchair and pull the hood up over him. He'll sleep on the plane all the way back to Scotland.

We find a place to eat not far away, and they bring wine. We clink glasses over Ash's toes, and drink to the city. In a way I feel better, as if I'm existing in the present for the first time in a long time, but I can tell Matthew's mostly thinking about his own next steps. Things have shifted here, even more than I thought they would.

1942

Dora works days and Davy works nights. She opens the door on her way out and finds him stinking of smoke and wiping his boots, his entire body blackened like a witch's cat, like something the night has left behind.

'Don't touch me,' she laughs, and they tiptoe around each other in the doorway, her on her way to the bus stop, him on his way to bed. The elderly landlady doesn't seem to mind. She winks and tells them to make the most of it, and Dora knows she's right. Davy could be called away again any day. The Royal Pioneer Corps does all kinds of dirty work, stretchering bodies, digging trenches. For now, Davy lights the oil-burners that put Luton under a blanket of smoke. He stands beside them all night, making sure they don't flame. Dora feels lucky he's here, for now, filling the town with black clouds whenever the stars are twinkling, hiding the factories from the Luftwaffe. The smoke clarts Davy as black as a miner from head to foot. When he coughs, he coughs up tar.

It's Saturday. Dora's done her hair up and put earrings in, dangling ones that show off her long, pale neck. She's picked a summer dress, light blue with a white collar and large buttons up the front. At the weekend, she likes ditching her work overalls and looking like a girl again, showing herself off. Her hands aren't very ladylike, but they haven't been pretty since she was at school. She finds it hard to get the oil out from under her nails.

The bus takes her into town. She can see people looking at her, wondering where she's from with her brown eyes and dark hair. She gets off at the High Street and stands in front of the studio, looking at the portraits in the window and trying to check her hair in the reflection.

Getting the photo doesn't take long. The photographer is an old man. He positions her on a stool and tucks her hair behind her ear.

'Beautiful,' he says, and goes behind the camera. 'Is this for your sweetheart?'

She doesn't answer. She just smiles and the shutter clicks.

'Lovely. I think we got it in one.'

The man clicks his camera a few more times, for luck, he says.

'Shipping out again, is he?'

She nods.

'I'm sure he'll treasure this.'

Dora presses her thumbs for luck.

When she picks up the photograph on Thursday, she isn't sure what to write on the back. They don't usually do sweet talk.

'If you see Shitler when they ship you out, kill the swine,' she tells Davy that evening as a news report drones through the wireless. This is how they speak to each other. She's lying next to him, watching the smoke from his cigarette curl into the air. They have an hour together tonight before he goes to his post. His uniform hangs over a chair. She's gotten used to the smell of it, the muck that never really comes off.

Her overalls are lying where they fell when he unbuttoned her and she stepped out of them. She can still smell the assembly line on her body, the metal and oil. Davy doesn't mention it. The smoke from his own oil has ruined his senses.

He turns his head and kisses her shoulder. His soft lips are warm and his stubble grazes her skin.

'I dreamed you were driving a tank,' she says.

In the dream she was right at the top of the thing, building it, looking down the front of the gun. And Davy was inside it, the tank swivelling on its bogie wheels to take aim. The ricochet shook the men in their seats, the smell of the explosion, the dust flying up around it, then settling.

'Pioneers don't get to drive tanks,' Davy says.

Strange dreams had been a sign she was expecting with Ruthie, but morning sickness was the real give-away. Now she can't ignore it any longer. She'll be due in May, a late Spring baby. Davy still doesn't know. She watches him pulling his overalls on. He gets another cigarette, closes the case, and slips it into his pocket. It's always the last thing he does when he gets dressed.

'Are you okay?' he asks. 'Aren't you going to see me off?'

She shushes him. The news has come back on the wireless, talking about bombs in Berlin.

'Hey,' he says, and moves his hand over her belly. 'See you later. I have to go.'

She hears the door open and his feet stamping down the stairs and out into the street.

She looks around the room. She should make up the double bed. Davy never tidies it. The counterpane is kicked back, and the sheet wrinkled underneath. There's a dark wardrobe and a mirror by the window. The little table where she sits and smokes is here too. She likes looking out at the houses opposite, the countryside behind, the puffs of cloud, and that pale, watery sky of England that she's never quite gotten used to.

Davy has left the bedside light on, and the photograph she gave him has gone from the table. On the back she wrote *Dearest Davy, from your ever-loving friend forever, Dora.*

She put seven kisses on it. One for each day of the week.

7 July

I've driven the road between our house and the hospital a hundred times, but this morning my mind is wandering. I've taken a wrong turn. There's a long, old wall that hems in the forest. The wall hunches from the pressure of the trees overhead. I wonder what Matthew is doing right now, if he ever imagines driving back along this road.

When I get up the hill, I turn into the hospital car park and speed through the parking bays. I park, get out, open the boot and pull open Ash's pushchair, the one we bought in Berlin. He grumbles when I lift him out of the car. Once he's strapped in the pushchair, I take one last look so as not to forget where I've left the car. I won't forget. It's in the same place Matthew parked the van the last time I was here to be scanned. That was in April. The lambs were being born in the fields around our house, and he was about to leave.

Today is my four-month follow-up. They want to check the fibroids aren't growing.

We're just out of town here, but you can still smell the fields and the sky. Some gulls are making a clear, sharp cry as they fly in arcs above us, swooping from the hospital roof to the tall posts that run the length of the car park. Ash points and grins at them. His eyes seem better than they used to be. He blinks at the blurry shine reflecting off the cars, and interrogates the hospital building.

'No buddy,' I say. 'We're just here for me today.'

I didn't want to bring Ash with me. Last time, I had Matthew to help. He was busy packing his bags, but he still came along, and he held Ash in the waiting room while they did the scan.

This time I had to ask someone else. My in-laws are away visiting Shrewsbury, where another grandchild has just been born, so I spent last week scrolling through my contacts. Most of them I'd not seen in years, male colleagues who didn't have kids, friends from my time in Manchester, a couple of Elgin friends from school, or tradesmen who'd come to the house once to repair something. It was all a bit pathetic.

I landed on Roberta. I'd not seen her since the day she found me at the supermarket. I didn't call her straight away. I thought about it overnight, wondering what to say and whether she'd mind. I still owed her for the tinsel she bought that day.

When she picked up, she sounded her old self. She was right in the middle of things, her kids shouting, telly on, a neighbour round for a chat, choosing a new settee, but she sounded pleased that I'd called. When I asked her if she'd mind helping at the scan, maybe grabbing a coffee after, she said yes straight away.

We're meeting at the hospital shop, beside the balloons on sticks that they put in the doorway. As soon as the doors slide open I see her. She waves, and wraps her arms right around me. It's hot in the hospital, just like the days we spent together here. Holding her hand is her little boy, Marc. He has blonde hair and a vest that says *Ultimate Spiderman*, a lollipop in his mouth and crocs on his feet. She tells him to say hello, but he just stares at Ash. Ash stares back. He jiggles his feet in his blue boots, just a little movement, but it's there. Even Matthew saw it, just before he went away. It made him happier than I'd seen him in months, and he swung Ash all around the room in his arms.

'Can you believe that's two years since they were born?' Roberta laughs, and she bends down and grins at Ash and squashes his cheek between her fingers.

'Mine's not much of a talker yet,' she says, nodding at Marc.

'Nor is he,' I smile.

Normally Ash doesn't like strangers, but maybe he remembers Roberta, or maybe he just likes Marc, who comes closer now, touching the edge of the pushchair, reaching for Ash's fingers. I remember Roberta holding Ash for the first time, sitting in the hospital chair with the blue balloon bobbing over her head. It feels like yesterday and a lifetime ago.

Marc bobs over Ash now, the same way that balloon once did. Gentle, curious.

A trolley with a patient on it whizzes past and Roberta tells Marc to stay close. We start walking. I still hate the insipid paintings they put up all the way down the corridor. I hate the smell, the sight of people hooked up, pulling their drips on wheels, the linoleum, the awful coughing. But Roberta is just like I remember her, and with the sound of her chatting and laughing all the way to the lifts, I don't notice so much.

When I'm called through to the imaging department, Roberta flaps me away. She lifts Ash right out of his chair and bounces him on her knee, while Marc fetches everyone in the waiting room little cups of water from the drinking machine.

In a cubicle I change into the faded surgical gown they've given me. I wonder how many other bodies have worn it, at what points in their lives, at beginnings and at endings.

When the ties of the gown are knotted, I choose the music that I want them to play through the headphones. There's no one in front of me in the queue, so I don't have to wait long. They take me through and I follow the same steps as last time. I lie on a narrow tongue that sticks out from the MRI scanner, waiting to be sucked into its dome-shaped tunnel. I close my eyes, pretend I'm somewhere else. The table I'm lying on begins to move.

I wonder if the sonographers can see me naked when the music starts. Beethoven. The machine adds its own syncopated beat, a percussion of thumps, clunks, and screeches, a noise like a laser printer.

The last time I was in here Ash was tired and hungry and fussing, and Matthew was in a bad mood. He probably felt guilty about it being his last afternoon with us.

'The job's only for a while,' he kept promising. We didn't even talk about a visit. We didn't do anything special to see him off. He brought back fish and chips from Ayr, and while we ate, he explained himself again, saying the space, the peace, and a new project was something he needed. He wanted to get better at carpentry. It's good money, that's true enough. Matthew calls a couple of times a week. He asks about Ash's appointments and tells me to send more photos. He says he misses us, but he seems fine.

I thought about going back into town or moving nearer my parents, but I really have got used to the house in the woods. I like being a bit out of reach now. I like the trees. I even like the ravens, and the trespassing sheep in our garden.

'What, so Matthew just went?' Roberta says.

I nod and breathe in deep over my coffee cup. I fell asleep during the scan. The tech woke me up and told me it all looked fine to her eyes, but the doctor would confirm on the phone. I needed a coffee.

'He'll be back, I bet you. I give it till the end of the summer, honey.'

The coffee's great here. I didn't know this café was Roberta's uncle's place. It's proper Italian coffee, and wee pastries filled with cream. A satellite channel is tuned to Italian pop over our heads.

I look at Ash and Marc playing. They don't look anywhere near the same age, but they're finding a way to get on, the way kids do. Ash could still pass for twelve months. He lies back in his pushchair, strapped in, and Marc bounces up from the floor, trying to make Ash laugh, making himself laugh. Ash screams with surprise every time Marc appears.

'Too bloody much for him, is that what he said?' Roberta snorts. 'They're all useless. Honestly we're better off without them.'

I shrug.

'I'm sorry, honey,' she says.

We watch the kids mirroring each other, copying sounds and making faces. Roberta takes her phone out and records them. Ash is joining in.

'Yoo-eeee!'

'Oooo-yee!'

'Marc,' Marc says, pointing to himself.

Ash tries to copy him.

'Are you worried about the talking?' I say.

'Oh God, no,' Roberta says, putting her phone back in her bag. 'Listen to them. They are talking. That's how it starts.'

I ask her if she's bumped into any of the other mums that were in the hospital.

'I've seen TLC,' Roberta says. 'What a case. Remember she didn't want a blonde baby?'

I nod.

'She's fine.'

'What about Stacey?'

Roberta shakes her head. 'No idea, honey,' she says. 'I saw her leave the hospital. There were two taxis, one for her, one for the wean, and they went different ways.'

I spin my empty cup on its saucer and look at the kids. Marc is holding Ash's hand.

'Poor Stacey,' Roberta breathes. 'God love her.'

Roberta's uncle comes over with a refill and puts a plate down with three more pastries. Roberta's friends are his friends, he tells me.

By the time we leave, the sun's retreated behind the clouds. Lawns are being mowed in the gardens opposite and the air is filled with the smell of cut grass.

'Where's the day gone?' Roberta says.

'I know,' I tell her.

We agree to meet up soon and not leave it so long.

'Anyway, I owe you one,' I say.

'Don't be daft.'

We strap the kids into their seats, then fold our pushchairs and lift them into the boots of the cars. I let her drive away first, waving as she pulls out of her space. Once she's out of sight I feel a pang at the sun starting to go down and the sudden quiet. Perhaps I should move into town after all and try to see more people. I could look at the nursery schools and contact work about taking the medical assessments, doing the training, if there's any chance I'll ever get my license back. Maybe a support role instead. I could take Ash and flit, do something new, work another airspace together. Maybe I'm just hanging onto the house, mooching because I want Matthew to come back.

I still sometimes get a sense that there's someone around, but it's hard to explain. It could be Dora, or something else. I know my mind plays tricks.

There was one night in particular though. I was up late, drinking too much coffee, and I got the feeling she was there. It was just a feeling. I'd found a website with old street maps of Berlin, and I was zooming right into Weißensee to find Meyerbeerstraße, the address where Dora grew up. But I checked and double checked, and in the end had to accept that I'd made a mistake. Meyerbeerstraße wasn't where it was supposed to be. The street I had walked down, where Matthew had taken a photograph of me under the street sign, had a totally different name on the old map. This street had never felt right though, and I kicked myself for not trusting my gut. Now I'd have to go back to Berlin to steal another cobblestone for my grandmother's headstone, one from a different street.

The real 9 Meyerbeerstraße wasn't far away and it didn't take long to find. A street only ten buildings long, it was just a little further to the south, tucked below the St Nicolai and St Marien cemetery. The street it adjoined was Mendelsohnstraße, where Dora's mother gave birth to her in 1916, at another number 9.

I found the two old streets, Mendelsohnstraße and Meyerbeerstraße meeting at right angles, and there were two number nines sitting directly opposite each other. Finding the right door must have been a nightmare for postmen and visitors. Rosa lived at 9 Mendelsohnstraße, and Uscher lived at 9 Meyerbeerstraße. Maybe this was how they met. Nearly a century ago they were neighbours swapping misdirected letters in the street.

The puzzle piece fitted.

*

I shove my CD into the slot on the dash.

'*Ich werde mich daran gewöhnen*,' says the voice on the recording. 'Now you say it. *Ich werde mich daran gewöhnen.*' BEEP.

The German CD is too advanced for me, but I listen to it every time I'm in the car. My mouth is starting to find its way around the sounds. I don't know what this sentence means, but I try saying it before the teacher's voice cuts in with the translation.

'I'll get used to it.'

I look in the rear-view mirror at Ash. I click my seatbelt on, and while I pull out of the car park and follow the road home, I let the CD play through a couple more scenarios.

There are a lot of small moths in the house. I don't know how they've come in. Maybe it's normal for houses in the woods, but we've never had them before. Every time I open the cupboard by the door one seems to fly free, and today there's one fluttering around my face as I arrive home. They like the quiet early evenings best.

I bend down to pick up the post. There's a bank statement, and junk mail underneath, a catalogue from a company we ordered something from before Ash was even born, and a pastel blue envelope. Our address is written on it in a loopy, old-style hand.

I put the post by the kettle, thread Ash's legs into the leg holes of his highchair, peel a banana and put it in front of him. Then I make tea. While the kettle boils, I find the unstuck corner of the blue envelope with my nail and slide a finger along the top, tearing the seal. Inside there are three sheets of white notepaper and a photograph of a picture-perfect farm. The rolling landscape in the photograph is covered in lush grass with tiny red flowers sprouting in it. In the distance, trees grow around a small cluster of outbuildings and a white farmhouse. There's a large barn, painted red like a barn in a children's book, and a green tractor is driving along a single-track road leading to and from the buildings. The sky is saturated, pure blue. Standing in the foreground is an older woman wearing thick glasses and a white, short-sleeved sweater with red and white stripes across the front. She has tightly curled, faded red hair and strong arms, and she is laughing, looking up at the camera. In her hands she's carrying a box full of bright yellow chicks.

On the back of the photo, I find these words: *Me on the farm with hatchlings*. Underneath, like an afterthought, it says *Kitty*, and then another name, this time in brackets: *(Gittel Rowelski)*.

My grandmother was also a person in brackets. A person inside another person.

'Look Ash,' I say to him. 'It's Kitty.' There's no one else to tell.

'It,' he says, pointing to the photo.

'Yes! Kitty! Isn't her farm beautiful!'

I read the letter over and over and I stare at Kitty's face. I look for shared features. The shape of the mouth, definitely. Maybe something in the eyes. She looks like one of my aunts, I think. She has the exact same gaze. Kitty has children, grandchildren, and a great-grandchild. She has no memory of her parents or her brother, she says. All she knows is that she was nearly blind, and maybe that's what saved her, being in the hospital, then in a camp for three years, orphaned, till finally the camp was liberated and she was flown to England by the RAF.

Till now, no one had made the connection between Deborah Tannenbaum, who lost her daughter, and her baby cousin Gittel Rowelski, who lost her parents.

Kitty underlines her phone number. She wants me to call, and then she wants me to visit.

'What do you want for tea?' I say to Ash.

'Eh,' he says.

I follow his eyes to the counter where a box of eggs is open. Eh.

Eggs.

I might call Matthew later to tell him about Ash's words. I'm sure they are words. For now, I text Roberta instead.

I put the radio on while the eggs boil. Soft music plays as I stand over the pan watching the little bubbles on the shell, feeling the evening sun streaming through the window. Outside, in the patches of shade under the trees, insects are starting to swarm. Birds are feeding. A tractor working somewhere in the fields nearby cuts its engine. The sheep bleat, and far above a plane journeys west at high altitude, drawing a white line over the sky.

1943

There's a long whistle. Doors slam. The engine is already chugging and there's a hiss and a shout. People are running up the platform.

'The train's about to go,' says a man in uniform. 'It won't wait. You'll have to go back to the ticket office.'

They don't listen. Davy takes Dora's case and runs ahead with the bags while she pushes the tickets deep into her coat pocket. She goes as fast as she can, but can't keep up with him.

'I'll hold it,' Davy shouts over his shoulder.

The walk to the station tired her out, and her hand underneath her swollen belly isn't enough to ease the pain in her hips. She holds her coat closed over her front. She can tie the belt but not the buttons. Do babies get bigger each time? She still has another two months to go.

He's taking her home to his mother, to her new home. They'll have to change trains and they'll spend the night in Edinburgh before heading north. Davy is excited to be going home on leave. He has taken his jacket off, and as he runs, she can see the muscles in his arms just under the short green sleeves of his uniform. He doesn't seem to notice how heavy the cases are. When he reaches their carriage he flings them in through the door and stands holding the train, one foot on the platform and one foot on the step. The flag's waving and the whistle's blowing.

'On you go, Mrs Wilson!' he says, as if he's encouraging a horse or a cow into a shed. He lifts her in, gesturing an apology to the men on the station and laughing as they both catch their breath. He puts a hand on her stomach. 'Are you fine?'

'Yes,' she laughs with him. 'I thought we'd missed it.'

Other passengers throw them looks. A British soldier and a pregnant woman with a German accent isn't something you see every day. There are a few whispers, but they settle down once the train starts to move. It gathers speed.

'Are you going to do your knitting?' Davy asks.

'Yes,' Dora says. 'But later.'

He takes her wool and needles out of the bag and hands them to her. She's making a pram blanket, and by the time they reach Scotland she'll have it finished. Dora takes the seat by the window. She stares at the outskirts of Luton sliding by. I'm moving again, she can't stop thinking, everything slipping even further away, another country, another home, another name. She is no longer Stateless. She holds her hands in her lap, feeling the tickle of the wool, and twists the ring on her finger. They were married in the town hall, just the two of them and three witnesses, nothing fancy. At least this is something she'll always have.

She used to feel a pull, as if she were still connected to Berlin by some invisible string. Now all she feels is lost, as if that string has been constantly unravelling. It lies loose all around her as she travels further and further away. She knits to keep her mind straight, for the baby's sake. She looks for things that make her happy: romance novels, chocolate, cigarettes, cross-stitch, the skin under her wedding ring that's gone smooth because she can't stop fiddling with it.

In the clumps of greenery beside the tracks there are early flowers already in bloom. Yellow and purple crocuses and thick banks of snowdrops, a few early daffodils. She loves this time of year. Winter's end is in sight. In Berlin, the skies will begin to clear now and soon it will start to get warm again. Ruth is five. She will be losing her milk teeth, and learning to skip with a rope, and growing her hair.

Dora offers Davy one of the sandwiches she has packed, but he's closed his eyes and is leaning back on the headrest. Knowing Davy, he'll sleep most of the way. He'll probably open his eyes somewhere on the border and drink some whisky from his flask, and that'll be the last she'll see of him until they arrive in Edinburgh.

Dora reaches over and puts a hand on Davy's knee. He's not fully asleep yet. He covers her hand with his and slips his fingers through hers, but still doesn't open his eyes. She puts her other hand on the baby, feeling it kick against her palm. She wants to call the child Rosa, after her mother. Davy has already said it will be Mary if it's a girl. Mary, after his mother.

Perhaps it'll be a boy. It kicks her again, as if to disagree. Soon the rolling movement of the train will send it to sleep. She will sleep too, if she can get comfortable.

The train follows the course of a river, and Dora admires

the green banks and the grey-blue swirls of the water. She imagines the fish lurking below. A long tunnel brings a rush of cold, and a light on the carriage wall flickers and goes out. Dora closes her eyes, waiting for the warm sun to pour back through the window and onto her face.

Further on, the train passes through more strange cities, and towns built with unfamiliar patterns of stone and brick. Dora dreams. It's a broken up, confusing dream. Some of it feels real, as if she's on a train in the dream as well, travelling on a long straight track. There's a stench of the fields, sharp and sweet at the same time, the farmers preparing to sow. She is beneath the surface of something, in complete darkness. Other people are there, so she puts her hands out, and her fingers find ears and hair, long and curled, tangled. Light flickers through tiny cracks, illuminating for a moment tiny splinters of the scene.

Near the edges of the dream, parts of many different faces flicker into view: eyes, chins, mouths, teeth. They appear for a split second, then disappear again in the darkness. Dora strokes her hands over a child's curls, and down the back of a knitted pullover. She feels the rows of stitches in the wool, tight little 'v's, and finds a loose strand. She starts to unravel.

Before she can see the child's face, another feeling takes over. This time it's Davy's child pressing out, stretching and tugging in the space that was once her half-sister's. How can an unborn baby know already that the world is so much more than her tight, watery space?

And in that moment there are two trains. One goes to the beginning. The other goes to the end.

Afterword

My grandmother hardly mentioned the family she lost. Whether she would have one day, we'll never know. Many survivors and refugees spoke openly about their experiences and their lives before the Holocaust, but others didn't. Some waited till they were much older to share their memories. Dora died relatively young. Her death was sudden, and it happened long before I or her other grandchildren were old enough to be curious about her different accent, or where she came from.

Shortly before she died, Dora started embroidering a tablecloth. Unfinished, it has been kept folded in a drawer since December 1980. Silky, stitched petals of green and pink remain joined only by her intention to continue, leaves and stems inked in blue biro, and her needle still threaded and pinned to the fabric. *Connective Tissue*, because it is based on my grandmother's life, was always going to be like her embroidery, a story forever half-told.

In today's terms, you might say that Dora didn't have a 'safe space' in which to give her testimony. She was always busy, not being a 'survivor', but surviving hand to mouth. She worked for decades at the Reid and Welsh woollen mill in Elgin, checking the cloth for flaws. At night she cleaned other people's houses.

She raised her four girls alone after my grandfather, a Scottish Traveller, died in a police cell in 1951. She was protective of her daughters, 'over-protective' they said, even to the point of it feeling 'suffocating' at times, but it's clear she tried hard not to burden them with her own suffering. How she felt about raising her girls as non-Jews is another unknown. She continued to wear her Star of David, and she served Kartoffelpuffer, also known as Latkes (my mother's favourite), once a week. But in Elgin, there was no Jewish community for miles, and the bus to Aberdeen was unaffordable. Holocaust testimonies were not yet being widely recorded, but even if they had been, who would have found Dora?

I have been researching my grandmother's early life for over a decade and interviewing those who knew her. I also spoke with survivors who remembered the institutions in Berlin that my grandmother had once belonged to. They told me about their experiences of becoming refugees in the UK. I have made trips to many places connected to my grandmother, scoured old maps, chatted on Jewish genealogy forums, and met distant relatives whose DNA matches mine. I've trawled international archives and photographic collections for hundreds of hours. The true events of Dora's life matter to me, and recorded facts provided the framework for the historical narrative in this book. Whenever I found new information, I did rewrites. But however hard I tried to be accurate, I knew that imagination, my vastly different life experience, and my personal interpretation of history would interfere with my telling of Dora's story. The line between fiction and non-fiction is an ethical tightrope that many grandchildren of Holocaust refugees and survivors end up on as they tell family stories. I decided to write *Connective Tissue* as fiction because of everything I will never know. With archives around the world digitising their collections, my knowledge about my relatives' lives and their vanished community keeps expanding, but this book can only reflect what I know as it goes to press.

'Third-generation Holocaust narratives' (books about the Holocaust written by grandchildren of survivors) have become a recognised literary genre. I didn't know about this when I began writing *Connective Tissue*, and later I was surprised at how much I had in common with other '3G' writers, as we are sometimes called. Most other authors had close relationships with their grandparents, unlike me, and there were other differences: culture, geography, language, religious practice, and age. But I recognised time and again the same shared experiences, familiar obsessions, and similar narrative choices. Their words which chimed with mine were a comfort, as if here I'd found something rare, a group of people a bit like me. Very seldom in my life have I experienced such a sense of fitting in.

However, there are also differences. The most significant is my grandmother's social class. In Berlin, she was a young, single mother who had left education in 1932 at the age of sixteen. She worked as a cook's assistant in the Jewish Old People's Home in Große Hamburgerstraße. No one in her family owned property or a business. She and her cousins were workers. Their parents' generation had come to Berlin from towns in East Prussia, Lithuania, and a village that today lies in Western Ukraine. They survived month to month on what they earned.

My sense that Dora's story was in some way unusual started only as an inkling. The more pre-Holocaust accounts I read or listened to (whether they were told by first, second or third-generation writers), and the more Holocaust museum exhibits I stood staring at, and the more descendants I spoke to on forums, the more obvious it became: no one was talking about working-class Jews. The stereotype of the wealthy German Jew has endured to the point that even academic studies of pre-Holocaust Jewish life in Germany follow the same trend. Fortunately, I wasn't alone in noticing this. Historian Stefanie Schüler-Springorum noted that 40% of the Jewish community in Berlin was living below the poverty line even prior to Hitler's rise to power, and reading her words below, I understood at last why writing about Dora felt so necessary.

> 'Various authors have pointed out that it is high time to revise the old cliché of (upper) middle-class Jewish Berlin, since, even before 1933, the wealthy Jewish lawyer or doctor living in the western neighbourhoods of the city was by no means representative of the economic norm in the broader community...[in

*numerous studies] 'poverty' remains largely
an abstract statistical variable; seldom is
the fate of the individual highlighted and
made palpable.'[1]*

Perhaps it's unsurprising that the fate of Berlin's working-class Jewish community is largely missing from collective memory. Dora's family were among those least likely to survive the Holocaust, having no powerful friends, no means to buy the £50 ticket for the Kindertransport (thousands in today's money), and nothing material to barter with. I'm willing to guess that they probably had fewer non-Jewish contacts, so were less likely to find individuals willing to help them or hide them. On the branches of my extended family tree there are several large households, some with ten to fifteen children, yet none survived. Modern memorials to individual victims, such as the Stolpersteine,[2] are also less likely to be laid for people like my grandmother's relatives. This is because names on memorials are often suggested or sponsored by surviving relatives and descendants.

1 See Stefanie Schüler-Springorum *Fear and Misery in the Third Reich: From the Files of the Collective Guardianship Office of the Berlin Jewish Community,* Yad Vashem Studies Vol. XXVII, Jerusalem 1999, pp. 61-103

2 These are brass cobblestones that commemorate individual victims outside their last address freely chosen. Laid by artist Gunter Demnig , these memorials can be seen all over Europe. There are over 8000 in Berlin.

I went into the archives wishing for facts to help me tell the story of Dora's family, but I had low expectations. I thought I'd find little more than dates of deportation and train destinations, and nothing about life before that terrible moment. But there were pages and pages of information, entire files about ordinary families that were presented to me, cold to the touch, fresh from chilled storage rooms. Many of the words in those files still send shivers down me. In the absence of family photographs and oral histories, mundane details about every individual and household become precious: lists of belongings, other relatives, health, hints about their politics, religious observance, hobbies, and who their friends and neighbours were.

I didn't want to write a Holocaust book. I wanted to seat Aunt Dorothea at her oval table on one of her four chairs. Those pieces of furniture were real. Cousin Meta, a seamstress, and her husband Herbert, a tailor, had a dentist's chair and a bag of dentists' tools belonging to a brother-in-law stored in their living room. The most valuable item in the home of Cousin Max, who was a building site foreman, was the pram he and his wife Lucie bought for their three-year-old son, Efraim, and their baby girl, Gittel. Max's twin, Jette, worked in the laundry at the Jewish Hospital, and in July 1939, the youngest brother, Hermann, went to work in a Paderborn field where there was one single tap. He helped build a training school for Jewish youth, a place to learn skills for emigration to Palestine. Hermann's own emigration, which began a few months later, ended in tragedy. He avoided Auschwitz, where his mother and all his siblings were killed, but he was shot with hundreds of Jewish and Gypsy men in a massacre in 1941 in Zasavica, Serbia.

When I started this research, I hoped that one day I would find a photograph of my aunt, Ruth. My mother's sister. She was five when she was deported from Berlin with my grandmother's cousin, Meta. They were murdered on arrival in Auschwitz. No photograph of Meta or Ruth exists, but these words were pencilled faintly in the margin of a social worker's report: 'Ruth is loved as if she were Meta and Herbert's own child'. The same report told me that Ruth slept in a small bed in the room they all shared. After the family had been deported, when auctioneers were sent into the family home to list every last pot and pan and price them up for sale, among the items collected were 'several items of children's clothing' and a 'child's bed', echoes of Ruth's short life that are worth far more than the assigned values.

It is a modern fictional narrative in *Connective Tissue* that connects Dora's story and all its unknowns. Helena is the embodiment of the interplay between what I know and what I'll never know, my personal interpretation of the past, and how my family history is stitched into the way I view the present. Luckily for me, as I disappeared into a rabbit hole of historical research, my husband Chris, my parents, my cousins, and my aunts, were much more supportive of the project than Helena's fictional family. Aspects of our life did twist into Helena's narrative, however, not least the traumatising genetics investigations that my daughter underwent when she was born with a disability for which no cause could be found.

Like Helena, I was the first person in my family to 'return' to Berlin. Just before I left, my late friend Rosa Sacharin, who arrived in Scotland from Berlin on the Kindertransport, told me I would love it. It felt like she was giving me permission, and love it I did. I also realised that I shared something with others of my generation in Germany, not just with the 3G Jewish writers. Many non-Jewish Germans grew up aware of a dust that had been left to settle, a backdrop of questions about the past, or a family history that was unspoken and hard to reconcile. We are alike.

Fresh home from my first research trip in 2013, I enquired about obtaining dual German citizenship. At the time I was told this was impossible, but in 2022, three generations of my family finally acquired it after a change in Germany's citizenship law, Staatsangehörigkeitsgesetz (or STaG) 15. The events in my grandmother's life and the archival documents I had gathered for this book, were used as evidence to support a thorough revision of the law. It had previously allowed some persecuted people and their descendants to obtain or reinstate German citizenship by way of restitution, but it excluded many others, including some first-generation survivors and refugees.

People ask me how Dora would feel about my mother, myself and my children taking German citizenship. As a former Stateless resident with no material wealth, Dora was never eligible for restitution during her lifetime. I regard German citizenship as a form of restitution for the family, since after Brexit it restores our rights to live and work across the entire European Union. I also view Jewish people returning to Germany as a good thing, if only for the simple fact that it would have incensed Hitler.

Finally, there is a story I want to share about Dora which I couldn't fit into the book. It hints at what my grandmother's opinion may have been about our accepting German citizenship.

Dora was only twenty-six when she married my grandfather, and already pregnant with my mother, who in the real version of events was her third daughter. Dora had lost Ruth in Berlin, and a second daughter, Shirley, who had been born in Luton. It's not known who Shirley's father was, only that Dora was still single, and not yet a British Citizen. As such, she was unable to fulfil her visa requirements while looking after a baby. She was forced to put Shirley up for adoption.

My grandfather took Dora up to Elgin immediately after their wedding in November 1942. Then he returned to war. If she thought her living conditions in Berlin had been crowded, this made what came before seem luxurious. The three-room house in Lady Lane was shared with her Traveller mother-in-law, several of her husband's sisters and sisters-in-law, seven children, a steady flow of relations visiting, and another branch of the family, numbering ten or so, who resided in a makeshift shelter on the back of the little house. For now, the men were all away fighting. Dora had been in England for nearly three years, but my grandfather's family deliberately spoke Traveller Cant to exclude her. In retaliation, she gave some of them unflattering Yiddish nicknames. One of these was used for two generations before anyone realised.

Instead of spending time in the house, Dora explored the local area and found her way to the perimeter of a nearby prisoner-of-war camp. This was where she spent her spare moments, standing at the fence, chatting to young German soldiers. It was much disapproved of by the women in my grandfather's family.

My grandmother never fitted in. She was a Jewish refugee unlike other Jewish refugees because of her working-class background, and a German Jew unlike other German Jews because she was Stateless. She was a mother forced to leave behind a child, twice. She raised Scottish daughters in a town miles away from any Jewish community. A Jew in a family of Travellers. Dora was Stateless in every sense of the word, an incredibly lonely thing to be.

When Dora visited the German soldiers who were held in the nearby POW camp, as well as the relief of conversing in her mother tongue, she passed cigarettes and chocolate through the fence. This was not an act of forgiveness. To her, these boys were not Nazis. Like her, they were lonely and displaced, just young Germans in Scotland, probably as miserable about the weather as she was, howking tatties for the entire War.

I would like my grandmother to be remembered for this act of kindness. She experienced sadness in her unbelonging, but in it she showed incredible resilience. She had the ability to look outward, and she nurtured others who were lost. In doing this, she brought people together. I'd like to think it's a quality that will keep travelling through generations of her descendants. I'm proud to call her my grandmother.

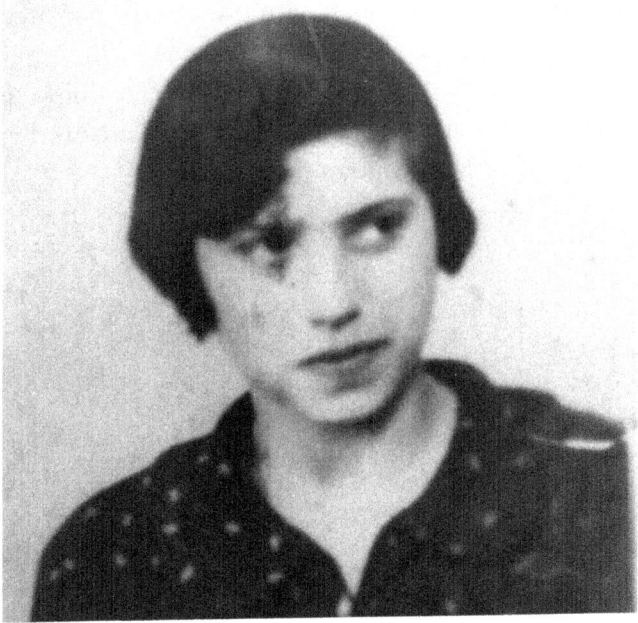

Dora in Berlin, c.1938

Elgin (c.1957) Dora centre, with daughters clockwise from left, Helen, Besty (the author's mother), Nancy and Elsie. Dora's husband, Duncan Wilson, was superimposed behind Dora and her daughters after his death in 1951.

Photo c.1920. Dora in Berlin with her parents. Her mother was Rosa Tannenbaum, née Rowelski (1879-1922) from Młynary, Poland, formerly Mühlhausen in Ostpreußen, Germany. Her father was Usher Tannenbaum (1868-1937) from Banyliv, Ukraine, (formerly Russ Banilla, Austria). This photo may have been taken in Weißensee, Berlin, likely wearing the studio's older-style, fancy clothing. Usher's coat is visibly too long in the sleeves.

One of several class photos. Dora, centre, seated on a sledge.
Photo c. 1928

Acknowledgements

Researching and writing this book has been a project throughout a large chapter of my life, and as such, I'm grateful to so many people who have shared knowledge, encouraged me, and supported me in different ways.

My mother, Betsy, and her sisters, Helen, Nancy and Elsie trusted me with a family story which is part of us all. Without their help and encouragement, I would not have been able to set it to paper at all. My cousin, Debbie, a constant companion in the archives, has experienced with me every joy and despair as we uncovered our grandmother's history. Thank you for sharing this search, and for making me not the only weirdo sitting up late at night squinting at two-hundred-year-old documents in German till my eyes hurt. We will continue.

I want to express my deepest gratitude to three late Holocaust refugees, Rosa Sacharin in Glasgow, who translated and transcribed large parts of Ruth's file, Edith Argy in London, and Kurt Friedlaender in Australia who conversed with me over email. Edith and Rosa invited me into their homes where they shared memories and answered my questions. It was the greatest privilege to meet with them. To Rosa in particular, whose outlook on life I so admired, and who offered guidance at a very difficult time, I owe my thanks.

There were many archivists, librarians, historians and fellow genealogists from Australia, Israel, the USA, and across Europe, who had a hand in this immense project, which is also the subject of my 2018 PhD,[3] There were also people who listened, offered expertise, helped track down records, or arranged access to places I was researching. I want to mention historian, Hermann Simon at the Centrum Judaicum in Berlin, Fabian Wendler who at the time was an intern at the Leo Baeck Institute, The Sonnenhof Children's Hospice in Berlin, Edinburgh Hebrew Congregation, the Adass Yisroel Synagogue in Berlin, and many members of the Facebook community Jews - Jekkes Engaged Worldwide in Social Networking in particular Vera Meyer, Evelyn Shnier, Milt Zweig, and Eran.

For academic support, I want to thank to Paula Cowan, and Professor Henry Maitles, whose early discussions with me guided my research and writing. Thank you most of all to my supervisor, Dr David Manderson, for his unrelenting belief that I would find a way to tell this story.

Thank you to my good friend, Alison Irvine, who read generously and offered astute suggestions on a new version of the manuscript after a big rewrite. Thank you to my friend, Esthi Thurston, for conversations about air traffic control. For further comments on the entire manuscript, my appreciation to Edna Oppenheimer,

3 Thom, EJ (2018). *Signal to Noise: The Holocaust and a Third Generation Perspective* (unpublished doctoral thesis). University of the West of Scotland.

Paula Cowan, my mother and my aunts, and my husband, Chris Dooks. Chris has supported me in immeasurable ways, with his beautiful photography and sonic archiving, his spirit of adventure, his creative slant on the everyday, reading my first and my final drafts, and being a social butterfly when I just can't face it.

My dad, Bill, and Mum (again), can never be thanked enough. My son, whose two-year-old hand gripped mine as I arrived in Berlin, is now a brilliant teenager. On the days I struggled with my grandmother's devastating history, I was so grateful for his laughter and love. Last but not least, thanks to my youngest, my Berliner baby, for changing the way I look at everything, from the bones in my body to the big blue sea.

Sources

For those interested in aspects of Dora's history, or the wider third-generation Holocaust narrative genre, referenced below are a few suggestions for further reading.

For anyone researching a similar personal history, I've listed some useful archives and online resources.

Texts:
- Aarons, Victoria (2016) *Third Generation Holocaust Narratives*, Lexington
- Dreifus, Erica (2005) *Ever After? Healing and 'Holocaust Fiction' in the Third Generation* in *Beyond Camps and Forced Labour: Current International Research on Survivors of Nazi Persecution*, ed. Steiner, Johannes-Dieter and Weber-Newth, Inge, Osnabrück: Secolo Verlag, pp. 524-30
- Gradwohl Pisano, Nirit (2013) *Grandaughters of the Holocaust*, Academic Studies Press
- Greenspan, Henry (2014) *The Unsaid, the Incommunicable, the Unbearable, and the Irretrievable*, Oral History Review. Sept 2014 pp. 229-243

- Gross, Leonard (1982) *The Last Jews in Berlin*, Simon and Schuster
- Hirsch, Marianne (2012) *The Generation of Postmemory*, Colombia University Press
- Kushner, Tony (1991) *An alien occupation: Jewish refugees and domestic service in Britain, 1933-1948* in *Second Chance: Two Centuries of German-speaking Jews in the United Kingdom*, Carlebach, Julius ed. et al Tubingen, Mohr Siebeck, pp. 553-578.
- Luton News (1947) *Luton at War* Volume 1, Home Counties Newspapers Ltd
- Luton News (1985) *Luton at War* Volume 2, The Book Castle
- Meyer, Beate, Hermann, Simon and Schutz, Chana (2009) *Jews in Nazi Berlin*, The University of Chicago Press
- Hirsch, Marianne (1993) *Family Pictures: Maus, Mourning, and Post-Memory* in *Discourse: Journal for Theoretical Studies in Media and Culture*: Vol. 15 : 2 pp. 3-29
- Hirsch, Marianne (2014) PMLA Presidential Address: *Connective Histories in Vulnerable Times*, *PMLA 129.3*, The Modern Language Association of America. pp. 330-348
- Schüler-Springorum, Stephanie (1999) *Fear and Misery in the Third Reich: From the Files of the Collective Guardianship Office of the Berlin Jewish Community*, English translation in *Yad Vashem Studies* Vol. XXVII, Jerusalem

Artistic works:

- Demnig, Gunther (1996 to present) Stolpersteine
- Photography of Jewish institutions in 1930s Berlin by Abraham Pisarek
- Photography of Jewish institutions in 1930s Berlin by Herbert Sonnenfeld

Film:

- *Berlin: die Symphonie der Großstadt* (1927) Directed by Walther Ruttmann, Fox Europa
- *Im Himmel Unter Der Erde* (2011) Directed by Britta Wauer, ARTE, Britzka

Archives and Online Sources:

The following links may help others researching personal histories, particularly those with a connection to Berlin's Jewish community:

- **Berlin's Historical Address Books**
  www.histomapberlin.de
  (listing head of household only)
  digital.zlb.de/viewer/berliner-adressbuecher/
  Berlin street names change frequently. This site offers historic overlays for the modern streets.

- **Landesarchiv Berlin**
  landesarchiv-berlin.de
  This archive holds historic birth, marriage, and death records, and lots more. To note: births taking place within the last 110 years, marriages within 80 years,

and deaths within 30 years are held in local registrars and are only accessible to direct descendants.

- **Brandenburgisches Landeshauptarchiv**
  blha.brandenburg.de
  This archive holds original documents completed by all individuals prior to deportation, as well as information about the auctioning off of deportees' belongings. In some cases, people who fled also completed detailed forms about what they took with them. These are also held here.

- **Arolsen Archives**
  www.arolsen-archives.org
  Search here for records of individuals

- **Yad Vashem Memorial**
  www.yadvashem.org
  Search here for records of individuals

- **Centrum Judaicum, Berlin**
  centrumjudaicum.de
  This archive holds roughly one hundred original files on individual Jewish children who became wards of the community, and much more.

- **Memorial Book**
  www.bundesarchiv.de/gedenkbuch/
  Search here for records of individuals

- **Adass Yisroel Berlin**
  adassjisroel.de/en/adass-yisroel-berlin/
  This small synagogue holds burial records and has some useful historical information on their website.

- **Weißensee Cemetery Berlin**
  http://www.jg-berlin.org/en/judaism/cemeteries/
  weissensee.html
  Search here for burial records of individuals

- **Mapping the Lives Project**
  Using data from the 1939 German Minority Census
  www.mappingthelives.org
  Search here for records of Jewish residents (all members of a household).

- **The Association of Jewish Refugees**
  ajr.org.uk
  Search here for records of individuals who came to the UK as refugees.

- **Leo Baeck Institute**
  www.leobaeck.co.uk

- **The Weiner Holocaust Library**
  www.wienerholocaustlibrary.org

- **United States Holocaust Memorial Museum**
  www.ushmm.org

- **Jewish Gen**
  www.jewishgen.org

- **Europeana Newspaper Colllection**
  www.europeana.eu/en/collections/topic/18-
  newspaper

- **The Scottish Jewish Archives Centre**
  www.sjac.org.uk

- **Bedfordshire Archives**
  bedsarchives.bedford.gov.uk/Archives-Service.aspx

- **1939 Register (UK)**
  www.nationalarchives.gov.uk/help-with-your-
  research/research-guides/1939-register/
  *Search here for records of individuals who were in the
  UK in 1939*

Facebook Groups:
- **Roaring Berlin. Die Vergessene Metropole**
  www.facebook.com/groups/798535277005208

- **Berlin - Auf den Spuren der Vorfahren**
  www.facebook.com/groups/369499039918004

- **JEWS – Jekkes engaged worldwide in
  Social Networking**
  www.facebook.com/groups/1556357284602836